MW01128152

ANGEL'S FLIGHT

LEGION OF ANGELS: BOOK 8

ELLA SUMMERS

ANGEL'S FLIGHT
Legion of Angels: Book 8

www.ellasummers.com/angels-flight

ISBN 978-1-0800-7626-0

Copyright © 2019 by Ella Summers
All rights reserved.

CHAPTER 1

VISIONS OF ANGELS

*F*aris stood before me, his armor shimmering in the light that streamed in from my apartment window, his mouth curled into a superior, godly smile. The people of Earth knew him by many titles—the God of Heaven's Army, King of Sirens, Slayer of Demons—but to me he was also something else. He was my father. Not Dad or Daddy or anything that would imply warm, fuzzy feelings. I wasn't even sure Faris was capable of any. I harbored no delusions about my origin. I was a product of war, not love. Faris had created me for one reason and one reason only: to be his greatest weapon, a warrior who possessed both the gods' light magic and the demons' dark magic.

"You think you can trust Nero Windstriker?" Turning away from the glass window that looked down on the city of New York and all its people, he glanced back at me. "Then ask him why he interviewed you the day you came to this office to join the Legion of Angels. Ask him why he oversaw your training. Or did you think it's common for an angel, the head of a Legion office and a large territory, to concern himself with a lowly initiate?"

I opened my mouth to rebuff his words, but that protest died on my lips. Honestly, it *was* strange that Nero had overseen my initiation training. I'd been too enamored with him to see it back then, but now that Faris pointed it out, I couldn't deny that he had a point.

"There is much more going on here than you know, child," Faris told me. "And Nero Windstriker is entrenched neck deep in it all."

And with that said, Faris vanished into thin air.

"You will be hearing from me," his voice echoed, filling my living room.

As the echoes faded, Nero reappeared beside me, standing precisely where he'd been the moment Faris had spelled him away.

"What's wrong?" Nero asked, stepping toward me.

I just stared at him. He looked no different than before. His hair shone the same shade of caramel; his hard, unyielding emerald eyes had the same magic-charged glow. He still wore black leather armor, a suit that perfectly hugged every muscle in his body, a body built for battle, honed over the centuries.

In every way, he still looked completely like my Nero, the archangel with whom I shared my apartment—and my heart. And yet, there was something different about him. Was my mind playing tricks on me, brought out by Faris's words? Or was I simply seeing the real Nero for the first time?

"Leda?" Nero took my hands.

I withdrew.

His brows drew together. "What did Faris do to you?"

"It's not so much what he did, as what he said."

"He threatened you."

"It wasn't a threat. It was a warning." I took a deep breath, then met his eyes again. "About you."

He folded his arms over his chest, his face impassive. "He told you not to trust me."

I braided my sweaty fingers together. "Nero, why did you interview me the day I applied to join the Legion of Angels? And why did you take charge of my initiate class? Angels do not train initiates."

I watched and waited for Nero to respond.

"Faris is trying to isolate you from everyone who cares about you. So he can control you."

"I know he is," I said, frowning. "But that's not the answer to my question."

"The answer is complicated."

My heart thumped erratically. My whole life, everything I knew and felt to be true, was in danger. It was at the brink of collapse. "Is that a refusal to tell me?"

"No," he said cautiously. "I have no secrets from you, Leda. I've wanted to tell you this for a while, but I thought you might react badly."

"Whatever it is, I can handle it."

Ok, so that was not at all true. If Nero told me he'd been manipulating me all this time, that he didn't really love me, that I was just a tool to him, just as I was to Faris... I took a few calming breaths. No, I couldn't handle that.

But I didn't think it was that at all. The love in his eyes, the caring caress of his hand, the concern in his voice—they were all too real, too true.

"Good or bad, I have to know, Nero."

"Very well," he agreed. "The night before you walked into this office and applied to join the Legion, I had a dream about you."

"You had a dream about me?" I blinked in confusion. "But we hadn't met yet."

"No, we had not," he said. "But in my dream, we knew each other very well. I had very strong feelings for you, feelings that felt completely real, that didn't fade away when I awoke. I had never experienced such strong feelings, so much love for anyone, even in real life. And in this dream, I felt so much love for you that I couldn't shake the feeling."

A happy ache in my heart replaced the sad, heavy ache. "What exactly happened in this dream?" I winked at him.

He chuckled, deep and dark. "Nothing like that, Pandora. In my dream, we fought side-by-side, united against a great invading army. You were an angel."

"That must have piqued your interest."

He brushed his hand down my cheek. "You always pique my interest."

I smirked at him. "I don't get it, Nero. This sounds like a great dream—well, minus fighting the impossible army. Why did you think I would react badly?"

"Because of what we were fighting for: to protect our daughter." He watched me closely for my reaction.

"Our…daughter?" My voice cracked.

"In my dream, she looked about seven or eight years old, and the world had gone to war over her," he told me.

"Why did we need to protect her? Who was after her?"

"Everyone," he said. "She already had wings, Leda."

"She was a child angel? A born angel?" Which meant she was unimaginably powerful, to have enough magic from birth to be born an angel. My anxiety returned, bringing all-out panic along for the ride. "But it was only a dream, right?"

Nero's mouth tightened into a hard line.

"Right, Nero?" I asked, my voice barely breaking a whisper.

"The day after my dream, your application form crossed my desk," he said. "I recognized your name. I had to know if you were the same Leda. When I walked into that office where you were waiting, I saw the Leda from my dream staring back at me. I knew right then that my dream would come to be."

"You believe you saw our future in your dream?"

"Yes, I do," he confirmed.

"But is that even possible?"

"There are people who can catch glimpses of the future," he replied. "It is a rare magic some powerful telepaths possess."

"And you have this power?"

"No," he said. "I believe someone with that power sent me future visions of you."

"But why?"

He shook his head. "I don't know. Someone obviously wanted us to meet. This someone wanted me to take a closer look at you. And I did. As you noted earlier, I don't usually train initiates."

"Someone is playing us. They pushed us together."

Nero took my hands, gently unfolding my clenched fists. "No, someone merely nudged me in your direction. But it was you who ensnared my heart, Leda. And what I'd thought were overwhelming emotions in my dream, now pale in comparison to how you make me feel in real life." His lips brushed softly against mine. "You are my destiny. One way or the other, dream or no dream, we would have ended up together. The dream just brought me to you sooner."

I smiled against his lips. "You're such a romantic, General Windstriker."

When he chuckled, his chest buzzed delightfully against mine.

My smile faded. "But why did this mysterious someone want us to meet?"

"I don't know."

I tried to think it through. "Faris said you are neck deep in this. But you don't even know what *this* is."

"Faris sows discord. He breaks people apart, as our recent training demonstrated," Nero reminded me.

I hardly required the reminder. In those training challenges, Faris hadn't simply pitted the angels and soldiers of the Legion against one another; he'd exposed the other gods' secrets and turned them against one another as well.

"True," I said. "But this feels different. It doesn't feel like Faris's doing. You did take an unusual interest in me. Faris is right about that. We're both playing this game; we just don't know what the game is. But Faris does."

"You can't trust anything that comes out of his mouth, Leda. Everything he says is carefully crafted to manipulate everyone."

"Oh, I know," I laughed. "I know exactly how Faris is. He likes to hold all the pieces, and he plans and plots until he does. He manipulates everyone. But two can play at that game. I will find out what he knows."

Nero looked at me, pride pulsing in his eyes. "I believe the God of Heaven's Army has finally met his match in you."

"You bet he has," I declared. "Faris, I'm coming for you."

A knock sounded on the apartment door.

I frowned. "That was a quick response to my challenge."

"It's not Faris," Nero told me.

He was right. Faris wouldn't have bothered with doors —or knocking, for that matter.

Nero walked to the door and opened it. Harker stood on the other side. The two angels exchanged a loaded look, then Nero stepped aside. As Harker walked across the living room, his eyes honed in on me—and more specifically, on my wings. Like my hair, my wings changed color to reflect my magic and mood. Right now, they were predominantly ivory white, with dark pink tips, as though I'd dipped them in a paint bucket.

"Pandora, you're a vision in white and pink—and angel wings," Harker told me.

I'd only just become an angel. Most people, Harker included, hadn't seen my wings yet. And with every passing moment that he continued to stare at them, I grew more and more self conscious. A red flush touched my cheeks, spreading down my hair and across my wings. My whole body was blushing.

"You have the most badass wings, Leda," Harker said.

"If only I could control them," I sighed. "They keep popping out when it's not convenient."

Harker shrugged. "Control will come with time."

"Says the guy who'd already figured out flight two seconds after he became an angel."

Harker winked at me. "You have other skills. Like being snarky. And defeating your opponents in battle by tossing water bottles at them, or setting their shoelaces on fire."

I planted my hands on my hips. "Be nice to me, or I'll set *your* shoelaces on fire."

Harker chuckled.

"Careful, Sunstorm," I warned him. "I'm an angel now too. I can totally kick your ass and not even get punished for insubordination."

Nero's brows arched. "Since when have you ever worried about the implications of your insubordination?"

Harker laughed so hard that *his* wings popped out.

I glowered at them both.

Nero patted Harker on the back. "What brings you to our doorstep?"

"Besides catching my first glimpse of Leda's wings, I have a message for you, Nero. From Nyx."

The humor faded from Nero's face, leaving only a hard, unapproachable mask. It was the sort of expression that every sane person on the planet hoped they'd never see on the face of an angel. Because it spelled calamity for them.

"Nero, why is the First Angel sending me to deliver your new orders to you?" Harker asked. "Why doesn't she send them directly to you?"

"She likely feared I would ignore any message from her."

Harker's eyes went wide. "You're ignoring messages from the First Angel?"

"Only her last thirty-six."

Harker looked at Nero like a stranger lived inside of him. "What's going on between you and Nyx?"

"It's a long story."

Harker's gaze shifted to me. "This is about Leda, isn't it?"

"What makes you say that?" Nero said casually—*too* casually. He only ever sounded so calm when he was burning with anger.

"There's only one thing that could possibly incite you,

the perfect soldier, to insubordination," Harker said. "And that's protecting Leda."

"As I said, it's a long story," Nero replied.

Anyone else would have seen the look on Nero's face and abruptly ended the conversation right then and there. But Harker wasn't just anyone. He was Nero's best friend.

He turned to me now. "Leda?"

"It was Nero and I who found the weapons of heaven and hell, back in the Lost City," I told him. "The recent training revealed that Nyx and Ronan stole them from Nero before Faris stole the immortal artifacts from them. Nero isn't overly pleased with either of them right now."

"And?" Harker prompted me.

"And what?"

"This has something to do with Faris."

"Yes, Faris stole the weapons from Nyx and Ronan. I said that already."

"No, this has to do with Faris's secret," Harker pressed on.

"I don't know what you mean."

"I know."

"Know what?" I asked.

Harker pulled an object out of his pocket. It was roughly the size of a blueberry and silver in color. The silver orb rose from his open palm. When it was hovering a few feet above our heads, it began pulsing with yellow light.

"I've cloaked the area from prying eyes and ears," Harker said.

"Where did you learn that spell?" I asked him.

"Bella made it for me."

"Did she? My sister must be warming up to you."

His forehead crinkled. "Actually, I paid her to design it."

"Why did you do a stupid thing like that? You should have paid her to help *you* design it. Then you could have worked with her, spending time with her."

Harker chewed on his lower lip, considering my idea. "You're right."

"Too late now. Now you've set a precedent of her working alone on your projects, not together with you."

"Leda, you are attempting to sidetrack me," Harker said firmly.

"I was trying to help you, Harker. But if you'd rather not have my help in winning Bella's heart…"

He scowled at me. "You don't fight fair."

"No," I laughed. "I absolutely do not."

"This is important." Harker looked from Nero to me. "I know what you are, Leda. The daughter of Faris and Grace."

I laughed.

"I'm serious." His voice scraped like gravel. "We all saw what Faris was trying to do: create a living weapon with light and dark magic, with access to the entire spectrum. More powerful than a god or a demon. That's you."

Nero moved toward him, but I stepped between them. "How do you know?" I asked Harker, my arm braced against Nero's chest, blocking him.

"I told you that the need to protect Leda incites you," Harker told him. "Would you kill me, Nero?"

"Of course not," I answered for him.

Nero ignored my sensible answer. "That depends entirely on you," he told Harker.

"No one is killing anyone," I declared. "Especially not best friends." I glanced at Harker. "Who told you?"

"No one told me. It's obvious. You have perfectly balanced magic, Leda. And Faris has been protecting you."

"*Protecting* me?" I nearly choked on the words. "Is that what you call what Faris is doing?"

"Yes, in his own twisted way, Faris is looking out for his investment," said Harker. "That's how he sees you."

I didn't doubt it.

"I know Faris," Harker continued. "Not completely, of course. No one truly knows him. But I know him more than anyone at the Legion does, except for Nyx."

He was probably right. Harker had worked for Faris before he'd realized that Faris was actually working against the other gods.

"I think Faris suspected what you are from the time you joined the Legion," Harker said. "And his suspicions were confirmed at Crystal Falls, during the recent training challenges, when he gave you the Nectar and you didn't level up."

I felt like an iron fist had just clamped down on my heart. "Faris wants to train me to be his weapon."

"Leda, listen to me." Harker set his hands on my shoulders. "Don't for a single second trust Faris. He doesn't care about others, even his own blood. Just look at how he treats his brother. He exposed Zarion's secrets. Daughter or not, he would do the same to you if it furthered his agenda."

"I am well aware of Faris's immorality."

"I'd help you, try to warn you if I get a sense he's about to do something to hurt you," Harker said. "But I am in the dark. I believe Faris suspects my duplicity. Lately, he hasn't let me close to any of his plans. I was as shocked as everyone else at what happened at the Crystal Falls training."

Harker had been working as a double agent, pretending to still be in Faris's pocket, all the while spying on his activities and reporting back to Ronan and Nyx.

"I've got your back, Leda," he told me. "No matter what."

I sighed. "Nyx and Ronan know what I am."

Harker's brows peaked.

"They want me to wield the weapons of heaven and hell for them," I continued.

"They want to turn her into a weapon. Just like Faris," Nero growled.

"In the gods' eyes, we're all weapons for them to wield, to throw at problems, to use as they see fit," said Harker. "That's why they give us magic. That's why they level us up as far as our potential allows."

"Leda is the daughter of a god and a demon," Nero replied. "Her potential is high. If the other gods find out what she is, they will either try to use her or kill her. I'm not going to allow either of those things to happen."

"Nor will I." Harker's hand squeezed my shoulder. "You are my friend." As his gaze shifted to Nero, he set his other hand on his shoulder. "You're both my friends. More than that, you're like family."

I believed Harker, that he would stand with us, keep our secrets, even against the other gods. He'd kept my sister Bella's secret. And he'd been there for me through so many tough situations.

Nero appeared convinced too. His body noticeably relaxed. He didn't look like he was preparing to charge into battle against his best friend.

"You'd better talk to Nyx," Harker told Nero. "And then head out on the mission she assigned you."

"He's right, Nero," I said. "You have to act normally,

like nothing is wrong. The gods might be busy licking their wounds right now, but they will start asking questions if we act strangely. If the Legion stops working perfectly, if angels stop following commands, they'll take a closer look at us all. If Harker put together what I am, so can the gods if they watch us long enough."

Nero set his hand over mine. His eyes still on me, he asked Harker, "What is Nyx's mission for me?"

"She is sending you to the Forsaken Desert."

The Forsaken Desert was on the plains of monsters, one of the areas overrun by beasts, a place few people dared to go.

"The First Angel wants you to investigate the sudden surge of monsters in the area," Harker said. "If their numbers continue to grow, they will soon threaten three nearby major cities."

"Meda has been experimenting on monsters and growing their magic," I said. "I wonder if this is related."

That was one of the secrets we'd learned in the Crystal Falls training: the goddess Meda was trying to regain the control the gods had lost over the monsters. Like a true god, she was jumping the gun, powering up the monsters in anticipation of her regaining control over them. More and stronger monsters meant it took more magic to keep them out of the Earth's cities. Sometimes, it felt like the gods were welcoming the apocalypse with open arms.

"Meda claims this monster surge is not her work," Harker told us.

"And gods never lie," I said drily.

"Nyx is thinking along the same lines." Glancing at Nero, Harker added, "That's why she's sending you to investigate and get to the bottom of this. Your mission is to ascertain whether Meda is behind this or someone else is."

"How big is my team?"

"You have no team, Nero. Just you. Nyx doesn't trust anyone else."

"But she trusts me?" Nero snorted.

"Despite your conflict, Nyx knows you will always do the right thing to protect the Earth and its people," I told him.

"Stop being so optimistic, Leda." He pretended to look grumpy, but I knew better. "It's contagious."

"A little optimism never hurt anyone." I traced my fingers softly across his lips.

His mouth responded to my touch, drawing up. "Tell that to the monsters. An attitude like that would get you killed on the plains of monsters."

"Oh, I'm invited along on your mission?" I smiled, my hand trailing down his neck. "I thought Nyx wasn't giving you a team."

His hands caught mine. "That would not stop me from bringing you along."

"But something else is?"

"Yes, something much more important: your safety. You're a baby angel, Leda, newly made. Your magic is wild and unpredictable. As are your moods. No, I'm certainly not bringing you along with me on a dangerous mission, not in your current state. You would just get yourself killed. You're going to stay here and train yourself to control your magic and moods better."

I pouted out my lips. "Like a good little angel?"

Wickedness flashed in his eyes. "Absolutely. Becoming an angel has pumped your body with explosive new magic. Rebuild your self-discipline."

"Rebuild? You say it like I ever had it." My grumpiness

was not feigned. I wanted to go with Nero, and I was annoyed that he wasn't bringing me along.

"Harker will help you," Nero said.

Harker nodded. "Of course."

I leaned into Nero. "I'd much rather train under you," I whispered against his lips.

Magic sparked in his eyes. "As would I."

I linked my hands behind his neck, drawing him in closer. "Don't stay away too long." I kissed him softly.

"I find myself unable to stay away from you for too long."

I smiled. "Good." I kissed him again, slowly, leisurely. Drinking in every moment, every breath.

Harker cleared his throat loudly.

My hands still around Nero, I glanced over my shoulder. "You don't have to stay," I told Harker.

"Alas, I do. Nyx ordered me to stay with Nero until he leaves on the mission."

Great. So much for good-bye, won't-see-you-for-who-knows-how-long sex with Nero.

Nero kissed me, quick and rough, then he pulled back abruptly. I could still taste him on my tongue.

He pulled out his phone and quickly typed out a message. "I told Nyx I'm heading out to investigate the monsters," he said to Harker.

Harker just stood there, watching him.

"You're really going to stay with me until I leave, aren't you?" Nero's smile was wry, his eyes bright.

Harker matched his expression, point for point. "Pretty much."

Nero glanced at me. "You'll be all right?"

"I don't know." I smirked at him. "Who will I cuddle at night when it's cold?"

"Basanti has a cat named Storm to cuddle when she's away from Leila," Harker said helpfully.

I snapped my fingers. "Now, that's an idea."

Nero watched us with obvious disapproval. "I hope you two aren't implying that a cat is a suitable substitute for an angel."

"Would you rather I cuddle another angel?" I asked with an innocent smile.

Harker laughed so hard that his wings burst out of his back again.

"This isn't funny," Nero said coolly.

"It really is, Nero," Harker chuckled.

"I have to go." Nero's hand brushed my cheek. "Try not to cause any trouble while I'm gone."

"I always try."

Sighing, Nero looked at Harker. "Keep an eye on her."

"I will."

Nero stepped onto the balcony. His wings burst out of his back—a beautifully dark tapestry of black, green, and blue—then he jumped off the ledge and soared high into the air.

I watched him shoot across the city, moving with the grace of a swan and the power of a dragon. "I wish I could do that."

"Fly?" Harker asked me.

"Yeah. And look so cool doing it."

"Get dressed."

I looked down at the tank top and shorts I was wearing. "For what?"

"I'm going to introduce the Legion's latest angel to everyone in the New York office. And then I'm going to teach you how to fly."

CHAPTER 2

ANGEL'S FATE

I looked across the blackened, burnt terrain of the Black Plains. It was a wild and feral prairie beyond the borders of civilization, a land where monsters reigned, a place that no sane person ever visited.

No one had ever said the soldiers at the Legion of Angels were sane. After all, we risked death every time we tried to level up our magic.

I shifted my gaze upwards, staring into the dark storm clouds swirling overhead. The air was hot and sticky. Not a single drop of rain had fallen during our drive across the plains, but it was only a matter of time. A storm was coming. It might come in a minute, an hour, or even a day from now—but it would come.

"Glowering at the sky again, Pandora?" Basanti commented beside me, a wry smile drawing up one side of her mouth.

She was a major now, as the small metallic flower pin on her jacket broadcast loud and clear.

"Do you think the sky will obey and hold off on unleashing the storm upon us if I glower at it long enough?" I asked her. "I don't want to drive back into town drenched to the bone."

"Doubtful," Basanti chuckled.

"Are your wings waterproof?" Ivy asked me. "How do you get them to be perfectly straight all the time? Is there a brush for that? A beauty kit? Do you stand in front of the mirror for hours at a time?"

Along with Basanti, Ivy, Drake, and Alec had joined me on my mission across the Black Plains.

I smirked at Ivy. "Maybe my wings are just perfect by design?"

She laughed.

"What's so funny?" I asked.

Ivy patted me on the shoulder. "I was just remembering how often you used to complain about angels' egos. And here you are, the perfect angel, ego and all."

"I still complain about angels."

Delight sparkled in Ivy's eyes. "Irony is a dish best served cold."

"That's revenge," I told her. "Not irony."

She shrugged. "Same difference."

"Do you even know what you're talking about?" I laughed.

"I'll have you know that most people find me quite charming."

I grinned at her. "Most people are focusing on the lyrical sound of your voice."

"Or on something else," Alec said, his eyes dipping to her chest.

Ivy got that reaction a lot. With her tall and slender figure, perfect complexion, and long crimson hair, Ivy looked more like a supermodel than a soldier in the gods' earthly army.

Ivy set her hands on her hips and shot Alec a stern scowl, the expression of a mother telling off an unruly child.

"Don't encourage him," Drake told her.

Where Ivy was slender, he was bulky, built like a football player. He and Ivy had been best friends since they were kids, long before they'd joined the Legion of Angels.

"I wasn't encouraging him," Ivy said. "I was reprimanding him."

"Such subtly is lost on Alec," replied Drake.

Alec nodded with glee. "He's right, you know."

Ivy ignored them, instead looking at me. "And?"

"You want me to weigh in?" I shrugged. "Ok, then. Alec is as subtle as a battle axe."

Alec winked at me, as though I'd delivered the world's best pickup line.

"No, I wasn't asking about Alec," Ivy said. "I want to know about your wings—and how you make them look that way."

My wings, currently a glossy blend of green and black, had popped out during our last battle with the monsters of the Black Plains. My blood was still pumping fast from that fight. I hadn't yet calmed down enough to force my wings to disappear again. Before I'd become an angel, I hadn't realized how much trouble wings could be. I'd seen them as a useful accessory, something that would allow me to fly. Maybe other angels' wings were useful, but mine more often than not just got in the way. At least they were pretty, though.

"And how do they look?" I asked Ivy.

"They look cool. Earlier today, they were purple. Now they're green and black. How do you control the color?"

19

"I don't know. They're just that way. Must be magic," I added, winking at her.

"That is not a helpful answer," she told me.

"And that's not a pertinent question to ask an angel," Alec pointed out.

"Ten minutes ago, you asked her how many times an hour an angel can have sex," Drake reminded him.

Alec shrugged. "And?"

"That's not pertinent either."

"Neither am I." Alec's amused eyes flickered to Ivy. "But she is. So diplomatic. Always saying the right thing. She is the perfect counselor. So she has to be pertinent."

Ivy shook her head. "Alec, your weird logic makes my brain hurt."

He rolled back his shoulders, standing taller. He looked mighty proud of that accomplishment.

"Enough chitchat," Basanti snapped at them. "Stay focused."

Basanti was here to keep my team in line—and to make sure I behaved as an angel should. That was probably Nyx's idea. Not that it was a bad idea, honestly. I'd been volatile before becoming an angel; my new magic had only increased my destructive capacity.

"Yeah," Ivy told Alec sternly. "Your mischievous joviality might attract more monsters. And I'm still recovering from the excitement of the last attack."

Ivy worked as a counselor in the Legion's New York office. She didn't usually come along on missions, so she wasn't used to the 'excitement' of being in the field—especially when the field was the monsters' playground—but the nature of this mission necessitated her presence.

"Bring on the monsters," Alec said. "Our fearless angel leader can handle them."

"Thanks for the vote of confidence," I said drily. "But I wouldn't be so quick to invite disaster."

"Why not?" His brows arched. "It's so much fun. You, of all people, should appreciate that."

"And why is that?"

"Why? It's written on your jacket." Alec's eyes dipped to the name on my jacket—or to my breasts. Probably both, knowing him. "I love your angel name. Pandora. It's perfect."

"I certainly think so," I said.

When a Legion soldier became an angel, they gained a new surname, an angel name meant to reflect what kind of angel they were. I'd been an angel for just over a week now, but I still didn't have one. At least not technically. The Legion couldn't figure out what to call me. Apparently, I was the kind of angel that defied definition.

Short an angel name, in the meantime I'd had the seamstress at the New York office embroider my uniform with a single word: 'Pandora', the nickname Nero had given me shortly after I'd joined the Legion. The seamstress hadn't even argued. That was one of the perks of being an angel. People tended to do whatever you said and didn't ask questions.

"Do you think they'll let you keep the name Pandora?" Ivy asked me.

"If Nyx were here, she'd probably make the seamstress undo her work," I admitted. "And the First Angel would punish me for having the gall to not only name myself, but to select a very un-angelic name for myself."

"I think the name is funny," Ivy said.

"So do I," I agreed.

An angel name wasn't all I was missing. The Legion also hadn't yet assigned me a territory or position. They didn't know what to do with me. First off, there weren't even any territories available. Jace, who'd leveled up with me, had gotten the South, the territory controlled by Colonel Battleborn before his untimely death.

The Legion had a strict one-angel-per-territory rule, a necessity since angels didn't get along all that well with one another. They were very territorial, dominant; the need to command and lead was written into the very fabric of their magic. *Our* magic. I was an angel now. That meant I had the same powers *and* the same failings.

What was my fate? What would the First Angel decide to do with me? With no territories available, she might still assign me to Colonel Fireswift's Interrogators or General Spellsmiter's Vanguard of front-line warriors. Neither option was particularly appealing.

Of course, Nyx might not give me an official position at all. She and her lover Ronan, the God of Earth's Army and Lord of the Legion, wanted to use me to wield the weapons of heaven and hell. My balanced light and dark magic made me uniquely qualified for that task, but I wasn't any more interested in being a living weapon than I was in being an Interrogator or Vanguard warrior. The only reason Nyx and Ronan hadn't yet put their plans for me into motion was the two of them weren't speaking to each other at the moment.

And then there was Faris. I hadn't heard from Daddy Dearest since he'd visited my apartment in New York last week. Like Nyx and Ronan, he planned to use me and my magic as a weapon, but right now he was busy overseeing the punishment of his brother Zarion, God of the Faith, and Stash, Zarion's demigod son. Their sentence was one month of hard training in the gods' army. Faris's army. I didn't expect to hear from Faris until the month was over.

"I wonder what Soren is doing way out here," Ivy said.

Her words brought me out of my own circle of worries —and back to my immediate problem.

Last night, Captain Soren Diaz, a loyal Legion soldier, had suddenly gone missing from the New York office. We'd tracked his movements here to the Black Plains. No one knew what had led him here, but our mission was perfectly clear: to bring Soren back with us.

And I was assigned to lead it. Nyx had told me that the best way to master my new magic was to channel it into my work. The Legion took a very throw-you-off-the-deep-end approach to things. After all, every time we went through a promotion ceremony, we either leveled up our magic or died.

"This place gives me the creeps," Ivy commented, looking across the feral terrain. Her body shuddered.

I couldn't remember the last time Ivy had been in the field. Her position as a Legion counselor didn't generally throw her into the heat of battle. She excelled at talking to people, at calming them down. I had a sinking suspicion Nyx had sent her here to babysit my volatile new-angel emotions.

But right now, she was the one who needed comforting. "It will be all right." I set my hand on her shoulder. "We'll find Soren and bring him back. And no monsters will eat us."

Ivy shuddered again. "You call that a pep talk?"

I countered her frown with a smile. "Of course. Now, chin up. All this gloom and doom clashes with your outfit."

She laughed.

A chorus of beasts howled in the distance, as though in response to her laughter.

Drake's eyes scanned the plains, looking for the noisy monsters. "Soren sure picked a great spot to make new friends. What was he thinking?"

The plains of monsters were dangerous areas, consumed by the beasts when they'd overrun the Earth centuries ago. Only Magitech walls separated civilization from these wildernesses. Hunted criminals fleeing from the gods' justice sometimes hid out here in desperation, when no place in civilization was safe for them. They rarely lasted long. What had made Soren, a respected Legion soldier, come all the way out here?

"I guess we'll find out soon enough," I muttered.

I pointed out a figure leaning against a boulder. Soren. Blood stained the rock face and his clothes. It was *his* blood. He wasn't in good shape.

"Careful," I said as we made our way toward him. He was still so far away. "There are monsters nearby." I couldn't see them, but we could all hear them. And I could feel their minds buzzing in the background.

For a week now, ever since I'd woken up to find I was an angel, I'd been setting off on one short mission after the other. And when I was not out on a mission, I trained.

Nero had left a week ago to go on Nyx's mission. He was still away—I got a message from him every day or so, depending on whether he was close enough to civilization for his phone to have reception—so Harker had been training me.

The first few days had been the worst, but with a lot of training and even more self-discipline—gods, I hated self-discipline—I was managing my explosive magic. Managing, not excelling at it. Yet. But things had to get better, right?

I still couldn't fly. Well, at least not in a straight line

and not without crashing into things. Lots of collateral damage was pretty much where my flying was at right now. Flying was a lot harder than angels made it look.

On the plus side, the other gods had been mostly quiet lately. They were undoubtably still licking their wounds following the Crystal Falls training—and plotting their next moves. That meant they hadn't yet questioned me about becoming an angel without their blessing. I was not looking forward to that interrogation.

Lightning flashed across the sky, trailed by the rumbling roar of thunder. It was followed a few moments later by the hard patter of hail hitting the ground. The hail stones were as large as tennis balls.

"I knew I should have brought a shield," I commented.

A different sort of roar echoed across the plains now: a chorus of angry beasts. A hundred feet up the hill, a forest of spiky yellow trees shook and shuddered. A herd of razor-backed bulls burst out of the trees, their nostrils puffing noxious green fumes, the tips of their tails streaming trails of purple fire.

They beelined straight for us, dozens and dozens of beasts. Lightning flashed every second, in sync with every stomp of their heavy metal hooves. The monster tsunami stampeded around us, swirling closer with every loop they made around us.

CHAPTER 3

THE GREAT MONSTER FLOOD

I extended both my hands. Fire flared up in each open palm. Flames surrounded me in a fiery aura. It pulsed over my skin, along my hair, across my wings, down to the very tips.

A ribbon of fire shot out of me like a shockwave, torching every monster it touched. There was a loud, resounding pop, like a drum in an echo chamber—and then the fiery ribbon was gone.

"Cool," Alec sighed as burning monsters fell to the ground all around us.

"Now we know why the plains are black," Drake said.

Alec nodded with glee. "Because Leda scorched them with her magic."

"No time for jokes, you comedians," I told them. "More beasts are coming."

It seemed every monster on the Black Plains had responded to the razor-backed bulls' howling call to battle. The land was flooded with beasts, and not just bulls. There were wolves and birds and dinosaurs—and even a huge, hulking marine creature on legs that looked like a cross between a whale and a frog. The great monster flood rushed toward us, growing and growling.

Ivy glanced at me hopefully. "Any chance you can do that fire ribbon trick again?"

"Sorry, no."

It was a cool spell, one that I finally had enough magic to pull off, now that I was an angel.

"At this point, it's a once-per-battle trick," I said.

That was the downside of the spell, the once-per-battle problem. Maybe in time, I'd grow powerful enough to pull it off more frequently.

"Performing the spell completely blew out my elemental magic," I said.

"But you have other powers," replied Ivy.

"Yes." I grinned. "Yes, I do."

My team was fighting hard, giving the monsters a run for their money, but it wouldn't be enough, not without some angel magic to even the odds. There were just too many monsters.

I targeted the whale-frog with my shifting magic.

"You made that thing even bigger?" Drake gasped, his eyes wide as he stared up at the enormous beast that towered over us like a skyscraper in a village of cottages. "What is that good for? It will just step on us."

I cast a psychic wave. It exploded out of me, throwing back everything in sight—including the whale-frog. The gigantic beast flopped onto its back like a toppled turtle. I gave it another nudge with my psychic magic, and it began to roll uncontrollably, crushing every beast in its path.

Then, its momentum finally spent, its destructive capacity fulfilled, it flopped to a stop and shifted back to normal size.

Alec took out the monster with a sharp slash of his

sword. "You are the most badass angel ever, Leda," he said, his eyes alight with excitement. "I've never seen an angel fight so deliciously dirty."

Basanti was shaking her head slowly. I wondered if she was shaking her head at my dirty tricks or at Alec's appreciation of them. Probably both. If Basanti could have afforded the time to take her eyes off the battle, she certainly would have squeezed in a little face-palming for good measure. As it was, the storm of monsters was not subsiding. In fact, it seemed like the more beasts we killed, the more new ones rushed in to take their place.

I watched the monsters' advance, trying to decide what to do about them. Having blown the fuse of my elemental magic, my psychic magic, and then my shifting magic, my options were becoming more and more limited.

"Have any more magic tricks up your sleeves, Leda?" Ivy asked, panic streaking her words.

"I could curse them," I said. Curses and healing were the magical domain of fairies. "*If* I can remember the spell."

"If you can remember the spell?" Ivy repeated in disbelief as her arrow took down a purple wildebeest.

"Hey, give me a break. Curses are tricky business." I'd read through a few curses printed in old fairy spell books, but they were all complicated. "And there are so many of them to keep straight. You wouldn't want me to mess up and curse one of you, would you?"

"That depends," Ivy said, a small smile touching her lips. "Can you curse Alec with a sensitive personality?"

"I heard that, Ivy," Alec growled over the whistle of his swinging blade.

Ivy ignored him, her eyes trained on the new wave of

beasts crashing toward us. "Any day now, Leda. I don't think we can hold them off much longer."

"Curses are always overly long and complex," I said, mentally searching through my paltry library of curses. I hadn't possessed fairy powers for very long, so I was horribly ill-equipped in that branch of magic.

"This is why I have a desk job," Ivy muttered, continuing to shoot arrows at the beasts.

"A desk job that involves counseling elite soldiers, who have been powered up by the gods *and* possess major personality defects," Drake said, fighting beside her. "Legion soldiers are far more dangerous than monsters."

"There is one curse in particular that might work well here," I said, more to myself than to anyone else.

I wove the curse together, creating a spell that rolled over the monsters, knocking them all unconscious. Then the sparkling blue cloud puffed out. Fairy curses were generally very pretty.

"It is not an exciting spell. In fact, it's so dull that it put the monsters to sleep." I smirked at my team.

They all stared back at me blankly, clearly not amused by my joke. And they weren't alone. The next wave of monsters was storming toward us. They hadn't even paused to smell the humor in the air.

Performing that fairy curse on hundreds of monsters had overloaded my fairy magic. That was four fields of magic gone now. I was burning out my magic powers at an alarming rate. See, that was the problem with having the extra power boost that came with being an angel: if I accessed all the power I had, it overloaded my magic.

Basanti watched the approaching monsters. "It's almost like they're drawn here."

"Don't look at me," I said, holding up my hands. "I didn't invite them."

Basanti snorted softly and charged at the monsters, swinging her sword. I ran beside her. With four of my magic powers out of commission, I turned to witchcraft, tossing potion bottles at the beasts. And when I ran out of those, I turned to my vampire magic, using that strength and speed to power every strike of my sword.

Behind the curtain of reptilian beasts and hairy spiders closing around me, a flock of giant feathered monsters slashed at a barely-standing Soren. We'd found him! But would he last long enough for us to get to him? He wasn't in any condition to defend himself. The beasts barreled him right over.

Basanti sheathed her sword and caught my arm, pulling me back as I tried to run toward Soren. "There are too many of them. They're everywhere. We need to leave while we still can."

"Soren is still alive." I could see him twitching beneath the stampeding hooves and clawed paws. "I'm not leaving him behind."

"This is about more than losing one soldier. If we stay, we will all die." She gave me a pointed look. "Including an angel."

"The rest of you will take the truck," I said. "But I am staying. I will clear a path through the monsters for you to get away safely. And then I'll get Soren out of here."

"You don't fly all that well," Basanti pointed out. "There's no way you'll be able to fly a few hundred miles while carrying another soldier."

"Hey, don't you know me by now? I've been getting myself into trouble since I could walk, and I always find a way out of it." I shot her a crooked smile. "I never needed wings before. I can get along without them now."

Basanti drew her fighting staff and faced me down.

Smirking, I glanced from her weapon to her hard face. "Are you going to try to stop me?"

Basanti tapped her staff against her open palm. "If I have to. For your own safety."

"This is insubordination."

The corners of her mouth drew up. "Ironic words, coming from you."

I shrugged. "The attitude came with the wings."

"The wings you apparently don't need," she snipped.

"Well, I don't exactly *need* three double chocolate sundaes either, but that doesn't mean I don't appreciate them."

Basanti snorted. "Being on a mission with you is never dull." Her lips might have been smiling, but her eyes were as hard as granite. She wasn't backing down—and now the rest of my team was falling into line around her, facing me down.

"I was wrong," I said, frowning. "This isn't merely insubordination. It's a full-out mutiny."

"Harker told us to knock you over the head with a pole if we got in a hopeless situation and you predictably and stubbornly refused to leave," Basanti told me.

"Damn you, Harker," I muttered, then raising my voice, declared, "Harker and I have the same rank. He isn't in command of me."

"Maybe not, but he is in command of us," Basanti replied. "And if he orders us to save you from your own stupidity, we must comply."

I tracked their movements closely as they closed in.

"I'm sure there must be a Legion rule against calling an angel stupid."

"Those were Harker's words, not mine. Take it up with him."

"Oh, I will," I promised darkly.

More monsters poured over the horizon. Soren wouldn't survive if we didn't leave now. The monsters would devour him.

No, I refused to allow that to happen. I was going to save him. We were *all* getting out of here alive. I didn't know what had possessed Soren to run off and leave New York, but he was my friend. So was his girlfriend Nerissa. She would be heartbroken if he died. I couldn't allow that to happen either.

Desperate to save Soren and protect my team—yes, damn it, I wanted my cake and to eat it too—I wrapped my siren magic around the beasts, capturing their minds, their will, their magic. For a moment, all the monsters just stopped, frozen in place. Then they turned tail and retreated back across the plains as fast as their legs or wings could carry them.

"What just happened?" Alec asked in confusion, watching the beasts flee.

"The monsters all ran off." Drake looked at me. "She made them leave. She compelled them to go."

"Come on, guys. Monsters cannot be compelled," I laughed. "They were simply afraid of us."

Ivy's sculpted red brows arched. "Right before they were going to eat us?"

"See? I told you no monsters were going to eat us." I grinned. "They saw my wings and got scared."

"Your wings." Drake's gaze panned across my wings. They were currently a bright mix of red and orange, reacting to my emotions, which were running hot from battle. "Each angel has special powers, abilities unique to that angel. Is one of yours the power to compel monsters?"

No, it wasn't. I'd been able to control beasts long before I'd become an angel. But I didn't want to get into that now —or ever, for that matter. It would only lead to blowing open all my other secrets.

"We need to help Soren." I turned and walked toward him.

Soren rose slowly to his feet. He looked at me, blinking rapidly. "What happened?" His voice was scratchy, his eyes bloodshot. If he'd been human, he'd have died beneath that monster stampede.

"Monsters attacked us," I told him. "Thousands of them."

His eyes panned across the dead monsters lying all around us.

"There were more. They're gone now," I said.

Basanti closed in behind me and gave me a pair of handcuffs.

I glanced down at the silver cuffs in my hands. "I like Soren."

"I like him too," she said. "But we both know that wishful thinking isn't one of the cornerstones of the Legion."

She was right.

"No," I sighed. "It's not."

And I'd seen far too much to not exercise caution.

I slapped the cuffs over Soren's wrists. "It's nothing personal, Diaz. I have to do it. Procedure and all. You did desert the Legion."

"Desert," he muttered, as though he were chewing on the word—and didn't like the taste of it on his tongue.

"What happened?" I asked him. "Why did you run out of the New York office yesterday?"

"I…"

"You don't remember?"

"I remember *everything*," he gasped. "In perfect detail. The need to flee, to get out of there. Like my life depended on it."

"Do you still feel that way?"

He shook his head. "No. I do not. One moment, I was fine, and the next, I was totally consumed with panic. And then the panic left as quickly as it had come." His eyes quivered with fear. "Leda, I can't explain where those feelings came from. What if they come again? What if I'm broken?"

I patted his back. "You're not broken, Soren."

"How can you be sure?"

I couldn't be sure. Maybe Soren had just had a simple panic attack, and that was it. Except Legion soldiers didn't have panic attacks. My gut told me something else was going on here—something world-changing-big—and my gut was rarely wrong.

CHAPTER 4

THE GIFT

*M*y discussion with Soren during the long drive back to the Legion's New York office yielded nothing to shed light on his mysterious behavior. He claimed to have no explanation for his hasty departure yesterday morning. I had no reason to doubt him. I knew Soren well, and the baffled, powerless look on his face was not feigned.

Right before his desertion, he'd been resting in the New York office's medical ward, recovering from injuries incurred during training. Then panic had suddenly spiked in him, the feeling that it was imperative to get away immediately.

"Whatever ailed him was only temporary," I told Dr. Nerissa Harding in her lab as she began running a series of tests on Soren. "There were no signs of another outburst during our drive back here."

"This feels familiar," Nerissa replied.

"You're referring to what happened with Stash."

Many months ago, the supernaturals throughout the city began acting oddly, caught in a mad rage. We'd eventually tracked it down to my friend Stash, whose demigod magic was affecting them.

"Except Stash isn't even on Earth right now," I told Nerissa.

He was training with the gods on another world, under the weight of Faris's iron fist.

"And it's different this time," I continued. "Stash's warriors didn't even remember doing what they'd done. Soren remembers every moment, every thought that he had, every feeling that burned through him. He was over-loaded with panic. That's what caused him to desert. I wonder…" I glanced from Soren to Nerissa. "Could this be a new demon weapon? A weapon that fills a person with an overwhelming sense of panic? The Legion wouldn't be very effective if its soldiers all turned and ran from battle."

"I don't know, Leda." Nerissa shook her head. "I won't know anything until I've run some tests on Soren's body and magic." She flicked her hand, shooing us away. "Which I can't do as long as you are all breathing down my neck."

"Sorry." I stepped toward the door, motioning for my team to follow me. "It's just that Soren's my friend, you know."

"I know," Nerissa sighed. "And I will figure out what's going on with him."

Her face was hard, her eyes determined. She and Soren had been dating for nearly a year. She cared about him—maybe even loved him. She wouldn't stop until she'd found an explanation for his odd behavior.

"Where to, boss?" Alec asked me with a wicked smile. It was a smile that had incited its fair share of incensed behavior—and broken more than a few hearts.

"To Demeter," I replied.

Demeter was our canteen, and I was famished. Trekking across the Black Plains and battling monsters had a way of sparking one's appetite.

"Good. Your stomach is growling so loudly that it's shaking the walls," Basanti said.

I rolled my eyes. "It's not *that* bad."

"Oh, it is," Ivy told me.

Drake grinned. "It sounds like someone is firebombing the building."

I folded my arms over my chest. "I have the sinking suspicion that none of you respect my authority."

"Sure, we do," said Drake.

"Right," Alec said, nodding eagerly. "You're the angel with the prettiest wings. They look like sparkly little rainbows."

I shook my head slowly. "What did I do to deserve this mockery?"

"Do you really want an answer to that?" Ivy asked.

I snorted. "Probably not."

"I'd love to stay, but I have to welcome our newest batch of initiates," Basanti said.

"You'll be training them?" I asked.

She nodded. "For the next month."

"Well, in that case…" I smirked at her. "I suppose I'll need a new babysitter."

Basanti's laughter trailed her all the way down the hall. The rest of us continued toward the canteen.

Demeter was bursting with life. Nearly every table was full of Legion soldiers, chatting as they loaded up on food before the long day began. Those conversations sizzled out the moment I stepped into the room. Every pair of eyes locked onto me. Every step that I took echoed off the absolute silence.

"Haven't they ever seen an angel before?" I commented softly.

"I think it's safe to say that they've never met an angel like you before," Drake told me.

"Nor will they ever again," Ivy added with a rosy smile.

Soldiers peeled away, making room for me as we approached the food counters. They continued to stare, watching my every move. It was downright eerie, and after two weeks as an angel, I still hadn't gotten used to it. I didn't think I ever would.

My tray filled with food, I sat down at the nearest empty table with the rest of my team. The silence hanging over the canteen shattered like a glass ball against a marble floor. The buzz of the soldiers' rapid whispers filled the room.

"They're certainly excitable today," I commented.

"You're an angel now, Leda. You're supposed to sit at the head table, not here with us," Ivy reminded me.

"Yes, I'm an angel, damn it, and so I'm going to sit with my friends," I said, challenging the idea of assigned seats. "There's no one at the head table right now, and I don't want to sit alone. Sitting and eating alone sucks. There have to be some perks to being an angel, right? Something better than brooding in solitary silence."

"Not that you could ever keep silent, Leda," Drake teased me.

I frowned at him. "I'm already starting to regret my decision to sit with you guys."

A shadow rolled over my breakfast. I looked up at the skylight, but the shadow's source was closer than the sky. A soldier stood beside the table.

"Yes?" I asked him.

The silent soldier set down the big box in his hands,

placing it on the table right in front of me. He bowed deeply to me, then he turned and left, all without saying a word.

"He sure looked devoted," Drake said, his eyes twinkling.

"Yeah, he was staring at Leda like she farts rainbows and walks on sunshine," Alec added.

My so-called friends were shaking with laughter.

I glared at them. "Oh, shut up." I turned my attention to the box.

"What do you think is in it?" Ivy asked me.

I leaned in for a closer look at the box. "I haven't got a clue."

The box looked like a normal plain delivery box. It was the sturdy sort that the Legion used, not a flimsy cardboard box that would turn soft and spring holes in the sides if it happened to rain too much during transit.

I glanced at the shipping label. "It's from Nero."

His name wasn't on the box, but I recognized his handwriting on the label, which read: 'Pandora, The Legion of Angels, New York'.

"General Windstriker sent you a present," Ivy told me in a sing-song voice, fluttering her eyelashes.

The soldiers in the canteen had returned their attention to their breakfasts, but at Ivy's words, every person in the room spun around to stare at me once more.

"Do you think you can say that louder?" I said to Ivy in a hissed whisper. "I think there might be a few initiates in Basanti's class that didn't hear you."

Ivy chuckled.

"I wonder what's inside," Drake said as I slid my hand across the box's smooth surface.

"Jewelry," Ivy declared with confidence.

"Jewelry?" I repeated. "Have you noticed how big the box is?"

She smiled. "Room for a lot of jewelry. Angels like to make a big statement."

"Do you know what makes a big statement? A rocket launcher." Alec's lips curled up, and a dreamy glimmer slid over his eyes.

"A rocket launcher wouldn't fit in that box," Drake told him.

"It would if you disassembled it."

"General Windstriker didn't send Leda a weapon," Ivy told Alec.

"Why not?"

"Because weapons aren't romantic."

Alec shrugged. "They are to an angel." And from the look on Alec's face, he found the idea of weapons pretty damn romantic himself.

Ivy pointedly looked away from him, turning her attention to me instead. "I bet there's lingerie inside."

"Just a few seconds ago, you were sure it was jewelry," said Drake.

"There's space for both jewelry *and* lingerie. As Leda pointed out, it's a big box." Ivy turned a demure smile on me. "Maybe it's an engagement ring."

"The Legion arranges all angels' marriages," Alec pointed out.

"Stop it," Ivy snapped at him. "You're such a party pooper." She slid the box toward me. "Leda, give the box a shake and see what you hear."

"Or she could, you know, just open it," Drake said.

Ivy looked positively scandalized at the suggestion. "That is *not* how you savor a present." She held up her index finger. "First, you make wild speculations regarding its contents." She counted off a second finger. "Then you poke and prod and shake it while you speculate some more." She popped up a third finger on her hand. "And only then, after all that, do you open it and see what's inside."

"What a ceremony." Drake frowned at Alec. "Is that how you savor a present?"

"Nope. I rip the box open right away and pull it out. You can't savor something you can't touch."

Ivy pressed her lips together. "That is a man's answer."

"I am a man, honey." Alec wiggled his eyebrows at her. "If you doubt me, a demonstration can be arranged."

Ivy made a face. "No demonstration is necessary, Morrows. Or wanted. Keep your pants on."

Alec chuckled like a panther hiding in the bushes, sneaking up on an unsuspecting deer.

"Well, what are you waiting for?" Ivy asked me. "Give it a shake."

I shook the box. A rustle of movement responded to my action. I quickly set the box back down on the table.

"What is it?" Ivy asked eagerly. "What did you feel?"

"Something is alive in there." I stared at the box with trepidation. "And I think I just woke it up."

Alec flashed me a bright, shiny grin. "Aww, how romantic. General Windstriker sent you a monster."

Drake squinted at the box on the table. "That would be a small monster." He measured the box with his hands.

"You're both being ridiculous," Ivy told them. "General Windstriker did not send Leda a monster."

"Why not?" Alec asked.

"Because…well, because that would be the lamest gift ever! That's why!"

Except Nero was currently investigating a surge in the

monster population. Maybe he'd sent me one of those monsters, so I could take a look at it, maybe test it in the lab. I glanced at the package. The origin city was Judgment.

Judgment was a Frontier town, situated along the Magitech wall that separated civilization from the plains of monsters. In Nero's last message to me, he'd mentioned being there. Since there were no high-end Legion facilities out there on the edge of civilization, he'd probably sent the monster to me in New York.

I couldn't help but feel disappointed. I would have much preferred a present to a monster.

"Well, there's only one way to find out what's really inside," I sighed.

I began opening the box's many locks. There was probably a note inside, complete with testing instructions to accompany the monster.

Beside me, Ivy was bursting with excitement. "Oh, the suspense is killing me."

"Let's hope the monster inside doesn't kill you," said Drake.

"Very funny."

Drake smirked at her.

The two of them were so cute together. No one understood why they still weren't a couple.

"And?" Ivy demanded, practically bouncing in her chair.

I stared into the box and chuckled.

"What is it?" Ivy asked me.

I pulled a fluffy white kitten out of the box.

Alec watched the cat for a moment in confusion, as though he weren't sure what to make of it. The kitten blinked its blue eyes. Then it sneezed.

"Oh, yes, a very ferocious monster, to be sure," Ivy laughed.

It was Alec who blinked now. "It's a cat."

"A very adorable cat." Ivy rubbed the kitten under its chin. "And look at its cute little collar. Are those real diamonds on it?"

I took a closer look. "I believe so."

"See?" She smiled at Drake and Alec. "I told you there was jewelry for Leda inside the box."

"Technically, the jewelry is for the cat," Drake told her.

"And the cat is for Leda," replied Ivy. "Hence the jewelry is hers. Come on, Drake. You're a soldier. You know how a hierarchy works."

Alec rose in his chair and stared into the box. "What, no lingerie?"

"No," I told him.

He looked disappointed.

"The cat would have torn holes in the lingerie anyway," I pointed out.

"Even better," he said, his eyebrows wiggling.

I looked at Ivy.

She shrugged. "Did you honestly expect a different response from Alec?"

"No," I admitted.

Alec shook the box. "Anything else in here?"

"Like what?" I asked.

"Like maybe a rocket launcher."

"No," I said as Ivy nearly choked on her orange juice.

"Why on Earth would General Windstriker put a rocket launcher in a box with a cat?" she coughed.

"In case the cat got bored, of course. Cats need toys too."

"Yeah, like a toy mouse or a feather on the end of a

string. Not a military-grade weapon. Cats like to play, not make war."

"Sounds like a boring animal. If I had a cat, it would have a rocket launcher."

Ivy dropped her face to her open palms. "I don't think anyone here doubts that, Alec."

"Why exactly did General Windstriker send you a cat?" Drake asked me.

I petted the kitten on the head. "To cuddle."

"To cuddle?" Drake repeated, confused.

"Yes, Nero sent me a cat to cuddle when he's not around. Basanti has a cat to cuddle when she's away from her angel. I told Nero that I needed one too." I chewed on my lower lip. "Actually, I wasn't completely serious. I don't even know how to take care of a cat."

"It's usually a good idea to feed it," Drake told me helpfully.

I presented the kitten with a slice of orange.

"That won't work," said Drake. "Cats don't like citrus scents. They overload their sensitive noses."

"Since when are you an expert on cats?" Alec asked him.

"Cats, dogs, even bunnies. I worked part-time at a pet store when I was in high school."

The kitten opened its mouth and took a bite out of the orange slice.

"Apparently, you're not as much of an expert as you thought," Alec told Drake.

Drake frowned at me. "That's a weird cat you've got there, Leda."

"Of course she is. She's mine." I grinned at the kitten. "And I love her already."

"I prefer dogs," said Alec. "They do what you say. Cats are so unruly. So chaotic."

I arched my brows at him. "Sound familiar?"

Alec snorted. "Yeah, it does."

"Is there anything else in the box?" Ivy asked me. "Like maybe the kind of toy a normal, not-owned-by-Alec cat would enjoy?"

I looked into the box. "No toys, but there is a note."

"Well, don't leave us hanging, Leda. Read it."

Ivy was leaning forward so far that her chest nearly crashed into the tabletop. But so was everyone in the canteen. Gods, I felt like I was on display. I guess that was just the reality of being an angel—an angel with an archangel lover, for that matter. The Legion hadn't had something this juicy to chew on since Nero's parents had gotten together.

I unfolded the slip of paper I'd found inside the box. Nero wouldn't have written anything he'd mind if others saw, in case the package was opened by someone else. Of course, that didn't mean *I* was comfortable with others hearing what he had to say.

Well, if it was too racy, I just wouldn't read it aloud.

But what was written on Nero's note wasn't racy. It was funny.

"Pandora," I read. "I purchased this kitten for you from a pet store in Judgment. The pet store owner claims it's a purebred, but its insubordinate behavior brings that statement into question."

I imagined Nero trying to order the cat to quietly step into the box. I couldn't imagine the cat had been pleased with the command. It had most certainly fought back. I had a feeling the cat hadn't been unconscious solely for its own comfort during transit. It had probably been the only way to get it into the box.

I read the rest of the note. "P.S. The pet store owner named the cat Creampuff. You should rename the animal immediately. A pastry dessert is not a dignified name for an angel's cat."

Before I'd tucked Nero's note into my jacket pocket, everyone at my table was laughing—and they weren't alone. Isolated chuckles punctuated the room's silence. When I turned to look, however, everyone pretended to be really interested in their food.

"General Windstriker is right, you know," Drake told me.

I smirked at him. "There's no point in sucking up to Nero when he's not here, Drake."

"Sure there is," he chuckled. "Angels are always watching."

"That's gods, not angels. And I think the gods have better things to do than watch us eat lunch."

I scratched the kitten behind its ears. It purred deeply, nestling up against me. The act of petting it was surprisingly soothing. It was then that I realized Nero's gift of a kitten was about more than having someone to cuddle when he was gone. Petting a cat was relaxing, soothing. Nero knew my emotions were all over the place after becoming an angel, and he was trying to help me regain some equilibrium. It was such a sweet gesture that I nearly cried.

Ivy set her hand on my shoulder. "Are you all right?"

Swallowing my bubbling emotions, I wiped my wet eyes. "Fine," I told her brightly. "Just fine."

I'd thought I'd been handling my wild angel emotions pretty well for the past week, at least in public. And now here I was again, weeping in front of everyone. Talk about regression.

Something crashed. My kitten sprang up into the air, then scuttled under the table. I looked down at the trembling white fur ball hiding between my feet.

I scanned the canteen for the source of the crashing noise. Across the room, a table had overturned. Two female soldiers were locked in a wrestling match, rolling over the scattered remains of broken plates and glasses.

Every soldier in the room was watching them fight. No one even tried to stop them. Weird. Granted, fights didn't break out that often in the middle of lunch, but if they had, they were quickly subdued. What were the guards waiting for?

"They are waiting for you, Leda," Drake told me. "You have to step in and stop the fight. You are the ranking officer here."

Oh, right. Harker wasn't here, and I was an angel. My transformation had come so suddenly, so abruptly, that it was easy to forget what I was now.

I waved to the pair of Legion security guards standing on either side of the door. They moved in to stop the fight, but the dueling soldiers pushed them back, tossing them right through the window.

I jumped up and moved between the two fighters. They blasted me away with a barrage of firebombs.

"For two people who are trying to kill each other, you sure coordinated that well," I grumbled under my breath as I pushed free from the debris they'd buried me under.

I pushed out my hands. A powerful, explosive pulse of psychic magic punched out from me, knocking the dueling soldiers unconscious.

A hundred pairs of eyes gaped at me. No one in the

canteen was talking, but they were all staring. Some of them were looking at me with wide-eyed devotion. Over the years, I'd seen many people look at angels like that, but it felt so weird to be the object of that devotion.

"It seems like Soren's weird behavior is no longer an isolated incident," I told my friends as they closed in beside me.

CHAPTER 5

ANGEL OF CHAOS

I levitated the two unconscious soldiers with my telekinetic magic. "Finish your meal," I told my friends. "I'm taking them to Nerissa." I took a step, then glanced over my shoulder, looking at my kitten huddling under the table. "Here, kitty, kitty."

She must have decided I was an acceptable companion because she abandoned the shelter of the table to come to me.

As I left the room, my magic carrying the two soldiers down the hall, my little kitten trotting by my side, voices burst to life in the canteen. I knew they were gossiping about me, but I didn't care to listen.

"Go away," a harried voice called out from behind stacks of books as I stepped into Nerissa's office.

"Nerissa?"

Nerissa peeked over the top of the book stacks. "Oh, it's you, Leda." She stepped out from behind her desk. "I thought it was Dr. Young again. He's been nagging me every five minutes, trying to commandeer my magic microscope for his silly vampire blood study. He had a perfectly functional one until this morning. Is it my fault he spilled the leftover milk from his chocolate puffs cereal all over it, now I ask you?"

"I didn't even know we had chocolate puffs cereal."

I would have totally gone for that kind of breakfast. It sure beat the unflavored oatmeal the canteen usually served.

"The offending chocolate puffs came from Dr. Young's private supply. I told him it's not good to eat where you w—"

Suddenly, Nerissa, the Legion's gossip queen, stopped and looked at me—or, more accurately, at what was floating in the air before me.

"Leda, why are you bringing me bodies?" Her eyes narrowed, and she added, "*Again.*"

"They're alive this time."

"Well, that's an improvement at least," she said drily.

"That remains to be seen. They suddenly started fighting in the canteen." I set the sleeping soldiers down on two of the cots in Nerissa's lab. "They were at each other's throats. I think they would have killed each other if I hadn't stepped in."

Nerissa glanced down at them. "More soldiers acting strangely. Like Soren."

"There are similarities," I agreed. "Soren fell into a blind panic. These two soldiers fell into a blind rage. They wouldn't listen to anyone. They knew only attacking."

"In both cases, their emotions overpowered their minds, their higher reasoning," Nerissa said. She glanced down at my kitten. "What's this?"

"My cat."

"When did you get a cat?"

"Just now. Nero sent her to me."

Nerissa considered the cat. "She's cute."

I grinned. "I know." I returned my attention to the sleeping soldiers. "Let's see what they have to say for themselves." I slapped their faces. When that didn't wake them, I grabbed two drink glasses and headed for the sink.

"What are you doing?" Nerissa asked me.

I filled the two glasses with water.

"You can't mean to—"

I tossed cold water on the soldiers' faces. They both jumped up like they'd been electrocuted. Their eyes darted around wildly, looking for the person who'd attacked them with cold water. Their gaze fell on me—and the fight went right out of them, like a deflated balloon. Rather than murderous as they'd been in the canteen, they looked merely confused.

Right then, Ivy walked into the lab. Her eyes immediately honed in on the puddle. "Why is there water all over the floor?"

"Leda," Nerissa replied with a sigh. She glanced at the puddle and muttered something about liquids and sensitive magic equipment.

"Take my cat back to my apartment would you, Ivy?" I asked my friend.

The two soldiers were blinking and looking around in apparent confusion. They seemed to be normal again, albeit a bit dazed, but I wasn't taking any chances. If they went berserk again, I didn't want them trampling my little kitten.

"Sure thing," Ivy told me. She lifted the cat into her arms and carried her out of the room.

"Do you know who I am?" I snapped my fingers at the dazed soldiers to get their attention.

"Pandora," said one of them.

"The Angel of Chaos," added the other.

"The Angel of Chaos, you say?" I nodded in approval. "I like that. I like it a lot. In fact, I think I'll adopt it." I made a mental note to have the seamstress stitch the title onto all my jackets. Then I returned my attention to the two soldiers. "Do you know where you are?"

"In Dr. Harding's office," said the second soldier.

"And do you know how you got here?"

"We were talking. Then I was suddenly overcome with rage," said the first soldier.

"As was I," said the second. "I jumped at her."

"And I jumped at her, right over the table between us."

"We pushed back the guards."

"We pushed you back."

They looked at me, guilt painted across both their faces. They were worried that I'd punish them.

"And then what happened?" I prompted them.

"You knocked us out."

"And then we woke up here."

"And the rage that overcame you?" I asked.

"Gone."

"Nothing but a distant memory."

"Just like what happened with Soren," Nerissa said.

I glanced at her. "Did you learn anything from your tests on Soren?"

"There was nothing unusual in his magic or body. No signs of any foreign influence."

I nodded at the two soldiers. "And them?"

Nerissa looked at the magic samples she'd collected from them. "They are normal too."

"This is different than what happened with Stash's army," I said.

"Yes. I can find no evidence of anything controlling any of them."

"Nothing you can detect," I pointed out. "But maybe you can only detect it when they are acting strangely."

"Where are you going with this?" Nerissa asked me.

"The next time someone goes berserk, we need to test them *while* they are berserk."

"How do you know it will happen again?"

"Experience," I replied. "I'm the Angel of Chaos, remember? Disasters are pulled in by me. They gravitate toward me. Trust me. Whatever weird thing is going on, it will happen again. And we have to be ready."

Nerissa returned to testing her patients, and I returned to my room. But first I took a quick detour to the kitchen to grab some snacks. The disturbance in the canteen had cut my meal short.

I met Harker on the final staircase up to the top floor, a corridor reserved for angels and highly ranked Legion officers.

"I heard what happened in the canteen," he said. "Where are the soldiers involved in the altercation?"

"In Nerissa's office. She is examining them. They remember doing everything and feeling they *had* to do it, but they can't say what made them lose control."

"That's strikingly similar to what you wrote to me about Captain Diaz's odd behavior."

"Yes, it seems we have an epidemic."

"But what's the cause?" Harker said. "And what's behind it?"

"The demons," I decided. "I think they are testing a new weapon on us, one that causes our soldiers to lose control over their emotions. Panic in Soren's case. Anger in the incident with the two soldiers in the canteen. Because

53

if we have no control, it doesn't matter how much magic we have. The demons' army will be able to run us right over, and we'll be too busy cowering in fear or fighting one another to stop them. We'll never put up a fight."

"It does indeed sound like the sort of underhanded strategy the demons would employ," Harker agreed. "Very cloak and dagger."

"We should have our scientists start working immediately on a way to detect this influence," I said. "The cause could be anything. Infecting people with a potion. A curse. Telepathic manipulation."

"That's a very broad spectrum. We need to narrow it down. Leda, I want you to investigate what the three affected soldiers were doing in the days leading up to these incidents. Try to find similarities. What missions they were on. What they ate. What people they interacted with."

"I'll get started as soon as I get changed." I indicated the slashes in my uniform, courtesy of the two fighting soldiers in the canteen. Rolling over broken glass wasn't any more fun than it sounded.

"Leda, be careful. There's a chance whatever this thing is, it's contagious."

That was a definite possibility. The demons' weapon would be most effective if it spread quickly, and the best way to accomplish that was to let us infect one another. It would spread through the Legion like wildfire, consuming us even before we knew it was there.

I smiled. "Am I not always careful?"

"I'm going to pretend you didn't say that."

"Harker?" I said as he moved away.

He turned back toward me.

"You ordered my team to subdue me and haul me back

here if things got tough out there," I said, and I wasn't smiling this time.

"I ordered them to save you from your own foolishness."

"It was not your call to make. Nyx gave me the mission to find Soren and bring him back here, not you."

"It was Nyx who instructed me to protect you. With force if necessary," he added.

I wasn't surprised. Nyx had her own plans for me. Those plans were pretty contingent on my survival.

"Don't take it personally, Leda. Nyx's priority, the Legion's priority, is to protect the Earth. And that means not letting angels throw away their lives in hopeless situations."

"It wasn't hopeless. I saved Soren, and I brought him back alive."

"Indeed you did," Harker agreed, smiling.

He looked proud of me. I knew he hadn't enjoyed telling my team to bring me back alive, in chains if necessary, but he had to follow Nyx's orders.

"And if I had left when things got tough, if I hadn't brought Soren back, we would be even further from figuring out what the demons are up to," I pointed out.

"Everyone is talking about what you did on the Black Plains," Harker said, his voice low. "How you compelled the monsters to run away, right at the moment when they had you all completely cornered and were moving in to kill you."

"News travels fast," I muttered.

"That kind of news does. How did you do it?"

I looked up and down the corridor. No one was around —that I could see. That didn't mean someone wasn't listening. I opened my apartment door and waved at Harker to follow me inside.

He frowned. "As you said, news travels fast. I don't need Nero to hear rumors of me following you into your apartment."

"Better that than the rumors that would spread if we continued this conversation out here. Besides, Nero knows you only have eyes for Bella."

"What a man knows means little when emotions flare. These recent incidents have shown us that." But Harker followed me into my apartment anyway.

My new kitten was waiting inside, perched atop a giant cat cushion. A toy mouse held securely between her paws, she purred in victory. My living room was filled with cat trees, jungle gyms, toys, and food dishes. Wow, Ivy worked fast. How had she gotten all these cat things already? She'd only left Nerissa's office half an hour ago at most.

Harker's gaze fell on the kitten. "You have a new roommate? Or did you shift Nero into a cat?"

"No," I laughed. "Nero sent me a pet cat to cuddle."

"It's smaller than the cat Leila sent Basanti," Harker said, amused.

"She's still a kitten. She'll grow."

"But I have to say that Basanti's cat doesn't have a diamond collar." Harker chuckled. "Nero probably knew that when he made a move to upstage Leila."

I shrugged. "Well, no one ever accused angels of being subtle."

"Neither is your friend Ivy."

He glanced at the kitten's giant purple sleeping cushion. It was made in the shape of a mouse with angel wings. It looked completely ridiculous, but my kitten seemed to love it.

"Ok, Leda, spill the beans. What really happened with the beasts on the Black Plains? Rumor has it that controlling them is your unique angel power."

I gave him a pointed look.

In response, he pulled the blueberry-sized Magitech device out of his jacket pocket and put up a magic privacy screen.

I watched the pulsing yellow ball hovering between us. "Have you acquired any unique powers since becoming an angel?"

"Not yet."

"Neither have I. Controlling beasts isn't some new power I've acquired with my transformation. I did it before, back when I wasn't an angel at all."

"When?"

"I first learned I could control monsters last year when Nero and I went to the Lost City. He showed me how to do it."

Harker blinked in surprise. "Nero can control monsters too?"

"Yes, but not as well as I can. I can control them because of my magic. It's light and dark, just like the beasts. And the stronger my light magic and dark magic get, the better I can control the monsters."

"And Nero? How can he control them? He has only light magic."

I shook my head. "I don't know."

"Your ability to control the monsters grows as your magic does."

"Yes."

"The gods must know by now what happened on the plains," he said. "You saved your team by driving back the monsters, without even lifting a sword, just by looking at them."

"I had to protect my team."

"Everyone is talking about it, Leda. You did what the gods have been trying to accomplish for centuries: regain control over the monsters. They will come calling."

I crossed my arms over my chest. "Then I'd better be ready when they do."

"Leda…"

"Will you train with me?"

"You know I will, but I'm not sure it will be enough if the gods come."

"Maybe not, but it would help considerably if I could at least fly in a straight line."

"Indeed," Harker laughed.

"I have to get changed and then get to work tracking the three affected soldiers' movements over the last few weeks," I said. "But let's train tonight."

"Ok." He set his hand on my shoulder, looking at me like he was standing in the presence of a doomed woman.

"I'm not dead yet."

"It's not your life I'm worried about, Leda. I don't think the gods will kill you if they find out what you are, not once they realize you can control monsters. It's your freedom that's in danger."

"Thanks for being a good friend. Again."

He collected his magic orb. "Don't mention it."

After he left my apartment, I pulled a fresh leather uniform out of my closet. I emerged from my bedroom clean, shiny, and fully decked out in black leather.

"Ok, kitty," I said, petting her softly on her head. "Now let's get to the bottom of the demons' scheme."

CHAPTER 6

PHANTOM WEAPON

*L*ike a good angel, I sat in my designated spot beside Harker at the head table in the canteen, eating pasta with vegetables, which was supposed to be very healthy. Even before the first bite, I was already wishing for a dessert. But what kind of example would that set for the other soldiers, an angel eating dessert for dinner?

I sighed. Setting a good example wasn't all that much fun.

"In the past two days, Nerissa has run every test on the three soldiers that she could think of, and she's found nothing," I told Harker. "All three are acting perfectly normal again. No one else has been affected either. If this thing is contagious, it works slowly. The two soldiers went berserk two days after Soren, so we might be due for another incident soon."

"Have you found any possible explanation for their odd behavior?" Harker asked me.

"I found that all three soldiers were in the New York office when the incidents occurred. No other Legion office has reported a similar incident, and there have been no reports of soldiers acting oddly anywhere on Earth. All three ate at this canteen in the days leading up to their outbursts, but so did all the rest of us. Two of the soldiers have not been out of the city in the last month; the third went on a mission to the Black Plains last week."

"The Black Plains." Harker rubbed his chin, his face contemplative.

I knew what he was thinking. "She wasn't the first soldier affected, though, so this isn't some curse she brought back from the wilderness. Basanti was in charge of that mission, and she's just fine. So is everyone else on the team. Not a single one of them has displayed any symptoms."

"Not that the three affected people are showing any symptoms anymore either," Harker pointed out. "What else did you find?"

"I thought the Nectar might be contaminated, but none of them were promoted in the same cycle. Soren was promoted last year. Sergeant Mackerel was promoted two months ago. Corporal Dunn has not been promoted in years."

"You're grasping at straws now, Leda."

"Straws are all this thing's made of."

Harker made a give-it-to-me gesture with his hands. "Continue."

"Sergeant Mackerel works as a nurse in the medical ward."

Harker perked up at that. "Has any unusual illness gone through the medical ward recently?"

"No."

"Leda, do you enjoy torturing me?"

I gave him a half-smile. "Maybe?"

"Did you find anything of note?"

"No. I couldn't find any origin for the demons' weapon, and I don't have any idea how it spreads. Nerissa couldn't find any sign of anything in their bodies or in the bodies of anyone with whom they work closely. It is a phantom weapon."

"You seem to have covered all the bases."

"For all the good it did us," I said glumly.

Sighing, he glanced down at his dinner like he suddenly found it as unappetizing as I found mine.

"Two days, and I didn't accomplish anything." I gritted my teeth. "It feels like crashing into a wall. Repeatedly. Or like treading in water, not going anywhere but down, struggling just to keep my head above the water."

"You've mastered many magics, Leda," Harker said. "But not patience."

"I guess it's more fun to blow things up than to sit by, helpless and idle."

"So true," Harker laughed. "So what's your plan now?"

"Wait for another incident, and bring the affected soldier to Nerissa so she can test them while they're still acting strangely."

"So, wing it?"

I smirked at him. "The perfect strategy for an angel."

"Speaking of winging it, in the meantime, I have some exercises to keep you occupied."

"Not flying exercises, I hope."

He cocked an eyebrow at me. "I thought you wanted to fly."

"I do. I just always thought flying involved more being in the air and less falling out of it and crashing into things."

"It will," he assured me. "Just give it time."

"You could fly right away after becoming an angel."

"And you can play 'O Come All Ye Faithful' on yogurt containers. We each have our own special talents."

He was referring to my performance at the Legion talent night in the New York office a few months ago. Most people had showed off their prowess with a weapon or how they could masterfully weave spells. I had gone for a decidedly different approach—much to the amusement of the audience, but not the angels. Harker had buried his face in his hands. While Nero had looked positively scandalized.

"Do these exercises of yours include pushups?" I asked Harker.

His brows lifted.

I sighed. Of course the exercises involved pushups. This was the Legion of Angels.

"Wing pushups," he told me.

Goody.

"How many?" I asked.

"That depends."

"On whether or not I've been a good girl?"

He laughed. "On how long you can stay conscious."

"You're as bad as Nero," I told him.

"The wing pushup routine is actually Nero's. He gave it to me to strengthen my wings so I could prolong my flight time."

"How many wing pushups can you do in a row?"

"Two-thousand-three-hundred-and-fifty-two is my record."

I stopped my jaw before it dropped. "I guess I'll knock out a quick three thousand and then see how I'm feeling," I said casually.

"You're crazy," he chuckled.

"It sure beats being boring."

A ripple of excited whispers buzzed across the canteen. The soldiers parted away from the main aisle, making way for a new arrival. A small white kitten trotted down the aisle, her tail poised in the air, strutting like she owned the place. Like she was the queen.

"Her Majesty has returned from the hunt," Harker commented.

My cat had something in her mouth. Her prey. I took a closer look. It was a dead seagull. The little kitten had grown a lot in the last two days. Her new abode suited her. She hunted in the gardens, catching her own food.

"Have a good hunt?" I asked her.

Purring, the kitten sat at my feet and dropped the dead bird into her ivory dish.

"Angel?" Harker read the name on the dish. "As in the cat of an angel? The property of an angel?"

"Angel, as in the name of an angel's cat," I told him.

"You named your cat Angel?"

"Yes."

He snorted.

"It's better than Creampuff."

He watched the kitten eat her seagull. "She can't be a creampuff. She's not even white anymore. There's blood and dirt all over her."

"Well, she is a paws-on kind of angel."

Harker's shoulders shook with suppressed laughter.

Dramatic opera music sang from his pocket.

"I know that opera," I said. "It's the Airship Queen."

A soprano voice trilled over a dramatic orchestra.

"It's the story of a witch who is as beautiful as she is clever. Were you thinking of someone in particular when you made that song your ringtone?"

Like my sister Bella.

But Harker wasn't laughing—not this time. He was staring solemnly at his phone screen.

"What is it?" I asked him.

"There's been another incident." He looked up from his phone, meeting my eyes. "Two hours ago."

"Why are we only hearing about it now?"

Gossip spread faster than that. Within five minutes of an attack at the office, everyone would have been talking about it.

"Because it didn't happen in New York," he said. "It happened at the Legion office in Chicago."

Chicago. That was the next closest Legion office.

"The demon's curse is spreading," I realized.

Harker's eyes panned back and forth across his phone. "The Legion soldier involved in this latest incident went into a rage. They barely stopped him in time."

"In time for what?"

"Before he blew up the Legion's Chicago office."

"Was anyone hurt?" I asked, my stomach clenching up.

"There were a few minor injuries. No one was killed."

"And the soldier involved?"

"He's been locked up," said Harker. "He remembers doing everything and being completely overwhelmed with fury. But now he's acting completely normal again. The fury is gone."

"And with it, our chance to test him while he was under the curse's influence," I sighed. "To detect it, to figure out what exactly we're dealing with—and to try to come up with some way to counter it."

"You should take a team to Chicago anyway, to see if you can find any clues that you missed here."

He was right. Before I could abandon my dinner, however, a brisk flick of sharp telekinetic magic threw the doors to the canteen wide open. Colonel Fireswift strode into the room, followed by four soldiers with bright, shiny Interrogator pins on their uniforms. Every person in the canteen fell silent and watched the Interrogator procession storm down the main aisle.

Colonel Fireswift stopped before the head table. "No, you won't be going to Chicago," he told me. He turned to address the whole room. "In fact, none of you are going anywhere. Until this situation is neutralized, no one leaves this building. And I promise you, we *will* get to the bottom of it, even if I have to interrogate every last one of you."

CHAPTER 7

THE INTERROGATOR

The Legion's New York office had grown considerably in the last year. There were five thousand soldiers stationed here. Interrogating them all would take weeks, if not months. To tackle this task, Colonel Fireswift would need a lot more than just the four Interrogators he'd brought with him. Perhaps, more of his people would be arriving shortly. I shuddered at the thought.

The Interrogators started off by confiscating the complete contents of my investigation. They then worked their way through the list of anyone I'd marked as a potential connecting person between the infected parties. I didn't see the point, given that the latest incident had occurred outside this office, all the way in Chicago. And besides, I'd already gone over everything a million times and found absolutely nothing. What we needed was to test someone while they were acting strangely, not waste time chasing flimsy connections.

Which was exactly what I told Colonel Fireswift when I was called into the Interrogation chamber.

"You are here to answer questions, not to tell me what to do," he said coolly. "When you are an Interrogator, you can have a say in how these investigations proceed."

I seriously doubted it. Colonel Fireswift did not strike me as someone who operated his division by popular vote. He commanded and expected his Interrogators to do whatever he said. Blindly following orders was not my forte, nor would I be happy doing so day in and day out.

"You can't make me an Interrogator, Colonel," I said. "I'm an angel now. And Nyx doesn't ever put two angels in the same division."

"I don't know how you pulled off this feat—"

"It wasn't me. I didn't pull off anything. It was the Everlasting telepath Athan. Unbeknown to me, he slipped Nectar into my drink to make me an angel. Then he placed Aleris's glasses over my eyes, so I'd see where his sister was being held and save her."

Which was mostly true, except for the very important difference that Athan had slipped me not just Nectar, but Nectar *and* Venom together. That had made me an angel and a dark angel in one, something Colonel Fireswift definitely did not need to know about. It was a good thing my magic had calmed down again, so I could mask my thoughts. Colonel Fireswift had no qualms about reading my deepest, darkest thoughts and condemning me for them.

"But I *will* find out how you skipped the queue to become an angel," Colonel Fireswift continued, ignoring my interruption. "Frankly, I'm surprised the gods haven't killed you for it."

I slid my hands over the cold surfaces of the wide silver metallic chair arms. Thankfully, the restraints were currently disengaged. But in my time at the Legion, I'd witnessed how quickly that could change in the Interrogation chamber. A single word, a single glance, could doom me. My pulse quickened, a nervous pop against my skin.

Colonel Fireswift would hear my racing pulse. He would smell my panic. So I covered my uneasiness with a little humor to distract him—and myself as well.

"Maybe the gods were just so impressed with my performance in the trials that they've decided I'm an invaluable asset they simply can't do without," I said, smiling,

Colonel Fireswift frowned. "Doubtful."

"Why?"

"You are wild, unruly, and completely replaceable."

"If I'm so replaceable, then why are you pushing Nyx so hard to get me into your division?"

He opened his mouth, then snapped it shut. He seemed to be trying to find a hole in the logic I'd wrapped around myself like a suit of armor.

"Speaking of trials, when are yours?" I asked him.

"The gods have set my archangel trials for next month." As soon as he spoke the words, his face hardened, as though he were upset with himself for being drawn into my smalltalk. "But we were not speaking of me. This is *your* interrogation. And if you survive it, you might just learn something that will help you when you become an Interrogator."

He sure was certain he'd get me in his division, even though I was an angel now. I really hoped he was wrong. Two angels weren't generally assigned to the same office or division, but I wasn't just any angel. And Nyx knew it. She would put me wherever she could use me best, and if that meant Colonel Fireswift's division, that's where I'd end up. There weren't any territories available for me to command, so she'd come up with something else for me. I really hoped she didn't think the place she needed me most was with the Interrogators. Or with General Spellsmiter's Vanguard.

Thinking about that made me uneasy, even more so than this interrogation.

"What would you like to know?" I asked Colonel Fireswift.

"That's better," he said, nodding. "Your own investigation condemns you as closely linked to the infected soldiers."

Wow, *condemned*. That was a telling word, like the dour dong of a funeral bell. Nice to know he wasn't jumping to wild conclusions.

"I definitely did not use the word 'closely'," I replied—calmly, I hoped. "I believe it was more like 'loosely'. And that same investigation listed over two hundred other people in this office who'd come into contact with all three affected soldiers in the month leading up to the incidents."

"Just over two weeks ago, you became an angel," Colonel Fireswift said, as though I hadn't spoken at all.

"And what does that have to do with anything?" I asked in exasperation.

"Shortly thereafter, strange things started happening at the Legion," he continued.

"You ate bacon and eggs and a glass of orange juice this morning for breakfast."

"How did you—"

"And a few hours later, one of your soldiers went berserk and tried to blow up the Chicago office and everyone in it."

"My breakfast had nothing to do with that," he snapped at me.

"And neither did my becoming an angel."

"Flippant remarks won't save you."

"But my innocence will," I said. "I had nothing to do with these strange incidents."

Clearly unimpressed, he continued, "Nine days ago, Major Holmes, the soldier who went berserk in my office this morning, visited the New York office on his way back to Chicago. You had lunch with him that day."

"So did the seven other people who were sitting at the head table in the canteen."

"Among them, Harker Sunstorm, Basanti Somerset, and Soren Diaz. They are suspects as well."

Gods, he was annoying.

"None of us have any idea how the demons' curse came to us, how it spreads, how to cure it, or even how to detect it," I told him, my patience crumbling against my fake smile.

His eyes narrowed. "You seem quite certain this is a demon curse. Why is that?"

"I am not certain, but given the facts at hand, it's the best guess I have. The demons are powerful enough to design a magic curse like this, and they have the most to gain from the Legion imploding in on itself. They are the most likely culprit behind these occurrences."

"You have a lot of experience with demons."

I had a bad feeling about where this was going. "I've faced them before," I said cautiously.

"For instance, when you spent several weeks with the demon Sonja."

Yep, my bad feeling was spot on. 'Spent' several weeks. Like it was a vacation.

"I was Sonja's prisoner," I ground out. "Not her guest."

"So you say."

"I was being held against my will, tortured by the demon and Soulslayer, one of her dark angels."

"Soulslayer, also known as the Legion deserter Balin Davenport, whose magic was inverted by the demons and made a dark angel," said Colonel Fireswift.

"Yes, that charming fellow."

"You were a prisoner, trapped far away, not even on this world. And yet here you now are, safe and sound, no longer trapped in a demon's dungeon."

"Nero and my family rescued me," I told him.

"And with them, the archangel Damiel Dragonsire."

I blinked.

"General Dragonsire has recounted to the Legion his involvement in your rescue."

"Well, there you have it," I said. "Straight from the mouths of angels."

Colonel Fireswift's mouth was tight, his eyes as hard as granite. "It's too easy."

"What's too easy?"

"Your escape from Sonja. Becoming an angel. These convenient, orderly explanations.

I kept my expression neutral. "I thought the Legion appreciated orderliness."

"In my many years leading the Interrogators, I've found that simple explanations are generally flimsy facades that mask seditious schemes."

"And what seditious scheme do you think I'm involved in, Colonel?"

"That's what I intend to find out," he told me.

"And if I'm innocent?"

"No one is completely innocent."

"Not even an angel?"

"You aren't like other angels." It sounded like an accusation.

"No, I'm not," I agreed. "But I'm not guilty either."

"We shall see."

I sighed, letting my back sink into the hard, unyielding chair.

"Let's start with the army the demons were *coincidentally* gathering in New York right around the time you joined the Legion," Colonel Fireswift said. "And we'll go from there."

CHAPTER 8

WILDFIRE

I sat with Harker at the head table in Demeter. It was just the two of us this morning. Basanti, who usually ate with us, had already eaten with her initiates earlier this morning, and now she was putting them through drills that were literally a matter of life or death. Soren was still under observation following the desertion incident. Everyone else who could sit at this table was away on some mission or another, Nero included.

I missed him, but his absence wasn't the only reason I was irritable. I was tired. I'd spent most of last night in the interrogation chamber, being grilled by Colonel Fireswift on every little thing I'd ever done since joining the Legion of Angels. I hadn't slept at all. And I was *still* wearing the clothes I'd had on yesterday. I'd come straight to the canteen from the interrogation chamber, my hungry tummy screaming for food.

"Colonel Fireswift conducted a similar interrogation on me," Harker told me. "He also asked me about everything I've ever done at the Legion."

"You've been at the Legion much longer than I have," I pointed out. "Two centuries is a lot of ground to cover."

"Fortunately, my first two centuries at the Legion were mostly uneventful—up until about a year and a half ago, when the future Angel of Chaos joined the Legion."

My new nickname sure had spread fast.

"So Colonel Fireswift is going over everything we've ever done. But why?" I asked. "What is he looking for? Does he really think something that happened so long ago would have any relevance to these recent incidents?"

"I think this is more about interrogating us than it is about the actual investigation, if you know what I mean."

"The recent incidents have finally given Colonel Fireswift the excuse he needs to interrogate angels and other key people," I realized. "He's using the investigation as a shield, so that he can dig into our secrets. So that he has the authority to do what he's never been able to do before."

"That's what I suspect," Harker said. "Fireswift tried something like this once before, many years ago, but Nero shut him down right away. Colonel Fireswift didn't have an excuse back then, but these recent incidents have given him all the ammunition he needs. When Legion soldiers start losing control of their minds, Nyx gets worried. The gods get worried."

"Then it's even more crucial that we get to the bottom of the incidents," I said. "The *true* reason, not wild conspiracy theories. Honestly, after all Fireswift and I have been through, I thought he'd at least leave me be for a month."

"It's not in his nature."

"Yeah, I know," I sighed. "I guess that's what I get for trying to see the best in people."

"Continue seeing the best in people, Leda. If anything else, it disqualifies you for the job of Interrogator."

I snorted. "Yeah, they always have to see the worst in everyone."

The doors to the canteen opened, and Angel strode into the canteen.

"Look at what the cat dragged in," Harker chuckled.

Angel trotted down the aisle, dragging a dead turkey.

"That looks like one of the wild turkeys that wander through the gardens around the office," I said.

Though my kitten had grown considerably since she'd arrived inside a present box two days ago, the turkey was bigger than she was. Even so, Angel dragged it with poise and grace, like she was a bride walking down the aisle, her long veil trailing after her.

Several people in the room laughed as Angel pulled the dead turkey toward the head table. A few even captured snapshots with their phone. I was one of them.

Harker looked at me. "What are you doing?"

"I'm going to send the picture to Nero so he knows his gift is being thoroughly appreciated." I added a caption to the photo I'd taken with my phone. "Gods, I love that cat. She makes me laugh. Just what I needed after last night."

A sly grin curled Harker's mouth. "Make sure you get the feathers all over the floor in the background of your shot. Nero will really love that.

"I thought you're supposed to make me behave, not encourage my bad behavior. Inciting naughtiness is not very becoming of an angel."

"You're right." His voice teetered on the precipice of a sigh.

I snapped a second shot, this time with the turkey feathers all over the floor. "You're right too," I told Harker as I sent the two photos to Nero. "Your idea made for a brilliant shot. You have a real eye for art."

Angel sat down at my feet and proceeded to eat the wild turkey she'd caught. How had she managed to catch a bird twice her size? I supposed that, like me, she was an underdog. Or an under-cat.

I'd finished my first plate of food and moved on to my second. Dessert was the dominant theme on my breakfast platters this morning. I wasn't overly worried about setting an example at the moment. After the shitty night I'd had, I wanted sweets and lots of them. Hey, even angels needed comfort food. Perhaps, *especially* angels.

"You're eating like this meal might be your last," Harker chuckled.

"If Colonel Fireswift has his way, it just might be." I ate a bite of blueberry pancake. "I missed most of dinner and a whole night of sleep stuck in that interrogation chamber. I'll need my strength when Colonel Fireswift pulls me in for round two."

"Good point," he said glumly. "I should do the same." He eyed my overflowing dessert plate. "Are you going to eat your marble cake?"

"Yes."

"All *five* pieces of marble cake?" he asked, reaching for my plate.

"Every single crumb." I lifted my fork in a warning gesture, ready to skewer his hand if he made a move on my cake.

Below the table, Angel hissed at him. It was nice to know she had my back.

Harker withdrew his hand. "You need to learn to share with your friends."

I forked a steamed carrot and put it on his plate. "You're welcome," I said with a smile.

Why the canteen was serving steamed carrots for breakfast was anyone's guess. Probably because they were healthy. But sweets were better. And the best part was that since I was immortal and immune to most ailments, all that sugar couldn't even kill me.

Harker frowned at the carrot I'd given him. "That is not cake."

"It's healthier than cake."

"Leda, you really shouldn't give health advice." He looked pointedly at my dessert plate—and the mountain of sweets piled onto it.

"You know, you could always get your own piece of marble cake. You don't need to steal any of mine."

"There isn't any more marble cake. You took it all."

I shrugged. "Ask the kitchen to make more. They have to listen to you. You're in charge here."

"Yes, I'm in charge here." He sat taller in his chair. "And I'm telling you to give me one of your pieces of marble cake."

"No." I took a bite of my cake.

"Why not?"

"Because they're all mine. And you're not in charge of me or my cake."

"It's my cake. My building. My city. My territory. Everything in this office is mine, including that cake." He sounded angry.

"You damn angels, always so possessive," I said, raising my voice. "You think everything you see is automatically yours. You are sick with Mine Syndrome."

"I hate to break it to you, Leda, but you're an angel too. You suffer from the exact same syndrome."

I arched my brows. "Then it was pretty stupid of you to try to steal my cake, don't you think?"

He growled.

"Very scary," I said sardonically.

"Don't test me, Leda." His nostrils flared in anger; his voice was a scathing hiss that scraped across my eardrums.

"No, you don't test me," I shot back.

Our stares locked for a few seconds. Then he reached for my cake. I slammed my fork down, right through his hand.

He looked at the fork in his hand, then up at me. His eyes were wide with shock. "I can't believe you just did that."

"And I can't believe you tried to steal my cake. What the hell has gotten into you, Harker?"

Before he could answer, a scream roared through the canteen, "She is mine, not yours!"

I scanned the room, searching for the source of the outburst. I found them right away, two male soldiers standing on either side of a long dining table, glaring at each other.

"She was never yours! And she never will be!"

Their agitated eyes flickered to a female soldier who stood at the end of the table, watching them both in surprise. She was obviously the object of their affection— and the source of their conflict.

"She doesn't want you. You're not good enough for her. Not strong enough."

"Let's just see who's not strong enough."

The two enraged soldiers jumped at each other, colliding in a punching, wrestling, rolling, kicking mess on the floor. Tables toppled. Dishes shattered. Food spilled all across the floor.

And the craziest part of it all was that everyone else in the canteen was cheering them on. The captive, incensed audience was roaring for blood and action. The rage spread like wildfire across the canteen, consuming everyone. They went from watching to participating. They were all acting like street fighters, not soldiers in the Legion of Angels.

I looked from that barbaric scene, to the fork I'd just put through Harker's hand. Suddenly, our cake dispute seemed pretty trivial. "I think the demon's curse has struck again." I freed the fork from his hand. "And it's escalated."

CHAPTER 9

AN ELUSIVE KIND OF MAGIC

*T*wo hundred highly-trained and disciplined Legion soldiers were engaged in an all-out brawl with one another in the middle of the New York office. A moment ago, I would have declared such a thing to be impossible, even after the recent incidents. Because there was a big difference between one or two soldiers losing control—and two hundred of them simultaneously going berserk. Two hundred wasn't a mere brawl; it was a civil war.

Harker and I moved in to break up the fight. The enraged soldiers didn't take kindly to that. In fact, anyone we got too close to tried to punch us in the face. Under normal circumstances, not a single one of them would have dared to strike an angel, let alone two angels. This was the demon curse at work all right. These soldiers were all running on raw emotions and base instincts, not rational thought. Even Ivy, Drake, and Alec were entrenched in the brawl, their eyes burning with magic, their minds completely overwhelmed by primal emotions. They didn't even seem to recognize me.

"We need to get one of these fighting soldiers to Nerissa for testing before the curse's effects wear off," I told Harker as a soldier fell unconscious at our feet.

In the previous incidents, the curse had seemed to wear off when its victim fell asleep. We needed a conscious soldier to test.

Angel leapt into the war zone, pouncing on a soldier who tried to get the jump on me. The soldier threw her off, howling as he freed himself from her claws, dug in deep into his back.

Angry that he'd attacked my cat, I blasted him with magic. I hit him too hard. The spell knocked him out— and sent him straight through a window. Oops. Every day since I'd become an angel, my magic seemed to grow stronger. It was kind of hard to get used to something that was constantly in flux.

I picked up Angel. "Are you ok?"

She replied with a meow, then jumped back into the fray. Apparently, I needn't have worried. She regularly hunted creatures many times her size. She was tough. A fighter. And she fought dirty—just like me. I witnessed that dirty fighting firsthand. Angel egged on a soldier, getting him to take chase. She jumped out of the way at the last minute, and the soldier crashed through a glass wall.

Another soldier swung a punch at me. I grabbed his swinging arm, then the other arm as he spun, twisting them both behind his back. I dragged him toward the door, where Harker was grappling with three security guards.

"I called them here to subdue the fight, not join in," he told me. "Whatever this curse is, it's highly contagious. The guards were affected within moments."

"Then why aren't we affected?" I asked.

"Angels are more resilient to curses, poisons, and diseases."

We left the canteen, holding the struggling soldier between us as we hurried down the hall. Or at least tried to hurry. The soldier made every step a battle.

"Enough," Harker said as we reached the stairwell. He cast a spell around the soldier, encasing him in magic.

In response, the enraged soldier banged his head hard against the glowing gold cocoon, knocking himself out.

I looked down at the unconscious soldier at the base of the stairs. "Now, that wasn't very clever, was it?" I told him.

Harker dragged the sleeping man off the stairs, and we backtracked to the canteen to grab another infected soldier. As we entered the room, I saw Angel dragging a kicking, thrashing soldier down the aisle by his collar. Wow, that cat was strong. No wonder she could take down a turkey. I wagered she could even take down something a whole lot bigger.

Angel dropped the soldier at my feet, her blue eyes looking up at me expectantly.

"Good job," I told her, grabbing the soldier before he could get away.

Angel purred at me.

The soldier tried to kick me in the shin. I evaded, and as I dragged him out of the canteen, Harker sent a psychic punch through the room that knocked out everyone at once.

"Cool," I gasped. "How was the spell powerful enough to knock them all out, and yet you didn't break any windows or furniture?"

He grinned. "Collateral damage is overrated, Pandora."

"Very funny." I stuck my tongue out at him.

"I know." His gaze slid over the struggling soldier I was restraining. "I will hold him."

"Like hell you will." An angry, possessive urge raged in my blood. "I caught him. He's mine."

"You didn't catch him. The cat did."

"*My* cat caught him. So he's mine."

"You're being ridiculous. I am stronger than you. I'm better able to restrain him."

"You didn't restrain the first guy all that well," I snapped.

Harker hit me with a glower—and then with his fist. I hit him back. Since my hands were full, I had to use my magic to do it. My spell slammed his head against the wall. The impact was powerful enough to leave him dazed.

Now was my chance. I hurried past him, taking the stairs up. I would be the one to deliver the soldier to Nerissa's office, not Harker. My prisoner. My victory.

"Leda, wait!"

I kept running up the stairs. Harker was right behind me. As I reached the final step, he grabbed my foot and gave it a rough tug. I slid down the stairs, and Harker grabbed my prisoner. My head bounced off a hard step. The anger burning inside of me fizzled out.

I rose slowly. Harker stood at the top of the stairs, watching me. The anger had gone out of his eyes. However, the soldier he held was snarling and struggling like a savage, enraged animal.

"We were affected," I said, rubbing my head. "I snapped out of it when my head hit the step."

"And I snapped out of when my head hit the wall."

I shivered. "This—whatever this is—is getting out of hand."

"Yeah," he agreed, and together we dragged the struggling soldier to Nerissa's office. Miraculously, we made it the rest of the way there without any further excitement.

"We got you an active sample, Doctor," I declared as we stepped into the room.

Nerissa immediately jumped up and circled to the frontside of her desk, her tools in her hands. "Bring him to the cot." She snapped her fingers at two of her assistants. "Hurry. Hold him down as I run some tests on him."

They pinned him to the cot, but one of the thrashing soldier's hands broke free and knocked the tool out of Nerissa's hand.

She picked it up. "A little help, Leda."

I clamped my hands around the soldier's free arm, locking it down. He tried to break free, but he couldn't move an inch. His face red, he glared daggers at me. I merely smiled.

Nerissa glanced at the four holes in Harker's hand. The shape was undeniable. "He slammed a fork through your hand?"

"No." Harker waved his glowing hand over the wound and it healed. "Leda slammed a fork through my hand."

Nerissa looked at me, a worried wrinkle forming between her eyes.

I let out an exasperated sigh. "I only did it because he tried to steal my cake."

"And she slammed me against a wall," Harker added. "You'd better test Leda," he told Nerissa. "She might have been infected as well."

"Me?" I shot back, my anger simmering again. "No, she should test you, Harker. You were the one acting strangely. I was just defending my property. Twice."

"Angels." Nerissa rolled her eyes. "See, this is why the First Angel doesn't put two angels in the same territory."

My anger died, replaced by embarrassment. She was right. I was acting just like an angel.

"The territorial urge is too strong," Nerissa continued. "The angels quickly start fighting over every little scrap. I warned Nyx it wasn't a good idea having you here now that you're an angel."

"Trying to get rid of me, Doc?" I winked at her.

"Now, why would I do that? You make such an excellent restraining device." Her gaze flickered to the soldier I was holding down.

"Why do I have the feeling I'm being mocked?"

"Must be those highly-developed angel senses," she said.

I snorted. "Must be."

"So you don't think Leda is infected with the demons' curse?" Harker asked her.

"Neither of you are. You're both acting far more rational than he is." She indicated the red-faced soldier on the cot, his muscles bulging under the strain of trying to break free. "You two seem to be just engaging in normal angel territorial conflicts. But just to be safe, I'll take a look at you both when I'm done with him."

Awesome. Just what I needed: someone to test my magic.

"Now that we got your conscious sample in here, I need to go quell the fight in the canteen," Harker said. "While the canteen is still standing."

I could hear the noises filtering up the stairs from the level below. It sounded like the sleeping soldiers had all awoken and restarted their fight.

"Isn't knocking them out supposed to end the curse? It always worked before," I commented.

The sparkle in Harker's eyes had dulled. "Apparently, we can no longer count on that."

The demons' curse was growing more powerful, more complex. It was evolving. If we didn't stop it, it would tear the Legion apart. And if the curse didn't tear the Legion apart, Colonel Fireswift's interrogations would.

"Do you need any help?" I asked Harker. I had to do something. I had to stop this.

"No, you have your hands full as it is," he said as the soldier shouted and thrashed against my hold.

Harker left the room, passing Nerissa on the way out. She was looking through her magic microscope and frowning.

"What is it?" I asked her.

"There are no foreign potions or spells in his body."

"No sign of the demons' curse?"

"His magic is incensed for sure. I just can't explain why. It's streaked with color."

"Streaked with color?" I asked.

"Our magic changes color with our moods."

"And you can see that?"

"Only with this." She indicated the magic microscope on her desk. "Though there is one person whose magical changes are visible to the naked eye."

I thought of my hair and wings. Both of them reacted to my moods and magic, changing color. "Me."

"Yes." She looked contemplative.

"What does your microscope tell you about this soldier?" I asked, putting her back on track. She needed to focus on the curse, not on my very odd magic.

"The colors of his magic are indicative of someone in a jealous rage," she said.

"The battle in Demeter began when two soldiers

fought over a woman. First, it was just the two of them, but soon everyone was fighting, including the security guards who came into the room later."

"Those feelings of jealousy and anger transferred to others?" Nerissa was clearly asking herself the question.

I answered anyway. "That's what it looked like. They were all expressing the same emotion."

"I can see he's agitated. I can see that emotion painted here, right in front of me." She frowned. "But I can't find the cause. Besides his agitated mood, his magic is completely normal… Wait a moment." She adjusted a few dials on her microscope. "There's something going on inside of him. A weird echo."

"Weird echo?"

"A foreign echo in his mind," she clarified, then adjusted more dials and knobs. "Triggering these emotions." She looked through the microscope. "It almost looks like…"

"Yes?" I asked. "Like what?"

She looked up from her microscope and met my eyes. "Like it's telepathic."

"Telepathic? The demons are administering the curse telepathically," I realized. "Is there any way to trace a telepathic spell to its source?"

She shook her head. "No. Telepathy is a strange and elusive kind of magic. It's the branch of magic we understand the least. It's so intangible."

"So you can't find the source of the curse, the person or thing telepathically attacking our soldiers." I chewed on my lower lip. "But can you block it?"

"No. There is no Magitech that can block telepathic signals. Only a ghost, a telepath, can block them."

"Or a telepathic angel."

The man on the cot suddenly stopped struggling. A dazed expression washed over his face, and his eyes darted around the room.

Harker stepped through the door.

"The fight in Demeter?" I asked him.

"Is over. When I walked into the canteen, everyone just stopped fighting. They don't even know why they'd suddenly grown angry."

"We do," I told him. "Someone is sending out telepathic signals targeted at manipulating emotions, flooding our soldiers with strong negative feelings, ones that bury their rational thoughts and make them lose control."

"A telepathic attack." Harker's phone buzzed. He glanced at the screen.

"Trouble?"

He looked at me, his expression dark. "There's been an incident in the Legion's New Orleans office."

The New Orleans office. That was in the South, the territory commanded by my friend Jace.

"A fight?" I asked.

"Yes. At precisely the same time as the one here broke out. And one broke out in the Chicago office as well, also at the same time."

"It's escalating, growing with each wave, with each telepathic attack."

"If it's spreading, it will soon reach the next Legion office," said Harker.

"Los Angeles. Legion headquarters."

"The first incidents occurred in this office," Nerissa said. "I think the source of the telepathic curse is in New York, branching out as the spell gains momentum. You need to call the First Angel here immediately. I don't have any Magitech that can shield our soldiers from these attacks, but Nyx is a demigod. She might be powerful enough to block the curse long enough for us to find a cure."

"Can it be cured?" I asked her.

"I hope so," she replied. "The curse is escalating fast, reaching out further with each wave. And if we don't figure it out soon, in a few days there won't be anything left of the Legion's formidable fighting force."

"The demons won't even have to lift a sword," I hissed. "All they have to do is wait and watch us wipe ourselves out."

CHAPTER 10

Six hours had passed since the battle in Demeter, and Harker and I had spent nearly every moment in motion, putting down fights. The curse was hitting the Legion's New York office every hour now. Reports from the Chicago and New Orleans offices confirmed their soldiers were always being affected at exactly the same time. Nyx was off world right now, but I hoped she got here soon. The Legion wouldn't survive much more of this before it imploded.

There were no accounts of incidents like these outside the Legion of Angels. This curse did not seem to affect the normal population of humans and supernaturals—only Legion soldiers. That made it pretty likely it was an attack targeted directly at the Legion, rather than someone just trying to create general mayhem in the world.

Harker, Colonel Fireswift, and I went to meet the First Angel when she finally landed on the rooftop of the New York office. She didn't waste any time getting down to business.

"I have been following your updates on the situation. I

am taking over the investigation," she declared, much to Colonel Fireswift's chagrin.

I hadn't seen such a sour expression on his face since the gods had assigned him to be my partner in the Crystal Falls training.

"Well, what did you expect? After all, your own team has been compromised," I pointed out to him.

One of the Interrogators had been caught up in the Battle of Demeter. That's what everyone was calling the incident in the canteen.

"Compromised," Colonel Fireswift repeated, his nose crinkling up as though he'd smelled something foul.

We followed Nyx to her office, the opulent room set aside for the First Angel. Except it wasn't looking particularly opulent right now. During one of the recent outbursts, several affected soldiers had found their way inside and trashed the place. The curtains were burnt, the paintings on the walls slashed, and the furniture in pieces. And since the outbursts were happening every hour now, we hadn't had any time to clean up the place.

Nyx stepped over the shattered remains of the chandelier and leaned her hands back against her mahogany desk. Only the sheer impracticality of throwing something that massive had saved it from mutilation.

"Close the door," she said.

The door to her office was half off its hinges, but Harker managed to set the lock in place.

"This situation has completely spiraled out of control," Nyx declared, a hint of reproach in her voice. As though it were our fault the demons had cursed the Legion. "How are you three faring?"

"We seem to be resistant to the curse's effects," Harker

replied. "Though I would be lying if I claimed I wasn't feeling a bit testy myself lately."

"So you think the curse is affecting you?" Nyx said. She was looking at all three of us.

"Well, I did stick a fork through Harker's hand," I admitted, feeling altogether embarrassed that Harker and I had fought over something as silly as a slice of cake.

Nyx wasn't laughing, but her eyes were. "That is just your territorial angel instincts—most likely aggravated by what's going on here."

"Angels are immune to this ailment afflicting the Legion's lower ranks," Colonel Fireswift proclaimed, casting a sidelong glance at me and Harker. "Some of us more than others."

I frowned at him. "What is *that* supposed to mean?"

"You don't possess the power of Ghost's Whisper. Your resistance to telepathic attacks is minimal."

"You didn't think my resistance to telepathic attacks was minimal the last time you tried to read my mind," I shot back.

He gave his hand a dismissive wave. "Everyone gets lucky occasionally."

"Maybe if he ever got lucky, he'd be in a better mood," I muttered.

Harker choked down an emerging chuckle.

"Luck is a fickle ally," Colonel Fireswift continued, oblivious to my bawdy joke. "And unlike other people, it is not something I'm forced to depend upon to shield me from this telepathic curse."

His narcissism, his sense of absolute superiority, hung so heavy in the air that it made me want to gag.

"You're forgetting something, Colonel," I told him.

He let out a short, derisive laugh. "I doubt it."

"You're forgetting how magic at the Legion of Angels works."

His forehead crinkled with agitation. "You dare—"

"Yes, I dare. I *always* dare." I smiled. "We might not yet possess the power of Ghost's Whisper, but we Legion soldiers train our resistance to a power before we gain it." I nudged Harker in the shoulder. "In fact, after this ordeal is over, I'd say our telepathic resistance will be pretty well trained."

He picked up on what I was getting at. "Bringing us both closer to the next level."

"Yep."

I'd been working on my resistance to telepathic attacks for a while now actually—at least when it came to blocking people from reading my thoughts. I guess you could say that I was very motivated to keep both angels and gods out of my head.

Colonel Fireswift favored us with a scathing look. "It's not prudent to strategize your path to promotion in front of the First Angel."

"You mean, to strategize how to be stronger, so the Legion can be stronger," I said. "How is that not prudent? Don't we want the Legion to be stronger?"

Colonel Fireswift glowered at me.

I smirked at him. "Come on, admit it, Colonel. You've missed conversations with me since we went our separate ways after the gods' challenges."

"Hardly."

"Sure you have. You couldn't stay away. That's why you came here. You were aching for a good laugh."

His fists clenched.

"Don't kill her," Nyx told him.

As Colonel Fireswift stepped back, I commented, "People keep having to tell him that."

"And you stop provoking him," Nyx told me sharply. "We need to get to work. You will all report to Dr. Harding's office for a full examination. Angels are apparently resistant to this curse. We might be able to create a magic vaccine to protect everyone else from the malicious telepathic signals. It would buy us time, so we can find the source of this curse and put an end to it."

Her voice vibrated with frightening conviction. Whoever had cast this curse should be very worried. Nyx's Legion had been attacked, and she was going to hunt down the guilty party and obliterate them. Just like a mother dragon protected her young.

Colonel Fireswift nodded briskly to the First Angel, bowed, then unlocked the broken door and left the room. He was undoubtably heading straight to Nerissa's office as ordered. I lingered in front of Nyx's desk.

"What is it?" she asked me.

Harker was already halfway to the door, but he stopped at her words.

"Is there something else, Pandora?" Nyx asked me, her brows lifting.

Her gaze dipped to the name I'd taken the liberty of putting on my jacket: Pandora. Amusement twinkled in her bright blue eyes. Unlike Colonel Fireswift, the First Angel, scary mother dragon of the Legion, actually had a sense of humor. That was Nyx's duality; she had a foot each on Earth and in heaven, standing between the worlds of humans and gods. That's what I liked about her. She could somehow be both; she could balance both. If only she hadn't stolen from Nero and tried to manipulate me—if only I could truly trust her—we would have been good friends.

"Yes, there's something else," I told Nyx. "Aren't you worried what Nerissa will find if she does a full examination on me?"

Nyx glanced at Harker.

"He already knows," I said. "He figured it out."

"You are fortunate Colonel Fireswift did not figure it out as well."

"We are both fortunate," I told her with a forced smile.

Nyx sighed. "Leda, you take everything so personally."

She wanted to use me as a weapon. She'd tried to blackmail me, promising to keep my secret if I wielded the weapons of heaven and hell for her.

"Of course I take things personally. Because it's *normal* to take these sorts of things personally," I said. "And, just so we're clear, you take things personally too."

Nyx frowned at my reminder that she and Ronan weren't getting along right now—and that everyone knew it. But she immediately shrugged off her discomfort and went right on with business.

"Dr. Harding is your friend." She stopped to let the words settle on her tongue, like she was sampling a taste of wine. Then she pulled out her phone and quickly typed out something. "I have just forbidden her from discussing the results of my angels' tests with anyone except me."

Apparently, Nyx wasn't putting all her eggs in the friendship basket. I wasn't surprised. Unlike Colonel Fireswift, she understood and appreciated the bonds of love and friendship, but that didn't mean she had complete and absolute faith in them. Nyx was someone who always needed a backup. She needed layers of armor, of protection

—probably now more than ever, after learning Ronan had kept secrets from her.

As Harker and I left Nyx's office, going back to see Nerissa, he commented, "Nyx is even scarier than Fireswift."

"Yeah," I agreed. "Colonel Fireswift ignores his emotions; he bottles them. But Nyx doesn't. She feels every bit as much as we do. I know she sympathizes with my situation—with me—and yet that doesn't stop her from seeing her plans through. It doesn't freeze her. And it doesn't stop her from manipulating me if she feels that's the best way to ensure the Legion's survival."

We reached Nerissa's office as Colonel Fireswift left it.

"What are you two doing, skulking about?" he demanded gruffly.

"We weren't skulking," I replied. "The First Angel just wanted to have a few words with us."

Colonel Fireswift looked like he didn't believe a word I said. His ego wouldn't allow for the possibility that Nyx would want to speak to us, but not him, the ranking angel of us three.

"I will be watching you," he told me, then left.

No, Colonel Fireswift wasn't at all like Nyx. Because he always suppressed his feelings, he couldn't handle them when they reared their ugly head. Like when his daughter had died. The emotions that he kept prisoner had broken free, overloading him completely.

"Are you just going to lurk in the doorway, Leda, or are you coming inside?" Nerissa called out to me, drawing me out of my reflections.

"Sorry. I was just…"

"Daydreaming," Harker said with a roguish wink.

Nerissa was already drawing blood from him. "Isn't she

always? Honestly, I've never met an angel with her head so much in the clouds."

"Haha. Very funny," I said drily.

She chuckled.

"How is Soren?" I asked her as she took samples of Harker's blood.

"He's doing fine. Thankfully, he wasn't affected during any of the curse's later outbreaks. It seems almost random who's affected."

"The attacks at the other offices don't seem connected either," said Harker. "Some of the soldiers haven't been in close contact with the other affected people. Some who were unaffected were friends or worked closely with the affected soldiers."

"Are we still assuming the curse originated here?" I asked.

"The first affected soldier was in New York. And more soldiers are affected in the outbreaks here than anywhere else: five times more than in Chicago, ten times more than in New Orleans."

"It's bleeding outward from here," I realized. "The incidents are more concentrated here, at the curse's epicenter."

"It would seem so," Nerissa said as she moved on to testing me. "Telepathic range is limited. Its effects are stronger the closer you are to the source."

"Well, whoever is doing this, their range is growing."

"What do you mean?" she asked me.

"The curse started here, then it spread to Chicago, then later to New Orleans. In addition, the frequency in all offices is increasing, but the attacks are still concentrated mostly here. So the person cursing people must be somewhere in this city or close to it. With each passing outbreak, their range is growing, their power increasing."

"Maybe it's multiple people. Multiple telepaths," Harker said. "One person might have started the curse."

"And others joined in later," I said. "You know, there is someone who's been collecting telepaths for years. Someone who is constantly growing his army of ghosts."

A dark look crossed Harker's face. "Faris."

"Right."

He frowned. "So you don't think a demon is behind this curse?"

"I'm not so sure anymore. It's just…well, ever since we determined that this is a telepathic attack, it got me to thinking. It's no secret that Faris is collecting telepaths. And he did create all that disarray at the Crystal Falls training a few weeks ago. Maybe this is his next move, the next step in his grand scheme."

"But to cripple the Legion…" Harker shook his head. "It's just so risky. Without the Legion to protect the Earth, the demons could more easily gain a foothold here again. Why would Faris risk that?"

"Maybe he has a plan in place to counter the demons. Or maybe he wants them to take over the Earth. Maybe *that* is part of his plan. After all he's done, would that really surprise you?"

"No," Harker admitted bleakly.

"Well, whoever is behind this curse, we have to stop it."

I glanced at Nerissa, who was staring into her magic microscope like she didn't believe what she saw.

"Nerissa?" I asked. "What's wrong?"

She met my gaze, her eyes haunted. "I've finished reviewing the results of all your tests. I checked three times just to be sure."

"Sure of what?" I smirked at her. "Am I dying or something?"

"No." She didn't return my smile. "But I know what's causing these incidents."

"Demons? Faris?"

She swallowed hard. "No, Leda. *You* are."

CHAPTER 11

A FEVERED RESPONSE

"*Y*ou are?" I repeated Nerissa's words. "What do you mean by 'you'. You, as in me? Or 'you', as in all the angels you've tested?"

That would be a dose of dark irony indeed if someone had found a way to make the angels' magic attack the other Legion soldiers. There was no solution to that problem.

The Legion wouldn't kill its angels to protect its other soldiers because it needed us; it needed our magic. Angels were the cornerstones of the Legion, its most powerful soldiers, its strongest weapon against the demons.

But the Legion also couldn't very well stand by and allow the angels' magic to throw the rest of the soldiers into disarray. The effects of the telepathic curse were intensifying with each new outbreak. Soldiers were growing more violent, more explosive. Sooner or later, someone would die—and soon after that, a whole lot more people would die.

The Legion was nothing without angels to command it and lots of soldiers to make those commands happen. Both were necessary.

"I've already said too much." Nerissa shook her head. "The First Angel ordered me to speak about her angels' results with her directly—and only her."

Who could have known that the order meant to protect my secret would end up keeping us all in the dark? The ironies were piling up fast lately. What an unprecedented convergence of unlikely events. It must be raining unicorns today.

The cynic in me wondered if maybe Nyx already knew what was causing the outbreaks. Maybe that's why she'd ordered Nerissa to share the results only with her. If Nyx did know, she was keeping all the knowledge in her court. The old saying was so true. Knowledge really was power, especially when angels and gods played the game.

"She should be here soon," Nerissa said.

Nyx stepped into Nerissa's office. Her black hair, long and glossy, swirled around her in slow, languid waves, as though she were underwater.

It seemed like forever had passed since Nerissa had messaged Nyx, but the clock told me it had only been a few minutes. It was funny how time stalled when hell was busy freezing over.

"Everyone out, all except for Dr. Harding and my angels," Nyx declared loudly. Her voice, pulsing with authority, echoed through the lab.

All of Nerissa's staff immediately stopped what they were doing. They set down their work and rushed out of the lab as fast as they could move, which was pretty damn fast, being that they were all soldiers with god-gifted magic. Harker closed the door behind them.

Then, when the four of us were alone, Nyx's gaze zeroed in on Angel. My kitten had made herself comfortable perched atop Nerissa's computer, her eyes surveying her territory. The cat really was an angel, through and through.

"Who does this animal belong to?" Nyx asked us.

"Angel is mine," I told her.

Nyx's slender dark brows arched. "Angel?"

"That's her name."

Nyx met the kitten's bright blue eyes. Angel yawned, completely unconcerned by the badass First Angel.

"You have found yourself a worthy companion," Nyx told me. "She does not scare easily."

"Plus, she's adorable," I said, trying to lighten the mood, most of all my own.

Nyx petted Angel on the head. The kitten purred, nudging her fluffy white head against Nyx's hand.

"I had no idea you were an animal person," I said.

"There's a lot you don't know about me, Leda." The almost wistful look on Nyx's face hardened. She stopped petting the cat and looked at Nerissa. "You said you've discovered the cause of this curse."

"Well, yes," Nerissa said cautiously, her eyes flickering to me and Harker.

"Out with it, Dr. Harding," Nyx said sharply. "We need to sort it out now, before the Legion tears itself apart."

It sure didn't sound like the First Angel already knew what was going on, but then again, she was a skilled actress with deity-level shifting magic. She could become anything. Look like anything. Sound like anything.

The power of shifting wasn't only about changing your physical attributes. It was about changing your mannerisms, your voice, your body language and facial expressions. It was about choosing what emotions you showed others. That same power was used to craft others' perceptions of you. A skilled shifter was an actor. They could choose what story their body told.

"I tested the magic of the three angels currently present in this office," Nerissa said. "I looked at their magic levels as a whole, as well as specifically their signs of telepathic resistance."

Gods, this prologue was going on forever. Nerissa was my friend, but right now I was sorely tempted to grab her by the heels and shake the answers out of her.

"Everything was normal in Colonel Fireswift and Lt. Colonel Sunstorm," Nerissa continued. "There was an increase in telepathic magic activity, more specifically the magic that defends against telepathic attacks. Just as we'd suspected, their magic is warding off the effects of the tele-pathic bombardment."

"And me?" I asked, almost fearing the answer.

Nerissa's gaze flickered to Nyx, who nodded. Right, for a moment there, I'd almost forgotten that I needed the First Angel's permission to hear about my own test results.

"Your magic is all over the place," Nerissa told me. "It is completely overstimulated, bouncing up and down, all over the chart."

"That's typical for a newly-made angel, Doctor," said Nyx.

"Leda's magic is not like any magic I've ever seen, and certainly not the magic I'd expect to see in an angel."

Nyx looked at Harker. She must have issued a tele-pathic command to him because he nodded, then reached into his jacket to pull out the now-familiar-to-me magic orb. He tossed it into the air, casting a privacy screen around us.

"Go on, Doctor," Nyx told Nerissa.

"Leda's magic is completely balanced, both light and

dark. At the same time, she is an angel and a dark angel." A perplexed crinkle formed between Nerissa's eyes. "How can that be? It should be impossible. Everything I've ever read, everything I've ever seen, tells me this cannot be. And yet it is."

"I am well aware of the nature of Leda's magic," said Nyx. "And it's classified."

Nerissa looked like she had a million questions buzzing on her lips.

"Is Leda's balanced light and dark magic relevant to the outbursts of uncontrolled emotion currently plaguing the Legion's soldiers?" Nyx asked her.

"No."

"Then speak no more of it—to *anyone*," Nyx added harshly, her words backed up by a potent punch of magic.

Nerissa swallowed hard. "Yes, First Angel. I understand."

Nerissa was one of the Legion's reigning queens of gossip. She loved to drink it in and to dish it out. Still, I knew she would keep my secret, and not just because Nyx had ordered her to do so. I knew she would keep my secret because she was my friend. And I trusted in friendship, even if Nyx didn't. I supposed that in her position, she felt like she couldn't afford to feel that way.

Nyx's forehead crinkled up in thought, and her black hair responded, swirling faster now in the air. On top of Nerissa's computer, my cat stretched out her back and rose to bat at the hair. Nyx didn't seem to care. She took Angel into her arms and began to pet her. It seemed petting a cat calmed her too, just as it did for me. Maybe Ronan should get her a cat as a present. I'd make sure to suggest it to him the next time I saw him.

Nyx turned sharply to me. "Why are you laughing, Pandora?"

Was I? I hadn't even realized it. Maybe laughter was my body's natural antidote to the worries building up in me.

I pointed at her swirling hair. "Angel likes your hair. How do you make it move like that?"

"It's a reality-shifting spell."

"It's a cool spell," I told her. "Someday, I really should learn it."

"It's a difficult spell, one not found in any book. It's of my own design, in fact. If you're good, I might teach it to you."

I smirked at her. "Oh, come on, Nyx. Since when have I ever been good?"

Harker choked down a laugh.

Nyx cocked a single brow upward at him. "Something in your throat, Sunstorm?"

"No, First Angel."

Nyx caught his magic orb, zapping out the privacy spell. She tossed it at Harker, then glanced at the closed door to the lab. "Come in, Colonel." She nodded at Nerissa. "Now go on with your analysis, Dr. Harding."

Colonel Fireswift entered the room, shutting the door behind him. The privacy spell must have worked because while he viewed me with his usual suspicion, he didn't pull a sword on me and declare me a freak of magic.

"Leda's magic is erratic, but not like those of a new angel," Nerissa said. "The classic post-transformation erratic patterns are weak now, almost gone. From the looks of her magic, it basically settled down about a week ago."

"Before the first incident," Nyx said.

"Yes. But there's something else happening inside of her, a buildup of all her magic across the board."

"You make it sound like I'm a bomb ready to blow," I told Nerissa.

I hoped this buildup wasn't my body unable to handle all the light and dark magic now pumping through it—that I wasn't a failed experiment gearing up to self destruct. Damn Athan for giving me double shots of Nectar and Venom. That magic cocktail had skyrocketed my magic across the entire magical spectrum, light to dark. Vampire, witch, siren, elemental, shifter, psychic, fairy…and all the angel and dark angel abilities waiting to be revealed. Maybe my body couldn't handle that sudden spike in magic.

Or, worse yet, perhaps Athan had known this would happen. Had he made me an angel not only to find his sister, but to get revenge on the gods? By turning me into a magic bomb that destroyed the Legion, ripping control away from its soldiers, burying them in negative emotions until they imploded? And then, when everyone else was gone, would I self-destruct, my body unable to handle my new magic?

I wouldn't have thought Athan capable of something like that. He'd been desperate to save his sister. Everything he'd done, including exposing Aleris and leveling up my magic, had been to save her. He wasn't a malicious man. Or at least, he hadn't seemed malicious.

But 'seemed' was the key word here. Admittedly, I didn't really know Athan beyond the few brief conversations we'd had—conversations that had been mostly focused on me and the gods' games. Athan could very well be more than he seemed. He could be someone capable of all this and more.

"Show me Leda's test results," Nyx commanded Nerissa.

Nerissa handed her a tablet. Nyx's eyes panned across the screen. Then they both stared long and hard at me.

"If I'm going to die, at least tell me now," I said.

"You're not dying, Leda," replied Nyx. "Not at all. This isn't about death. Quite the opposite actually."

"Meaning?"

"When the reports of these incidents started coming in, I suspected this might be the cause."

"What is the cause?"

"But for it to happen so quickly is completely unprecedented."

My impatience overrode my propriety. "Spit it out already, Nyx!"

Colonel Fireswift looked horrified that I'd address the First Angel in such a manner, but Nyx was clearly unbothered by my outburst.

"You have the Fever," she told me.

Nyx's words didn't process. My brain couldn't grasp them.

"I have the what?"

"Your magic is building up, your moods growing more turbulent as your body prepares to become fertile," Nyx said. "And as we always see when a female angel has the Fever, it's affecting all the Legion soldiers around you."

CHAPTER 12

"*Y*ou claim I have the Fever and it's affecting the Legion soldiers around me," I said to Nyx, keeping my voice calm. "But there have been incidents in other offices far from here." My heart was pounding so hard in my ears that I could hardly hear myself speak. "The soldiers involved in those incidents weren't anywhere near me when their emotions went berserk."

Her eyes slid over me, giving me a long, assessing look. "Your magic is different. Its reach is obviously larger than that of other female angels who've had the Fever."

"But female angels aren't fertile right after the transformation," I protested, grasping for something else, *anything* else that would kill this wrong theory where it stood. I couldn't have the Fever. I just couldn't. It was impossible. It *had* to be impossible.

Nectar was a poison, the strongest that there was, save the demons' equally-potent Venom. The dosage of Nectar or Venom required to create an angel or dark angel was enormous. It flooded the new angel's body, consuming it, overloading it. It took decades for the poison in the female angel's blood to quiet down enough for her to become fertile.

And I'd had an angel-sized dose of Nectar *and* Venom, both at once. With two potent poisons like that raging inside my body, my first Fever shouldn't have hit me for another forty or fifty years from now—at the earliest. A whole century was more likely. And after that, the Fever would recur only once every few decades or so. Angels were notoriously infertile, courtesy of the poison that gave us our magic.

"The Fever couldn't have hit me so soon. So immediately." I shook my head vehemently. "It goes against everything we know about the laws of magic."

"I think we've established that you don't follow the normal laws of magic, Leda." I could have sworn I caught a hint of sympathy in Nyx's eyes, peeking through her facade of professional detachment, but it vanished even before she'd shifted her gaze to Nerissa. "How long before she peaks, Doctor?"

"I'll have to run tests every few hours on her to determine her surge pattern." Nerissa glanced down at her tablet. "But based on her magic and hormones right now, she doesn't have more than a week before she peaks."

Nyx read the screen of Nerissa's tablet. "She is spiking fast."

"Yes," Nerissa agreed. "It usually takes at least a month."

"We don't have much time. We must get started immediately. Dr. Harding, I need you to coordinate magic tests at all Legion offices. Every male soldier is to report for magic testing."

"Wait," I said.

Nyx didn't wait. She continued firing off commands to Nerissa. "As the samples come in, I need you to run them with Leda's samples for magic compatibility. You—and no one else—are to handle Leda's samples. Do you understand?"

Nerissa bowed her head. "Yes, First Angel."

"Stop," I told them.

"Until this is sorted, all medical personnel are assigned to the task of testing the Legion's male soldiers," Nyx said. "The clock is ticking. Let's get it done."

"You will listen!" I shouted, my magic bursting out of me.

A glass wall between two of the labs shattered. The potions inside the vials on Nerissa's shelves began to bubble. Papers blew off the desks, froze suspended on the air for a moment, then all simultaneously caught on fire. They dove to the floor, streaming black smoke.

Hissing, Angel jumped straight up through the burning pages and landed on the floor. She turned around in sharp, agitated pivots, her back arched, her tail up, ready to attack whatever phantom force had made all the furniture and tabletop accessories suddenly go berserk.

Everyone stared at me.

"What the hell do you think you're doing?" I demanded, glaring at Nyx.

Colonel Fireswift glowered at me. "How dare you speak to the First Angel in this manner of—"

"It's all right, Colonel," Nyx said, cutting him off. "The Fever is known to bring out uncontrolled emotions in even the most disciplined angel."

Colonel Fireswift frowned. He certainly did not consider me one of those highly-disciplined angels.

Nyx stepped forward and addressed me, "We have only

one week at most to find you a compatible mate and bring him here."

I folded my arms across my chest. "I already have a mate."

"Leda," Nyx said patiently. "We have to be realistic here. Nero is an angel. You are an angel. You know angels are rarely magically compatible with each other."

"Nero's parents were magically compatible," I pointed out. "But that's beside the point. You are not going to marry me off to someone simply because my magic is dinging like an oven timer."

"This is how we do things at the Legion," she told me. "It's how we safeguard the Legion and the people of Earth. The Legion needs soldiers with high magic potential. That means the children of angels. *Your* children, Leda. You're an angel now. You have a responsibility, a duty to the people of this world. Now more than ever, as gods and demons are clashing, edging closer to an explosive confrontation. The Earth is sitting at the center of the immortal war. The gods have this world. The demons want it. And both sides are fully prepared to tear it apart to keep it out of the other side's hands. Centuries ago, when gods and demons first came here, they clashed, and the Earth suffered. That clash gave us the plains of monsters. Are you willing to wait and see what catastrophe rocks the Earth next? Are you truly that selfish?"

I really had to hand it to Nyx. She was a master guilt-tripper. Even knowing that she was manipulating me into following the path she'd laid out for me, I couldn't help but feel how horribly selfish I was being for wanting something else, like I was a truly terrible person.

"Well, what would you do in my place?" I demanded, planting my hands on my hips.

"I think you already know the answer to that."

"And Ronan would just be all right with you marrying someone else?"

"No, he would most definitely not be all right with that. But it's never come up. I've never had the Fever."

"Not in all this time?"

She was the First Angel, the Earth's first angel. She'd been around before any of us. Before the Legion of Angels. She should have been fertile at least a few times by now.

"Female angels' fertility is unpredictable and rare. And that's why we can't pass up this chance." She glanced at Nerissa. "Have all the male angels tested too. Just in case." As Nerissa nodded, Nyx returned her attention to me. "I will contact Nero myself. He's deep within the plains of monsters right now, out of contact. Our last communication was two days ago, so I can't promise he'll be here in time. Or that your magic is compatible with his."

I shot her a defiant look. "Maybe my weird magic isn't compatible with anyone's."

Nyx laughed. "If that turns out to be the case, I wouldn't be the least bit surprised." She pointed at Colonel Fireswift, then at Harker. "I'm putting you two in charge of chaperoning Leda. Don't let her out of your sight."

In other words, they had to make sure I didn't run away and escape the Legion's plans for me. Wow, two angel chaperons. Nyx must have been really worried that I'd run.

I supposed it made sense. Right now, I was potentially the most valuable asset the Legion had: a fertile female angel. Well, unless I turned out to be completely incompatible with anyone. Then I was just a dud, the Legion's very own lemon angel.

"I don't need chaperones," I told Nyx.

"Of course you do."

"What if I have to use the toilet?"

Her response was immediate and unapologetic. "Then they go with you to the toilet. No exceptions."

She favored me with a sharp, do-not-bullshit-me look. She was telling me that she wouldn't be fooled by such an obvious trick. It figured. At the Legion, male and female initiates bunked together in large open rooms. We learned to shed our modesty along with our humanity. Nyx fully expected me to pee under supervision.

I moved toward the door. Angel strutted after me, her tail held high. She turned up her nose at the debris on the floor, then shot me a withering look, like she knew the mess was all my fault.

"As though you don't ever make a mess," I laughed.

She meowed in protest.

"After you dragged a wild turkey into Demeter, there were feathers all over the floor," I reminded her.

She licked her paw and began to groom her coat.

"That's your excuse?" I snorted. "That you can clean the turkey off your own fur? Well, what about the canteen floor? Who's supposed to clean up that mess?"

She meowed again.

"My own messes are beside the point," I replied.

"Why are you talking to your cat?" Harker asked me, his blue eyes twinkling with amusement.

"Because she's the only one who makes even a lick of sense in this madhouse."

Angel meowed again to punctuate my point. Then she followed me out of Nerissa's office.

The two angels trailed me through the doorway, matching me step for step. They kept pace behind me, one on either side, matching even the slightest shift in my speed or direction, like we were all moving in a tight attack formation. This was ridiculous. They were so close that I could feel them breathing down my neck.

I spun around, looking back into the room. "Is this really necessary?" I asked Nyx.

Her face was humorless. "I think we both know the answer to that, Pandora."

Yeah, we did. I didn't want to marry some random Legion soldier, and Nyx knew it.

I had to get out of this. I had to escape my chaperones and find Nero. I had to contact him myself. We'd promised each other that we would always stick together and not let anyone break us apart, even if that meant fleeing the Legion.

I just hadn't expected this to come up so soon. I'd thought we had all the time in the world.

I'd been so wrong. We had only a week—one week before my immortal future was set in stone.

CHAPTER 13

MS. REVOLUTIONARY

ith my two zealous chaperones on the job, there wasn't anywhere to go, so I visited the canteen. I was starving, annoyed, and consuming large quantities of sugar made me feel better. I asked my angel chaperones to carry the loaded plates for the duration of the walk back to Nerissa's office.

"I am not a server," Colonel Fireswift snapped.

"No, you're a leader," I replied. "But you don't want to endanger my fragile fertility by being mean to me, do you? The First Angel would not be pleased."

His mouth opened in outrage, but he snapped it shut again immediately.

I gave him a pleasant smile that seemed to bounce right off him. Looking rather sour, he picked up two of my loaded plates. Harker took the other two plates, and we made our way back to Nerissa's office.

When we reached it, Angel trotted in first to check for threats. She found a few bugs throwing their bodies against the glass window in a futile attempt to get outside, and she promptly busied herself with the task of catching them. As

I ate my nutritious meal of cookies and ice cream, I watched my kitten launch her tiny body high into the air, mouth open and ready to swallow the first bug. Launch and swoop. It was thus that she rid the office of the insects, one by one, with perfect accuracy. She didn't miss a single one.

"That cat isn't normal," Harker commented. "She jumps like a spider."

"No, not a spider. An angel." I grinned. "She can fly."

"Ridiculous." Colonel Fireswift sneered. "A cat cannot be an angel."

"Oh?" I slid my tongue across the top of a mini cupcake, licking the icing right off. "And why is that?"

He glared at me—and the cupcake. "A cat cannot be an angel because it cannot survive the Nectar. It's impossible."

"It's also impossible that an angel catches the Fever right after her transformation, and yet here we are," I pointed out with a sigh.

Harker pulled a large box out of a drawer. "Fancy a game of War?"

I glanced at the brightly colored game box. "War?" I snorted. "That's sure a creative name for a game."

"I didn't make the game, Leda." Harker pulled the game board out of the box. "I just found it."

"I think Sergeant Jarden designed that game last year when he was cooped up in here for a month with a particularly virulent case of Pooka Pox," Nerissa said.

"What are Pooka Pox?" I asked her.

"Very unpleasant. Pray you never find out," she replied.

I could either try to figure out what she meant by that, or I could play a game of War with Harker. Hmm, decisions, decisions.

"I'll play," I declared, hoping Sergeant Jarden's game was long.

I needed something to keep my mind off things while we all waited for Nerissa's magic tests to determine my fate. I really hated sitting by and doing nothing. At least playing a game was doing something.

Harker handed me a small tray with beautifully crafted and painted wooden pieces. "How about you, Colonel?" he asked Colonel Fireswift.

"I don't play games," he stated coolly.

I grinned at him. "Why not? Afraid of losing?"

"I am not afraid of losing or anything else."

"Really? Is that so?"

"Leda," Harker warned me.

But this was too much fun. "You're not afraid of anything?" I asked Colonel Fireswift. "Not even a mission report rife with spelling mistakes? Or a wardrobe stuffed full of only dirty uniforms? Or maybe if someone were to set back all the clocks in your office building by precisely one minute? I bet that your soldiers have tried that prank on you once or twice."

"They wouldn't dare."

"Not even on April Fool's Day?"

"No."

"On your birthday? The Gods' Feast? Halloween?"

"Absolutely not," he ground out.

"Your soldiers sound like a real dull bunch," I told him. "Don't they ever have any fun?"

He puffed out his chest in indignation. "Of course not."

"Well, that has got to change. Next time I'm in the area, I'll stop by the Chicago office and throw you all a party."

"You will do no such thing."

"Sure I will. You'll love it. I promise."

"Be careful, Leda," Harker said.

I gave my hand a dismissive flick. "Oh, I'm just teasing him."

"I don't think Colonel Fireswift has a sense of humor."

"No, I most definitely do not," Colonel Fireswift agreed.

I smiled at him. "Now, I just don't believe that, Xerxes. May I call you Xerxes?"

"No," he growled.

"Oh, come on. Let's drop protocol for a moment. In fact, let's throw it right out the window."

Colonel Fireswift looked positively scandalized.

"We're all angels here." I propped up my elbows on the tabletop and balanced my chin atop my braided fingers. "Well, except for Nerissa."

Nerissa was anyway too caught up in her work to pay any attention to us.

"Babysitting Leda is a long and tedious task, Colonel." Harker spoke like he was slowly and carefully defusing a bomb. "And sitting idly by is very unbecoming of an angel."

Colonel Fireswift grunted in agreement. "What is the goal of this game?" His eyes fell over the big box.

"Taking over the world."

"Such a goal is definitely worthy of an angel," I added.

"Very well. I shall play." He said it as though he were doing us an enormous favor.

"Wow, Leda, that's a lot of food," Nerissa commented, pulling her head out of her work long enough to notice the plates of food in front of me. "When did you notice your increased appetite?"

"Why do you ask?" I said, my suspicions piqued.

"Angels with the Fever eat a lot. It fuels their peaking magic. I've read all about the Fever, but I've never seen it in an angel with my own eyes. Fascinating." Her eyes were glowing with excitement. Hell, her whole body was glowing. "Maybe I should write a paper about it."

"You are *not* writing a paper about this calamity."

Angel had just finished catching all the bugs in the room. She looked around for something else to hunt.

"That cat is very efficient," Nerissa commented. "Those bugs have been bothering me all day."

Having found nothing else worthy of an angel cat huntress, Angel pranced over to me and plopped down on my lap. She ate what was left of my last piece of cheesecake, so I slid one of the other plates across the table toward me.

"Why do you let her eat your desserts?" Harker demanded. "You drove a fork through my hand when I tried to do the same."

"Well, she always brings me gifts," I said, petting her fondly.

"She brings you dead birds," he pointed out.

"It's the thought that counts."

"So if I brought you a dead bird, you would share your cake with me?"

"Maybe." I grinned at him. "But why don't you try it with Bella instead?"

"Bring her a dead bird?" He frowned. "I don't think she'd appreciate that as much as you would."

"I guess that depends on the quality of the bird."

"The quality of the bird?" he repeated. "Ok, now I know you're joking."

"Girls like gifts," I said solemnly. "Look at how much

I'm enjoying Angel." I scratched my kitten under her chin, and she purred in appreciation.

"Last time I tried bringing Bella a gift, she overreacted," he sighed.

"I know. She called me in a state of total panic."

"What did you tell her to do?"

I smirked. "To blow into a bag and count to ten."

"Very funny."

I laughed. "I told Bella angels are crazy and not to let it get to her."

"Wow, Leda, thanks for the help. No wonder she's been avoiding me."

"She hasn't been avoiding you," I told him. "She is studying for exams. And I happen to know that she is in desperate need of a set of Red-tipped Inferno Bird feathers for her chemistry exam."

Surprise flashed in his eyes. "You were actually serious about the bird."

"Am I not always serious?"

"No," he said, deadpan.

"Red-tipped Inferno Birds are highly magical, but they're damn near impossible to find, let alone catch. You'd have to go to the Black Plains to find one. I know Bella would *really* appreciate the feathers."

A cynical crinkle formed between his eyes. "You're trying to get rid of me by sending me off on a wild goose chase."

"Not a wild goose chase. A wild Inferno Bird chase," I corrected him.

"Nice try."

I shrugged. "You wanted to know the way to Bella's heart, and the answer is Red-tipped Inferno Bird feathers.

What you choose to do with that information is entirely up to you."

He looked thoughtful.

"Don't listen to anything that silver-tongued siren is saying. She is trying to manipulate you," Colonel Fireswift told him.

"Yes, I realize that, Colonel," Harker replied. "And it won't work."

"Just be sure that it doesn't. I will be watching you. And if your personal feelings make you negligent in your duties, I will act accordingly."

Harker shot me an exasperated look. "You're always getting me into trouble, Leda."

Smiling, I took a big bite of strawberry cake.

"Back to your question, Leda started eating her weight in food a few days ago," Harker told Nerissa.

"Hey," I protested. "Stop helping her make me the subject of a magic research paper."

"Why?" He flashed me a wide grin. "You could be famous."

"I am already infamous. And that's good enough for me."

"She started eating her weight in food a few days ago, Doctor," he repeated, adding on, "But by now, she's eating *my* weight in food."

"Whose side are you on, anyway, Harker?"

"On the side of science, of course."

"Your revenge is swift and merciless."

His nod was crisp and satisfied. "You bet it is."

"See if I ever again give you tips on the way to Bella's heart," I grumbled.

"Abnormally-increased appetite," Nerissa said, oblivious that our conversation had left the station without her. "Interesting." She scribbled down some notes.

"Hey, who do you think you're calling abnormal?" I demanded. I leaned back in my seat, trying to catch a glimpse of the paper she was scribbling notes on. "What are you writing about me?"

She buried the piece of paper beneath a notebook. "Nothing of any consequence to you."

"Not of any consequence to me? It's about me!"

"I'll change your name in the paper," she promised. "No one will ever know."

"*Everyone* will know," I countered. "In the Legion's long and glorious history, just how many angels have gotten the Fever immediately after getting their wings?"

The answer was one: me.

Nerissa gave her hand a dismissive wave. "It will all work out." She eyed my dessert plate. "Are you craving sweets in particular?"

"If I say yes, will you give me that box of cookies sitting up on your shelf?"

She recovered the paper and scribbled down more notes. "Fascinating."

"Aren't you supposed to be looking at magic samples?" I reminded her. "Not tormenting me."

"I'm still waiting for the test results to come back." She rubbed her chin thoughtfully. "In the meantime, maybe I should test your magic again to see how it's grown."

"Again? It hasn't even been an hour since the last time you tested me," I protested.

"The more data points, the better."

I rubbed my sore arm. "Says the one who hasn't been pricked by twenty million needles already."

"Besides, you have eaten a lot in the last hour," she

said, brushing off my protests. "It would be interesting to see what effect that had on your magic readings."

"If you're going to prick me again, I'm really going to need that box of cookies," I told her.

She grabbed the box off the shelf and tossed it to me. "You don't have a very balanced diet, Leda."

I offered one of the cookies to Angel and took another for myself. "I'm immortal. It won't kill me," I said as Angel chowed down on the chocolate mint cookie; she really did have unusual food preferences for a cat.

"I'm going to give you a prenatal vitamin."

"I don't need a prenatal vitamin. I'm not pregnant."

"You should start taking them before conception." She popped open a bottle and shook out a vitamin. "I have a special variety laced with extra sugar."

I shot the vitamin on her open palm a stony look. "I'd rather eat cake."

"Cake isn't good for you."

"Sure it is. It's feeding my magic. You said so yourself."

"Stop being so stubborn, Leda," she sighed. "Vitamins are good for you." She tried to hand me the vitamin.

"Get that away from me, or I'll tell Nyx that you're disrupting my magical equilibrium."

"Take this vitamin, or I'll tell Nyx that you're interfering with the Legion's procreation initiative," she countered, smiling.

Checkmate. Frowning, I begrudgingly accepted the vitamin from her. I showed it to Angel. She sniffed it, her nose crinkling up in disgust.

"My cat, who eats raw meat and licks her fur, thinks your vitamin is disgusting," I told Nerissa. Then I swallowed the pill, washing it down with some chocolate milk.

"Way to take one for the team, Leda," Harker said.

I frowned at him. "Oh, shut up."

Chuckling, he moved around several of his game pieces on the board.

"So, there was never a demon or god curse," I commented as Nerissa drew blood from me. "All these outbursts were me the whole time."

"The Fever has made your emotions unstable and you are projecting those emotions onto others," she said.

"Telepathically?"

"Yes."

"I don't possess the power of telepathy," I pointed out.

"It's inside of you, just as it's inside of all angels," she said. "That buried power has been magnified by your peaking magic, because of the Fever. It's quite fascinating actually. You know how you train a power before you gain it, priming it for your next dose of Nectar?" The question was clearly rhetorical; she continued speaking without waiting for a response. "But in this case, it was the Fever that primed your next power, rather than you training to increase your resistance to the power. You've become partially empathic—at least temporarily—and you're projecting emotions, influencing the moods of others. It's actually a quite common phenomenon in female angels with the Fever."

I remembered Nerissa once telling me about the effects of a female angel having the Fever, how it affected the Legion soldiers around her. Unlike humans and normal supernaturals, Legion soldiers had taken Nectar; and so their magic was keyed to an angel's influence. They were getting the bleed-off of my turbulent emotions.

"What's not common is that soldiers in other offices, thousands of miles away, are affected," Harker commented.

"That is indeed most unusual." Nerissa looked at the

sample she'd just taken from me. "But it makes sense, given these readings. Your magic is accelerating fast, Leda. There are no records of a female angel with the Fever who's possessed this high of a magic level. However, your hormones are still on track to peak one week from now, just as I predicted."

"What does that mean?"

"It means that by the time your magic peaks, it will reach a higher potency than anything we've ever seen. Even an archangel doesn't have magic that high." She nibbled reflectively on the end of her pen. "Maybe this has to do with your magic—" Her eyes darted to Colonel Fireswift, then she snapped her mouth shut.

Ever the Interrogator, he demanded, "What about her magic?"

Nerissa shook her head. "Nothing."

"You are hiding something." His eyes narrowed. "I will find out what it is."

"Then you'll have to go through the First Angel." Nerissa's voice was clear and strong, but she did cringe slightly under his hard glare.

"The First Angel knows something about you," Colonel Fireswift realized, looking at me. "And she's concealing it."

No one said anything.

"You *all* know what it is." His scowl deepened. "This is completely unacceptable. I am the head of the Interrogators. I should know everything you do."

"My favorite flavor of ice cream is mint chocolate chip," I told him.

His forehead crinkled in confusion.

I smiled. "Now you're one step closer to knowing everything we do."

His confusion melted away to annoyance.

"Actually, I didn't know that about you already," Harker said. "Mmm. Mint chocolate chip."

I grinned at him. "I bet you're glad you only tried to steal my cake, not a bowl of my mint chocolate chip ice cream. If you had, I might have used something a lot bigger than a fork to defend my property."

He snorted.

"That is not an appropriate sound for an angel to make, Sunstorm," Colonel Fireswift snapped.

Harker pretended to look repentant. He did a much better job of it than I could. For some reason, no one ever believed that I didn't enjoy misbehaving.

"Leda, you became an angel two-and-a-half weeks ago." Nerissa looked over her notes. "You had a boost of magic, which unsettled you for a time. Then your magic settled down, equalizing."

She didn't seem to be talking to me or anyone else, so I didn't say anything.

"Then, once your magic had settled from your transformation, the Fever hit you," Nerissa continued talking to herself. "Like the Fever was waiting for that moment when your magic was calm, like it needed that serenity. Your fertility seems to work differently than any other angel's. I wonder how often this cycle will repeat."

"Hopefully not ever," I said. "It kind of sucks to have my magic and emotions all over the place."

"I wonder whether we can induce the state at will by simply settling your magic."

"No. Absolutely not," I told her. "We are most certainly not going to do that. We're not even going to *try* to do that."

"This could be a new breakthrough in angel fertility—

something as revolutionary as Nyx's birth, which showed the gods how to make angels out of humans."

"Let's stay clear of anything revolutionary. The gods aren't overly fond of revolutions."

"Leda, your condition could show us how to make female angels fertile at will," Nerissa pressed on, my joke not even breaking through her scientific euphoria. "This could shake the very foundation of the Legion."

I glanced at Harker. "She keeps saying 'you' and 'Leda', but I don't think she's really talking to me."

Harker laughed. "It's your move, Ms. Revolutionary."

I moved a few of my pieces around the game board.

Colonel Fireswift gave the board a thorough once-over. "That move makes no sense. Why did you make it?"

I smiled demurely. "Wait and see."

Colonel Fireswift was watching the board like it would at any moment jump up and bite him. He was likely trying to figure out what dirty stratagem was preparing to attack him from the shadows.

"Careful, there, Colonel," I said. "You're glaring at the game board so hard that it might just spontaneously combust."

"Nothing inside my circle of influence is spontaneous. It's all carefully planned."

It sounded like a line from a self-help book, something you were supposed to repeat to remind yourself that you were the master of your own destiny. I wished I felt like I was the master of my own destiny right now, rather than just another piece on the Legion's playing board.

"And what about the things outside your circle of influence?" I asked Colonel Fireswift.

He looked at me like there was nothing outside his circle of influence. You'd have thought our recent experience with the gods' challenges would have reshaped his perspective, at least a little. But old habits died hard, especially for stubborn angels.

Maybe he needed a reminder. As the game cycled around to my turn again, I made my move. I swept in behind him with a magic-cloaked army twice as large as my visible force on the board. They wiped out one of Colonel Fireswift's strongholds.

"Maybe your circle of influence doesn't stretch as far as you think?" I suggested, cocking a single brow.

He glared at me, his eyes shooting fireballs. Not literally, thankfully.

"Just call me Ms. Revolutionary." I stood up, stretching out my arms over my head.

"Where are you going?" Colonel Fireswift demanded as I walked toward the door.

"To stretch my legs and get some air."

He rose immediately, motioning for Harker to do the same. "We're going with you."

"Of course you are," I sighed.

Nerissa's clock clicked, then began playing an upbeat jazz song.

I looked at it, then at her. "Is that your dinner alarm?"

She was always so engrossed in her work that she often forgot to eat. I regularly brought her a dinner plate along from the canteen, just so she wouldn't starve.

"No, not the dinner bell," she said. "The test results I've been waiting for are ready."

She eagerly rolled her chair to the computer on the far end of her desk, the one running magic compatibility tests on me and the Legion's male soldiers. I had to admit that since learning I had the Fever, I'd been tempted at least once a minute to blow up that computer. Of course, it was a futile wish. All her tests were run on the Legion's servers, which she only accessed from her own computer.

But the idea of blowing things up made me feel better. It made me feel less hopeless, like I was doing something, like I was taking steps to stop this insanity. That maybe I could really become the master of my own destiny.

"And what's the verdict, Doctor?" I asked as she typed on her keyboard.

"Weird," she muttered.

"I'm not compatible with anyone, am I?" I said hopefully.

"No, you're not," she said in surprise. "At least not anyone we've tested against your magic. It's not even close. There is absolutely no compatibility. Zero percent with anyone."

I breathed a sigh of relief. "And that's weird?"

"Yes, that's very weird." She stared at the screen. "In each case that we tried putting your magic together with another soldier's, your magic overpowered theirs, gobbling it right up. That's why their magic isn't compatible with yours. Your magic consumes theirs, absorbing it to make itself more powerful."

My magic sounded like a parasite. Or a vampire.

"So my magic doesn't play well with others?" I said, daring to hope.

"Apparently not."

"How completely expected," Colonel Fireswift said drily.

Nerissa's timer went off again. It was an operatic tune this time, not a jazz one.

"Your toast is ready," I told her.

"No, those are the angel group magic compatibility results. They just came in."

"Let me guess. My magic is not compatible with any of the angels' magic either."

Nerissa glanced up from the screen, her wide eyes meeting mine. "Actually, Leda, according to these results, you are compatible with them all. Every single angel."

CHAPTER 14

CHAMELEON MAGIC

"Every angel at the Legion?" I repeated in shock. "My magic is compatible with every angel at the Legion?"

"At least every angel who's sent in a new magic sample so far," Nerissa said.

Magic didn't stay fresh for long, so you needed a very recent sample to test magic compatibility.

"It's truly remarkable. The angels' magic must be powerful enough that yours doesn't consume it. It blends with it in seamless harmony—well, at least to varying degrees." Nerissa's eyes panned across her screen. "Your magic is a blender. A chameleon. This is just...fascinating."

"You're doing that thing again, Nerissa," I told her. "The thing where you talk to me but don't really talk to me."

"Sorry." She turned her monitor toward me. "Look at the test results. Your magic seems to be a kind of universal blend that goes with anything powerful enough to handle it, adapting itself to complement another angel's magic sample. I've never seen anything like it. I haven't even heard of anything like it."

That must have been my balanced light and dark magic at work. It was pretty adaptive.

"Your magic is universally compatible, but it does blend better with some samples than others," said Nerissa. "Your compatibility with other angels seems to depend on the magical spectrum of your abilities, on which powers are strongest for you. Your siren and vampire magics are way ahead of the rest."

Because of who my parents were.

"But look at your telepathic magic!" She pointed at the graph on her screen. "You haven't even yet had the Nectar for that power, and see how strong it is. It's nearly up to the level of your weaker talents, which have been activated by Nectar."

Well, that explained how I could usually block people from reading my mind, but it didn't tell me why my telepathic magic was so strong to begin with.

"You must have ghost blood in your lineage," Nerissa said.

No, not ghost blood. Deity blood. My siren magic was strong because of my father Faris, God of Sirens. My vampire magic was strong because of my mother Grace, Demon of Dark Vampires.

But neither gods nor demons possessed powerful telepathic magic. It wasn't one of their native powers. They'd acquired it later in their magical history. So why was that power strong in me? And why had it never expressed itself in me before I'd joined the Legion? My siren and vampire magic had—albeit in an odd way."

Before my Legion days, the glow and shine of my hair had mesmerized vampires, filling them with an irresistible urge to chow down on my neck. Nowadays, it responded to my mood and magic, changing color. And so did my new wings. Chameleon hair. Chameleon wings. Chameleon magic—that was the phrase Nerissa had used. This was all connected. My hair and wings and magic. The reason they changed color, and the reason my magic was compatible with every other angel's magic.

As for my telepathic magic…well, the only way it had expressed itself before now was my ability to mask my thoughts from telepaths. I'd thought that was sheer stubbornness—and desperation—on my part. I had a lot of secrets to hide. But what if there was more to it than that?

Nerissa's gaze slid from the screen, to Colonel Fireswift. "You are compatible with her."

Colonel Fireswift's disgusted face mirrored my own.

"But your compatibility is higher," Nerissa told Harker. "Ninety percent. Not bad. Do you know what this means?"

"That Nero is going to kill me," Harker said glumly.

"It means that if we can figure out why Leda is compatible with so many angels, this will completely change the Legion of Angels." Nerissa's whole face was lit up with excitement. "Maybe we could learn how to make more angels compatible with other angels."

Wow, I'd revolutionized the Legion a lot in the last few minutes.

"Do you have a magic sample from Nero?" I asked Nerissa.

"No, the First Angel has been unable to reach General Windstriker."

My last message from Nero had been two days ago when he'd been out on the plains of monsters, about to close in on a monster breeder, a profession I hadn't even known existed. Since then, there had only been silence from his end. Phone reception was notoriously bad out there. He might not even know what was going on at the Legion—and with me—right now.

Nyx entered the room. "Interesting results, Doctor?"

She said it like she already knew the answer. She'd probably been listening.

"Leda seems to be universally compatible with other angels," Nerissa reported. "These unprecedented results are very exciting."

I could forgive my friend's enthusiasm—she was a scientist who'd discovered something new and novel—but that didn't mean I would go through with this. Whatever 'this' ended up being. I had to find Nero. I had to contact him and get out of here before…well, just before. We would run away together as we'd promised each other.

"Walk with me," Nyx said to me.

I followed her out of the room. As we walked down the hallway, we passed other soldiers, but no one appeared to be fighting or going otherwise berserk. They were all acting with the dignity and reserve expected of a soldier in the Legion of Angels.

"They all seem fine," I commented.

I'd thought the incidents had been caused by a demon curse, but these troubles had been my fault all along. I couldn't help but feel guilty about that. Some of the affected people were my friends, and I'd hurt them. The fact that I'd done it unknowingly did little to assuage my guilt.

"The spell I cast around you has effectively blocked your emotions from telepathically bleeding onto others," Nyx told me. "There have been no further incidents in this Legion office or any other. But the spell won't be effective forever. At the rate Nerissa projects your magic to be building up, it's only a matter of time before tears form in my spell. Soon after that, it will dissolve completely."

"You can recast it."

"By that point, the Fever will have made your magic too wild, too potent, for any ward that I can cast around you."

Wow. The First Angel was admitting her magic wasn't up to the task of countering mine. I guessed the problem was my dark magic. I bet she could have held back my light magic, but she and everyone else here possessed only light magic. And light magic was weak against dark magic. It was a wonder her light magic spell was holding out against my dark magic at all, a testament to how powerful Nyx truly was.

"It sounds like you might want to explore cooperative options," I said.

Her dark brows drew together.

"You know, like casting the spell together with someone else," I clarified. "A god perhaps. Like Ronan."

And to do that, she'd have to talk to him again.

"Pandora, you should not meddle in my personal affairs. What happened between Ronan and me is between Ronan and me."

"Unless it affects the whole Legion. Aren't we supposed to not allow our personal feelings to get in the way of our duty? And besides, you love him. You can't let a few secrets stand in the way of that."

Her mouth drew into a hard, flat line. "I doubt you would be so forgiving in my place."

Not so long ago, I *had* been in her place. Faris had cast doubt on Nero's intentions. After a few unsettling moments, I'd calmed down and just asked Nero about it. We still didn't know who'd sent him the dreams of me before we met, the images that had caused him to take an interest in me, but I trusted Nero. Whatever was going on, he wasn't master-minding it, no matter what Faris wanted me to believe. Faris was just trying to create a rift between us, so it would be easier for him to ensnare me, to make me his weapon.

"You'd be surprised how forgiving I can be," I told Nyx.

"I'll remember that."

She was thinking of herself now, of how she'd lied to us and stolen the weapons of heaven and hell from Nero. She expected my forgiveness.

"Of course, forgiveness must be earned," I added.

She dipped her chin. "Naturally."

"You know, there's actually a very simple solution to our current predicament, Nyx. There's a way we can protect the Legion's soldiers from my emotional bleed-off *without* using magic wards."

"Oh? And what is that?"

"You simply give me the potion that nullifies my magic until the Fever has passed."

A slight smile twisted her lips. "You must know that is impossible."

"Yeah," I sighed. "I know."

The Legion would never waste an angel's fertile time. Nyx needed to plan for the future, to create new soldiers to fill her army's ranks. She especially wouldn't block my magic now, not after Nerissa had found me to be compat-ible with other angels.

"Or you could go with the usual solution: you send me away so I can't affect others."

"Your condition is different than other angels with the

Fever," she said. "Your reach is wider. At the rate your magic is building up, I'm afraid there's nowhere on Earth I could send you where you wouldn't affect at least two Legion offices."

That wasn't exactly true. She could send me out into the middle of the plains of monsters. That wasn't a possibility I found particularly thrilling, but out there were vast stretches of nothingness far from any Legion office.

"Besides, I can't send you out of my sight," Nyx continued. "I need you where I can keep an eye on you. You're a flight risk."

She said it like I was a criminal she was refusing to release on bail.

"A flight risk? I can't even fly. At least not in a straight line," I joked.

Nyx, the Legion's mother dragon, looked at me like she was scolding me, one of her baby dragons, for setting the whole nest on fire. "You're staying here, Pandora, until your magic peaks and your Fever has run its course. And I'll be right here beside you, watching you."

Being under Nyx's watchful eye would certainly make it difficult to flee. She sure wasn't fooling around.

"You know, Nyx, this really isn't necessar—"

Magic rocked the corridor, throwing open the doors at the other end. Everyone stopped and stared as Nero stormed through them, his wings spread high and wide. Magic burned in his green eyes. It hissed and snapped across his dark feathers.

"You will test my magic with Leda's," he told Nyx, his voice cutting like a lightning whip.

He spoke the words like he was giving an order to the First Angel of the Legion.

But Nyx appeared neither annoyed nor upset. She merely replied, "You're late, General."

"I was detained by monsters, but I'm here now." A fresh wave of magic flared up around him, igniting his aura, lighting up the sword he held in his hand. "And I have no intention of allowing any other angel but me to marry Leda."

CHAPTER 15

THE RULES OF ENGAGEMENT

*I*t turned out that neither Nero's sword nor his magic was necessary to back up his heroic proclamation.

"Congratulations. Your magic is more compatible with Leda's than any other angel's," Nerissa declared after testing our magic together.

"Of course it is," he said with a charming absence of humility.

I couldn't seem to keep the smile off my face. "You were so sure, were you?"

His hand softly brushed my cheek. "I have experience on my side, Leda. The benefit of always being right for centuries."

"You've said that before."

"And yet it's still true."

I chuckled.

"Your magics fit so well together," Nerissa commented, her eyes darting between us and our test results. "Almost like they'd been designed to complement each other. You were never compatible with any soldier at the Legion before, General. So why Leda?"

That was the scientist in her, going at it again, digging for answers.

Nero didn't answer her. His eyes locked with mine, he leaned in closer to kiss me.

Nyx intercepted us before our lips met. "Come with me, both of you," her voice cracked, jolting us out of the moment.

Sighing, I followed her out of the room. Nero walked beside me, looking pretty damn amused. Wherever Nyx was taking us, he found it particularly funny.

"Now what?" I whispered to him.

"Now comes the spectacle," he told me.

"What kind of spectacle?"

"The angel kind."

Which meant big, flashy, and full of fanfare. Oh, goody. I sighed again.

Nyx led us through the ballroom's doors. All soldiers in the New York office—and any visitors from other offices too—were packed inside. Harker and Colonel Fireswift waited on either side of the raised stage. Nyx headed there now, motioning for me to follow her.

"Soldiers of the Legion," she began when we were standing atop the wood stage. "As you all know, we've discovered the cause of the recent incidents involving soldiers at three Legion offices." Her eyes flickered briefly to me. "Our newest angel has the Fever."

Awesome. My fertility was being broadcast to everyone. Sure, they all must have known it as soon as Nerissa's staff began submitting all male soldiers to magic tests, but Nyx putting me on stage and publicly announcing my condition to everyone as they all gawked at me—now, that was something else entirely.

"A match for her has been found," Nyx said.

Excited, eager whispers buzzed from several of the male soldiers, including a few that I knew for a fact could not stand me. But things were different now. I had become an angel. Maybe the prospect of having sex with an angel was enticing enough to make them forget their dislike for me. And the Fever was a special phenomenon. Lots of guys eagerly embraced the idea of being screwed until they couldn't walk. I guess you could say it was built into their biology.

Nyx motioned toward Nero. "General Windstriker's magic is the best fit," she declared as he came to stand beside me.

The whispered words were decidedly more shocked than excited now. It was understandable. Angels were basically never compatible with other angels.

Well, at least none of the guys were leering at me anymore. However, some of them were looking upon Nero with trepidation, as though worried he would punish them for daring to look at me.

None of them looked scared of me—which they totally should have been. I was an angel too. Just because I had breasts didn't mean I couldn't kick all their asses.

Nero lowered to one knee before me and presented me with a large box. The audience fell so silent I could hardly hear them breathe.

What is it? I asked him silently, taking the box.

An engagement gift. A token of my devotion.

I opened the box to find a sword inside, a weapon that required no introduction. I recognized it immediately. The sword was an immortal artifact. It was a piece in the weapons of heaven and hell set. How had Nero gotten it back from Faris?

Brushing my hand across the blade, I glanced at Nyx. Her face was impassive. If she knew anything about this, she wasn't showing it.

"It seems your trip was eventful," I said to Nero.

"Yes." He rose from his knee, taking my free hand. I held the sword in the other.

"For the first time in over two centuries—and only the second time in Legion history—two angels will be joined." Nyx's voice was as clear as a bell. She looked upon our audience. "You are all charged with the task of making sure everything proceeds as I have laid out."

Hundreds of phones chimed.

"You have your assignments," Nyx told them. "Now get to it."

As the soldiers left in a swift and orderly fashion, Nyx went to speak with Harker and Colonel Fireswift, leaving me and Nero alone on stage.

"Have dinner with me," Nero said to me.

"Only if we're eating in."

"I've already instructed the kitchen staff to send the food to our apartment." His smile was delightfully roguish. "It will arrive in ten minutes."

I squeezed his hand harder, leading him off the stage. "Then we'd best hurry. I'm famished."

"As am I," he replied, his voice rough and impatient.

We moved toward the exit, our pulses pounding hard —and in perfect synchronicity—through our joined hands.

Nyx was waiting at the door, barring our path. "Where do you think you're going?"

I presented her with my most innocent smile. "Having dinner."

Her counter-smile was as hard as dinosaur-scale armor. "Nice try. But I'm going to have to put some distance between you two. General Windstriker, I've arranged another apartment for you."

"Why?" I demanded, unable to keep the exasperation out of my voice.

"Because we all know you two weren't going off to eat dinner," replied Nyx.

"We'd have gotten around to the dinner part eventually," I muttered grumpily.

"You can't have sex with Nero," Nyx said. It sounded suspiciously like an order.

I frowned at her. "I thought that was the whole point of marrying us."

"You're not married yet. Your magic hasn't peaked; it hasn't reached the peak time of fertility, the best chance of conception. Until then, no sex. No kissing. No touching of any kind." She looked pointedly at our joined hands.

Nero dropped my hand.

"Those are the rules of engagement," Nyx declared.

"No touching of any kind?" I repeated, frowning. "What if I accidentally bump into him in the corridor?"

"There will be armed guards posted at every doorway, exit, and intersection to make sure you don't *accidentally* bump into each other," she informed me. "Bumping leads to kissing, which leads to sex."

"I think they had those exact lines printed on a poster at my high school," I quipped.

"And having sex prematurely, before your magic peaks, disrupts the upward trajectory of your magic, fizzling out the Fever," Nyx continued. "I will be assigning chaperones to you and guards to Nero to make sure you comply with these rules."

"There's no need," I snapped at her. "I can behave myself."

"Leda, you've *never* been able to behave yourself. And as you approach your Fever's high point, as your magic peaks and your hormones surge, it will grow increasingly difficult to do so. Even now, I can feel a weakening of the spell I cast to shield others from you. Your magic feels my ward—and it's fighting back."

I wasn't surprised. My magic didn't like being told what to do any more than I did.

"But I haven't seen Nero in a long time," I protested.

"You can still see him. At a distance," she amended. "Or, when a face-to-face meeting is absolutely necessary, it will be in the company of armed guards."

"This is ridiculous. I don't need a babysitter."

"You do, in fact, and many of them. Or would you prefer that I locked you up in a cell?"

I threw my hands up into the air in exasperation. "Fine. Assign your chaperones."

She nodded in approval. "Good girl. Now, according to Dr. Harding's latest magic readings, your magic should peak in five days. Your wedding will be held in the afternoon of the fifth day. Do you think you can control yourself for that long?"

I looked at Nero, rolling my eyes to let him know how I felt about this. I could keep my hands off him for five days if I wanted to. I wasn't a complete nymphomaniac.

The smoldering look Nero gave me in response set my magic on fire, testing that assertion. I could feel my body moving toward his, like there was a taut rope linking us, drawing us together.

I resisted that draw—and all the fun that came with it. "Now, if you'll excuse me, listening to all this nonsense has made me hungry," I told Nyx.

She didn't move from the doorway. "You will eat your meals in the canteen."

"Great," I said brightly. I pasted a broad smile over my immense annoyance at her overbearing micromanagement. "I'll head there at once. I hear they're serving lasagna today."

"Go with them," Nyx told Harker, then she stepped aside.

Harker followed me and Nero out of the ballroom.

"So you're first on bride babysitting duty," I said.

"So it would seem," replied Harker.

I glanced sidelong at Nero. "If it comes to a fight, I think we could take him."

Harker shook his head. "So much for behaving yourself. This is going to be a very long five days."

"Relax. I was just kidding."

"You might be kidding now, but just wait a day or two. You won't be kidding then," Harker promised me. "I remember when Leila had the Fever. Nyx assigned me to chaperone her. Leila stapled my hands to a post."

"But Leila is so nice," I said in surprise.

"Exactly. And if a nice angel can do that, imagine what the Angel of Chaos can do."

"Angel of Chaos?" Nero asked, the corner of his mouth twitching.

"That's what people are calling me," I told him.

"It's very fitting."

"So true." I glanced at Harker. "You want to imagine what the Angel of Chaos can do? How about tie your shoelaces together? Or glue your butt to your office chair?

Perhaps spike your morning orange juice with sneezing powder?"

Harker looked horrified. "That wasn't an actual invitation to imagine the possibilities, Leda."

I laughed.

"But even if you got through me, Nyx has posted guards every twenty feet in all corridors and rooms," he warned me. "You won't make it far."

So those were the assignments she'd given everyone back in the ballroom. That's why everyone's phone had chimed. I wondered if anyone here in the New York office was doing anything else besides babysitting me right now.

"Why do I feel like I'm in prison?" I said to Nero.

His wide shoulders rolled back in a slow, unbothered shrug. "Did you expect anything else from the First Angel?"

"No," I admitted. "Not really."

I reached for his hand, but Harker moved between us.

I scowled at him. "We aren't even allowed to hold hands?"

"Holding hands qualifies as touching," Harker reminded me.

"Barely."

"It's for your own good, Leda."

"Why do people always say that when they're doing something decidedly *not* for my own good?" I grumbled.

"Just because something is good for you, that doesn't mean it's enjoyable. Like the vitamin Nerissa gave you."

"What vitamin?" Nero asked me.

"Nothing," I said. "Nerissa doesn't approve of my dessert diet, so she made me take a vitamin."

"A prenatal vitamin," Harker told Nero.

Nero glanced at me, his expression decidedly blank.

I blushed. I couldn't even say why I did it. We all knew why the Legion was marrying me to Nero: procreation. But somehow it was easier to concentrate on how much I wanted to have sex with Nero than it was to think about why we were supposed to do it.

"I wonder what they're serving for dessert in Demeter today," I said quickly.

Nero watched me as I stepped up my pace, but he didn't comment on the vitamin, my fertility, or the Fever at all. I wondered what he thought of any of it. He'd flown in, my angel in shining armor, to rescue me from marrying someone else. That meant he wanted to marry me. Right?

Just a few weeks ago, he'd proclaimed that he would do anything to keep us together, even if it meant leaving the Legion he'd dedicated the last two centuries of his life to. But we hadn't discussed marriage. He hadn't told me his thoughts on it. I didn't even know my own thoughts on it.

But thinking about it now, I realized that I did want it. I wanted to be with Nero forever. And that's what marriage was. Well, maybe that wasn't the Legion's idea of marriage; they used it to create future soldiers with the potential to become angels. But that's what it meant to me. I wanted Nero to be mine and only mine. I wanted every woman who dared look at him to know what would happen to her if she made a move on him.

"Whoa, Leda," Harker said, stepping back. "Where did all the wrath suddenly come from?"

I realized rage and wrath and jealously were burning inside of me. That was the Fever, spiking my emotions. My feelings were bleeding off me again, and Harker had caught a whiff of them. It was safe to assume Nero had too.

I wondered what Nero thought of my insanity. There was no one here, no one who had incited these emotions.

It was just my own mind, considering the possibility that someone might try to take Nero from me. The thought of it made me murderous.

Gods, the Fever was making me crazy. Nyx had been right. With every passing hour, my emotions were growing more turbulent. And I had five days to go of this. Right now, I could resist. My mind was stronger than my emotions. But how long would that last?

"I hate the Fever," I growled.

"I heard it's not all bad." Harker winked at Nero.

Nero watched me, the magic in his eyes swirling. And just like that, in an instant, my anger and wrath and jealousy melted away, replaced by pure, undiluted lust.

"I was wrong," I told Nero. Every hard throb of my pulse pumped that lust through my body, from the soft flesh of my lips, to the tingling tips of my toes.

His brows lifted. His lips twisted into a sexy smile.

"Five days is an eternity," I moaned.

Harker cleared his throat and moved between me and Nero.

I swallowed hard and took a step back from Nero, trying to allow my head to settle. My pulse was still pounding, my skin tingling, like I could feel every whisper of the gentle breeze coming down the corridor, every particle of dust. Every brush of Nero's lips against my… I stopped, shaking my head. No, that hadn't happened. I realized I'd taken a step toward Nero again, so I moved back, putting some distance between us.

"You two can't even keep your hands off each other under normal circumstances. And Nyx wants me to keep you apart when Leda has the Fever." Harker shook his head like the task she'd set him was impossible.

Maybe it was. Every part of me, every inch of my body

inside and out, every beat of my magic, wanted Nero. To be one with him. To join with him. To mark his body and magic and soul as mine. So that everyone knew he belonged to me and me alone.

"I prefer your hard training sessions to this agony," I told Nero earnestly.

His eyes shone with wicked promises. "A hard training session can be arranged."

"How hard?"

His voice dipped lower, darker. "As hard as you need it to be."

Every word he spoke was a whisper of fire across my feverish skin. Any training we did would have to be harder and tougher than ever before. I had a lot of lust to work off.

"How can we train if we're not allowed to touch?" I gasped.

"I have a sword," he proclaimed silkily.

My eyes slid down his hard body, tracing every hard muscle, every ridge and valley, as my tongue flicked out and slid slowly across my lips.

"Leda."

The sound of my name on his lips set off an explosive cascade inside of me. My wings burst out of my back, a sunset tapestry of dark pink and orange and yellow. His dark wings unfolded from his back. The tips of our feathers kissed, and a splash of liquid fire rippled down my wings, igniting every nerve ending in my body. I gasped.

"Oh, for the love of the gods," Harker grumbled and gave us each a rough shove backward.

I looked up and down the hallway. Seven soldiers were within sight, and they were all watching every move that Nero and I made. That realization jolted me back to Earth.

My hair and wings turned as red as my cheeks. I couldn't believe I'd nearly had sex with Nero in the corridor.

We've had sex in more public places, he said in my mind.

Stop it. You're not helping.

Then how can I help you, my love?

The thought of him helping me out of my clothes was particularly appealing.

A satisfied smile curled his lips. *That would be acceptable.*

Gods, if I made it through these five days, they would have to declare me a saint.

We were almost at the canteen. As we approached the doors, Angel closed in beside me, strutting like the queen she was.

Nero glanced at her. "That cat has grown considerably since I shipped her to you."

"It's all the fine cuisine available here," I said. "Fish. Seagulls. She's even caught a wild turkey."

Nero nodded in angelic approval. "A worthy hunter."

His approval dissolved the moment his eyes met the track of dirty footprints Angel was leaving on the marble floor. "What has that cat been getting into?"

I gave her a fond look. "Trouble, of course."

He frowned. "She isn't even white anymore. You must wash her immediately."

"Believe me, I've tried."

"Try harder."

"You try getting a cat into a bathtub. The harder you try, the less successful you are."

"I am completely confident in your ability to command a cat," he said.

"Wow, great. I'm glad you're confident. That really helps a lot."

I took my usual seat at the head table. I frowned at Harker when he moved between me and Nero, claiming the seat between us. He merely shrugged and smiled.

"Cats are notoriously independent, but you have tamed her well," Nero said to me as Angel sat down at my feet. "Just as you tamed those beasts on the Black Plains."

"You heard about that?" My heart sank. My mood soured, washing the lust right out of me.

"The whole Legion has heard about it by now," said Nero. "And the gods too, I'm sure."

Nero had warned me not to show anyone my unusual ability to control beasts. He'd warned me that the gods would take me captive to use me if they found out what I could do. They'd been trying to regain control of the beasts for centuries without success. They would not pass up the opportunity to realize their goals.

"I didn't have much of a choice," I said to him, my voice low. "It was either compel the beasts, or let them eat me and my team. What are the gods going to do about it?"

"Nothing for the moment, but now the cat is out of the bag." Nero glanced at my cat. "Eventually, the gods will react. And we have to be ready when they do."

"I'm always ready," I said. "In fact, I've been in a state of constant readiness since I joined the Legion."

Nero reached for my hand, a sign of support and comfort for what I'd been through—but he froze, then withdrew his hand. Harker was watching us. We weren't supposed to touch. Kisses, hugs, and even comforting hand squeezes were forbidden. It felt like there was an invisible wall between me and Nero, a wall we could not cross.

"This sucks," I sighed.

And I wasn't just referring to my unsatisfied desire. I wanted Nero to be allowed to offer me a comforting

151

squeeze or a pat on the back. And I wanted to do the same for him.

"I can't wait until the five days are over," I said.

"Neither can I."

Right now, his mind wasn't thinking of comforting squeezes or pats on the back. I could see it in his eyes, the promise of what would happen when the wait was over: the two of us, together, and days of passion as my Fever peaked. He was anticipating it, wanting it. I felt it through the bond that connected us—and it spiked my magic, and my desire.

I cleared my throat. "How was your trip? Did you figure out why the monsters' numbers are swelling?"

"No," he replied. "I thought the path would lead to Meda, considering her experiments on monsters and magic, but I found no evidence of her involvement. I did track a monster dealer to the Frontier town of Judgment, and from there onto the plains of monsters. I caught up with him there and interrogated him."

"What did he say?"

"After several minutes of proclaiming his complete innocence, he admitted to selling monsters to wealthy humans in need of guard animals."

"People buy monsters as guard animals?" I just couldn't get my head around that kind of sheer stupidity. "You can't be serious."

"I am completely serious, Leda. In fact, two of the monster seller's clients live right here in New York. And tomorrow morning, we're going to pay them both a visit."

CHAPTER 16

I walked beside Nero in the Cauldron District of New York. A change of pace from the city's tall skyscrapers, the Cauldron District was an old-money neighborhood populated by wealthy witches living in white stone villas with tall metal fences designed to keep anyone and anything out.

"They must have forgotten that angels can fly," I commented to Nero.

"Well, at least some of us can," Harker teased me.

I glanced back at him, frowning. "I can fly. Sort of. I just can't control which way I fly."

Ivy, Drake, and Alec laughed. Along with Harker, they made up my chaperone squad.

Honestly, I was surprised that Nyx had let me out of the office to track down monster buyers with Nero, even with this heavy escort. On the other hand, she must have realized I needed to do something, or I'd go stir crazy. And if I got agitated, my emotions would bombard her ward around me, which would reduce its longevity. If Nyx's ward fell, my emotions would spill out and affect other Legion soldiers in New York and beyond.

"No fence could keep an angel out, flight or no flight," Nero told me.

I didn't know about that. A Magitech bubble could keep out an angel, but those required a lot of energy to run. And right now, there weren't any Magitech generators outside the Legion's control. We were diverting most of the power to the walls that separated civilization from the plains of monsters. It kept the monsters out and humanity safe. The fate of humanity was definitely a much higher priority than a single person trying to keep out his nosy neighbors.

I surveyed the neat and trim hedges beyond the street-facing fences. They were thick and high enough to keep prying eyes from peering inside.

"The fence might not keep an angel out, but those hedges would slow us down," I commented.

"They are not mere plants," said Nero. "They are hedge monsters."

"The branches move, grabbing and choking anyone who gets too close," Harker added with unnatural enthusiasm. "And the thorns on the branches are poisonous."

A moment ago, the hedges had looked so nice. Now they appeared rife with hazards. Clean and proper on the outside, feral on the inside.

"Are hedge monsters actual monsters, or is that just a fanciful name?" I asked.

"They are monsters," Nero replied. "In fact, they are among the most common monsters sold by monster breeders and traders."

I shook my head. "I still can't believe there's an actual business in selling monsters."

"Wealthy humans buy them to guard their properties, believing they can control them," said Nero.

"The gods can't even control the monsters. What makes these people think that they can?"

Nero shrugged. "Hubris."

When it came to capital offenses, hubris ranked even higher in the gods' eyes than buying monsters on the black market.

"Does Wildfoot sell hedge monsters?" I asked Nero.

Wildfoot was the name of the monster trader Nero had interrogated on the Black Plains. He'd obviously given himself that fanciful title, likely considering it a very clever name for a monster merchant.

"Wildfoot used to sell hedge monsters," said Nero. "But he's since moved on to more mobile beasts."

I nodded. "Yes, I'd imagine you can't very easily redeploy hedges."

Behind me, Alec snorted.

I turned around to look at him. "Something funny?"

The sunlight bounced off his shiny white teeth. "I never thought I'd see the day where an angel talked about redeploying hedges."

I flashed him a grin. "Just you wait. I expect I'll shock you at least five times over before the day is up."

"I can hardly wait. I love missions with you, Leda." Alec's gaze flickered to Nero, then he hastily amended, "Uh, I mean Pandora."

Legion protocol was pretty strict on these things. You weren't supposed to call an angel by their first name. Since I didn't have an angel name yet, that complicated matters somewhat. People were mostly just referring to me as 'Pandora' since that's what I'd put on my jacket. I wondered how long Nyx would allow that to continue. Probably until she could come up with an angel name that fit me and instilled fear into the hearts of our enemies. I didn't envy her the impossible task of coming up with a name that made people fear me. I could imagine it was giving her a massive headache.

"And what is it you enjoy about my missions so much?" I asked Alec. "Well, besides the enormous honor of being in my presence and basking in my angelic light?"

Ivy made a choking sound.

"Too much?" I asked her.

"You passed 'too much' by about twenty times," she told me.

"I thought I was being ironic."

"Angels aren't supposed to be ironic. They're supposed to take everything completely seriously."

"Oh, I take a lot of things seriously. Like ice cream." I glanced at Nero and Harker, an angelic expression on my face. "And doing my wing pushups every morning."

Neither of them laughed—we were in public, after all —but I knew they really wanted to. I'd found that humor was helping me keep my wild moods under control. A joke here and there deflated the burgeoning tempest of Fever-induced emotions.

Alec was laughing, though. "I enjoy your missions so much because they usually deteriorate into chaos within the first half hour."

Drake glanced at his watch. "Twenty minutes to go."

The light caught his watch as he turned it to read the clock face. Angel pounced at the reflected flickers of silver light on the sidewalk.

"Good girl, Angel." I smiled at my cat. "You show that wayward light who's boss."

"You named the cat Angel," Nero commented, his face impassive.

"You told me to rename her. And I can think of no name more befitting of an angel's cat than Angel."

Nero said nothing.

"I don't think General Windstriker appreciates irony," Drake told me.

"Nonsense, he has a fantastic sense of humor." I glanced at Nero. "Show them, honey."

Nero's face was deadpan.

Sighing, I shifted my gaze to the monster hedges. "So, all of the people who bought the monster merchant's guard monsters live in this little slice of privilege tucked away inside the city?"

"His hedge monsters are popular," said Nero. "Most of the Cauldron District residents bought them, but only two of them splurged on his experimental new monster guard dogs. And Maxwell Plenteous is one of them."

I read the gold plaque fixed to the iron fence of the house we'd stopped in front of. The gold letters read 'Maxwell Plenteous'.

"Maxwell Plenteous?" I snorted, which was admittedly not particularly angelic or regal. "He totally made up that name."

Nero rang the bell. Roughly half a minute later, the gate doors parted. Through the opening stepped a woman dressed in a navy-blue business suit and a wide-brimmed hat with a big navy-and-white polkadot bow. Her high-heeled shoes clicked against the beige cobblestones.

Her eyes widened when she saw us, three angels and their three soldiers. She must never have seen that many angels in one place. Unable to speak, she merely stared at us. She might have been a bit less shocked if she'd known

157

that Harker was only here to babysit me. Then again, there was nothing comforting in the knowledge that I and my wild magic were more of a threat right now than any monster.

"Do you know who we are?" Harker asked the witch at the gate.

"Yes," she said cautiously. "Harker Sunstorm. Nero Windstriker." Her gaze shifted to me. "And the Pandora."

Oh, I was *the* Pandora now, was I? I tried to decide whether that was a step up or down.

"We are looking for Maxwell Plenteous," Nero told her.

"My husband died last night." Her voice broke. "His dog went berserk and killed him."

And now I felt bad for mocking Maxwell Plenteous's name, even though it was his own fault for buying a monster.

"This dog was not a dog at all," Nero said, undeterred.

The witch's lip quivered in fear.

"It was a monster, smuggled past the wall into the city," Nero continued.

Maxwell's widow looked like she didn't know what to say that wouldn't make everything worse.

"Where is the beast?" Harker asked her.

"Dead." She swallowed hard. "Maxwell shot the beast as it jumped on him. The creature died of its wounds shortly after Maxwell did."

"When did Mr. Plenteous purchase the beast?" Nero asked.

"Last Thursday. The beast was completely obedient—until it went suddenly berserk last night."

"We need to see your husband's and the beast's bodies," Harker told her.

She stepped aside. "This way."

We followed her past the gate, following the cobble-stone path that cut through the garden. The toolshed behind the house was splattered with blood. A giant furry dead beast was floating facedown in the pool. Maxwell Plenteous's corpse lay propped up against the fence.

"I was afraid to move them," the widow said, her voice shaking.

"We'll take care of it," Harker assured her. He was already on his phone, calling in a team to come pick up the bodies.

Meanwhile, Nero was interrogating the witch. He wanted to know where her husband had bought the monster, whether it was really Wildfoot who had sold it to him, and what had happened in the lead-up to the monster going berserk.

Angel's tiny meow drew my attention. I followed her across the grass, to where Maxwell lay. Broken shards of metal were scattered around his body. I leaned down for a closer look. The pieces were bloody—and they looked smashed, like something heavy and strong had crushed the metal flat.

I picked up the shards—with my magic, of course, not my hands. I didn't even know whose blood it was, or what diseases it might contain. Ivy, Drake, and Alec closed in behind me.

"What do you think they are?" I asked them.

Ivy watched the metal fragments floating in the air in front of us. "They look like the remains of a necklace or bracelet."

Alec rolled his eyes. "Everything looks like jewelry to you."

"Just look at that." Ivy pointed at the shards. "Those are pieces of some kind of big ring."

"Something magical?" Drake wondered.

"If it was magical, it didn't help him much." Alec glanced down at Maxwell's body.

I gave the broken metal pieces a nudge with my magic, dropping them into a small bag I'd pulled out of my jacket. The Legion team Harker had called in was just arriving. They immediately got to work loading the dead beast and Maxwell into their truck.

"Bring these shards to Dr. Harding for testing," I said, handing the bag to one of the soldiers. "Tell her they were found close to Maxwell Plenteous's body."

Then we left them to their work and headed to the next house on Nero's list, Wildfoot's second New York client. It was not a long walk. In fact, the house was just two streets over, still inside the Cauldron District.

"It takes a lot of guts to buy a monster and bring it into the city, especially one with a Legion office," Harker commented as we walked. "Most citizens of Earth are not that bold, at least not those who belong to one of the world's old money dynasties."

"I don't think we're dealing with typical citizens," I said, pointing at the monster tied to a grand villa's front gate.

It appeared that we'd found the second guard beast.

CHAPTER 17

*A*ngel turned up her nose at the dead headless monster tied to the front gate. She stepped back, clearly not caring to get too close to it. I was totally with her on that. The stench was almost unbearable.

But Nero didn't back up. Instead, he moved forward and rang the bell. His willpower was remarkable. His nose didn't even crinkle up in disgust, even though I knew he could smell it every bit as much as I could.

The house door opened, and out walked a man dressed in a pair of denim tights, high leather boots, and a tan suede jacket with tassels. The cowboy witch wore a coat of black eyeliner so thick and heavy that I could see it from the other side of the gate, clear across the expansive front lawn.

Unlike Maxwell, this monster buyer was still very much alive. He took one look at us—and our Legion of Angels uniforms—and made a run for it, his tassels swaying wildly around him.

The cowboy witch made it only two steps before he

slammed face-first into the invisible psychic wall Nero had cast. He bounced back off the magic wall and hit the ground with a thump and a grunt.

As the man lay there, dazed, Nero cast a lightning spell to fry the security system. The gate opened, proving his earlier point that no amount of security could keep out an angel. The witch rose wearily from the ground, his silver eyes darting around. He knew he'd been caught. And that there was no escape.

Nero's gaze shifted from the monster on the gate, to the man before him. "You bought this beast from Wildfoot."

"Yes," the witch croaked out.

"And not only did you buy a monster, you snuck it into my city," Harker continued.

The man swallowed like there was a lump the size of an egg wedged in his throat.

"Then, to top it all off, you lost control over the monster," Nero added.

"That wasn't supposed to happen," the man protested, his eyes shifting nervously from one angel to the other. Nero and Harker were doing a very thorough job of scaring him out of his wits.

I looked at the beast crucified to the gate. "How exactly did it happen? And how did you survive the beast's attack?"

"I decapitated the monster with a shovel."

That would do it.

"And then you mounted the beast on your front gate for all to see," I said.

That hadn't been a very clever move. He'd effectively broadcast to everyone in the neighborhood that he'd brought a monster into the city. Not that the guy had to be particularly smart if he'd bought a monster as a guard dog in the first place.

The witch frowned. "I was angry."

Right now, he was having an obvious 'oh, shit' moment. He seemed to have just come to the unhappy conclusion that putting the monster there had implicated him.

"The dead beast is keeping intruders away even better than the live one did," he said meekly.

I could believe that. The smell was positively rancid. I frowned as the wind shifted, blowing the smell my way. My stomach flopped. Acid rose in my throat.

"What made you think you could control the monster?" Harker asked the witch as I tried my hardest not to throw up.

Vomiting all over one's shoes was not very becoming of an angel. Unfortunately, becoming an angel meant my magic was stronger than ever, and among other things, more magic meant a more sensitive nose. The dead beast's stench was testing my willpower in ways that even Nero's training sessions couldn't.

"Wildfoot had the monsters completely under control. He was using special control collars," said the witch. "My beast was outfitted with one. Wildfoot promised the collar had made the monster tame, controllable."

"It seems it didn't work at all," I said.

"The collar *was* working," protested the cowboy witch, his tassels swishing in irritation.

I gave the monster on the gate a pointed look.

"At least the collar was working *until* it short-circuited when the beast went for a swim on the property."

I arched my brows. "You would think he'd have thought to make the collar waterproof."

"The collar was waterproof," said the witch. "The beast had swum in that very same pond many times before. But something was different this time. Something triggered the incident."

"Where is the collar?" I asked him.

He reached his hand into an inner pocket of his suede jacket. He handed the collar to me—or at least what was left of it. It was in pieces—three pieces, to be exact. What a strange thing to carry around.

The fractured collar bore a striking resemblance to the pieces of metal I'd found at the previous house. Maybe it was the remains of a broken control collar that I'd discovered beside Maxwell's body.

I looked over the broken collar in my hand. Though it wasn't nearly as shattered as the pieces from Maxwell, both collars seemed to have broken in the same way. Maybe the collars possessed the same design defect.

"Potions and Poisons?" I read off one of the pieces.

"The name of the company that designed the collar," the witch told me.

"That company sounds totally aboveboard," I commented.

"The collar is black market stuff," he admitted.

Real shocker.

"Potions and Poisons makes experimental tech like the collar," said the witch. "The collar monitors the beast and injects a potion when needed. That potion controls the beast. You can buy refill potion cartridges for the collar."

Trust it to a witch to understand the science behind the product that he'd bought. Maybe he wasn't so stupid after all. He must have studied the tech and decided the science was sound. So what had gone wrong?

"Where can you buy refill potions for the collar?" Nero asked.

If we followed the refill potions trail, it might lead us to Potions and Poisons, the company behind the collars, the company whose collars were encouraging people to import monsters beyond the wall. To bring beasts into our cities, endangering everyone.

"You can buy the potion cartridges at the waterfront, right at the border between the city's witch and vampire districts," the witch said reluctantly.

Harker looked at Nero. "We should pay that market a visit."

"Agreed." Nero turned his hard, granite stare on the witch. "When is the market in operation?"

"Between two and four o'clock each afternoon."

The witch was certainly quick to share information. Maybe he hoped his cooperation would save him from being punished for his crimes. But that wasn't how the Legion worked. Surely, he must have known that. On the other hand, hope might not be a particularly good strategy, but it was all he had left at this point.

"Do you still have any of the refill potions?" Nero asked him.

The witch pulled a vial out of his jacket. How much else did he have stored inside those hidden pockets?

Nero turned the small glass vial over in his hand. "Look familiar?" He showed it to Harker.

"The bottle does," replied Harker. "It's the same shape —has the same design—as the vials of Nectar we confiscated from another black market operation two years ago." He popped the cap and took a sniff of the potion. "Smells like there's Nectar in the mixture too."

Nectar? How the hell had someone gotten hold of that? Neither gods nor angels would sell it on the blackmarket.

The substance was very difficult to produce—too rare to waste by selling it off to the highest bidder. And it was too powerful to risk it falling into an enemy's hands.

"What do humans and supernaturals want with Nectar?" I wondered. "It's poison to them."

"The most effective poison known to man," said Nero.

"You're saying people bought Nectar and then used it to kill others," I realized.

"Yes. Shortly before you joined the Legion, Harker and I stopped one of these blackmarket Nectar traders and confiscated all his goods."

"Did you interrogate him?"

Nero gave me a flat look. Of course he'd interrogated the man.

"Well, did he say where he'd gotten the Nectar?" I asked.

"He claimed he'd stolen them from a Legion storehouse," Nero said. "And there had indeed been a break-in recently that seemed to confirm his story."

"It sounds like it was all neatly wrapped up."

Nero frowned. "Too neatly, come to think of it. Back then, an explanation was right there and obvious, and so we took it. We closed the investigation and moved on to other pressing matters. In retrospect, perhaps we were too quick to accept the easy solution, especially now that it seems more Nectar has found its way onto the market. No Legion storehouses have been hit lately." He stroked his chin thoughtfully. "At least not that I know of."

Harker's cleanup crew had finished up at Maxwell's house and joined us here. They cuffed the cowboy witch and loaded him into their truck, along with the dead headless beast, broken collar, and the Potions and Poisons vial.

The rest of us headed for the waterfront between the city's witch and vampire districts. It was nearly two-thirty in the afternoon, so the black market should be in full swing right now.

CHAPTER 18

*N*ero, Harker, and I took the lead. Ivy, Drake, and Alec walked behind us. Alec had a gun in each hand and a broad smile on his face. We hadn't done much more than glower at criminals and look at dead monsters today, so I'm sure he was excited at the prospect of a battle at the black market.

As we passed out of the residential Cauldron District, into the witches' business district, private villas gave way to high-tech high-rises made of steel and glass. Beyond that— standing tall, dark, and gothic in the background—were the vampire district's stone palaces and spiked towers. Sculptures of angels, monsters, and vampires adorned the buildings' roofs and windows.

Like a valley, a few square blocks of squat buildings were nudged between the witches' and vampires' high structures. The market at the waterfront between these two districts was not any different than any other I'd seen. Homemade crafted goods, fruits, and vegetables were being sold from canvas stalls. I scoured the rows of merchandise, looking for anything illicit. I found nothing. Angel, however, found a cat toy that she liked. She pounced up onto the pet stall counter, purring at a little toy mouse.

"She seems very taken with it," said the pet stall lady. She was an elderly woman with a weathered, wrinkled face —and bright blue eyes.

Maybe there was catnip hidden deep within the fluffy stuffing. That would have been a very clever sales trick to pique a cat's interest.

"She really doesn't need it," I said.

The woman smiled, deep dimples forming between her wrinkled skin. "I'll give it to you, free of charge."

Angel meowed in approval.

"Move along, Angel," I told her.

The kitten hissed at me.

I sighed, looking at the pet stall lady. "Why would you just give it to me?"

"You're an angel."

She looked at me with deeply devoted eyes. *Worshipping* eyes. I won't lie. It made me feel terribly uncomfortable. I had to remind myself not to squirm with discomfort. Angels didn't squirm. They didn't get embarrassed by others' admiration. They basked in it.

"Thank you," I told the woman. "But she really has enough cat toys."

Ivy had seen to that. The cat had more accessories than I did.

"Please, angel. I insist. You would honor me by accepting my offering." The woman held out the cat toy in her open palms, head bowed.

I kind of felt bad for mesmerizing her. Though I hadn't *meant* to mesmerize anyone. I sighed. Well, what the hell. I guess I could find room for one more cat toy.

"At least let me pay you for it," I said to the woman.

She shook her head. "Your acceptance of my gift is all the payment I require."

I tried to haggle, but she wouldn't take my money, no matter how many times or how much—or little—I offered her for it. When I finally acquiesced, she packed up the cat toy in a nice bag, happily humming the Hymn of the Gods the whole time. She even put a bow on the fancy bag. Angel would enjoy tearing the bow off the package almost as much as she'd enjoy the toy inside. I should just buy her a bag of ribbons and bows instead of cat toys.

Harker came up to me as I left the pet shop stall. His gaze fell on the bag in my hand. "Shopping for wedding lingerie?"

"Haha. If you must know, Angel took a fancy to a cat toy, and the seller wouldn't let me leave without accepting it as a gift."

"You'll get used to it."

"To what?" I asked.

"To the way people look at you like you're holy. To the way they try to win your favor in the desperate hope that you'll erase all their sorrows. And make all their wishes come true."

"I'm not a genie."

"No, you're an angel, immortal and all-powerful. An elite soldier in the gods' army. One of the chosen ones, an angel made and selected by the gods themselves."

I shook my head. "It's more complicated than that."

"I know that. You know that." Harker's eyes panned across the marketplace. "But they need something more powerful than reality: faith. The gods do not show themselves to the people of Earth. We are the closest these people will ever come to the gods. You have to play the part they need us to play."

"Who needs us to play? The gods? Or the people of Earth?"

"Both. You are an angel now, Leda. Embrace it."

"It would be easier to embrace without the feverish consequences that come with it."

"That will pass." Harker moved toward Nero.

"Did you find any signs of illicit activity?" I asked Nero as we closed in beside him. Harker, my ever-vigilant chaperone, positioned himself between us.

"Not yet." Nero's eyes honed in on the bag in my hand. "But apparently you did."

I tucked the small bag into my jacket. "No, it's nothing illicit. It's just a toy that caught Angel's eye. The pet stall lady insisted on giving it to me."

"You'll get used to it," Nero said, mirroring Harker's earlier words.

"People looking at me with, at the same time, blind devotion and gripping fear? Like I might kill them on the spot because I feel like it? And yet they are so happy just to catch a glimpse of me? How can you possibly get used to that?"

"With time. It's not a bad thing, Pandora. Their adoration and fear is what keeps the Earth safe, keeps them safe. It keeps them from doing things that endanger everyone. Just look at what happens when they forget their adoration and fear for even a moment."

"They buy monsters and bring them into the city as guard dogs."

"Or worse. The second monster buyer we visited today was fortunate to escape with his life."

Of course, by now the cowboy witch was in a Legion Interrogation chamber, which most people considered a fate far worse than death. Not that I wanted him to be free.

He was suffering from a severe lack of good common sense. Who knew what dangerous thing he'd try next.

"And the first buyer lost only his own life," Nero continued. "If he hadn't fatally wounded the beast, it might have killed his wife. Or broken out and gone into the city. Many could have died before we got there to put it down. That's why we angels need to maintain this image. That's why people must fear and adore us. That's why they must desire our favor and fear the consequences of any misdeed. Because the moment they stop worshipping and fearing us, the cities of Earth become far more dangerous than even the plains of monsters."

I nodded. "I understand."

Not that I liked it. But Nero was right. We needed the people to love and fear us. Their love balanced their fear. Their fear checked their love. If they felt only fear, they would eventually rise up and strike back. If they felt only love, they would commit terrible acts, trusting in our magnanimousness to forgive them.

A part of me couldn't believe how easily I had come to see the logic in angels' ways since joining the Legion. The old Leda would have resisted the very notions I now had to uphold. Because I was an angel. And being an angel was about a lot more than glowing halos, pretty wings, and flaming swords.

Nero moved between me and Harker. He took my hand, kissing it. "You will get used to it," he assured me again. "You might even come to appreciate the rewards."

"Well, I suppose you can never have enough cat toys."

Nero chuckled, low and deep. His hand stroked my cheek. I looked up, meeting his eyes. We stared at each other, our gazes locked.

Sweat beaded my brow. "This is some unseasonably hot

weather we're having, don't you think?" I could have sworn I could hear the water bubbling beneath the dock.

"If you two don't behave, I'm going to electrocute you both," Harker warned us.

Sighing, I stepped away from Nero. "We weren't doing anything," I promised Harker, smiling.

"There was touching."

"Not nearly enough of it," I grumbled.

"You're really terrible at following the rules, Leda."

I snorted. "How long did it take you to figure that out?"

"About two seconds after I met you."

"I knew it just by reading her Legion of Angels application form," Nero told him.

The two angels looked mighty amused.

I folded my arms across my chest. "Well, I'm glad I'm such a great source of entertainment for you both."

Drake walked up to us, his expression cautious. He looked from Nero, to Harker, to me. "Am I interrupting anything?"

"Yes," I said. "Angel laughing hour."

Drake's face crinkled with confusion.

"What is it, Sergeant?" Nero asked Drake.

"We've found something suspicious."

He pointed at four people dressed in long jackets and hoods. They were keeping to the shadows, trying to stay out of sight.

"Suspicious indeed," I commented as the hooded figures slipped through a narrow gap between two buildings. "The way to the secret black market within the normal street market?"

"Let's find out," said Nero.

We took the narrow passage, emerging into a small

paved lot. But we didn't find any people back here, hooded or otherwise. And we didn't find a market, though stacks of empty boxes and a torn tent hinted that someone had hastily cleared it away. And positioned in the middle of the discarded wood and canvas was a pack of monsters with shining magic collars, as though they'd been waiting for us.

CHAPTER 19

BATTLE AT THE BLACK MARKET

*T*he pack of monsters stalked forward, fifteen wolf-like beasts with black fur and red eyes. The small paved lot was feeling smaller with every step that they took.

"They look familiar," I commented, my eyes panning across the spiky-furred ridges of their backs.

The beasts were the same kind of monster we'd found dead in Maxwell Plenteous's backyard—and also tied dead to the cowboy witch's front gate.

"The beasts' accessories are familiar too," Harker noted.

Each wolf in the pack—no, in the attack squad—was wearing a silver collar that looked identical to the one we'd recovered at the last house, that was currently heading back to the Legion for analysis.

Nero watched the pack advance on us. "There is no pack leader."

"Because the beasts aren't acting of their own accord," I said. "Someone is controlling them with those collars."

You could see it in the way the monsters were moving. Their movements were precise, their steps calculated—like they couldn't breathe without someone commanding them to do so. So they were all breathing in unison. Their eyes moved in unison too. Each step they took was perfectly in sync. They were more like machines than monsters.

"Whoever is controlling them, he is very bold to attack angels right here in the city in broad daylight," said Nero.

"They must fear we're getting close to something," I realized. "Something bigger than a few monster traders selling a few guard beasts."

"It would have to be some massively big plot or some massively stupid person to risk taking on the Legion of Angels," Harker commented.

The beasts moved toward us in perfect formation. Another ten beasts leapt over the rooftops behind us, leaving no room for escape. Flames blazed to life on my and the other angels' swords.

A monster jumped at Harker. He slashed at it, and his sword went through it like a hot knife through a piece of New York cheesecake. As the beast fell dead to the ground, its collar exploded, blowing up itself and what was left of the beast.

"The collars explode if we kill the beast," I stated the obvious.

Over the snarling wolves, I heard Nero's phone chime.

"The cleanup crew just messaged me," he said. "The team was ambushed on the way back to the office. Their attackers took the potion, as well as both sets of collar fragments."

"And the cowboy witch?" I asked.

"They shot him. He's dead. The Legion team was unable to save him."

"That's another check in the big fat conspiracy column," I said.

Harker pointed at the beasts all around us. "We need one of those collars. Intact."

He was right. If we could get an intact collar to Nerissa, she might be able to figure out how it worked. Then we might be able to track the parts and potions to their sources. We could find out who was behind the collared monsters. I hoped this whole thing wasn't Meda's latest experiment. I really didn't want to fight a god.

I promptly put out the fire on my blade and sheathed my sword. Neither fire nor swords were particularly useful for capturing monsters alive, which was the only way we could get ourselves a collar. The exploding collars were most likely a failsafe to keep the technology out of enemy hands.

We moved toward the monsters, trying to subdue them rather than kill them. But it was pretty damn difficult to capture a beast without the use of deadly force, especially when whoever was controlling them had no qualms about using deadly force against us.

Movement in the shadows between buildings drew my attention. The hooded figures we'd tracked to this alley were here—and they were escaping.

"These monsters are just a distraction to keep us busy while they get away," I realized.

Nero's eyes darted to the cloaked procession. "Take the rest of the team to head them off," he told Harker. "Leda and I will hold off the monsters."

"Alone?"

"We won't be alone," I said. "We have Angel."

Harker glanced at my cat as she sprang into the air and thumped her hind paws against a monster, forcing it back with her strong kicks. That was my Angel: the kickboxing cat.

"A pet cat is not a proper escort, no matter how… eccentric she is," Harker said. "Nyx assigned me the task of chaperoning Leda. I'm not supposed to leave her alone with you, Nero."

"Look around, Harker." I blasted a psychic spell at a monster, knocking it back. "This is hardly a romantic getaway. We are not having a picnic under the stars. We're fighting monsters. And a lot of them too. Nero and I will have our hands full. Trust me, there won't be any time to play footsie."

"It's not just about making sure you two behave," Harker told me. "It's about keeping you safe. And alive."

"These monsters are a nuisance, not a threat," I replied. "We'll handle them. It will just take time. We're not in any danger. The most challenging part is not killing them by accident, so we can actually get a collar back to the lab for closer examination."

Harker frowned. "Nyx won't like it."

"Nyx also won't like it if you let suspects connected to the monster trade slip through your fingers," said Nero.

Harker's face was contemplative, but at last he turned and blasted the monsters behind him, clearing a path. "Very well. We'll pursue them. But don't make me regret this, Leda." He waved at Ivy, Drake, and Alec, commanding them to follow him.

"Me?" I asked Nero as Harker and the others pushed through the remaining beasts that blocked their way to the fleeing hooded figures. "Why does everyone always think everything is my fault? It takes two to tango, you know."

"But it takes only one very persuasive angel to incite her mate to madness and merriment."

"When this is over, I want to hear more about this

178

madness and merriment of which you speak." I winked at him. "It sounds like my sort of scene."

"I won't just tell you. I'll *show* you," he said, promises burning in his eyes.

It was enough to almost make me forget the monsters all around us, closing in for the kill. But only *almost*.

Nero and I battled the beasts, trying to capture one. It was a lot harder than it sounded. Every time we trapped a wolf inside a magic field, the other beasts immediately changed direction and beelined for the barrier. They pounded, scratched, and kicked it until its magical bonds broke and their pack mate was once again free. I sighed. Killing monsters was so much easier than trying to subdue and capture them.

Excited voices from above drew my mind out of the battle. I looked up. Four kids were sitting on the rooftop of a nearby shed. They'd obviously come to watch the angels in action.

I pointed out our audience to Nero. "They don't understand how dangerous this situation is."

"I was the same when I was a boy," he told me. "I used to sneak up to battles, hoping to catch an angel in action. We all did it. We trailed them as they fought, envisioning ourselves as angels."

That was the love-and-fear angel dichotomy at work again. People idolized them. They wanted to be with them. To be in their halo, caught inside the pull of magic around them. Because they felt that being close to an angel put them one step closer to becoming one of them.

"Little Nero went chasing after angels?" I chuckled. "That was rather reckless of you."

"I was being reckless long before we met, Pandora. You only took that recklessness to new heights."

I smirked at him. "Don't flirt with me, Nero. If Nyx finds out, she will put us both in timeout."

I cast an elemental gale between my hands, spinning it, winding it tight. Then I released it, sending it whirling at a monster. I tried to capture the beast inside a whirlwind, but it darted away too fast.

The beasts' formation was changing shape and direction. I wasn't the only one who'd noticed our captive audience. The beasts turned toward the children. Two of the wolves broke off from the pack and jumped at the kids on the shed's rooftop.

"Run!" I shouted at the children.

They stayed right where they were, smiling at me.

"Why aren't they running away?" I demanded, sprinting toward the shed as fast as I could. I only hoped I got there before the pair of wolves did.

Nero ran beside me. "They are confident that we will save them."

"They need to save themselves, not depend on others to do it for them."

I tried to catch up to the beasts, but they were too far away. I wouldn't make it to them before they made it to the kids. The beasts kicked the shed, and it fell apart. Children and broken wooden planks rained to the ground. The two beasts closed in on them. I couldn't risk using magic. The beasts were too close to the kids. If I cast a spell at the wolves, it might hit the children too.

That left just one final option.

Tapping into my siren magic, I grabbed control of the minds of the two beasts circling around the kids. The monsters froze in place. Magic flickered across their collars, then the silver rings exploded, taking the wolves with them. The explosion splattered the children with monster guts, but at least they were still alive.

I blinked. "What just happened?"

"When you seized control of the beasts' minds, it must have overloaded the collars already controlling them," Nero said. "And they exploded."

Ok, I couldn't use that trick again, not if we wanted to capture a beast alive. The explosion had pushed back the remaining wolves. I moved in front of the kids, shielding them.

But the beasts weren't moving at all. They were just standing there.

I heard a tiny click. One of the wolves exploded. Then another.

Nero looked at me.

"I didn't do it this time," I said, watching helplessly as the monsters continued to explode one by one.

I hadn't even so much as touched their minds, let alone tried to seize control over them from the collars. And yet the collars were self-destructing en masse.

Nero and I grabbed the kids, two in each arm. We ran, carrying them out of the path of explosions. The final beast blew up, leaving us with twenty-five dead beasts and a graveyard of metallic debris. What remained of the wolves and collars was scattered all across the cobblestone ground —in tiny little pieces.

We set down the kids we'd rescued. They gazed up at us, mesmerized.

"Nero Windstriker," a boy gasped, his eyes wide as he gaped at Nero.

A girl looked at me, her eyes just as wide as the boy's. "And the Pandora," she said with reverence.

Their enamored eyes fell on the monster bits, and

reality finally clicked in. They ran off screaming at the top of their lungs.

I looked down at the monsters and collars, asking Nero, "Do you think there's enough left of them to salvage anything?"

CHAPTER 20

THE PANDORA

*B*ack in Nerissa's lab, I looked through a box of broken parts, the remains of the monster collars that we'd managed to collect from the back lot after all the beasts had blown up.

Following the Battle at the Black Market, we'd returned to the Legion office to clean up. Angel and I had been a complete mess. Bathing my cat had been the highlight of my day. I'd enjoyed it even less than finding the dead monster tied to the gate—or all those monsters blowing up around me.

Angel ate things no other cat would, but she unfortunately didn't diverge from her feline brethren on the topic of baths. She hated them, and she'd made damn sure I knew that every step of the way.

Right now, Angel sat in front of one of Nerissa's ovens, which she used to keep her samples warm. My kitten was playing with the cat toy she'd gotten from the market, her back turned pointedly to me. I hoped she'd soon forgive me for daring to give her a bath.

"There's nothing I can do with these broken bits." Nerissa sifted through the box of collar parts. "You need to bring me an intact collar."

"Easier said than done, Doc," I replied. "Whoever is controlling these beasts has their finger planted permanently on the self-destruct button. If we kill a beast, the collar blows up. And if I try to seize control over any of the beasts, they *all* blow up."

A contemplative crinkle formed between Nerissa's eyes. "Someone really doesn't want you to get to the bottom of this."

"They should be scared of me. They sent their attack beasts after kids, Nerissa. *Kids.* When I find out who is behind this, they are going to rue the day they crossed paths with the Pandora."

"It's *the* Pandora now, is it?"

I shrugged. "Apparently." I glanced down at my jacket, where the name Pandora was stitched in silver threads. "I might need to modify my uniforms."

"You'd have to completely redo all the stitching to make room for the 'the' before Pandora."

"It might be worth it." I glanced at Colonel Fireswift, who was seated across the small round table from me. He was my current chaperone on duty. "What do you think, Colonel? Which name is better: Pandora or *the* Pandora?"

"What do I think?" he said with gruff indignation. "I think you are making a mockery of the Legion. I think you never should have been allowed to be an angel. And that you should most definitely not be allowed to walk around and embarrass the Legion, an angel without dignity or reserve."

"You really are a sourpuss, Colonel."

My kitten meowed in agreement.

"Ah, are we speaking again, darling?" I asked her.

She began licking her paw. I didn't know what to make of that, so I chose to be optimistic.

Colonel Fireswift's gaze slid from my kitten to me. "It is not dignified for an angel to speak to a cat."

"But since I'm just a dirty, usurping angel, it doesn't matter, right? In fact, everyone would be better off if I just disappeared?"

He scowled at me. "If you attempt to flee, I will nail your feet to the ground."

"Nyx wouldn't like that," I told him. "She wants me in top form for my wedding. I'm pretty sure she doesn't want me trailing blood down the aisle."

"Your injuries would heal before then. And in the meantime, they might just teach you a valuable lesson."

I glowered at him. "I'm really glad Nyx didn't order me to marry you."

"For once, we are in complete agreement." He watched me very closely, like if he blinked for a moment, I'd find a way to disappear.

"I'm not going to run away, Colonel. It was a joke."

"So you claim."

"I'm going to marry Nero in four days. Do you really think I would miss that?"

He remained thoroughly unconvinced, and I knew there was nothing I could do to change his mind. Admittedly, I had been thinking about running away, but that was before Nero had come back. That was before Nyx had declared that he would be my husband, not some random stranger—or worse yet, someone I couldn't stand.

I didn't like the way Colonel Fireswift was glaring at

me, so I changed the subject, hoping to get his mind off his suspicions. "What have you learned from the hooded people we saw fleeing the market this afternoon?"

"My Interrogators have questioned them."

Harker's team had been more successful than Nero and I. They'd brought back the suspicious hooded people. All I'd brought back were broken pieces of metal.

"The hooded miscreants were nothing but decoys," Colonel Fireswift continued. "They know nothing. They were merely hired to run off, to divert your attention."

"Divert our attention? From what?"

"I do not know."

"Surely, your prisoners must know something," I insisted.

"I assure you, my people were quite thorough."

I cringed to think what the Interrogators had done to those who'd been hired to don hoods and stalk through the shadows.

"But I might be willing to allow you to speak to them," Colonel Fireswift said. "You have proven how persuasive you can be. You are quite adept at revealing secrets."

I'd revealed a lot of secrets during the gods' recent challenges. It would seem, unfortunately, that I really was my father's daughter.

"And you would allow me to speak to the prisoners because…"

"It seems your delusions about the goodness of all people isn't as deeply rooted as I'd feared." Did he sound pleased?

"I assure you, Colonel, when it comes to you, I harbor no delusions." I flashed him a grin. "I know you for exactly what you are."

"Good." He nodded. "Very good."

Gods, his approval felt worse than his scorn ever could.

"What do you want?" I asked him.

"I have a price, of course."

"I'm sorry, but I'm fresh out of empty yogurt containers. So if your greatest wish in life is an encore of my 'O Come All Ye Faithful' performance played on yogurt containers, then I'm afraid I'll have to disappoint you."

Colonel Fireswift's nostrils flared up. I was surprised fire didn't shoot out of them.

I smiled demurely at him.

"If you want to speak to the prisoners," he began, his voice hard and unyielding. "You may do so as one of my Interrogators. Under my supervision."

That nonsense again?

"I thought you'd given up on the idea of breaking me and putting me back together in the form of one of your Interrogators."

"I do not give up," he said. "To do so—"

"Would be unbecoming of an angel." I sighed. Yeah, I should have known.

"So, what do you have to say to my offer?"

"I say that there's no way Nyx will put two angels in the same territory, let alone the same division. It's just not how things are done at the Legion."

"Things change. The Legion evolves."

I laughed. "So let me get this straight. If I try to change even the teeniest, tiniest thing at the Legion, you brand me a troublemaker. But you are allowed to change a fundamental element of the Legion's structure?"

"It's different. *I* am different than you."

"How?" I questioned him. "Why?"

His response was immediate, and packed with all due

arrogance. "Because you lack the wisdom and experience I've spent centuries cultivating."

"Just because you've been doing something a long time, that doesn't mean you're good at it. You've had two centuries to learn compassion, and look how well you're doing on that front."

"Enough of this," he snapped. "If you tell Nyx you want to be in my division, she will consider it."

"No thanks. If I wanted to speak to the prisoners that badly, I'd just sneak in and talk to them when you weren't watching."

"I am always watching."

"Perhaps," I allowed. "But are you seeing?"

He frowned at my statement, probably wondering how I could be so philosophical. The answer was less meaningful than he thought. I'd said it because it sounded like the sort of deep statement an angel would make, and I enjoyed confounding him.

Nero stepped through the door to Nerissa's office and headed right for me. I rose to greet him.

Colonel Fireswift moved between us. "Come no closer." He was taking Nyx's orders to keep Nero away from me until the wedding very seriously.

Nero ignored him completely. He didn't even pay enough attention to him to offer him a scowl. Nero kept his eyes on me the whole time, even as he lowered to one knee in front of me.

I looked at the box he'd set in my hands. "What is this?"

"Your engagement gift."

"You already gave me one."

"That was yesterday," he said. "This is today."

"A man courting an angel with the Fever presents her

with a gift each day leading up to their wedding," Nerissa told me.

I nodded, a smile stretching my mouth. "Not a bad tradition, at least as far as Legion ones go. It sure beats the tradition of punching a metal wall with my bare fists, like you made me do when I was an initiate, Nero."

"I have many more exercises for you."

I grimaced. "Do I have a choice in the matter?"

A savage smile curled his lips. For some reason, it made me think of sex. Probably because I had the Fever, and pretty much everything made me think of sex.

I lifted the lid and pulled Nero's second present out of the box. "Shooting Star." The gun that belonged to the immortal weapons of heaven and hell lay cold and dormant in my hand.

And I was glad for it. The last time Shooting Star and I had crossed paths, I'd been on the receiving end of its fiery bullets. It had left me with the scar on my abdomen.

"Do you have them all?" I asked Nero. "All the weapons of heaven and hell? The whole collection?"

"You'll need to wait and find out."

"But I'm impatient." I smiled coyly. "I don't like waiting."

His voice dipped lower. "Nor do I."

Magic crackled between us, a pleasant, impatient buzz against my skin. My lips moved toward his...

Colonel Fireswift was suddenly between us. He shoved us apart. He didn't say a word, but the look of total disapproval on his face spoke droves. Apparently, he had a big problem with the idea of losing yourself in the passion of the moment.

Angel fell off her perch atop Nerissa's oven and tumbled to the floor.

"Hey, silly," I chuckled. "Getting high off the catnip a bit early today, aren't you?"

But as I came around the table to look at her, the laughter died on my lips. Angel was convulsing on the floor. I lifted her tiny body into my arms and prodded her gently with my magic, trying to figure out what was wrong with her.

"She's been poisoned," Nerissa told me.

She began compiling ingredients from various jars on her shelves. It was taking too long. She wouldn't be able to make an antidote in time. I wrapped my magic around Angel. A golden glow pulsed across her white fur. The healing spell enveloped her from head to tail—then it flickered out. My kitten looked up at me, expelling a pitiful whimper. She was alive! Still weak, but alive just the same.

I hugged her body to me. "What happened, Angel? Did you eat something or…" My eyes fell on the toy mouse resting atop the oven. Angel had been nibbling on it just before she fell. "The woman at the market. She gave me the toy. She tried to kill my cat!" My anger ignited my magic, setting the toy on fire.

Nero caught my arm, stopping me as I rushed toward the door, determined to find the person responsible for poisoning my cat. "Not your cat. *You*, Leda," he said darkly. "They were trying to poison you."

"Me?" Surprise froze me. I stopped struggling against him. "Well, I guess I've made a few enemies."

"This isn't about you," Colonel Fireswift said. "It's about your magic. You are a fertile female angel compatible with another angel. That's why they targeted you. Someone wants to hurt the Legion. This was an attempt to cripple the Legion, to weaken us."

"The demons," said Nero, his voice something between a growl and a hiss.

"If the Legion figured out how to make more angels compatible with each other, the demons wouldn't stand a chance," Colonel Fireswift said to him. "It would be a new generation of soldiers—soldiers more powerful than ever before, their destiny to become angels all but assured."

Nero and Colonel Fireswift were on to something. The demons might not have been behind the Legion soldiers' emotional outbursts, but this latest poisoning attempt absolutely reeked of them.

Someone had poisoned my cat just to get to me. Anger churned through my veins, thick and volatile. My poor Angel. They'd nearly killed her. My anger exploded from me in a shockwave that shook the building. All at once, Nerissa and her assistants began fighting one another. Beyond the room, I could hear soldiers in the corridor slamming, shouting, and punching. Blades clashed.

"Control yourself," Colonel Fireswift snapped at me.

Nero glanced at his phone. "Harker says the whole office has suddenly gone mad."

"You are causing this," Colonel Fireswift snapped at me. His voice cut like a whip. "You need to stop it."

"I don't know how."

"Pitiful excuses from a pitiful girl given too much power to control. Power she does not deserve," Colonel Fireswift growled. "If you don't put an end to this, I will." He edged forward, magic hissing off of him.

Nero intercepted, his eyes cold with fury, his sword hot and fiery. The two of them looked ready to tear each other apart.

Nyx ran through the door. "Pull yourselves together!" she told them sharply. "We must concentrate on the actual crisis. My ward has shattered. The office is imploding in on itself, buried beneath the weight of Leda's emotional tempest."

Nyx's hands were a blur. She wove a spell around me, trying to contain my telepathic bursts of emotion. At the same time, I struggled to reel in my emotions. Neither of us made any headway. Nyx's ward split as soon as she cast it.

There was a flash of light, and then Ronan stood before us. Without a word, he added his own magic to Nyx's, and together they fashioned a tightly-knit spell around me. As they tied it shut, the magic silver threads flashed once, then faded from sight. Though it was invisible, I could still feel the weight of the ward around me, a telepathic barrier between me and everyone else.

Nerissa and her staff stopped fighting. The battle noises coming from the corridor ceased.

"The ward won't last long," Ronan told Nyx. "Leda's magic is spiking too fast. If she gets upset like that again, even our combined ward will not hold."

Nero held my hands, stroking deep, soothing circles into my palms. This time, no one complained that we were touching. They must have realized his touch was keeping me grounded.

"I'm fine," I said.

It was a lie. No, I was mostly certainly not fine. Not at all. They'd already nearly killed my cat. Who else would get hurt before this was over?

The demons! They'd try again. They'd go after my loved ones. My friends. My family. Nero. I had to stop them!

Anger with a side order of panic bubbled inside of me.

Nero squeezed my hands. Right now, only his presence was keeping me from blowing up again.

The demons might not have caused the disruptions in the Legion—that was my Fever—but they were definitely taking advantage of the situation. They'd poisoned my cat. They were trying to make me lose control of myself, so I'd make everyone else lose control too. But were they connected to the monster trade?

I had to find out. The determination to thwart the demons' plans, to get to the bottom of this, settled my mind. I was stronger than the Fever. Sure, the Fever might be the primal force beyond the future of the Legion, but I was Pandora, the Angel of Chaos. It was no match for me.

"I was going to wait on this, but it seems now is the time," Nyx said.

"The time for what?" I asked her.

"For your new Legion post."

I held my breath, hoping I was right, hoping that Nyx wouldn't assign an angel to another angel's division. I didn't want to be an Interrogator. Or a member of General Spellsmiter's Vanguard.

"Every angel needs a territory," said Nyx. "And I have just the one for you."

"A territory?" I said, confused. "But there aren't any territories available on Earth."

"That's not entirely true," she replied. "There is one available, in fact. One which you are ideally suited to command."

I couldn't think of a single place I was suited to command.

"Leda, I'm giving you the plains of monsters," the First Angel told me.

I laughed. "You're joking."

But there wasn't a hint of humor on her face. "You have demonstrated a unique ability to control the monsters. Your mission as the Angel of the Plains of Monsters is as follows: to regain the lost lands overrun by monsters centuries ago. And you will start with the Black Plains. To that end, the newest Legion office—*your* office —will be located in Purgatory, at the edge of the Black Plains."

Home. I was going home.

CHAPTER 21

THE ANGEL OF PURGATORY

Gold banisters and red carpets greeted me as I stepped through the front door of the Legion's newest office. *My* office, the first and only on the Frontier. Purgatory was my town now. The Black Plains were mine. Nyx had given them to me. Now I just had to figure out what to do with them.

The Purgatory office was housed inside the largest of the former district lords' 'castles'. The Legion had converted the building for our use, but its original flavor—the air of an opulent country estate—remained.

The other district lords' former residences were still being renovated. When the work was done, one of them would hold our training halls. Another would become a garage for the vehicles we drove out onto the Black Plains. A fourth would serve as our armory. It was a good thing there were underground tunnels that connected all the buildings because they were situated throughout Purgatory.

The spread-out design of this office was different than any other on Earth, but Purgatory wasn't a typical place. It wasn't a city located at the heart of civilization. And I wasn't a typical angel.

I followed Nyx through the arched doorway of my new apartment. A private suite that filled an entire wing of the castle, it was the former sleeping quarters of the district lord who'd owned this building.

"What do you think?" Nyx asked me.

I rubbed the lush cream-and-gold curtains between my fingers. "I thought it would be bigger."

Nyx's blue eyes pulsed.

"I'm kidding," I told her. "The room is so enormous I might need a map to keep me from getting lost."

"I trust you won't be so flippant when you address your soldiers at your introduction ceremony in half an hour."

"Introduction? They all already know me."

"That is beside the point."

"What is the point?" I asked.

"Traditions must be upheld."

"So, you want me to enter the room, declare I'm taking control over this territory, and then walk out?"

"Flying would be preferable to walking. It makes a statement."

I snorted. "Yes, it will certainly make a statement when I crash into the wall and get tangled in the curtains."

Impatience flashed in her eyes. "How is it you *still* have not learned to fly?"

"I can fly just fine," I told her. "I just can't land. Or navigate if there's anything within ten feet of me."

In my defense, my flying had improved a lot. If if hadn't been for the Fever messing with my equilibrium—and the monster-trading conspiracy keeping me otherwise occupied—I might have mastered flight by now. Or at least mastered not crashing into things.

Nyx sighed. "Ok, you will stride into the room, wings out and spread wide. Make yourself as big as possible. You must own the room. The ceremony is being filmed live. The entire Legion will be watching. You need to show everyone that you own this town, territory, and everything in it. That's the only way the other angels will respect you."

I smiled at her. "I had no idea you cared so much about whether the other angels respected me."

"I care a lot. If they don't respect you, they will undermine everything that you do. I don't have time to play angel referee. I need all my angels working together if we're to have any chance of protecting the Earth from the demons' forces—and from the monsters that threaten our borders."

She handed me a package.

"What is it?" I asked.

"A present for my newest angel."

I opened the package and pulled out a plaque plated in gold.

"An angel plaque. It's for your office room," Nyx said. "Every angel has one."

"Leda Pandora, Angel of Purgatory," I read. It sounded too cool to be true. "Pandora?"

Nyx nodded. "It's about time we made it official."

"My angel name is Pandora?" I grinned. "Like for real?"

"It seemed fitting. Besides, you already had all your uniforms embroidered with that name."

That wouldn't have been reason enough for Nyx. Not at all.

"No angel has a name like mine," I realized.

"Yes, and no angel has a territory like yours. "At last,

you have an angel name and an angel territory, Leda. Now it's up to you to hold on to them."

And with that said, she turned and walked out of my room. Two soldiers remained in the corridor just beyond my door. My chaperones.

I stepped up to the window and pushed the curtains aside to look outside. My suite had a singular view of the wall and the Black Plains, but right now, the action was closer. Beyond the cast iron gates that surrounded the estate, the people of Purgatory had gathered en masse.

None of them had seen me or the other soldiers arrive in town. The Legion had closed off the train station for our arrival, and from there, we'd been ushered into trucks and driven straight here.

From the bright, homemade signs the people outside the gates were holding, they were here to catch a glimpse of me, the Legion's newest angel. Many names were written on those signs. Pandora. The Angel of Chaos. The Angel of Purgatory. The Angel of the Plains of Monsters. I was certainly racking up titles fast.

I was the angel who'd brought civilization here to the Frontier, who was going to rid the world of monsters—at least if the handwritten text on their posters were to be believed. They had hope in their hearts and stars in their eyes. I didn't know how I could ever live up to their lofty expectations.

I turned away from the window and climbed the stairs. The top floor of this multi-level suite contained a bedroom and a bathroom.

I passed the bathroom first. Its shower was of waterfall proportions. A huge hot tub, large enough to fit at least twenty people, sat in the middle of the tiled room. What the hell had the district lord done in here? Parties? Orgies?

I shook the thought from my mind. I really didn't care to think about that.

I reached my new bedroom. The room's highlight was definitely the ornate canopy bed, where Angel was already making herself comfortable. It was larger than any bed I'd ever seen. A dinosaur could have fit in that bed. Maybe that was a good thing. More than once, I'd woken up tangled in my own wings. They sometimes came out during my dreams, a reaction to my emotions. With this big of a bed, I'd have more than enough space for my wings. In fact, Nero and I could fit easily, wings and all, and still have room left over. My mind latched onto that tangent, imagining Nero in my bed.

I stopped those thoughts cold in their tracks. I had only half an hour until I was supposed to address my soldiers—and the whole Legion, for that matter. I didn't have time to daydream about Nero, not when I still had no idea what to wear to my own introduction ceremony.

Most soldiers wore formal evening attire to official ceremonies. However, Nero always dressed in the standard black leather Legion uniform for these functions. I looked through my closet. My wardrobe wasn't large enough to fill the room-sized closet, but what I did own was already hung up along one wall. My clothes had been delivered and sorted before I'd even arrived. I flipped through my choices.

Angel slipped past me to enter the closet, rubbing her side against my leg.

"What do you think?" I held up the Legion's hot weather wilderness uniform: a tank top and hot pants.

She meowed.

"I know. It's not quite right," I agreed. I showed her the all-leather ensemble, the uniform that Nero preferred.

Angel hissed.

"I know, I know. It's far too hot right now for that." I glanced at the blue evening gown on the rack. "And I don't feel like an evening gown either. I'll be wearing a dress soon enough at my wedding."

Angel pounced on a brown boot.

"That's not a bad idea," I told her, nodding.

I pulled out a maroon-red singlet top. Next came a pair of high boots worn over hip-hugging denim tights. I accessorized with a thick leather belt. The outfit was casual yet stylish, sleek yet rugged—just what I wanted Purgatory to be.

The town should have all the perks of civilization, without any of the stifling, uptight seriousness. It should be a little rough and rugged around the edges. That was part of its charm. We'd maintain that charm, while at the same time, we'd polish up the place a bit, making it safer and cleaner. And we'd push back the monsters to reclaim a piece of our world.

That's the statement I wanted to make with these clothes.

"Well, what do you think?" I asked Angel, turning before her in my chosen outfit.

She purred.

"Glad you approve."

With my wardrobe sorted, I moved on to my hair. I did it up in a side braid. Then I moved on to something harder. I manipulated my magic until my wings were just the right shade: white on top, the color slowly bleeding to pink, and finally culminating in dark red tips.

By the time I had that all worked out, the clock told me it was time to go. I left my room, moving out of the west wing. I descended more stairs than I had in a long time, finally coming to the ballroom.

Past the gold-and-cream doors, a beautiful hardwood floor spread out like a tranquil, glossy lake. Twin sweeping staircases arched up to the upper level, the way lined in sparkling trees with branches that dripped strands of gold, silver, and diamonds. Outside these walls, there were people struggling to feed themselves on the streets of Purgatory, yet the district lords had hoarded decorations which could have fed the whole town for months. Or could have funded a hospital. Or done essential repairs to the sheriff's station so that it could actually contain the convicts inside. Disgust rose in my throat, angry and acidic.

Legion soldiers filled the ballroom, and all their eyes were on me as I walked to the center stage. Harker looked amused by my choice of outfit, like an angel had never before claimed her territory dressed in jeans.

Nyx was there too. And Ronan. She was turned pointedly away from him, still clearly hurt and angry at him for keeping secrets from her.

"Soldiers of the Legion," I said from the stage, my voice loud and clear. After all, I was speaking to the whole Legion now, to all its angels and soldiers. And I was speaking to all the people outside, the people of my territory, watching this ceremony being projected onto the Magitech wall.

"Today marks a new era not only for Purgatory, but for the entire Earth as well," I continued. "Centuries ago, our world changed, the day the monsters came. No one knew why the monsters came, and no one saw them coming. Within days, they had all but overrun the Earth.

"Some people said it was humanity's punishment for its

sins. Others said it was the demons who'd unleashed the beasts on us. But one thing we know for sure: powerful beings stepped in. They called themselves gods, and they stood against the monsters.

"They built walls between Earth's remaining cities and the plains of beasts. They gave us food and weapons—but most of all, they gave us magic.

"From the survivors of humanity, they built their army, soldiers with the magic of vampires, witches, shifters, fairies, and all kinds of other supernatural beings. And the best of the best, the top of their Legion, they made into angels. With this new army, the gods won the war against the demons, pushing them back into hell."

It was a simplification of the truth, but it was a powerful message, none the same. And it was good propaganda. After all, it wasn't just the world watching my speech. I didn't doubt the gods' eyes were trained on me right now too.

"The monster problem, however, was not so easily fixed," I said. "The beasts remained. Two hundred years later, the battle still rages on Earth, but piece by piece, we are going to take back our world."

I heard raised cheers from the people outside, beyond the gates.

"And Purgatory is where this battle begins. No more are the district lords who exploited you for far too long. Today, you become something greater: the bright spark of hope that will sweep across the Frontier, changing not only your lives, but the lives of every person on Earth. Purgatory will become a better place, a safer place. And you will all contribute to this glorious future. We'll build a hospital. We'll make much-needed renovations to the school. We'll build new shops."

More cheers.

"Because the monsters won't be pushed back by only weapons and magic," I declared. "They will cower before the light of hope shining from us, from our town, from all the Earth. We won't simply endure; we will thrive! That is the image we will show to the monsters, the criminals—to *anyone* who threatens the Earth. We will take our world back!"

The cheers from outside were almost deafening. I bowed to the cameras, then walked off the stage, hoping they'd all gotten my message. The soldiers of the Legion. The other angels. And the gods.

"The whole town seems to have joined in cheering your ascension," Ivy commented as the party began.

Dance music was already pumping out of the speakers, and the buffet tables were loaded down with enough food to satiate even me.

"I guess that means they liked the speech," I told her, winking.

She chuckled. "Indeed."

Drake and Alec stood on either side of her. Nyx had transferred them, among others, to my office. And Basanti had passed her initiates on to someone else at the New York office so she could join me here. Right now, she and her friend Claudia Vance were debating the dipping merits of the various fruit pieces beside the chocolate fountain. They'd drawn Lucy, one of the soldiers who'd been in the initiation group with me, into their discussion. Lucy had been transferred to Purgatory too. I'd requested her. She might not be a top fighter, but she was more organized than anyone I knew. She'd have the whole place running smoothly in no time.

"Very dramatic speech," Nerissa said as she walked up to me, her boyfriend Soren at her side.

"Nyx told me to make an impression," I replied.

"You certainly did that," Soren told me.

Harker joined us. "The people liked your speech."

"And the other angels?"

"Are you asking me if I felt threatened by your speech and am now going to make trouble for you?"

I shrugged. "Apparently, it's what angels do: vie for dominance."

"Well, it's pretty much built into our magic." A sly smile twisted Harker's lips.

"And when an angel senses weakness, he moves in for the kill."

"Something like that," he agreed. "But I don't think anyone sensed weakness in your speech. For one, not one of us can make our wings change color. They reverberated with every word you spoke. It was like watching a light and music show."

"I hope it makes up for my lack of a grand entrance. I didn't think I could pull off the flying-in-through-the-ceiling stunt as well as you could, Harker."

He chuckled at my reference to his own angel intro-duction ceremony, when he'd arrived to take over the New York office. "There's something to be said for doing things differently. No one will soon forget your ceremony—or the words you spoke. Your promise to defend your territory and the Earth was a clear warning to everyone that you would answer any threats to anyone who fell under your protection."

"Speaking of people falling under my protection," I whispered to Harker as the others left us to find food. "I need to steal Nerissa from you."

"Dr. Harding is here to monitor you and your condition," he replied, all humor drained from his tone. He had his business face on now. His angel face. "And as soon as your Fever has passed, I expect her to return to New York."

"Be reasonable, Harker. My office doesn't have any doctors. Yours has many."

"You have Poison Ivy."

"Ivy? She's a counselor. She heals minds, not bodies."

"Dr. Harding is needed in New York."

"She's needed more here," I countered, planting my hands on my hips. "I'm trying to change the world."

Harker folded his arms over his chest.

I frowned at him. "You're so stubborn."

"You should look in the mirror, Leda. You're the most stubborn of us all."

"And that's why I'll win." I flashed him a grin, then walked off.

Harker's laughter followed me all the way to the window. Nero stood there, watching the fireworks show that lit up the sky.

"Those are for you," he said. "The people of Purgatory liked your speech."

"Well, that, or they're trying to blow up the front gate to kill me."

He snorted softly.

"That wasn't a very dignified sound, General," I chided him.

"Dignity is overrated," he replied, a delicious curl to his lips.

"I was hoping you'd say that."

I didn't touch him, not even to brush my hand against his. Our chaperones were everywhere, and they were armed. They probably had orders from Nyx to shoot us if we got frisky.

Care for a little excursion outside these walls? I asked Nero silently.

What did you have in mind?

The last time you were here in town with me, I brought you to the fanciest restaurant in town, I reminded him. *But this time, I'm going to show you the real Purgatory, not the show they put on once a year for the tourists. I'm going to introduce you to the raw, uncivilized Purgatory.*

He cocked a single eyebrow up at me. *Well, when you put it like that, how can I refuse?*

You can't, of course.

Nero's gaze swept the ballroom. *How do you plan to lose your chaperones without making a scene?*

Oh, that's easy, I told him. *The district lords left this town poor, hungry, and altogether worse for wear. But they did leave us one useful thing.*

The tunnels, he realized.

Right. The underground tunnels don't simply connect all the district lords' villas; they connect all of Purgatory. And one of those tunnels just happens to have an exit directly next to the Witch's Watering Hole, Purgatory's favorite bar.

CHAPTER 22

WITCH'S WATERING HOLE

*O*ur faces masked by cotton hoodies, we followed the underground tunnels to the Witch's Watering Hole. The bar was one of my old haunts from my days in Purgatory, and there I introduced Nero to its terrible moonshine. As someone who had never consumed any alcohol that didn't come with a proper, legitimate label, he was rightfully horrified. We danced off our disgust to a humorous ballad—about a witch who'd fallen for a vampire—playing from the red jukebox. Overhead, the old fan turned slowly.

"We have an audience," Nero commented.

I followed his gaze to the crowd gathered in front of the bar, to the trio standing by the jukebox, to the people at the pool table. Every eye in the bar was locked on us, tracking our every move. So much for sneaking a few private moments alone with Nero. Our hoodies apparently didn't disguise as much of our faces as I'd hoped.

Whispers buzzed beneath the ballad's soft beat. The gist of it all was they not only knew Nero and I were angels; they'd realized I was the Angel of Purgatory, the one who had, only an hour ago, loudly and publicly declared she would free the Earth from the monsters.

One of the angel gazers stepped forward, a sixty-year-old man with a bald head and a big belly. I recognized him immediately. His name was Dale, and back when I'd lived in Purgatory the first time, he'd been my neighbor.

"The Angel of Purgatory," he said, grinning as he bobbed his head up and down. "You've come to push the monsters back from our doorstep."

"That's the plan."

"And while you're at it, could we get a hair salon too?" asked Cindy, Dale's curvy wife. "A hair salon and a few of those fancy clothing boutiques like they have in New York."

"And an ice cream shop!" added Jak, a former classmate of mine.

"And a spa!" exclaimed someone in the crowd.

"What is your strategy for reclaiming the wild lands?"

"Will the Legion of Angels be levying additional taxes on us to pay for this initiative?"

"All the roads in town need to be repaved."

"Bring real booze to Purgatory!"

"Can prospective soldiers join the Purgatory office, or must they still go to New York?"

"Can you do something about the smell in the streets?"

"I want a swimming pool!"

The questions and demands shot out of the crowd like kernels of popping corn. I felt like I was stuck at the cross-roads of a press conference and a kindergarten party. I did recognize some of the people in the crowd as reporters for the local paper, the Purgatory Times. Others were just bar gossips or curious citizens.

"Tell us about the big wedding," Cindy cooed.

"Tell us! Tell us!" the crowd chimed.

"There's nothing to tell." I held my index finger to my lips. "It's a big state secret."

"You are marrying Nero Windstriker," a young woman said, her big eyes devouring the sight of Nero.

"The sexiest angel in the Legion," her friend added.

I smirked at Nero. "You're the sexiest angel at the Legion? You never told me that."

"Careful." The dark timbre of his voice shot delicious shivers down my spine. "Do not incite me, Pandora."

"Why not?" My smile widened. "I'm so good at it."

His eyes burned with sinful promises that made me wish we were alone.

"Well, we have to be going," I told our captive audience.

A chorus of sighs rocked the crowd.

"So soon?" one of them moaned in bitter disappointment.

"But you only just got here."

"Pandora, let me touch your hand. It's good luck."

"Let us all touch your hand!"

Nero put himself between me and the adoring crowd.

"Don't hurt them," I whispered to him. "They're just excited."

"Leda, you have a lot to learn about being an angel," he replied, eyeing our audience. "And about crowd control. You let them get completely out of hand."

"*I* let them? I didn't let them do anything," I protested.

"Remember how we talked about the fear-love balance? How people need to fear us and love us?"

"Yes."

He pointed at the crowd. "This is what happens when they only love you. An angel's aura is very powerful, very seductive. And right now, they are all drunk on yours. They're completely out of their senses."

"So what do I do?" I asked him.

"You know what you must do."

Yes, I did. And I would hate every moment of it.

I flipped back my hoodie to expose my face and moved toward the crowd. A flame of black fire burst out of the floor where I'd stepped. I took another step. A second flame formed, this one composed of swirling spirals of white fire. Purple flames. Blue flames. Yellow flames. Red flames. Every step I took added more color to my surging halo. My admiring fans shielded their eyes.

"You dare touch me!" I magnified my voice until the walls shook, punctuating every syllable I spoke. "I, Pandora, Angel of Chaos, Angel of Purgatory and the Plains of Monsters! Chosen by the gods!"

They quivered, their absolute adoration now streaked with fear. The door to the bar swung open, and six Pilgrims filed inside. They'd probably been drawn here by my booming, magic-amplified voice.

"Do you think I overdid it a bit?" I asked Nero as the Pilgrims formed a human shield between us and the other people in the bar.

"If anything, you under-did it," he replied.

I would have chuckled if I weren't too busy maintaining my badass angel aura. Beyond the wall of dour-faced Pilgrims, the people in the bar were still watching us. Their eyes grew wide when I sipped from my glass of pineapple juice, as though it were the most amazing thing they'd ever seen. Their fear might have checked their barrage of questions—and their need to rub me for luck—but it had done nothing to dull their admiration.

"Well, this party is officially dead." I set my glass down on the counter.

"The novelty of people hanging on your every word wears off very quickly," Nero replied.

"That, plus the Pilgrims are a bit of a buzz kill."

I hid my head beneath my hood once more. Then I took his hand, leading him toward the bar's rear exit. The Pilgrims' line parted to make way for us, and closed again to prevent anyone from following us. Nero and I slipped out the back.

I brought him to a quieter, less lively bar off the main road. In fact, the place resembled a coffee house as much as it did a bar. Soft guitar music played from white ceiling speakers. Behind the bar, two fluffy armchairs and a whole wall of books formed a cute little reading cove that stood in stark contrast to the dance floor and neat row of shot glasses laid out across the bar counter.

I pulled out my phone and typed a quick invitation to Calli, Gin, and Tessa to join us here. They hadn't been allowed at my angel introduction ceremony, but I wasn't going to let them miss the afterparty.

The bar was quiet tonight. Which was good. Fewer people meant less of a chance of being recognized. This time, our disguises worked better. No one seemed to recognize us, and I hoped our luck would hold. I was wearing street clothes under my hoodie, but Nero was not. Beneath his hoodie, he wore a black leather uniform. Luckily, the only leather anyone could see were his pants. I supposed people just thought he was a biker with a soft side.

I ordered myself a pineapple juice then headed straight for the target board on the wall. The aim of the game was to shoot tiny toy arrows with a tiny toy bow. Nero frowned when I handed him that bow.

"You look positively scandalized, General," I teased him.

"I've been with you too long to be scandalized by anything, Pandora."

He leaned in to nip me on the lip. As he pulled away, his tongue darted out and slid languidly across his lower lip, licking off the crimson drop of my blood. For not the first time tonight, I found myself wishing the two of us were alone.

I was planning the path to make that wish a reality when my little sisters walked into the bar. Tessa and Gin spotted me immediately and rushed forward to trap me in a double hug.

"Leda, this is so exciting!" Tessa was practically bursting at the seams. "Remember our lovely conversation with Nero and Damiel last year? I just knew I'd soon be planning a Legion wedding!"

"Wait a minute. Since when are *you* planning the wedding? The Legion has regulations about how an angel wedding should go."

"Tessa paid the First Angel a visit," Gin told me.

I gaped at Tessa in shock. "You paid a visit to Nyx, the First Angel of the Legion of Angels?"

"Yes, I did," confirmed Tessa. "And she has really cool hair, by the way. In any case, she agreed to let me plan your wedding, embellishing as much as I want as long as I stay within the Legion's guidelines."

"How did you convince her of that?"

She smiled. "I can be very convincing."

I gave her my best don't-bullshit-me look.

"Ok, fine. It wasn't my charms that convinced her," she admitted. "It's you, Leda. The First Angel really likes you. I can tell. So she gave me enough leeway to create a wedding that would make you happy."

"Just try to keep the dancing acrobats to a minimum, Tessa. I don't want them losing their juggling balls inside the cake."

Tessa giggled. She'd had a hard time lately, discovering the dark horrors of her forgotten past, but planning my wedding had filled her with happiness once more. It had given her back her spark.

"Gin is creating the wedding sculptures," Tessa told me.

"Sculptures?" I asked. "As in more than one?"

"They are angel sculptures," said Gin. "And they move."

"They also smell like strawberries and cream," Tessa added.

"Just how many sculptures are there?" I asked them.

Gin shrugged. "Over twenty."

"Over twenty?" I turned to Tessa. "Exactly when did you speak to Nyx?"

"Just this morning, shortly after you all arrived in town. There was no missing that mass procession of Legion trucks. I took it upon myself to investigate, being that my own sister didn't give me a heads up as to what was going on in her life."

Oops. I'd been so caught up in my own issues that I'd forgotten to share them with my family.

I offered my sisters a guilty look. "Sorry."

"You can make it up to me by endorsing my wedding planning business."

"You have a wedding planning business?" I asked Tessa in surprise.

"Yes."

"Since when?"

"Since now. I predict a surge in population—and weddings—in Purgatory now that we're under the protection of the great Pandora, Angel of Chaos. I need to be positioned to take advantage of that. Wedding planning is just one component of that multi-tiered business plan."

"How many tiers are we talking about? And how many businesses?"

"Many."

"It seems you've been busy."

"A busy body quells a busy mind," Tessa told me.

It sounded like something our foster mother Calli would say. I could imagine that lately Tessa had been pretty eager to quell her busy mind.

"You've been busy too," I said to Gin. "How did you manage to construct over twenty mechanical angel sculptures in under a day?"

"Actually, I've been building them for over a year."

"But why?"

"For your wedding, of course, silly." Tessa's brows drew together in an obvious show of sisterly concern. "You need to relax, Leda. Kick up your feet and let me take care of everything. The wedding stress is clearly getting to you."

"There's no wedding stress, and it's not getting to me. I'm only baffled by why you began creating angel sculptures for my wedding a year before anyone knew I was getting married."

"Your family knew," replied Tessa. "I told you the first time I met Nero that you'd marry him—and that I was going to plan your wedding."

"Angels' marriages are arranged. You couldn't have known that Nero and I are magically compatible."

"Well, of course you're magically compatible." She rolled her eyes at me. "It's completely obvious."

I cast a look at Nero. As usual, he looked pretty damn sure of himself. When he'd dramatically swept in to rescue me from marrying any other angel, he'd also told me he knew our magic was compatible.

"The wedding of two angels! This is historic!" Tessa exclaimed, a bit too loudly. She was drawing the attention of the bar's other customers. "You two are on the cover of literally every magazine right now."

"How do I look in the pictures?"

I *hated* photos of myself. I always looked sort of lopsided.

"You looked hot, Leda. That whole angelic halo has done wonders for your complexion, sooo much better than any makeup." Her forehead crinkled. "Which is good for you because you always forget to put on any makeup."

"I don't forget to put on makeup," I told her. "I just get distracted doing more important things."

"Like what?"

"Oh, I don't know, like saving the world."

"There will be no saving the world on my watch, Ms. Angel of Chaos," said Tessa. "Not on your wedding day anyway. I forbid it. Nyx has put me in charge of your wedding, and I'm not going to allow monsters or villains to stand in the way of perfection." She glanced at Nero. "Speaking of perfection, Gin and I need to go over a few Legion procedures with you. The Legion rulebook is a rather meandering and long-winded read."

Tessa and Gin ushered Nero off to the cozy reading corner.

"Fancy a game of pool?"

I turned around to find Calli standing behind me. "Where did you come from?"

"The door, of course." She hugged me tightly. "Not all of us can materialize out of thin air."

"I can't do that either." I motioned for her to follow me to the pool table. "I'm just surprised that an old lady like you could sneak up on me," I teased her.

She teased me back. "Get your head out of the clouds, angel, and you might just notice what's happening here on the ground." Her voice grew more serious. "How are you doing, Leda? Really?"

"I'm all right, all things considered." I set up our game on the pool table. "I feel like I'm trapped in a whirlwind of madness, Calli. Becoming an angel. Being assigned a territory. The Fever. The wedding. I'm caught up in the gods' games, and I don't even know which way to turn."

She watched me closely. "But you're happy."

"Yes," I agreed. "I really am."

"There's something else troubling you."

"Yes. My origin."

Calli nodded. "Bella told us when she visited town last weekend."

I'd confided in Bella after waking up as an angel. The truth about my origin was too dangerous to leave to a phone call or text message. It had to be shared in person. In private.

"I'm caught in the middle of a tempest, of an immortal war that has been raging since long before I was born," I said. "And I can't help but fear that I ended up on Earth for a reason. I just don't know what that reason is."

"I've looked into the woman who cared for you when you were a baby," Calli told me. "There isn't much information. She went by many names. Once, she was a Legion soldier, before she disappeared. But I can't figure out how she got you, or why she died."

Her death had left me on the streets, up until Calli had found me and taken me in. That also seemed to have happened for a reason.

"What happened to your friend?" I asked Calli. "The one who led you to us all?"

"I haven't seen him in years, not since the mission that led me to you. He vanished without a trace."

"I feel like he has the answers I need."

"I won't stop looking," she promised me. "I won't give up."

"Of course you won't. You never give up."

"But maybe you should give up on this game," Calli commented with a crooked smile as I missed a shot. "Leda, with your supernatural hand-eye coordination, you should be able to crush me."

"You're the best shot I know, Calli. And becoming an angel has boosted everything. Honestly, I'm having a bit of trouble controlling my own strength. Now if you would just let me use magic, I could nudge that ball into the pocket. In fact, I could nudge them all in, all at once."

"No magic." She said it in the same stern way she used to tell me I couldn't eat dessert before dinner. "It's cheating."

"You only say that because you don't have any," I laughed. "But you possess a special kind of magic of your own: your deadly accuracy. If I can't use telekinesis, you can't use your special powers either."

Calli clicked her tongue. "Still trying to get away with breaking the rules on account of a technicality, Leda?"

I shrugged. "You taught me well. Fight dirty and fight smart."

217

Calli laughed. "If you fight dirty and smart in your new role, you might just succeed. Rumor has it you will single-handedly banish all the monsters from this Earth."

"Yeah, using only my pinkie finger." I snorted. "It's not that easy. We're going to try to reclaim some territory from the monsters, piece by piece. But it won't happen overnight. And I can't do it alone."

"I see the Legion is taking over the district lords' old buildings."

"It seemed like the best use of them."

"Oh, it is," she agreed. "I'm glad you're here, Leda, and not just because our town needs an angel with a heart. I'm glad you're here because it means I get to see you more often."

My throat was tight, my eyes wet. "That's the best part about my new position. I got to come home."

Calli wiped the tear from my cheek. "But with the Legion taking over here, you're going to put me out of business. The big, flashy Legion buildings and the terrifying angel reigning over Purgatory will keep the criminal element away. And if they don't come here, I can't snatch them and turn them in for a nice bounty. I'll have to open a bakery or a bookshop or something people do in civilized cities."

"I'm sure we can find a better use for your talents," I laughed. "How do you feel about contract work?"

"What kind of contract work?"

"I haven't figured it out yet, but I'm sure I'll think of some use for your extensive talents."

A calculating smile twisted her lips. "Extensive, huh?" She took a pretzel from the snack bowl and popped it into her mouth. "You must want something if you're flattering me like that."

"I *do* want something, in fact." I held out my hand. "And that something is that bowl of pretzels."

Chuckling, she handed me the bowl.

I took a pretzel. "How are Tessa and Gin doing?"

"They're getting better. Slowly healing."

I looked across the room, to the reading corner, where Tessa and Gin were enthusiastically chatting up Nero. "They're going to be all right."

Calli watched them too. "Yeah, they are. I'm glad you're back, Leda. We all do better when we're together."

I thought of my brother Zane, whose disappearance had set me down this path. I was going to get him back. Our family would be complete once more.

"I'm glad to be back too," I told Calli.

Nero closed in by my side. He dipped his head to Calli, his face serious. "I need to borrow Leda."

"Well, I suppose that's ok. You eventually brought her home, even though it took nearly two years." A touch of reproval flickered in her amused eyes.

Nero set his hand on my back, moving quickly as he led me toward the back door.

"What's the rush?" I asked him.

"We need to escape before your sisters return from the bar."

"Why are we running from my sisters?"

"Not we," he said. "I."

"Are their wedding preparations too much for a great warrior angel like you?" I laughed.

"It's not the preparations. It's the talking without interruption, a continuous, full-throttle logorrhea. They don't even come up for air."

"Nyx put them in charge of planning our wedding, and they have only three days left," I reminded him.

219

"I wish the First Angel had found a more humane way to kill me."

My laughter trailed us out the back exit. I looked around at the tiny, enclosed back alley, hardly large enough for the three garbage dumpsters.

"You know, this is the first place they'll look," I told Nero.

"You're right." His eyes panned up the chain-link fence that surrounded the alley; he looked like he was preparing to scale it. "Let's put some distance between us and the battlefield."

I was laughing so hard that my chest hurt.

"Do be serious, Leda. This situation is hardly funny."

"Sure it is. You—General Windstriker, Legion archangel, second only to the First Angel—can't handle a pair of eighteen-year-olds. I find that very funny."

He glanced back over his shoulder at me. "You're wearing a tiara at the wedding, you know," he said in a silky voice.

"A...what?" I stuttered.

"A tiara," he told me. "It's a kind of crown."

"I know what a tiara is. What I don't understand is why I will be wearing it."

"You'll have to ask Tessa. She decided for you."

"She decided? She decided what an angel will wear?" My voice crackled and boomed, rattling the metal fence. "You know what? I think I'll go demand an explanation."

He caught my arm. "You don't want to go back in there."

"No, *you* don't want to go back in there," I shot back. "I am perfectly happy to demand an explanation from Tessa."

"You're worked up."

"You bet I'm worked up. I don't want to wear a tiara. And I'm pretty sure the Legion doesn't want me to wear a tiara either. It doesn't exactly evoke fear in the hearts of our enemies."

Fire flashed in his eyes. "You're thinking like an angel."

"Damn right I am."

A smile twisted his lips, slow and sexy. "And you're reacting like one too. Angels are territorial, and they can't stand people telling them what to do." His hands settled on my shoulders.

"That's me. Check and check."

"But you're not just any angel," he said, holding me as I tried to turn back toward the door. "You're different. Your heart is different. You feel—and you can regret. If you fight with your sisters over a tiara, you will regret it later."

I shook the fluff from my mind. "You're right. All this new magic and the Fever—it's messing with my head." I took a deep, calming breath. "Ok, I'm better now."

"Even so, you're not ready to go back inside."

"Neither are you," I laughed.

"Agreed." He allowed himself a sigh. "So let's not go back inside. Let's just go…" His voice trailed off as he looked through the chain-link fence, toward the Magitech wall that stood between Purgatory and the Black Plains.

"Nero," I said, grinning. "Are you asking me to elope with you?"

"Would you accept?"

I looped my arms over his shoulders, leaning into him. "In a heartbeat," I whispered against his lips.

His mouth came down hard on mine. He wasn't slow or gentle, and he didn't tease. We hadn't shared each other's bodies in a long time, so I was more than happy to dispense with the pleasantries and cut right to the chase.

Rough, impatient, and savagely erotic—his kisses devoured, his touch seared. Heat flashed through my body, a perfect storm of wrenching pleasure and raw need. I grabbed his collar, pulling him in. His rock-hard chest slammed against mine.

His head dipped, his mouth tracing my neck. He expelled a breath, long and hot, against my skin. I shuddered, my blood surging beneath the surface. A cascade of feverish sensations crashed against me, pulling me under. My self-control lay unraveled at my feet.

"Nero." A soft moan brushed past my lips. "I'm ready to go."

He took my hand, intertwining his fingers with mine.

But our escape was intercepted before we could even kick off the ground. Legion soldiers hopped down from the fences from all sides. They closed in, their expressions detached, their guns pointed right at us. Our disguises obviously hadn't fooled them.

"So much for eloping. Thwarted by my ever-vigilant chaperones," I sighed.

Damiel landed in front of us, his dark wings spread wide. "Getting caught with your pants down, Nero? Very sloppy." His smirk was at once disapproving and amused.

"Why are *you* here?" Nero demanded, all disapproving and not at all amused.

"I'd meant to make it for Leda's introduction ceremony, but I got held up," Damiel said. "As it turns out, I have caught a person of interest."

He paused, obviously waiting for us to ask who it was.

I obliged. It was not like I had anything better to do. Well, I'd *had* something better to do, namely elope with Nero, but then all these Legion soldiers had surrounded us. Their guns were still pointed at us.

"So who is this mysterious person of interest?" I asked Damiel.

"The head of the black-market operation Potions and Poisons," he revealed. "And he's shared some very interesting information with me. For one, the person from whom his company bought the Nectar they were dealing a couple of years ago. The seller was an angel, and that same angel sold Potions and Poisons the complete set of Meda's research notes on monster manipulations."

CHAPTER 23

ON THE WRONG SIDE OF CIVILIZATION

At Damiel's statement, the annoyance on Nero's face faded, displaced by pure, dispassionate professionalism. "Who is this angel who betrayed us and sold Nectar to a black market magic supplier?" he asked his father.

Damiel proceeded to drop another surprise. "Gauging from the memories of the mastermind behind Potions and Poisons, the treacherous angel is none other than Colonel Battleborn."

"Colonel Battleborn couldn't be selling Nectar to monster traders. He died several months ago, in the battle at Memphis, killed by Venom-laced bullets," I pointed out.

Damiel shrugged. "And I died two hundred years ago, at the hands of my son, who was mourning the death of his mother, who it turns out is also not dead."

He had a point. You couldn't always believe what your eyes showed you.

"There's also the possibility that Colonel Battleborn sold the Nectar before he died," said Nero.

He had a point too.

"Where is Colonel Battleborn's body?" I asked Nero.

"There was no time to bring him back with us before the monsters overran our forces. Colonel Battleborn's body lies on the battlefield of Memphis."

And Memphis now lay on the plains of monsters.

"Then Memphis is our next stop," I decided. "We need to see if Colonel Battleborn's body is still there, if he's innocent—or if he has, in fact, fooled us all."

Nyx swooped down from the sky. She set down so close to me that the force of her landing nearly bowled me over. "We'll leave immediately."

Half an hour later, Nyx, Ronan, Damiel, Harker, Nero, and I were flying south in a Legion airship. And a few hours after that, we were standing outside the fallen city of Memphis. The hour was early, the ruins cast in shadow. The sun wouldn't rise for at least an hour, but a full moon dominated the night sky. It was particularly big and bright this night. I couldn't decide if that was a good omen or a bad one. At least it lit our way down the broken highway into the city.

At my back, a Magitech barrier sizzled across the stone wall. As the city had been lost, overrun by monsters, the former second line of defense had activated. It was now the *only* line of defense, all that separated civilization from the plains of monsters. Memphis now lay on the wrong side of civilization, in the wilds—and we were now heading into those wilds.

As we approached the city, Jace came down the old highway to meet us. Memphis, at least what was left of it, was located in the South Territory. Jace's territory.

As I watched his approach, I could hear growling monsters within the city that lay behind him. The sound of bricks, falling and shifting, mixed with the growls. I couldn't shake this cold feeling, like something sinister was looming over my shoulder, watching me. The ruined city felt like an old ghost town—with monsters.

"This place gives me the creeps," I muttered.

"Commentary, Pandora," Nyx said sharply.

She was chiding me for my very un-angelic comments. Angels didn't get creeped out. They had seen everything and could handle anything.

Nyx needed to relax. There were no subordinate soldiers here to hear me, no humans, no supernaturals. It was just us angels and the God of Earth's Army. And they were all used to my commentary by now.

Well, ok, so there were monsters nearby too. I didn't think they were eavesdropping—or could even understand my words, for that matter—but still I said nothing more about the creepy atmosphere. I supposed it wouldn't hurt to practice being angelic.

"I have six teams already in the city, tracking the monsters' movements," Jace reported to Nyx and Ronan. "And another team working on repairing the Magitech generators that power the wall."

Our mission here was twofold: to find evidence of Colonel Battleborn's death, and to repair the wall so we could reclaim the city from the monsters. The Legion was efficient like that. With a god and six angels here, we might just have a shot at reversing this recent loss.

"In the Battle of Memphis, Colonel Battleborn went down at the southwestern end of the city," Nero said.

"There is a lot of monster activity in that area," replied Jace. "They are also concentrated around the Magitech generators."

Ronan pulled out a map. He had it all color-coded and everything. "Windstriker, Dragonsire, you'll search sections one through ten for Colonel Battleborn. Sunstorm and I will take sections eleven through twenty."

The four of them spread their wings and flew off toward the southwestern end of the city. That just left me, Jace, and Nyx.

I glanced at Jace. "Maybe we should help the team repairing the Magitech generators."

"Not so fast, Pandora," Nyx said. "You're sticking with me."

"Jace said there are a lot of monsters around the generators. His teams might need our help. Why won't you let me jump into the thick of things?" I smiled. "It's good practice."

"You certainly don't need any practice jumping into the thick of things," she countered. "You do that far too frequently already. Flying, on the other hand, is another matter altogether."

"You can't fly?" Jace asked me.

"I can flap my wings and launch into the air. What happens after that is anyone's guess."

Nyx's granite stare cut Jace's laughter short. He quickly reformed his face into a serious expression worthy of Colonel Fireswift's son.

"The three of us will go up to the Obsidian Tower," Nyx decided. "Flying up there should give you all the practice you need, Pandora." She kicked off the ground, shooting into the air.

"The First Angel can be so cheeky," I told Jace, then flew off after her.

He flew beside me, looking considerably more coordinated than I did. "She can hear you, you know."

"I know." I winked at him, then closed in on Nyx. "Why are we going up here anyway?" I asked her, wobbling a bit in the air as a gust of wind bumped my body. "Afraid I'll run off screaming in fear of the monsters?"

"You? Run in fear? No, I'd rather expect you to charge straight at them and get yourself killed. I'm not about to let that happen."

"Come now, Nyx. Let's not get all sentimental."

"I am not sentimental," she said as we set down atop the Obsidian Tower. Besides the missing tip, the building was still pretty much intact.

I looked down across the entire city—and to the plains beyond, lit up by the big round moon. It was all so beautiful.

"Oh, maybe you're not sentimental about me," I said. "But you are *very* sentimental about my freaky magical compatibility."

She frowned, clearly unimpressed by my attempts at humor. "You don't take things seriously."

"If I did, I'd have your job.

This time, she did laugh. "Was that a challenge or a joke?"

"It was what you needed, nothing more or less."

She looked perplexed.

"You needed a laugh," I explained. "You've been stressed out lately. You really should talk to him."

"Who?"

"Ronan."

She closed herself off, her face devoid of expression, her eyes as cold as ice.

"Well, you should talk to *someone* at least," I told her.

Her dark brows arched together. "And you think that someone is you?"

"I'm here, you're here, and you've made it very clear

that you're not letting me out of your sight. As though I'm going to suddenly drop dead." I sighed. "Besides, we have a lot of time to kill. I'm sure we'll be here for a while. It's a big city, and there are a lot of monsters to kill."

Nyx gazed off into the distance, distracted, almost dreamy. Then, suddenly, her gaze snapped back to me. "Grab control of every monster you can and send them all at the Magitech wall beyond the city. Now."

"If you really don't want to confide in me, just say—"

"Our teams are in danger," she cut in. "They've been overrun."

She pointed down there, down into the city. You really could see everything from this spot, especially when you had supernatural vision. I watched Ronan and Harker as they were surrounded by monsters. Another pack of beasts was attacking Nero and Damiel.

Nero! Panic surged in me, the need to protect taking over. My magic, turbo-charged by the Fever, exploded. I grabbed for the minds of the monsters attacking Nero and the others. Then, my control over their wills locked in, I sent the beasts running at the Magitech wall. They exploded against the new border of civilization, like fireworks bombarding the night sky.

"I can't keep doing this for very long," I said over the booms and bangs of the wall's defensive magic.

"Running out of steam already, Pandora?" Nyx asked sharply.

"Not at all." Sweat dripped down my neck. "But the impacts of the exploding monsters will eventually overwhelm the Magitech barrier. And if the barrier goes down, this line of defense will fall and the monsters will advance deeper into civilization. Their territory will grow, not shrink, which isn't really what we're trying to accomplish here."

"Can you make the monsters fight one another rather than run at the wall?" Nyx asked.

"Just like my ability to fly, my monster control isn't that fine-tuned yet, at least not on the scale of thousands of monsters. I can make them all run mindlessly in a single direction. That's about it."

"How long before your team finishes repairing the Magitech generators?" Nyx asked Jace.

He glanced at his phone. "They are ready now. But the city is still swarming with monsters. If we put up the barrier now, we'll still have thousands of monsters on the wrong side of the wall, here inside the city with us."

Nyx looked at me. "Leda, can you send *all* the monsters out of the city, far out onto the plains?"

"I guess we won't know until I try."

I grabbed control over all the monsters now, not just those close to Nero and the others. The sheer weight of their wills, thrashing against my control, was overwhelming. I felt like I was drowning inside the storm of so many beasts.

Nyx caught me as I swayed sideways. "When the monsters are all out of the city, we'll activate the Magitech wall," she told Jace.

I directed the monsters toward the plains. Like rivers of moonlight, they streamed out of the city. I pushed harder, even as the monsters slipped from my control. There were just so many of them. A part of me was vaguely aware of Nyx talking on her phone, directing our teams to kill the monsters who'd broken free of my Siren's Song.

I kept pushing, my heart beating so fast I thought it might explode. It was like a sledgehammer pounding inside of my chest, shaking me. My whole body vibrated. Each beat of my heart rattled my ribcage.

I'd never expended so much magic at once. It was burning off of me so fast, my skin tingled, lighting up my halo. I was glowing like the sun's corona, the sheer brilliance of it blinding even myself. I tried desperately to hold on to every monster, even as more and more of them slipped away.

A thunderous roar shook the city. The Magitech barrier flared up across the inner wall that bordered the city's western perimeter. I collapsed to my knees, heaving in air, my lungs burning like I'd just run all-out for hours. Had it been hours? The rising sun was just now cresting the horizon.

Nyx locked her forearm with mine and helped me to my feet. "You did well."

I coughed. When it came to corralling monsters, I was seriously out of shape. As my heartbeat slowed, I could hear the steady, quiet hum of the Magitech generators down in the city.

"If it's all the same to you, I'm going to sit down for a few minutes." Exhausted beyond belief, I went over to a piece of debris and sat down.

Jace was talking on his phone to his soldiers who'd just arrived, directing those teams into the city to clean up the mess. Nyx was communicating with our existing teams on the ground. No one paid me any mind. I was totally fine with that. I just needed to rest my head against this pole for a few moments...

Someone shook me, and I jolted awake. I looked up, meeting Nero's eyes. I didn't know how long I'd nodded off, but the sun still appeared to be in roughly the same spot in the sky, so it couldn't have been very long.

Behind Nero, our airship was hovering over the Obsidian Tower.

"We're leaving?" I asked Nero.

"We are. Some of Jace's soldiers are staying behind to begin the city cleanup."

"Did you find Colonel Battleborn's body?"

"Yes. Ronan used Aleris's glasses, drawing out the memories imprinted on Colonel Battleborn's body to make sure he really is who he appears to be. And that he wasn't involved in any shady operations prior to his death."

"So Colonel Battleborn didn't sell Nectar to a black market operation?" I asked.

"No," Nero confirmed. "Colonel Battleborn did not. And he died here, at the battle of Memphis."

But if Colonel Battleborn wasn't the angel who'd sold Nectar to Potions and Poisons, who was?

CHAPTER 24

CONFESSIONS OF AN IMMORTAL

*M*onsters had reigned over Memphis for far too long. There was a lot of damage to repair. It would take months for Jace's soldiers to restore it to its former glory.

The airship carried us to the Legion's New Orleans office, from which Jace ruled over the South Territory. A breakfast fit for a king—or an angel or deity, as it were—waited for us there, tucked inside a private dining room. The room, awash with opulent marble, gold, and good old solid oak, was the equivalent of the New York office's head table. The room was normally reserved for angels and officers level six or above. This morning, it was reserved for six angels and the God of War.

A big, black box with a big, white bow was waiting at my spot. "My next present?" I asked Nero.

"Perhaps," he said. "Or perhaps it's another sleeping cushion for Angel."

I glanced down at the sleeping cat nestled between my feet. "Yes, watching the battle from the airship must have been absolutely exhausting," I told her.

She peeked up at me through half-open eyes, then went right back to sleep. And I returned my attention to the box. I unfastened the bow and lifted the lid to find a shiny silver-and-red shield inside.

"Not a very comfortable sleeping cushion." I turned the Shield of Protection, one of the weapons of heaven and hell, over in my hands. "Wait, there's more?" Silver armor, the final piece in that set of immortal artifacts, was at the bottom of the box. I now had the whole set.

"With all that went on yesterday, I didn't have time to give you your gift yesterday. So here are two days in one," said Nero.

"How did you acquire the weapons of heaven and hell from Faris?" Ronan said casually, as though asking Nero where he'd bought an umbrella.

"I asked him for them," replied Nero.

"And he simply handed them over?"

"Yes."

Ronan's brow furrowed with suspicion. "Faris never does anything without a reason. Without a carefully-crafted plan."

"Nor do I," Nero said stonily.

"What are your plans for the weapons of heaven and hell?" Ronan asked.

"What are your plans for Leda?" Nero countered.

They stared at each other, neither answering the other.

I helped myself to some pudding. Pudding for break-fast? This was my kind of place.

"You know, this is just what the demons want: for us to be fighting amongst ourselves," I told them. "A divided enemy is easily conquered. United, we are stronger."

Nero's gaze didn't waver from Ronan. "Unity requires trust, Leda."

"It also requires forgiveness. On all sides. Secrets and lies are what tore us apart. Well, I say, no more!" I tapped my fingers across the tabletop. "We're each going to share a secret with each of the people here."

Nero shook his head slowly. "This isn't a good idea."

"Nonsense!" I said brightly. "It's an excellent idea. We need to throw down all our weapons. We need to bare our souls. And someone has to take the first step." I glanced at Harker. "I think we could use some privacy, don't you think?"

"I hope you know what you're doing, Leda." He tossed his magic orb into the air, casting a privacy spell over the room.

"I do," I assured him, then looked at Nyx and Ronan. "I know why you stole the weapons of heaven and hell from Nero. You thought you could use them to protect the Earth from the demons. At the time, you didn't realize that only I could wield them."

Jace stopped eating. He just stared at me.

"You knew," I told him. "You knew that I'd charged the sword before you swung it at the demon."

"Yes, I knew," he said quietly. "And I took credit for it." He frowned, his face marred with guilt.

"Trust me, you did me a favor." My gaze panned across everyone seated at the table. "Trust. That's what we need— and far more than we need immortal artifacts or secret weapons. Trust is our sword, and it is our shield. The lies that exist between us are walls, closing us off from one another, sabotaging our unity, making us weak."

As I rose to my feet, Nero caught my hand. He looked at me like he knew what I was going to do—and he didn't like it one bit.

I smiled at him. "It's ok. We have to do this. We

cannot be divided. We must be honest. We must forgive so we can work together." I glanced at Nyx. "For the greater good."

She kept her gaze turned away from Ronan, unable to let go of her pain.

"There's a reason only I can wield the weapons of heaven and hell," I told Jace. Then I paused, preparing myself for the words I had to speak. "Because, of everyone, only I am of both heaven and hell."

"You're the one," Jace said, his eyes wide. "The daughter of Faris, the God of Heaven's Army and Grace, the Demon of Faith."

I nodded. "I am."

"That's why your magic is so different. Why *you* are so different."

"I'd like to think I'm the master of my own destiny. Yes, my magic comes from my parents, but I alone decide what kind of person I want to be. I am the bearer of my own moral compass."

Jace was quiet for a while. "You always did navigate by your own compass," he finally said.

Nero hadn't been reaching for his sword. His body hadn't even tensed. But through the magic that linked us, I'd felt his battle readiness. At Jace's words, he went off high alert. He'd now realized what I had recognized about Jace, that he was a good and loyal friend. That he would stand with me, not betray me.

"And everyone here already knew about this?" Jace looked around at the others seated around our table.

"Yes," I confirmed.

"I'm always the last to know about anything important," he sighed.

"Not the last," I told him. "Your father doesn't know, and we need to keep it that way. He wouldn't understand."

"You're right. He wouldn't." A dark shadow fell across Jace's face. "And I won't tell him."

"Thank you." I turned my gaze on Ronan and Nyx now. "We hid a lot of things from you. Some of them you've discovered, such as Damiel's survival and how we recovered the weapons of heaven and hell. Others you do not know."

Nero didn't try to stop me from confessing my secrets. He'd learned to trust me, even when I had crazy ideas.

"I would have left," I told Nyx. "If Nero hadn't come back in time, or if our magic hadn't been compatible, I would have left the Legion rather than marry anyone else. What the Legion does is important to me—keeping the people of Earth safe is important to me—but I just couldn't have done it. I couldn't be with anyone else. That sacrifice would have been too much to ask."

"I know," she said. "And I'm glad it worked out."

"It worked out for me *and* for the Legion."

"Indeed," she agreed.

"Do you know how Faris is always ahead of the rest of the gods?" I asked Ronan. "Do you know how he always comes out on top?"

Ronan's response was immediate and without doubt. "Because he's planned every move centuries in advance, and he has a chorus of telepaths to uncover others' secrets."

"That's part of it, but it's not all of it. That's how he wins the big battles, but it's not how he wins the little ones, the simple, small conversations where he always seems to end up on top. Neither scheming or telepaths help him there. The truth of it is Faris wins because you and the other gods let him."

Ronan stiffened. "We most certainly do not."

"You do," I told him. "You don't know it, but you are doing just that. I've watched you all. I was there when the gods' council declared they were taking over the Crystal Falls training. I watched as you fought over secrets and lies. I heard you speak with Faris before you confronted Sonja and Ava. Faris has a knack for getting under everyone's skin, for seeing everyone for what they truly are, for exploiting their weaknesses and negating their strengths. He does it with every word that he says, every movement of his eyes."

Ronan seemed to be mulling that over. His eyes shifted back and forth like he was scrolling through millennia of interactions with Faris. "You're right," he finally declared.

"Of course I am. Because I possess the very same ability," I confessed.

Ronan nodded. "You might possess some of Faris's abilities, but you are not Faris. You do not share his failings."

"Who is Faris really? He's wrapped himself in so many layers of deception, played games for so long, that I don't think anyone knows what lies beneath it all."

"Indeed," agreed Ronan.

I turned to Harker—and my next confession. "Earlier this year, when some mystery person rearranged the books in your office in reverse alphabetical order...yeah, that was me."

He rolled his eyes. "That's hardly a secret, Leda."

I frowned. "How did you figure it out?"

"Rearranging all my books in reverse alphabetical order must have taken hours. No one else at the Legion is that dedicated and systematic in their implementation of chaos."

"Ok, well...hmm... The only other confession I have

for you is I arranged for you to sit next to Bella at my wedding reception." I smirked at him. "So don't screw it up." I moved on to Damiel. "As for you, I must confess that you scare the hell out of me."

Damiel nodded, his smile serene. "Thank you."

What a response. Then again, I wasn't the least bit surprised.

"But you also make the world's best pancakes," I continued. "And Nero thinks so too."

Damiel glanced at his son.

"This is supposed to be *your* confession, Pandora," said Nero.

I smiled at him. "What's yours is mine, honey."

Harker coughed, in a totally transparent attempt to cover a laugh. Nero gave us both his best angel stare.

"The reason I keep visiting you at your apartment is to watch how you make the pancakes, so I can learn to make them for Nero," I told Damiel.

"And how's that working out for you?" Damiel's expression was mild, almost amused. Maybe archangels mellowed with age.

"How's it working out? Not well," I admitted. "My pancakes don't taste the same as yours. I don't understand. I watched every thing you put into the batter. I noted how much you used of every ingredient. I witnessed how you mixed the batter. I perfectly mimicked how you fried them. I even measured the diameter of the pancakes. But there's something missing. Something different."

Damiel's smile had reached his eyes. "You will just need to keep visiting me until you find out."

"You knew," I said, the heavy weight of the realization flattening me. "You knew I was trying to copy the recipe, and somehow you made sure I wouldn't figure it out."

Angels took sleight of hand to a whole new level.

"This is my confession to you, Leda. I knew that once you figured out my secret pancake recipe, you wouldn't visit me anymore."

"Maybe I would."

"Because you enjoy me scaring the hell out of you?"

"No, you crazy angel. Because you're family."

"Family." He blinked. Apparently, he hadn't considered that family was more important to me than my own fear. "But as family, you could have just asked me for the recipe."

I laughed. "Damiel might be family, but General Dragonsire is an angel. And I know better than to ask an angel for a favor, especially an archangel."

"You have come a long way." Damiel nodded in approval. "You've learned a lot. And I really enjoy our visits. So if you promise to continue visiting me, I'll promise to give you the pancake recipe. That's a deal even you can live with."

"I agree."

He pulled out his phone and hastily typed out something on it. A moment later, my phone dinged, hopefully signaling the arrival of the famous pancake recipe in my inbox.

I reached out my hand to take Nero's. "There are no secrets between us. You know that. So the best confession I can offer to you is that the cut of your shirt makes me want to tear it off you right now."

"I know. That's why I wore it." His eyes smoldered. "And that is my confession to you."

Like father, like son. They were knocking out their confessions with masterful efficiency.

Nero squeezed my hand. "Because I have no secrets from you either, Leda."

"Oh, I don't know. You have a few small secrets you could share, I'm sure. For instance, you could tell me what you're getting me for my final gift."

His brows lifted.

"I already have the complete weapons of heaven and hell, but there's still another day before the wedding. And another gift."

"I had no idea you were so materialistic."

"I'm not…I…I just…Nerissa said you'd bring me a gift every day. And I'm just so terribly curious."

"Your magic tingles so beautifully against mine when you're flustered," he chuckled, so low that if we'd been surrounded by humans, no one would have heard him.

"So glad to amuse you."

"I'm not amused, Leda."

The way his eyes, silver and gold swirling inside those emerald depths, bore into me backed up his words. No, he wasn't amused; he was aroused. And so was I. It flashed through me, hot and hard and persistent, devouring me inside and out. It was two days until our wedding night. It might as well have been two centuries.

"Switch places with Nero," Nyx instructed Harker.

Nero's eyes never left mine, even as he and Harker exchanged places at the table.

A shiver rippled down my spine. "You never answered my question," I told him.

"You'll have to wait and see what it is. It's a surprise."

"I love surprises." I curled a lock of hair around my finger. "Well, besides the whole agonizing wait part."

"And you'll love this one," he promised me.

"Give me a tiny hint?"

"Absolutely not." He looked offended.

"Give me a hint about my present, and I'll give you a hint about my wedding lingerie."

He mulled that over. "No," he finally decided. "I like surprises too."

I flashed him a grin. "You will really like this one. The lingerie has a…"

I allowed my voice to trail off. I could see his eyes moving, his mind clearly working to decipher the rest.

"You will tell me," he said, his voice ringing with the resounding note of command.

I laughed. "No."

"Yes." The word hit me like a hammer. "You will."

"Or what?" I challenged, planting my hands on my hips. I even gave my booty a sultry sway.

He opened his mouth to answer, his tongue tracing his lower lip.

"That's quite enough from both of you," Nyx snapped.

Nero leaned back in his chair.

I took my seat again. "It's your turn, General," I told Nero.

"To confess?"

"It's healthy for the soul. And only when we've laid everything out on the table, only when we've shared our secrets with one another, can we be truly united. Once that is done, no secrets will be able to divide us as they did the gods' council because we've already shared everything with one another."

"As you wish." His confession to me already made, Nero turned to Harker. "On the first day of training when we were initiates, I was the one who misplaced all your training clothes."

"I already knew that, Nero. One of our trainers caught

you in the act. He chastised us both in front of the whole group—you for playing the prank, me for being unable to defend my own stuff."

"Typical Legion," I commented. "Punish the victims along with the perpetrators to make them all stronger."

"Your husband-to-be was a real ass back in the day," Harker told me. "He and the other Legion brats. But he got better with time."

"No, I didn't," said Nero. "I'm still the same ass I was two hundred years ago."

They both laughed.

"So *that* is your confession?" Harker asked him.

"No. As you said, you already knew that. My confession is not that I stole your clothes, but that I made sure I got caught doing it."

Harker's face was utterly perplexed. "Why would you do that?"

"The Legion brats were annoying me, egging me on to prank you. They saw your talent and hated you for it, especially because of your humble origins. They demanded that, as the pedigree of two angels, as the top of the top, it was my duty to show you your place."

I glanced at Jace. "Sounds familiar."

"Yeah." His fellow Legion brats had often pushed him to act like that too.

"I wanted to get caught so I had an excuse to tell them when they pushed me to do things later: I'd been caught, and I didn't want that on my record, to be known as a silly prankster," Nero said. "But there was another reason too. I knew we'd be punished together, and I wanted to get to know you. I knew you were worth more than any of them, that you'd be something. And that you'd make a good friend."

I sniffled, my throat choking up with emotion.

Harker considered me. "What's this? The badass Pandora is crying?"

"It's just so sweet," I sobbed. "The birth of a beautiful friendship."

Harker and Nero exchanged glances, then they patted each other on the shoulder, hard and manly.

Nero looked at Damiel. "You were not a particularly good father."

"You're supposed to share a *secret*, Nero, not something everyone already knows."

"You were not a particularly good father," Nero repeated. "But I did not want to kill you. It plagued me long after I'd done it. And when I learned that I hadn't truly killed you, that you had staged the whole thing, I was relieved."

Damiel's smirk faded.

"Of course, when I found you alive, I was angry at you too," Nero added. "I was ready to kill you again if you endangered Leda."

Neither of them said anything. They just looked at each other. There were no back slaps this time. No humor. There was only the unspoken, intangible connection between father and son.

"You asked me what my plans are for the weapons of heaven and hell," Nero spoke to Nyx and Ronan now. "I gave them to Leda so she can fight off anyone who might try to do her harm or use her for her magic."

The way he looked at them made it clear he really meant *anyone*, gods and demigods included.

"We're supposed to be fostering unity," I sighed. "Is it really necessary to threaten one another?"

"Yes, Leda." Nero didn't take his eyes off Nyx and

Ronan. "As long as they are trying to coerce you, threats are absolutely necessary."

"I'm not going to coerce you, Leda," Nyx said. "I don't even think it's possible. I'd much rather work with you. We are on the same team. We have the same goal."

"You see, that's what I've been saying," I told everyone at the table. "We cannot allow petty things to break us all apart, as they fractured the gods' council. We need to be united, to promise one another that we will stand together. Because only then can we hope to protect the Earth and its people, as well as everyone on all the worlds left broken by this immortal war. Discord is what tore the universe apart. Unity will bring it back together."

"Good speech." Nero's eyes twinkled with a hint of insurgency. "You'd make an excellent First Angel."

I smirked at Nyx. "I heard the job's already taken. But I'd settle for First Angel of the Plains of Monsters."

Nyx laughed.

"Trust has to start somewhere," I told Nero.

"But are you sure you can trust them?" His gaze flickered to Nyx and Ronan, then back to me again.

"Yeah, I really do. It's not in their best interests to betray us. Not anymore."

That's one useful thing I'd inherited from Faris, the ability to see through the bullshit.

"Very well," Nero agreed, then glanced at Jace. "There's something you should know about the archangel trials your father will be facing." His gaze slid over to Ronan. "But it is not my secret to tell."

The Lord of the Legion remained silent.

"Trust doesn't flow only one way," I told Ronan.

"The Legion has been doing things this way for a long time."

"So it's about time for a change, don't you think?"

"You are trouble, Leda Pandora."

"Of course I am."

"To absorb the Nectar that will make you an archangel requires great resilience," Ronan told Jace and Harker, the only two people here who hadn't gone through the archangel trials or knew what they entailed. "But it also requires great sacrifice. An archangel's second, the one they love and trust the most, the one they choose to stand by their side as they complete the trials, must die for an archangel to rise. In so doing, an archangel demonstrates unerring devotion to the Legion, a willingness to sacrifice what they love most for the greater good."

Jace blinked. "I don't understand. Leda was General Windstriker's second in his trials. She didn't die."

"Leda doesn't fit into the natural order of things." Resignation strained Ronan's voice.

"During Nero's trials, we figured out what was going on and we circumvented it," I said.

"And the gods almost killed her anyway," Ronan noted.

"If not for the political in-fighting and scheming, they would have killed me," I admitted.

"The gods' council will not allow such an aberration to repeat," said Ronan.

Comprehension dawned on Harker's face. "Because then it would become a pattern. And the gods' order would break down."

"Just that," said Ronan.

"The one my father loves most...that's my mother." Jace's voice shook. "He asked her to be his second for the trials. She will die."

"No, she won't," I said with a sidelong glance at Ronan. "Things have got to change. There's no need to force a sacrifice on an archangel. Let them level up or die, just as it works everywhere else at the Legion."

"Not everywhere."

Jace was referring to me, to the odd impossibility that I had neither leveled up nor died when I'd drunk the Nectar for Fairy's Touch. It was because my magic was balanced, so now I needed Nectar and Venom together to gain new powers. As Ronan had said, I existed outside the Legion's normal laws of magic.

"We can't allow Jace's mother to die," I pleaded with the Lord of the Legion. "Too many have died already. These senseless sacrifices have to stop."

"The Legion changed the day you walked through its doors." Ronan looked reflective. "That was the impetus, and things have been spiraling out from there ever since."

I frowned. "Was that a yes or a no?"

"I will need to speak to the rest of the council. I'll do what I can, but I make no promises."

Well, it wasn't a refusal at least. I was right about Ronan. I knew I was. He might be a god, but he was still a good person. He would do the right thing.

"I should have put a stop to this sacrifice long ago." Was that regret I spied in Ronan's eyes? "It serves no purpose and robs the Legion of good soldiers. But I allowed the other gods to convince me otherwise. I allowed them to convince me of a lot of wrong things." Regret definitely burned in his eyes this time, as they fell upon Nyx.

"There are times when I wish you had never found me, never woken me, that I'd never remembered who and what I am," Nyx confessed to Ronan. "Things were simpler then."

"Simpler, but not happier," he replied.

"No, I wasn't as happy as I am now. But I also didn't hurt as much as I do now."

Nyx said nothing more. Neither did Ronan. But that short exchange between them had given me a much closer glimpse into who the First Angel truly was inside than I'd ever had before.

It was Jace's turn now. "Leda, when we first met, I thought you were a dirty street urchin from the edge of civilization," he told me. "I soon realized how very wrong I was. I came to admire your determination and marvel at your ingenuity. And most of all, I consider myself fortunate that you are my friend. You taught me more than anyone I've ever known." His voice dropped to a whisper, "Just don't tell my father that."

Jace looked around, as though Colonel Fireswift would suddenly pop out of nowhere and strike him down for making such a bold claim.

Fortunately, the leader of the Interrogators did not spontaneously appear. Colonel Fireswift was Faris's man, and if Faris found out what we were confessing here in this room, we'd all be in really deep shit.

"There is something special about you, Leda, but it isn't your divine blood," said Jace. "It's the person you are inside."

I wiped a tear from my cheek. "I thought you guys were saving the sappy speeches for the wedding."

"Pull yourself together, Pandora. The last thing I need is for Nyx's ward to break under the weight of your tears, and then have all my badass soldiers break down like a bunch of weeping willows." Jace winked at me.

I laughed and cried at the same time.

"General Windstriker, you scare me more than anyone, even my father. And even the gods." Jace shot Ronan an apologetic look, then his gaze flickered back to Nero. "Every time you look at me, I feel like you're thinking about killing me."

The faint hint of a smile hovered on Nero's lips. "The thought has crossed my mind once or twice."

Jace swallowed hard. "But you should know that while I love Leda, I love her like a sister."

I burst into tears again.

Jace smirked at me. "Seriously?"

"Sorry." I rubbed my wet eyes. "I blame the Fever for the emotional turbulence."

"You've looked out for her, Angelblood." Nero's smile was considerably less scary this time. It was almost amiable.

"Not even half as much as she looked out for me."

"I have experienced the same phenomenon," Nero laughed.

"On our first mission, she went off alone, across the Black Plains after you," Jace recalled.

"Indeed she did."

"I would have crossed the universe for you, Nero." Sure, it was a sappy thing to say, but I meant every word.

Nero chuckled. "Flattery will not save you from the consequences of your actions."

"You can't punish me for something from nearly two years ago, especially not something you *already* punished me for," I protested.

His lips curled with promise. "Oh, my dear Pandora, of course I can."

I stuck my tongue out at him.

"Do that again and see what happens."

I was so tempted. My tongue flicked across my lips.

"Pandora, go take a cold shower," Nyx ordered me.

"But we are finally all getting along so well."

Nyx's eyes panned from me to Nero. "Perhaps *too* well."

"I'll behave," I promised her.

Her brows peaked.

"As best I can," I amended.

"Flirt with Nero again, and I'll cast a cold shower over you both."

I shivered at the thought. Nyx's showers probably came with a copious serving of ice cubes.

"So that's your confession?" I asked Jace. "That you're scared of Nero?"

"I have very few secrets, Leda, and the ones I do have, you've already long since uncovered."

"Surely, there has to be something else," I probed him. "Something I don't know. This is about sharing, Jace. You'll feel better if you do it."

He was eerily still, like he was afraid of something.

"I knew you were holding back! Ok, out with it. Tell us."

"It's silly and totally embarrassing."

"My favorite kind of secret," I said brightly.

Jace took a deep breath. "I think Colonel Starborn is the Legion's sexiest angel."

"Leila?" I choked out in surprise. "You have a crush on Leila?"

"Teenage kids have crushes. Angels admire from afar."

"No angel I know ever admires from afar. They jump right in and get their hands dirty." I looked to Nero and Harker for confirmation.

"You just used the words 'angel' and 'dirty' in the same sentence." Harker frowned. "I'm sure there's a regulation against that."

"There is," Nero confirmed. "It's in article thirty-six, section twelve."

My mind sifted through the Legion's enormous rule-book. "There is no article thirty-six, section twelve." I frowned at Nero.

"No, there's not." His voice was a dark and dangerous caress.

I stole a peek at Nyx. A hint of magic crackled on her fingers. She'd promised to hit us with a cold shower if we didn't stop flirting, and I didn't doubt her for a second.

"So, Leila, you say. When did this happen?" I asked Jace quickly.

"During the gods' recent challenges. We spent a lot of time together."

"You're not alone," Harker told him. "Leila has been featured on the front of the Legion of Angels calendar more often than any other angel."

Jace's face turned red.

"Wait, there's a Legion of Angels calendar? How can I not know about this?" I asked.

"I'm sure the editor will approach you to model for it soon," Harker said.

I grinned at Nero. "Maybe we can share a spread."

His brow cocked upward at me.

I looked hastily at Nyx. "I meant a photo spread. Not any other form of...spreading."

Beside me, Harker's shoulders were shaking. "You're digging yourself deeper into that hole, Leda."

"Thank you for your helpful advice."

He shrugged off my sarcasm. "You're welcome."

"You're sitting between me and Nero, smartypants. If Nyx casts a freezing cold shower over us, who do you think will get hit the hardest?"

The humor drained from his face. "Being your friend is rife with hazards."

251

"But it's worth it?"

"Every moment of it." Harker told Jace, "You're not the only one who's ever been enamored with Leila. When she took me on as her apprentice, I have to admit I found myself appreciating her in utterly inappropriate ways."

My grin grew wider. "You know, I'm starting to wish I'd invited Leila along to this meeting."

Harker laughed, but Jace looked considerably less merry.

"You both do realize that Leila likes women, right?" I told Jace and Harker.

"Yeah, that hit me hard when I found out."

"I already knew. The knowledge didn't help me," Jace sighed.

"Leila is dating Basanti. I wouldn't share your appreciation of Leila with her," I advised Jace.

"Indeed," Nero agreed. "Basanti hits hard."

"I am not sharing it with anyone," Jace said, his voice rocky. "*No one* is going to share it. It's completely embarrassing."

"Are you in the habit of desiring unattainable women?" Damiel asked Jace casually.

Jace blinked. "Sorry?"

"First Leda, then Leila. There seems to be a pattern with the objects of your affection."

"I was never the object of Jace's affection," I told Damiel. "We've already cleared that up. Or did you nap through that part, old man?"

"I'm glad Nero is marrying you, Leda," Damiel laughed. "I want grandchildren with a lot of spunk."

At the thought of children, of bringing them into this dangerous world, my body grew colder than Nyx's promised icy shower. I could barely protect myself from the horrors and monsters that lurked around us. How could I hope to protect a child? My pulse pounded beneath my skin, like a metal hammer against a sheet of ice.

Nero shot Damiel a look laden with threat. "Stop annoying Leda, or I'll hang you from the ceiling at our wedding like a piñata and let all the guests take a swing at you."

Damiel laughed. He actually looked proud of his son for threatening him. Or was he proud at Nero for standing up for me?

"Your turn, Daddy," I said to Damiel.

One brow lifted, the other dipped. "Daddy?" He seemed amused by the title.

"Well, you're going to be my father-in-law. And as crazy as you are, I think I'm actually in less danger from you than from my own father."

"You're not wrong about that." A small smile touched his lips. "All right. I'll play. My biggest secret is already out: I'm alive." He glanced at Nero, declaring, "And I'm not the only one. Cadence is alive too."

Nyx dropped her fork. Ronan grew very still. So, they hadn't known.

"Cadence and I planned it all, down to every detail," Damiel continued. "I would stage my death and hers. And then we would meet up later. We never did. The Guardians got to her first. They took her, and I have spent every waking moment since then trying to find my way back to her."

Silence filled the room.

Ronan finally broke it. "The Guardians have Cadence Lightbringer?"

"That's what I said, isn't it?" Impatience tinted Damiel's voice. He was usually in complete control of himself, but when it came to Cadence, all bets were off. "I tried to link to her, but the Guardians' defenses are obscuring my spells, preventing me from telepathically connecting to her." His jaw clenched.

"Nero, Damiel, and I have been working toward getting her back," I said.

"We believe that if Leda gains the power of Ghost's Whisper, the three of us together would have enough power to break through the Guardians' defenses and find my mother," said Nero.

"And my brother Zane," I added. "That is the truth of why I joined the Legion. My brother, a ghost, was abducted."

"And you thought if you could gain the power of telepathy, you would be able to take him back from the Guardians," Nyx said for the others' benefit. She already knew about Zane.

"At the time, I didn't know the Guardians had him. But, yes, that was my reason, the spark that sent me down this path. The event that brought me to Nero." I looked around at the others seated at this table. "The event that eventually brought us all together. Here, where we are united, joined by the bonds of friendship, connected by a common purpose: a desire to protect, to be the true champions of the people, just as the Legion is supposed to be. The Legion has lost its way over the years, but we have the chance now to make it all right. To be not only the champions of Earth, but of all worlds. To be the ones who protect those who cannot protect themselves. To be the champions who hold off the monsters, demons, and even gods who threaten the people. But we can only succeed if we work together."

Their eyes were all locked on me, as though hanging on my every word.

"She is good," Nyx commented to Ronan. "Did you feel the siren magic reverberating from every syllable, drawing us in?"

"Yes," he confirmed. "Her magic sings even better than Faris's. Or at least it will once she smooths out the rough edges."

"You know, part of this whole unity thing is not talking about your friends as though they are not there," I told them.

"Sorry," Nyx replied, and she actually looked like she meant it.

"Old habits die hard," said Ronan.

I'd never seen either of them so contrite before. It was definitely a step in the right direction, and it made me glad that I'd shared my secret about Zane. I needed allies. I meant what I'd said. I could not do this alone. I needed help to save Zane.

And Zane really did need saving. I could feel it. He was in danger. Maybe he didn't realize it just yet, but I did. I could almost see the dark storm cloud closing in on him.

None of us could do all of this alone. We needed one another. Together we were stronger than any other force in all the worlds. I only hoped it would be enough to face the many challenges that lay ahead.

CHAPTER 25

DUTY AND SACRIFICE

*T*oday was running a little backwards. After breakfast, we all went to our rooms to sleep. Not that I could sleep. After an hour of tossing and turning in my bed, I finally admitted defeat and went for a walk through the corridors to clear my head.

The odd thing was all the corridors were completely abandoned. At this hour, they should have been bustling with activity. Jace must have cleared out everyone in this wing of the New Orleans office. I bet Nyx was behind that. Maybe she thought the ward she and Ronan had cast around me would spontaneously burst at the first sign of other people. Or maybe she was more worried about my tongue than about my magic; she'd always said I was a bad influence on others.

Speaking of Nyx, voices drew me in as I passed the First Angel's study. Every Legion office had a room reserved for her.

"I'm not interested in hearing more excuses, Ronan," Nyx said, her voice sharp and impatient.

Ronan was in there too?

"Ignoring this won't make it go away," he said.

"If I listen, then will *you* go away?"

"No, I won't. I left you once before, I chose the other gods over the only person I have ever loved. And because of that, I lost you for over a hundred years. I won't make that mistake again. It is the biggest regret of my immortal life," he said. "But I refuse to believe it was wrong to try to protect you from being hurt." His voice rang with conviction. "That was not a mistake. It wasn't a decision made out of fear but out of love."

Nyx said nothing.

"I know you, Nyx," said Ronan. "I know your dedication to duty, even at your own expense. If I'd told you about Leon, you would have interrogated him, and that would have hurt you. I chose to spare you that pain."

"How magnanimous of you." Her voice snapped with bitter sarcasm. "You don't make decisions for me, Ronan."

"No, *you* don't make decisions for you. You make them for the greater good, never taking your own happiness into account. You need to look out for yourself now and again."

"That is an outrageous statement coming from a god, particularly one who sits on the gods' council. Particularly, the Lord of the Legion. You designed the Legion of Angels, Ronan. It was you who made it all about duty and personal sacrifice."

"I know, and I designed the Legion wrong." Ronan's admission dropped like a stone.

The silence dragged on.

"I can't believe you just said that," Nyx finally spoke.

"Duty over happiness." His laugh was rough, cynical. "I created the Legion around the same time that I chose the gods over the woman I love. You can be mad at me all you want for hiding Leon from you, but I just want you to know that I did it for you."

"I know." Nyx sighed. "And I'm not mad at you, Ronan. Not really. I'm mad at myself. Seeing Leon there… It reminded me of everything that led up to his defection. It was a reminder of my own failings, of how things had gone so very wrong. I lost so many angels to the demons. I should have trained them better. If I had, they wouldn't have left."

"You need to stop blaming yourself for what Leon and the other defectors did. It happened long ago. It's done. We can't change what they did, and it's not your fault. We need to focus on the soldiers we have now."

"Our soldiers now are exactly what I'm worried about, Ronan. What if history repeats itself? The demons are already preparing to make a move on the Earth again. We've seen the signs. Things are playing out just like they did the last time. The demons' incursions into this world—they're recruiting people to their cause, building an army here on Earth. It starts with humans and supernaturals, then they begin stealing soldiers from our own army. Like Pandora."

I was about to leave, my guilt over eavesdropping at last overpowering my burning curiosity, but the sound of my name made me pause.

"Leda?" Ronan said. "What about her?"

"I can't shake the feeling that the demons are going to steal her from us."

"Well, of course they will certainly try. They know her worth as well as we do. Her ability to control monsters alone makes her a tempting kidnap target."

"Not kidnap, Ronan. Steal. Leda will be Leon all over again. The demons will make her theirs."

"You had a vision."

"Yes. And in that vision, I saw Leda at the head of a demon army."

Ronan was quiet for a few moments, then he said, "That doesn't mean it will happen."

"I once had a vision of Leon in the demons' army. I thought it was a nightmare, just a fear, so I ignored it. But it came to pass."

Nero had told me there were people who possessed the power to catch glimpses of the future. He believed one of these people had sent him future visions of me the day I joined the Legion. Someone had pushed us together, someone with this rare magical gift. Could this mysterious someone be Nyx? And if so, why?

"Leda is not Leon," Ronan said. "She loves her family, friends, and the people of the Earth far too much to betray them. She would not turn to the demons' side."

"Unless she didn't feel like she was betraying them," Nyx countered. "What if she felt that by joining the demons, she was protecting everyone?"

"Why would she feel that way?"

"Your comrades on the gods' council didn't exactly put their best foot forward at the recent Legion training. She might think the world would be better off without the gods."

"That was nothing but minor squabbles and bickering, Nyx. The demons abducted and tortured Leda. I don't believe she has any delusions about them."

"I hope you're right."

"This isn't just about losing an angel or a soldier."

"As we both know, Leda is more than just an angel or a soldier."

"This is about losing a friend," Ronan continued. "You care about her."

"I can't afford to care about my angels. Not like that. Not after what happened last time."

"So you've closed yourself off."

"That's just how it has to be. You, of all people, should understand that."

"I am not most people, Nyx. And I'm not one of your angels. You don't have to close yourself off to me."

"I'm not closing myself off."

"You don't think that I've felt it, the way you've been since you awoke? You are keeping yourself locked away from everyone. You are here, and yet you're not really here. Not even with me. You're holding back from me."

"I am doing no such thing."

"The whole no-lying thing goes both ways, Nyx. You are holding back from me. The least you could do is admit it."

"I…" Nyx sighed. "You're right. I am holding back. But it's easier this way."

"Easier but not better. Since when did the First Angel ever settle for ease at the expense of excellence. Or are you no longer the demigod who marched into Faris's training session as a young woman and fought tooth and nail to beat everyone there, to make it to the top? Because that is the Nyx I admire. That is the Nyx I fell in love with."

"I still am that Nyx."

"My Nyx?"

"Always," Nyx said, her voice for the first time unsteady.

I heard many small objects crash to the floor…and then kissing. Clothing tore. Something hard and heavy slammed against the wall. A moan shook the walls.

Wow, that had certainly escalated quickly.

I left just as quickly, hurrying back to my room. I'd already eavesdropped outside Nyx's office for too long. I'd just been so curious about what they had to say about me —and eager to gain any insight into the person Nyx was. I'd always admired and feared her, but now for the first time I thought I actually understood her. Everything she did was to protect her Legion, her soldiers. She was a mother dragon, and like a mother dragon, she feared losing her babies. She would do anything to hold on to us.

And that vision Nyx had seen of me at the front of a demon army... Ronan was right. It couldn't be real. It just couldn't be. I'd never join the demons.

My heart racing, I threw open my door and ran inside. I nearly slammed face-first into Athan. The telepath was standing in the middle of my room, and from the look on his face, he'd obviously been waiting for me.

"You're unsettled," Athan commented, ever cool and collected. Some would even call him dispassionate.

"I'm fine."

"While I can't read your thoughts, your body language tells me that's not true."

"My body language is just fine, thank you very—" I stopped. "Wait, you can't read my thoughts? How is that even possible? You're like the most powerful telepath in all the worlds."

"*One* of the most. Not *the* most," he said. "And you are an angel slowly blossoming into a deity. Your magic has grown significantly since we last spoke."

"Yeah, that's kind of the effect you'd expect from the double doses of Nectar and Venom that you gave me. I'm lucky that magic boost didn't kill me."

He gave his hand an easy, dismissive wave. "You were never in any danger of that."

I was pretty sure he believed it. He'd known what I was when he'd spiked my drink with Nectar and Venom, and he knew a lot about the nature of magic.

"I have the Fever," I said.

"Yes, I'd noticed."

Yeah, he must have been feeling the telepathic bursts of emotion pulsing out of me.

"No female angel has had the Fever so soon after her transformation. So why me?" I asked.

"These are uncharted waters, you understand, so I can't be entirely sure. But I'd imagine it's because Nectar and Venom are not a poison to your body. They merely help you realize what you truly are inside, what you were born to be. So instead of overloading your body, making it a barren wasteland of poison, the Nectar and Venom made you a fertile field. It made you blossom, not wither."

I frowned at the analogy.

"The Fever suits you," he told me. "You are glowing."

"Yes, my halo is glowing. I know. Woohoo." I swirled my finger around in an unenthusiastic circle. "So how do I make it stop?"

"Make it stop? Why would you wish to do that?"

"Because my Fever is affecting all the gods, angels, and Legion soldiers within a few hundred miles of me, making them go wild with emotion. Nyx and Ronan are having a hard time warding me so my emotions don't bleed off to others."

In fact, I was wondering if the ward was already splitting, if my rather raunchy state of being had affected Nyx and Ronan. Maybe my magic had been responsible for their sexy encounter in her office.

"Oh, you're affecting other people. Yes, I can see how that might be a problem."

Athan said it like it had only just occurred to him that my Fever might be affecting others. For a telepath who could read almost anyone's mind, he sure was sometimes oblivious to the other people around him.

"Yes, it's a problem," I said. "One I was hoping you could solve for me."

"How could I possibly help?"

"You're a telepath. I am broadcasting these emotions telepathically. Maybe you could block them from reaching others or something. As a powerful telepath, you should be able to cast the telepathic ward better than anyone else."

"You flatter me, Leda, but no, I can't help you."

"Can't or won't?"

Maybe my plight amused him.

"Can't," he replied. "I can read thoughts, but I can't cast wards or do any of those flashy spells. If I could, I wouldn't have needed you to rescue my sister, now would I?"

Oh, right. He possessed no offensive magic, just like his sister. Damn it.

"What are you doing here anyway?" I asked him.

"I am here to thank you for saving my sister, and to show you I'm sorry for manipulating you into doing it."

"You could have sent me a thank-you card. Or a sorry-I-screwed-up box of chocolates. Why come all the way here?"

"Because I've come to properly repay the favor. I don't consider cards or chocolates to be fair payment for my sister's life. I'm going to give you something far more valuable: answers. I'm going to help you figure out why Colonel Battleborn was seen selling Nectar and research notes on Meda's monster manipulations to a black market enterprise."

"It was a shapeshifter using Colonel Battleborn's face, undoubtedly," I said.

"Undoubtedly."

Wow, repeating after me. That was helpful.

"So are you going to tell me the answer, or are you going to make me jump through hoops for a few hours first?" I asked him.

I was placing my bets on the latter. Like the gods, the Everlasting enjoyed playing games.

"I don't know the answer to this mystery."

"You don't?" I said, surprised.

"I'm telepathic, not all-knowing, Leda. I don't know who is impersonating the dead angel, but I do know someone who knows more about magical artifacts, potions, and poisons than anyone."

"Who?"

"A magic smith named Arina. She possesses the ability to craft artifacts as powerful as immortal artifacts, yet she does not require an immortal soul to make them."

"That's possible?"

"I didn't think so, but apparently Arina has figured it out. She's a singularly gifted individual."

"And let me guess. She lives on another world far from here."

"She once lived on another world," he told me. "Currently, however, she lives in New Orleans."

"Right here in this city?"

It seemed fortune didn't just favor the brave; she favored the Angel of Chaos.

"Yes, she isn't far away," said Athan. "Come with me. I'm going to introduce you to her now."

Why did I feel like one of those children in the old fairy tales as the mysterious stranger led her to her doom?

"It can't be that easy."

"Who ever said it would be easy?" Athan said, a smile on his lips.

CHAPTER 26

THE LAST PHOENIX

*A*than, Angel, and I walked down the street, a box full of broken monster collar pieces in my hands. A clamor of blenders, coffee machines, and frying pans broke the early morning stillness, heralding in the new day. I inhaled, drawing in the spicy-sweet scent of cinnamon-swirled pancakes and French toast. My tummy rumbled in hollow protest. I was hungry. Again. My magic-charged body burned through food like the Legion's trucks guzzled fuel.

"What can you tell me about visions of the future?" I asked Athan.

"There's a particular vision that has you worried."

Gods, demons, and other immortals rarely asked questions. They made statements.

"Before Nero and I had ever met, Nero dreamt of me," I said. "And of our daughter."

"Fascinating."

"And Nyx dreamt of me leading a demon army. She had the same dream of Leon, the First Betrayer, centuries ago. Is any of it real?"

He braided his fingers together. "How should I know?"

"Aren't future visions part of the same branch of magic as telepathy?"

"Well, yes. Kind of. But the art of vision-seeing is a highly-specialized practice. Only some telepaths can do it."

"And you aren't one of them?"

"No, I am not," he said. "The power to go into a state that welcomes in the visions—a sort of dream state—is a very rare ability. And even for those who possess this ability, the vision is rarely concrete or coherent. You see, future visions are echoes of magic, rippling down the fabric of time. And sometimes someone with the gift manages to catch a future fragment as it passes by."

"Are the future visions real?"

"Yes. And no."

"Meaning?"

"Like I said, the visions are magic echoes. You don't know how many times they've bounced off things, how distorted they are, by the time they reach you. And then your mind has to interpret them. It's like trying to put together a puzzle without having all the pieces. Your mind naturally fills in holes with your own fears and dreams."

"So what we think is a future vision could be a complete distortion. When Nyx thinks she sees me, it might be someone else entirely leading that army. She just fears she will lose me to the demons, so her fears warp that vision."

"That is one possibility," he said. "Perhaps, you are leading a Legion army. Or there is no army. You might just be dancing at a party. Everything the First Angel saw could be true, or nothing of it might be."

Like a bunch of warped fears hanging on a skeleton image.

"And what about Nero's vision of me and our daughter?" I asked. "When he had the dream, he'd not yet met me, so his mind couldn't have filled in my image."

"That is indeed a very specific vision. There are two possibilities I see. Either it is a rare true future vision that made it to him intact. Or it is not a future vision at all, and someone projected those images to him as he slept. Given the timing of his having the vision right before he met you, I am tending toward the latter."

"That's what we thought, that someone sent Nero the vision. Someone wanted him to take an interest in me."

"Be careful, Leda," Athan warned me. "Just because the vision wasn't from the future, that doesn't mean it isn't your future."

I frowned. "I don't understand."

"Someone could have sent Nero that vision in order to make it your reality, to make it come true."

"And because Nero saw me in a vision, he thought I was important. Therefore, he took an interest in me."

"Thereby making you a part of his future."

I rubbed my head. "This whole thing is so messed up."

"The future usually is."

But who would send Nero visions of me? Who wanted him to meet me? I was back to the same old questions Nero and I had been pondering for days, and we hadn't made any progress. I didn't think it was Nyx's doing. She seemed as perplexed by her visions as we were by Nero's.

"Here we are," Athan declared.

We'd stopped in front of a colossal white building that dominated an entire city block. Artistic lighting lit up its face and stone columns. It looked like a bank—no, like a museum.

"The Museum of Magic," I read off a gilded plaque.

Athan was moving again, but he didn't head for the front door. He swung around the back of the building. I followed closely behind him. We entered the museum through a back door that was, surprisingly, unlocked.

A large office awaited us beyond the door. Shelves of neatly spaced and labeled boxes covered one wall, reaching up high into the vaulted ceilings. There was enough space up there for an angel to practice flying maneuvers. For those without wings, a tall sliding ladder offered access to each level of the storage shelves.

"The museum doesn't open until noon on Sundays," said the woman behind the desk. She didn't even look up from the device she was tinkering with. The tip of her high red ponytail tickled her shoulder as she worked.

"Arina," Athan said.

The woman *did* look up now, albeit hesitantly. "Athan." Her wary eyes watched him closely, cautiously. She did not look excited to see him. "What are you doing here?"

The smile Athan gave her was so serene that it was making even me feel nervous. "Arina, this is Leda. Leda, meet Arina Phoenix."

"Phoenix? What an unusual name," I remarked.

Or was it a nickname? A nickname that denoted her powers. Athan had told me the specialist we'd be meeting came from another world. Could this woman be a phoenix like my sister Gin, a supernatural being from another world with the power to be reborn?

"Arina's people possess quite striking family names. These names do not, however, indicate their magical abilities," Athan told me. "Phoenix. Griffin. Pegasus." He arched a single brow at Arina. "Dragon."

Arina scowled at him. "Tell me why you are here, or leave. I'm not in the mood to play games today, Athan."

"They live on many worlds, connected by magic mirrors," Athan continued with the anthropology lesson, oblivious to Arina's discomfort. "Each family runs a corporation by the same name. Phoenix Magic Technologies is legendary for its magical objects of power, counting even gods and demons among their customers."

"We *were* legendary," Arina said, her voice wavering beneath the armor of her sharp words.

I waited for her to clarify, but she didn't go on.

"Phoenix Magic Technologies is no more," Athan explained. "The company was lost in a hostile takeover."

"Like someone bought them out?" Financial terminology wasn't exactly my forte.

"No, we weren't bought out," Arina said, her eyes haunted. "We were invaded by another corporation's army."

So a *literal* hostile takeover.

"That was the day the Phoenix name died. My family's company was folded into the invading company. My parents and siblings were stripped of their name. They were assigned mid-tier positions unworthy of their abilities, an insult to our esteemed heritage. But I refused to give up my name. I refused to serve those who'd betrayed us, who'd destroyed my family name. I came here to Earth, far from their influence. Far from them. I am the last Phoenix."

From the way Arina spoke, that *them* sounded like a very specific person, and whoever it was, they were obviously at the very top of her shit list. I could understand her feelings. If someone had gone after my family, I'd have held a grudge too.

Arina shot the box in my hands a suspicious look. "Whatever you want to drag me into this time, Athan, I'm not doing it."

"Oh, but it's not for me," he said. "It's for her."

Arina's eyes slid across my body, snagging on the angel emblem pinned to my jacket, that which identified me as an angel in the Legion of Angels. "No way. She smells like trouble." Her nose crinkled up.

It took a lot of guts to say no to the Legion of Angels. It made me like Arina at once.

"Actually, that smell is my lavender potpourri." I flashed her a wide smile.

Arina glared at Athan. "Why have you brought the Legion here? Why have you exposed me?"

Exposed her? What did she mean? Was she running from something other than the pain caused by the end of her family's reign?

"Are you going to arrest me?" Arina asked me, her eyes hard, unafraid. She was terrified about something—and I could tell it wasn't me—but she wasn't flinching. She wasn't rolling over.

"Arrest you?" I asked, perplexed. "For doing what?"

"For working here."

"What's wrong with working for a museum—" I stopped. "Unless this is more than a museum." I glanced down at the device on her desk. "That looks like a personal shield."

She nodded. "Yes. The shield creates a skintight magic field around a person, protecting them from physical and magical attacks," Arina told me, her eyes twinkling with the excitement of someone in their element.

"You created this device?" I asked her.

"No, I just repaired it. It's very old. It's an ancient device, crafted by the Immortal Sunfire."

The smith at Storm Castle had told me about Sunfire, the most powerful magic smith to ever live. He was supposedly the first and only person who'd ever possessed the power to create immortal weapons, by channeling the power of immortal souls.

I looked into the box again. There were three other objects: a mundane communication headset, a first aid kit, and a gun that seemed to have been modified. I picked it up, turning it over in my hands.

"It doesn't shoot typical bullets," I commented.

"No," Arina said. "I modified it to shoot capsules, each one containing a spell."

I popped out the transparent capsules. Inside one of them, a miniature lightning storm raged. Another contained an inferno spell. A tidal wave. An earthquake. A blizzard. Each capsule held an elemental spell.

"When the capsule shatters against its target, the spell expands to full size?" I asked.

"Twice the size of a typical elemental spell actually. I designed them to be quite potent," she said with well-deserved pride in her work—and well-deserved trepidation. Modifying magical weaponry like this, outside the gods' control, was pretty illegal.

I set the gun down on her desk. "Why do you need such a powerful weapon?"

"To chase off the raccoons," she said solemnly. "They keep getting into the garbage dumpsters out back."

I grinned at her. "I just hate when they do that."

Gods, it was like we were twins separated at birth. Too bad it wasn't true. I'd much rather have Arina for a twin than Faris for a father.

"So, are you going to arrest me?" Arina asked me.

I arched my brows at her. "Are you going to tell me why you *really* need these guns?"

"The museum organizes adventure tours on the Black Plains."

"Why would anyone pay to take a tour of the Black Plains? There are monsters there."

"Yeah, that's the whole point of the tour."

"People pay to see monsters," I realized.

"The museum calls them Monster Safaris, and they aren't on the official menu," Arina said. "Each 'adventurer' is equipped with a survival pack that includes a personal shield, a spell-slinging gun, a communication headset, and a first aid kit."

"For when the shield fails?"

"For when a fearless adventurer trips over a rock," she told me. "Despite all the glitz and glamor they're shrouded in, the safaris rarely venture far from the Magitech barrier. They only ever go deep enough into the wilderness to allow an adventurer to set his foot on the wall's wild side and stick out his tongue at monsters. As soon as a monster growls back, the fearless adventurers scurry back to safety." She frowned at the shield device in her hand. "It's really a waste actually. This shield is powerful enough to hold off an onslaught of hundreds of monsters before it needs to recharge. And they are using it so silly tourists can capture snapshots of themselves on the Black Plains to send back home."

I looked up at the wall of boxes. "Each of those boxes contains a survival pack?"

"Yes."

I whistled, low and long. Those were a hell of a lot of survival packs.

"Hey, were you going to eat all of these?" I indicated the box of donuts on her desk. The aromatic explosion of sugary-sweetness was making my tummy growl.

"If I eat them, I'll have to pay back the calories later at the gym." She didn't look excited by the prospect. "So, by all means, help yourself."

"Thanks." I grabbed a chocolate donut from the box. "I thought the personal shield artifact was rare. How did you find so many?"

"I only found one of them. I used it as a model to create many more of them."

Wow, she wasn't just tinkering with ancient magical artifacts; she was recreating them. Athan had said Arina could craft immortal objects without needing to use an immortal soul to do it. So what did that make her? More powerful than the legendary magic smith Sunfire, for sure.

"I'm not going to do it," she said.

"Do what?"

"Make weapons for the Legion of Angels. I don't make weapons."

"You made spell capsules for that gun," I pointed out.

"I isolated the spells' destructive force."

"Meaning?"

"Meaning the spells only work on monsters. If you shot one of the capsules at a person, the spell would just fizzle out."

"How'd you manage to do that?"

She shrugged. "I'm smart."

I snorted. "No kidding. You really are."

"And I'm not going to work for the Legion," she said again.

"I'm not asking you to."

"And you're not going to arrest me?"

"No. It's not your fault people are willing to spend money to endanger their lives. Believe me, I've seen far worse recently."

Like people bringing monsters into the city, trying to use them as guard beasts.

She frowned, her brow crinkling up in confusion. "If you're not here to recruit me or arrest me, why are you here?"

"I brought Leda here because I owe her a favor," Athan told Arina. "She's not like the other angels at the Legion."

Arina looked me over, head to toe—from my glowing hair, to my black leather uniform, all the way to the tips of my purple wings. "I can see that." Her eyes froze on the name stitched into my jacket. "Pandora?"

"That's right," I replied brightly. My angel name was even official now.

"Pandora, the Angel of Chaos." Her eyes met mine. "I know what you are."

"An angel. What gave me away?" I smirked. "It was the wings, wasn't it?"

"You're the daughter of a god and a demon."

Her words dropped like a stone crashing into a tranquil lake.

"You have god *and* demon blood. I didn't think such a thing was possible."

"How can you possibly know this?" I wondered.

"I can see it in your magic."

"Arina doesn't just have the ability to craft magic to create immortal artifacts," Athan told me. "She can also sense the flavor and flow of magic, how it's composed, how it's blended together. Her ability to see the anatomy of magic helps her manipulate it."

I turned to Arina. "You must be the most powerful person in all the worlds."

"Or the least powerful," she said. "Because while I can manipulate magic, I cannot make it. Besides my ability to shape magic that's already there, I have no magic of my own. To create a new artifact, I need to take magic from someone else or something else."

"What could you make with my magic?" I asked her, curiosity getting the better of me.

"Something with enough destructive power to destroy this world." She shuddered. "But I won't do it. I won't make any weapons for you."

"I told you, I don't want any weapons from you. I'm already basically a living weapon."

"Yes, you were created with purpose." She looked at me like she could see through me to all the parts and pieces that made me what I was. "It was a rather heavy-handed job." Her hand captured a strand of my glowing hair, rubbing it between her fingers. "Your parents might have exercised a bit more subtlety when creating you."

"Yeah, well, since when were deities ever subtle?" I said, laughing to cover my unease at being referred to like an object of power.

"I don't know what scheme your parents were concocting when they created you, but I am not getting involved. I will not risk exposure."

There was that word again: exposure. What was she running from?

"Might I remind you, Arina, that you still owe me a favor," said Athan.

"How is it that every time I pay off a favor to you, I seem to accumulate two more?" she demanded.

He folded his hands together, his face perfectly serene. "One of the universe's great mysteries, I'm sure."

Her mouth drew into a hard, tight line. "I always suspected the universe was in your back pocket, Everlasting."

"So, let me get this straight," I said to Athan. "She owes you a favor. And you owe me a favor."

He nodded. "Indeed."

"For someone from a people of non-interferers, you sure interfere a lot in others' affairs."

With a smile, Athan bowed his head, then excused himself to the waiting lounge, where he immediately dove into a crossword puzzle printed in the newspaper. Angel sprang up onto Arina's desk and immediately made herself comfortable inside the survival kit box.

Arina considered my kitten closely. "I haven't tested my devices' resilience to cat hair."

"If the shield can hold off a hundred monsters, it can handle a little cat hair."

"I'm not so sure. From my experiences feeding my neighbor's cat, I've discovered that cat hair gets into *everything*."

"Maybe so, but she's so adorable." I looked fondly upon my purring kitten. "So, remember the 'worse things' I mentioned seeing recently?" I set the box of collar parts down on a free corner of her desk. "This is it. Some people imported monsters into New York City. They brought them into other cities as well."

A worry line formed between her eyes. "Here?"

"Not that I know of, but if we don't put an end to this operation, it's only a matter of time before it happens in all the Earth's cities, including New Orleans. The company that sells the tech has people convinced these collars can control the monsters."

Arina was already looking through the collar fragments. "From the state of these devices, I take it the 'complete control' is a bit less than complete."

"That's what we're trying to determine. Do the collars

277

simply not work? Or do they actually work, and their makers purposely turned the monsters on their owners?"

The door to one of the back rooms opened, and two children stepped into Arina's office. Somewhere around eight years old, the raven-haired girl and boy were dressed in bathrobes. Their hair was still wet. They must have just recently stepped out of the shower—or, I thought, noticing their brightly-colored flip-flops, the swimming pool.

"Mommy, I finished my weekend homework," the girl said. Her cute voice was soft and high-pitched. She sounded just like a cartoon fairytale princess. "May I color now?" Her manners were perfect, every element of her body language spot-on. This was a girl who could convince a sugar addict to give her his lollipop—and be totally happy with the decision.

Arina smiled at her. "Of course, Kalani."

The little girl carried her coloring book into the waiting room. My mouth nearly dropped as I watched her casually drop down into splits. My jaw inched lower when she pushed a stack of cushions under her front leg, stretching her splits beyond one-hundred-eighty degrees. She balanced her coloring book on her shin and began filling in a page.

I'd seen a lot of things at the Legion of Angels, but I'd never witnessed such a spectacular display of inhuman flexibility. And it was pulled off by an eight-year-old. Angel was apparently equally impressed with the girl. She hopped off the desk and joined Kalani in the waiting room.

Feeling suddenly terribly inflexible, I made a mental note to work more stretches into my exercise routines.

"And you, Cassian?" Arina asked the boy. "Did you finish your homework too?"

"Why do I have to learn about history?" he grumbled.

"It's all about people who aren't even alive anymore. This stuff is so boring and worthless. There's no way I'm ever going to use it when I'm an adult."

"Sure you will," Arina told him.

"Oh, really?" he countered, a roguish grin lighting up his face. "Give me one practical use for any of this."

"When you need to help your kids with their homework," Arina told him, her grin equally roguish.

I laughed.

"You're always such a smartypants, Mommy," Cassian told her.

She looked upon him fondly. "Well, where do you think you get it from?"

I really liked Arina. I was particularly fond of her sense of humor—and her doughnuts. I'd already eaten four of them, and I was still hungry.

"Let your mother work, Cassian," Athan called out to him. "I'll help you with your history homework."

Cassian went into the waiting lounge and sat down beside him. As an Everlasting, an immortal, I'd imagine Athan knew a thing or two about history.

"Is there anything you can tell me about how these work?" I asked Arina, directing her attention back to the broken collar pieces.

"There's not much left of them."

"Yeah, they kind of self-destructed."

"Self-destructed? It sounds like someone didn't want you to get your hands on them."

"So it would seem," I agreed.

Arina took a closer look at one of the larger pieces through her magnifying eyepiece. "This is my work," she said in obvious surprise.

"You made these collars?"

"No, not these exact collars, but they are based on my designs. Damn copycats, copying my work." She ground her teeth together. "The collar was one of the designs I was working on the day House Phoenix fell, the day our headquarters was seized by enemy troops."

"It looks like the family that took over your company sold your designs on the black market."

"House Dragon, the family that took over mine, did not lead the charge. They have many skilled warriors, but they prefer to pay others to do the grunt work. They hired House Leviathan to provide the troops. When the alarm sounded that we were being invaded, I destroyed all my designs. I didn't want them to get a single one of my inventions, so I blew up my lab—and all my prototypes." She frowned. "They must have salvaged one of the collars from the wreckage and sold it to the highest bidder. House Leviathan is a mercenary house. They don't create anything themselves. They don't strive to make the universe a better place." Her words dripped with disdain. "They're the wrecking ball you hire to unleash on your enemies."

As she spoke, she put the broken collar pieces back together. She moved quickly and flawlessly, like she could see immediately how the pieces fit together, without even thinking about it. Her spatial reasoning must have been off the charts. She'd make a great jigsaw puzzle partner.

"Any chance you can ask House Leviathan who they sold your collar prototype to?" I asked.

"No. Firstly, House Dragon would have specified in their contract that they claim any and all spoils of war. Breaking contracts isn't good for future business, and so House Leviathan would never admit that they'd pocketed anything. No one wants to hire mercenaries who skim off the top."

"Is there a 'secondly'?"

She took a deep breath. "Secondly, no one knows where I am, including my own family. And I intend to keep it that way."

"Why doesn't your family know where you are?"

"It's the way it has to be." She looked resigned, but hardly happy about it. "It's the only way to keep them safe —and me and my kids safe too."

"You're running from the people who did this to your family," I realized. "What would House Dragon do to you if they learned where you are? Would they kill you?"

"No, they'd do something far worse."

That was all she said, leaving me to wonder. Athan had said Arina was the most powerful smith in all the worlds, her skill unparalleled. Based on what she'd told me about these corporate magic houses, if they found out where she was, they'd find some way to force her to work for them. And so would the gods and demons if they found out about her abilities, I reminded myself. I had no intention of letting any of that happen.

"There has to be some way to figure out who bought your original collar from House Leviathan," I said. "If only it were an immortal artifact, then we could lift the memories from it."

"You seem to know a lot about immortal artifacts."

"I've had a lot of recent experience with them."

"Well, you're right. Unlike my original collar, none of these copycat collars are immortal artifacts, so none of them possess the power to store memories. And even if they had, the magic binding each collar together is shattered. There would be no memories left to lift from any of them." She indicated a metallic point protruding from one of the pieces. "This looks like part of an injection needle."

"You can insert a potion pack into each collar," I told her. "The collar injects the potion into the monster as needed, supposedly assisting in maintaining control over the beast."

"There's a residue here on the needle fragment." Arina set the magnifying glass in front of the piece. "Dragon root. Fire lily. A few other herbs." She looked up at me. "And Life."

"Life, as in the light and dark magic potion?"

"Yes."

"Meda's experiments."

She gave me a curious look.

"The Goddess of Witchcraft has been experimenting on controlling monsters," I explained. "She gave them a potion, and Life was one of the ingredients. She got the Life potion…from the Guardians." It hit me like a sheet of hard granite to the face. "The Guardians are behind these monster control collars. They stole Meda's research. They bought your collar from House Leviathan. And they are using the collars on monsters to control them."

The question was why. What were the Guardians trying to accomplish?

CHAPTER 27

IMMORTAL BLOOD

*A*rina held up the collar she'd reconstructed from fragments in mere minutes. "The Guardians made this collar all right. Look at the lines, the design. It might as well have their signature all over it."

I didn't know anything about the Guardians' designs, but I trusted that a master magic smith like Arina did. While her words were further confirmation that the Guardians had indeed made these collars, I was not any closer to understanding why they'd done it.

The door to the outside opened. Nero stood in the doorway, his caramel hair rustling dramatically in the wind, his leather-bound form lit up in an angelic halo.

"I've been looking for you."

"Well, here I am," I replied, smiling.

"How did you slip past your chaperones?"

"Athan distracted them by projecting the images of phantom spirits into their minds."

"Nyx will not be pleased by their lack of discipline."

I shrugged. "That's not my problem. Or yours. They are Jace's soldiers."

"I am obliged to report this to Nyx."

I couldn't fight the smirk tugging on my mouth. "Are you going to report me too?"

He stepped inside, and the door slammed shut behind him. "Eventually."

I stepped toward him. "Eventually?" I looped my arms over his shoulders.

He shot me a look that curled my toes.

"Unfortunately, we currently have an audience," I sighed.

Cassian peeked out of the waiting room. "You're an angel?" he asked Nero.

"Yes."

"Prove it."

Magic flashed, and Nero's dark wings unfolded from his back, stretching out behind him, larger than life.

"Wicked." The boy's eyes grew wider as they panned over Nero's wings, following the patterns of black, blue, and green feathers. "What would happen if I set your wings on fire, like if I shot a fireball at them? Would the feathers burn?"

His sister had joined him in the open doorway to the lounge. "Set them on fire?" She sounded horrified. "Why would you do such a thing? Why would you want to ruin such pretty wings?"

"There is little danger of that," Nero told the girl. "I am pretty much fireproof."

"Doubly wicked," said Cassian.

"Do not hurl fireballs indoors," Arina warned her son.

He frowned. "You never let me do anything fun."

"It is *not* fun to electrocute my goldfish," Kalani chimed in, her voice wobbling. The incident she was referring to obviously still stung.

"Sure it is. The fish had a great time." He shrugged. "Once they woke up."

Kalani's eyes trembled, as though she were reliving the experience. "They were *traumatized*."

"No, they weren't."

"You don't even know what traumatized means."

He stood up taller. "I do so."

"Then tell us." She smiled. "We're all listening."

"It means…" Cassian frowned. "Well, it means something really bad!"

Kalani giggled.

"You're just so…perfect," he said with obvious disgust. "All the time. And you're doing it on purpose, just to make me look bad."

"You don't need my help to look bad."

He growled, his fists clenching up. Fire burst up on his hands.

"Mommy! Cassian is trying to set me on fire!"

"Don't set your sister on fire," Arina said calmly. She didn't even look up from the collar she was examining.

"Why not?"

"Because if you waste all your magic hurting your family, you won't have any left when an actual enemy comes along."

Gods, the woman was positively brilliant.

"I have more than enough magic," Cassian declared.

The fire went out on his hands, but it continued to burn in his eyes as he glared at his sister. Kalani lowered into splits on the cushion pile again, the other leg in front this time. As she took up her coloring once more, Nero coaxed Cassian to return to his homework. The fact that the spirited boy complied wasn't half as surprising as my realization that Nero was really good with kids. All of a sudden, I recalled his words months ago back at the Party at the Wall, Purgatory's annual festival. He'd confessed that he wanted children someday.

I brushed off the memory. Honestly, given my current *feverish* situation, it kind of scared me shitless.

"Can you tell me more about how the collars work?" I asked Arina.

She hesitated.

"What is it?"

"I don't want to get involved in this," she said. "I can't afford to go up against the Guardians. They 'rescue' people with rare and unusual magic." She glanced at her kids. "I won't draw their attention to Cassian and Kalani. My kids don't need their kind of rescue."

"What kind of magic do your children have?" I asked her. Cassian obviously had some fire magic, but there had to be more to it. Elemental magic wasn't all that uncommon.

"The rare and unusual kind." That was all she said, and I could tell she had no intention of clarifying further.

"Why do the Guardians rescue people?" I asked her.

"I don't know what they're planning, but it's nothing good," Arina replied. "Their sordid past is littered with the skeletons of their betrayals."

"Betrayals? What betrayals?"

She watched me closely. "You don't know anything about the Guardians, do you?"

"No. That's why I'm asking you. Because you seem to know all about them."

"I know enough to steer clear of them," she said. "In the days of the ancient Immortals, the Guardians were the keepers of the Immortals' potions and caretakers of their armory of weapons. Hence the name Guardians. But they betrayed their masters, and it was that betrayal that led to the Immortals' demise."

"How? What did they do?"

Arina shook her head. "I don't know. I only know that they are bad news."

So I'd been right to be worried for my brother Zane, currently one of their 'guests'. Something about the Guardians had never sat right with me.

Nero closed in by my side. "You can't stay out of it," Nero told Arina. "None of us can. What's going on here between gods, demons, and the Guardians affects everyone on Earth, and on all the other worlds too."

"It's certainly affected you." Arina looked at him, her eyes narrowing.

I recognized the gleam in her eyes. It was the same way she'd looked at me before she'd declared me to be the daughter of a god and a demon. She was reading his magic as she had mine.

"In fact, what's going on between gods, demons, and the Guardians has shaped your entire existence," she told Nero. "It's the reason you were born."

Nero must have been bursting with questions, but he hid his curiosity well. I wasn't nearly as practiced as he was.

"What do you mean?" I asked Arina.

"From our recent conversation, I trust you know of the power of the Spymaster's Opera Glasses."

Of course I did. Those glasses had played a major part in the Legion trials recently, in revealing the gods' secrets.

"The glasses are an immortal artifact," I said. "They possess the power to lift memories off immortal artifacts, deities, and angels."

"Like future visions, echoes from the past also ripple across the fabric of magic. Since they have already

happened, the past visions are clear, solid, and unchange-
able. All the memories—your past, everything that
happened to make you who and what you are—are a part
of you. Those past events are woven into your magic.

"The Spymaster's Opera Glasses were crafted with lenses
that can lift those memories from the past, to uncover what
happened to the person who experienced them. But with a
few minor tweaks, the glasses could be modified to see
more. They could read memories that go back even further.
Your parents' memories, the memories of their parents…all
the way back to the beginning of your bloodline. Because
those memories are a part of your magic, of your soul. And
if they are potent enough, integral enough to the history of
your existence, they can be read off your magic.

"There are such memories in your magic," Arina told
Nero. "Memories crucial to understanding the true nature
of this immortal war."

"So if we brought you the Spymaster's Opera Glasses,
you could make the modifications required to read these
memories?" Nero asked.

"I could, but it's unnecessary." The corner of her mouth
curled up. "I can read magic. That means that, like the
glasses, I can also see the memories that form a person's
existence."

"And what do you see when you read my magic?"

"The Guardians watched your parents throughout their
Legion careers. They arranged for them to meet. They set
the scene so your parents would fall in love—and so that
you would be born."

I chewed that over. "Wait, so the Guardians are responsible for Nero being born? But why? What do they want
with him?"

"Unclear." Arina frowned. "But it has something to do with his magic. Have you ever wondered why Cadence Lightbringer and Damiel Dragonsire are the only two angels to have ever had a child together? The answer is in their blood. Their Immortal blood."

She said Immortal with a capital I, as in the original Immortals.

"Your parents have Immortal blood," she told Nero. "And, therefore, so do you."

"That's how two angels could be compatible. That's how they could have a child. It's the balancing effect of Immortal blood, of light and dark magic," I realized.

The next realization hit me harder. I looked at Nero. "This was what Faris meant by you being neck-deep in this all."

"Faris knows," Nero said darkly. "He knows I was born because of the Guardians' machinations. He knows that I have Immortal blood."

"For your information, the effect Nero's Immortal blood has on you is the same as Nectar and Venom, Leda. That's the reason you get drunk on his blood. That priest you drank from had Immortal blood too, albeit far more diluted than Nero's."

"Priest?" Nero asked me, his expression distinctly blank.

Damn it. When Arina had said she could read our past in our magic, she hadn't been kidding.

"It was part of the gods' challenges. Colonel Fireswift and I had to drink from one of Zarion's priests to gain entry into the temple. I assure you, he didn't taste even half as good as you, honey."

You could have bounced bullets off his hard face.

"He didn't taste even a hundredth—no, a millionth—as good as you," I amended quickly.

He folded his arms over his chest, looking somewhat appeased. "I take it my origin is the reason Leda and I are compatible?" he asked Arina.

"Yes, both light and dark reside in your blood as well as in hers." She looked at me. "Nectar and Venom have activated your light and dark magic." She turned back to Nero. "But your body is drowning in Nectar, a power so blinding that it's masking out the dark. To gain access to your dark magic, to realize your Immortal heritage, you will need the Immortal Life potion. It contains a balancing magic present in neither Nectar nor Venom."

"Life, the potion the Guardians use on the people it 'rescues'?" I wondered.

"Yes," she confirmed. "Like everything else they now possess, the Life potion was stolen from the Immortals."

"And if I take this potion, my dark magic will grow to match my light magic?" Nero asked her.

"Indeed, but getting it is an impossible challenge. Nowadays, only the Guardians know how to make the Immortal Life potion, and their Sanctuary is hidden away by ancient spells even the two of you can't break."

I smiled. "We live to defy impossible challenges."

"You're going to try to get to the Sanctuary, aren't you?" Arina looked incredulous. "Are you mad? Haven't you been listening to anything I've said? The Guardians brought about the end of the ancient Immortals, the originators of magic as we know it. If you go up against them, that will be the end of you too."

"Be positive, Arina." I turned away from her expression of utter disbelief. "Nero, in my dreams of your mother, the Guardians were giving her the Life potion, trying to build up her dark powers to put her magic in balance. And now they're building control collars based on designs stolen from Arina. They combined those collars with Meda's research on monsters."

"Controlling the monsters of Earth is clearly only the first step in the Guardians' plan," said Nero.

"But what is their plan? What are they trying to do? What do they want?" I tried to work it out. "Well, we know one thing they want. They want me dead. They tried to poison me. But why?"

"Because they cannot control you," Nero replied. "Whatever they're planning, they've obviously been planning it for a very long time. You are the wild variable they didn't plan for, the chaotic element they didn't predict in their equations."

But what was the Guardians' equation? What were they plotting? The answers weren't forthcoming, so I turned to a question that Arina might be able to answer.

"How do we stop the collars' influence?" I asked her.

"Use your magic to overpower the collars, to put the beasts under your spell."

"I tried that already. The result was the beasts blew up."

"You only need to be stronger than the collars, to overpower them completely and all at once so they don't overload and blow up. That's how you avoid the collars' self-destruct failsafe."

"Oh, is that all?" I laughed, my voice cracking with sarcasm.

"Your magic is up to the task," she replied. "When your mind is ready too, that is the moment you will succeed."

———

NERO AND I LEFT THE MUSEUM, PARTING WAYS WITH Arina and Athan.

"Nyx is afraid of losing her Legion soldiers to the demons, especially me," I told him as we walked back toward the Legion office.

"Nyx admitted this to you?"

"Well, not exactly. I kind of overheard her talking to Ronan about it."

His brows arched. "Eavesdropping, Pandora?"

"Not intentionally. I couldn't sleep, so I was getting some air. I didn't know the discussion would get all deep and vulnerable."

"You'd best hope Nyx doesn't ever find out that you eavesdropped on her admitting weakness."

"There was more."

"Oh?"

"I kind of caught the start of her and Ronan getting busy in her office. I ran off real fast when that started, but let's just say they didn't waste any time getting down to business."

It had all happened in a split second. One moment, they were just talking. And the next, tabletop ornaments were crashing and fabric splitting.

Nero was laughing.

"It's not funny." I frowned at him. "It's not my fault they suddenly went from arguing to having sex."

"Actually, it is *entirely* your fault," he said, amused. "As your magic peaks, your emotions do as well—enough, apparently, to overwhelm the formidable First Angel and the God of Earth's Army."

I opened my mouth to argue, to deny that it was my fault, but I popped it shut again immediately. Nero was right. I could feel my magic pulsing out, my emotions pounding. As I approached my Peak, my emotions weren't so much dominated by anger or fear or rage; they were settling decidedly in the lust category.

Nero brushed his hand down my face. "The urges pulsing out from you are very distracting."

I smiled coyly, trembling as his hands settled on my hips. I set my hand over his chest. My pulse seemed to beat in time to his heart. His mouth dipped lower, tracing the throbbing vein down my neck.

"Nero," I gasped.

My spine arched, my breasts hitting the hard wall of his chest, my pelvis rocking against his. I was no stranger to lust when it came to Nero, but I'd never before needed him so desperately. I felt like I was missing a part of myself, a part I'd only reclaim by joining with him, when my body merged with his, melting into each other.

My hands were at his belt. Suddenly, it wasn't so hard to imagine how quickly Nyx and Ronan had shifted gears. I couldn't get Nero inside of me fast enough.

"Put your hands up and stand away from each other!" a voice echoed off the building fronts.

I looked past Nero, to the army that had us surrounded. I dropped my hands from Nero's belt. His arms were folded around me protectively. His wings were folded around me too.

"She's mine." His voice hissed, hard and possessive.

"Step away from her, General," Nyx said coldly, her gun aimed directly at his head. "You are both under arrest for conspiracy against the Legion."

CHAPTER 28

CHOICES

It turned out that 'conspiracy against the Legion' were just some fancy words for our out-of-control libidos. We'd been caught red-handed getting frisky with each other before my magic peaked. I felt like a teenager caught making out in a parked car, except instead of the local sheriff tapping on my window, thirty highly-trained soldiers in the gods' army had their guns aimed at our heads.

All in all, it could have been much worse. Thankfully, Nyx didn't say anything about my overhearing her conversation with Ronan—or the sex afterwards. I hoped she'd been so caught up in the heat of the moment that she hadn't noticed me.

Nero and I were in timeout. We spent the entire flight back to the Purgatory office in separate compartments at opposite ends of the airship. This engagement was starting to get annoying. I'd much rather be doing shots with my girlfriends at the bar of the Witch's Watering Hole, while donning a pink feather tiara and a t-shirt that read 'bride-to-be'.

The moment we reached Purgatory, I was escorted to my room.

I'd now been confined there for the past five hours. My windows were barred, and guards had been posted outside my door. I was a prisoner in my own office, in the territory I was supposed to command.

Thankfully, there was now only one day left until the wedding. The thought was, at the same time, a relief and a source of paralyzing panic.

I was looking forward to shedding my chaperones. Nero and I could finally be alone, just the two of us.

But my panic was spiked by the whirlwind speed at which this was all happening. The point of this union was for me and Nero to have children.

Children. I couldn't bring children into this mad universe. Not with the gods and demons and their abominable Immortal War. Not with the Guardians trying to kill me because I didn't fit into their plans. I had no doubt that they'd try to kill any child Nero and I had together too. I wasn't sure I could protect a child. I hadn't even been able to protect my kitten. They'd poisoned Angel. It was only by sheer luck that she had survived.

The attack on Angel was an undeniable reminder that the Guardians could get to us, no matter how powerful we thought we were, no matter how safe we thought we were.

As my mind raced with terrible possibilities, I pet Angel and tried to remain calm. But even stroking her soft fur didn't calm me like it usually did.

"Moping doesn't suit you, daughter."

I jumped at the sound of Faris's voice. He was suddenly there, standing in the middle of my living room. I really hated when he popped in like that. And so, apparently, did

Angel. She jumped up and hissed at him, her back arched, her fur standing on end.

Faris regarded her coolly. "What a disagreeable animal."

"Don't you have better things to do?" I said grumpily. "I didn't expect you'd leave home until your month of subjecting Zarion and Stash to hard training was over."

"They are asleep. Torturing someone who's unconscious is considerably less enjoyable than torturing someone who is awake."

"You allowed them sleep? How magnanimous of you."

"A momentary relief from pain makes the next onset of agony that much worse."

Trust Faris to use a nap as a form of torture.

"If you kill Stash, I'm coming for you," I warned him.

"Your friend is a demigod." Faris sounded utterly unconcerned by both my threat and my friend's life. "He will not be irrevocably damaged."

"Irrevocably damaged?" I repeated in annoyance. "Stash is a person, not a toaster oven."

"Gods are not people. Neither are angels or demigods." He smiled at me. "Or more unusual deities, for that matter."

Unusual like me.

"So I'm not a person now?" I demanded, my voice growing louder despite my best efforts. Faris really excelled at getting my heckles up.

"Of course you're not a person. Nor have you ever been."

"Conversations with you make my head hurt."

"I've heard the same said about you," he replied.

"Don't."

His brows lifted. "Don't what?"

"Don't pretend that we have a connection. The only

reason you want me to believe we do is so you can manipulate me into doing what you want."

"And what do you know about what I want, child?"

"You want to use me as a weapon you point at anything that stands in your way. You want to conquer everything, to rule over all the universe, to have everyone on every world speak your name with reverence. You want them to worship you, for their faith and devotion to make you stronger, more powerful." I shot him a wry look. "Have I covered all the bases?"

His face was hard, his eyes humorless. "This would all be a lot easier on everyone if you just stopped fighting me and took your rightful place."

"What do you want, Faris?" I sighed. "Why have you come here?"

"Can't a father just visit his daughter?"

"No. Not you. You always have an ulterior motive, some scheme driving everything that you do."

"You will be marrying Nero Windstriker one day from now."

"If this is you fishing for an invitation—"

"A god does not need to be invited anywhere." His voice rumbled like thunder. "Any event is greatly improved by the honor of his presence."

I rolled my eyes.

"But this isn't about me," he said.

"How shocking," I muttered. "I thought everything was about you, that the universe revolved around you."

He continued, as though I hadn't spoken at all, "This is about you ignoring my warnings regarding General Windstriker."

"Unlike you, Nero isn't masterminding some grand plot to use me. He simply loves me."

"That is a naive attitude, one that does not befit a daughter of mine."

"No, it's not at all naive," I countered. "Because do you know what I did after you tried to push me and Nero apart? I talked to him. And I saw that I'd been right about him all along. Unlike you, he doesn't want to use me."

"He took an interest in you from the start. His parents, Damiel Dragonsire and Cadence Lightbringer, are of Immortal blood. And, therefore, so is he. Doubly so, in fact."

Faris watched me for my reaction. He thought to surprise me, but thanks to Arina, I already knew.

"You know," he said, frowning.

"The question is, how do *you* know?" I asked suspiciously.

"I have a lot of telepaths in my Orchestra."

"Orchestra?"

"Talented individuals who sing to me, who tell me the things others like to keep hidden," he explained.

Faris was known to collect telepaths and other special individuals. He could never find out about Gin and Tessa and their out-of-this-world rare magic, or he would try to collect my little sisters too.

"And my Orchestra has sung some troubling songs about Nero Windstriker," Faris told me.

I just shrugged. "He is the son of two angels with Immortal blood. I am the daughter of a god and a demon. It's a match made in heaven. Or hell, if you prefer," I added slyly.

"His parents were plotting something," Faris said. "*He* is plotting something."

"And what is that?" I laughed.

"His ancestors have been selectively breeding an army

to challenge the gods. And Nero went after you to bring your special blood into that mix."

"That's ridiculous," I said. "Just because that's the kind of ploy you would think up, that doesn't mean other people are that demented."

"Once again, Leda, angels are not people," he reminded me.

I growled in frustration. "Nero and his family didn't plot anything. It was the Guardians. They manipulated events and people. They wanted Nero, the person with the strongest concentration of Immortal blood since the Immortals walked these worlds, to be born. We just don't know why."

"How do you know this?" Faris said seriously. He actually looked like he believed me.

Oops. Arina had been worried I'd get her into trouble, that my investigation would expose her and her kids. No, I wasn't going to do that to her or her cute twins. So I lied through my teeth.

"Athan helped us modify the Spymaster's Opera Glasses to expose the memories of Nero's ancestors. The memories that shaped his existence are a part of his blood, of his natural magic," I told Faris.

"That is supposed to be a lost art," he said. "Trust it to the Everlasting to preserve the ancient practice. And his guilt compelled him to help you."

Faris seemed to buy my story. The best way to pull off a lie was to wrap it in a blanket of truth.

"The Guardians made the monster control collars," I added.

"That's all the ammunition I need to bring this to the gods' council."

"Bring what to the gods' council?" I asked him. "What are you going to do, Faris?"

But he was already gone. He'd vanished into thin air. I really hated when the gods did that.

His speedy departure left me worried. What was Faris going to do? What information was he bringing to the gods' council? Whatever it was, I had a sinking feeling it would stick me smack dab in the middle of the conflict between gods and gods. And between gods and demons. And now the Guardians were a part of this too.

I went to my door and opened it. The two soldiers stationed in the hallway shot me identical suspicious glares. That was the first thing I noticed. The second thing I noticed was that they weren't Legion soldiers. They were gods. From the markings on their uniforms, these godly soldiers belonged to Ronan.

"I need to see Dr. Harding," I told the soldiers.

They looked me up and down, obviously checking for weapons. Or maybe they were just checking me out. Nyx and Ronan had cast layers upon layers of wards on me, but my magic was growing stronger and more turbulent with every passing moment. The soldiers were standing so close to me that my emotions must have been bleeding off on them.

I snapped my fingers at the soldiers to get their attention. "Wake up, boys. I need to see Dr. Harding so she can perform a magic check. I feel a bit weird."

I must have said the magic words because the two soldiers motioned for me to leave my room. The Legion closely monitored female angels with the Fever to time things right. If they didn't bring me to Nerissa now, they could risk ruining everything.

As I passed in front of the soldiers, they closed in on

either side of me. They brought me to Nerissa's office, which was housed in a converted spa. It looked more like a relaxation room than a doctor's office. Not that I was complaining. I found the subtle aroma of mint in the air particularly refreshing.

"You can go now," I told the soldiers when they walked into the room with me.

They held their ground, silent and stoic. How very godly of them.

"There's no one but Dr. Harding here." I smirked at them. "And I promise not to get frisky with her."

"No?" Nerissa rose from her seat, doing her best to look disappointed. "Well, then why did I bother getting up from my chair?" She winked at me. "What can I do for you, Leda?"

"My magic feels weird. I was hoping you could test it?"

"Let's have a look." Nerissa shooed the soldiers away. "Stop hovering."

My bodyguards exchanged loaded looks, then took positions just outside the room. They must have decided I wouldn't get into trouble here. Besides the door they guarded, there was no other door in or out of here. The windows were stained glass. They weren't even openable. If I tried to smash through them and make a run for it, the whole building would hear it.

Nerissa brought me to the back of the room and sat me down on a massage table across from her desk. I didn't know how she'd managed to get that colossal piece of furniture into her office, but I had no doubt that magic had been involved.

"So your magic is feeling weird," Nerissa said.

I looked away from the water flowing down the serenity fountain behind the massage table, leaning forward to get a peek at the soldiers outside the door. "Actually, no, not really," I whispered to Nerissa. "At least, my magic isn't any weirder than it's been since I got the Fever."

"Then why are you here?" Nerissa asked me.

"I'm feeling concerned about what the Fever means."

"Yes, the prospect of days of sex can be quite daunting," Nerissa said with an amused smirk. "Especially with an archangel of Nero Windstriker's caliber. But I'm sure you'll endure it for the sake of the Legion."

I crossed my arms over my chest and pouted out my lips. "Very funny."

She grinned.

"But it's not the sex I'm worried about."

Nerissa stuck me with a syringe.

"What are you doing?"

"Just checking your magic and hormone levels," she told me.

"But I said I was fine. I only told my chaperones I was feeling weird because I needed an excuse to see you."

"Maybe so, but I need to check you out anyway as you draw closer to your Peak." She put the blood sample she'd taken from me under her magic microscope. "Keep talking. I'm listening."

"It's the 'for the sake of the Legion' part that bothers me," I said. "The Legion sees the Fever as an opportunity to breed angels, to create future soldiers, future angels."

She adjusted a few knobs on her machine. "Yes, that is the goal."

"The Guardians already tried to kill me this week. A few months ago, a demon kidnapped and tortured me. I'm constantly caught up in some kind of world-shattering danger or up to my neck in monsters. It's not a safe world

302

—or even universe—to bring a child into. So what if I'm not ready to make future angels?"

Talking to Faris had brought these dangers even closer to home. It had reminded me of the lengths he would go to in order to wield me, the living weapon that he'd created. Meeting Arina and her children had shown me how vulnerable being a parent would make me. Gods, demons, and Guardians would not hesitate to use my children to control me.

Watching Nero with Arina's children, seeing how good he was with them, had produced a very different and unexpected feeling: longing. I wanted that. Children. A family with Nero.

But not now. Not like this. Not when I'd only be bringing our children into a hazardous world. Before I had kids, I had to make the world a place where they'd be safe.

Nerissa looked up from her magic microscope. "Doesn't this issue fall more into Ivy's domain?"

Ivy was a Legion therapist. She helped talk people through their problems.

"Ivy can try to ease my concerns, but that doesn't change the danger of my reality, how my life and the lives of everyone around me are always at risk," I said. "This morning, I spoke to a woman who didn't dare get involved in saving the world because her involvement would put her kids in danger."

"I suppose that's what being a parent means: to sacrifice for your children, to keep them happy and safe," said Nerissa.

"I have already sworn to protect the people of Earth. What if it comes down to protecting my child, or protecting all the people of Earth? How can I make a choice like that?"

Nerissa shook her head slowly. "I don't have an answer to that."

"Neither do I," I told her. "Which is why I can't bring a child into this world. At least not yet. It wouldn't be fair to her."

"Her?"

"I like to think of the child as a she."

"The child you have not conceived." One side of Nerissa's mouth drew up into a crooked half-smirk. "And don't wish to."

"Not yet. Not until things are safe for her."

"But will they ever be safe?"

"I don't know. I am immortal, though, so I hope I do live to see that day, a day when I don't have to fear bringing a child into this world or any other." I frowned. "I'm not sure if I'm making any sense."

She took my hands and gave them a gentle squeeze. "I understand."

"So you'll help me?"

"In any way I can, Leda."

"Thank you." I gave her hands a return squeeze. "I was wondering if there was anything you could give me, a potion or injection or whatever."

"Birth control for angels?"

When she said it like that, it did sound weird. Angels were notoriously infertile. They never wasted a fertile cycle because they only came around every few decades at most.

I sighed. "Birth control for angels probably hasn't even been invented, has it?"

She leaned in to whisper softly in my ear. "Actually, there is a potion. It will prevent you from getting pregnant, but it won't get rid of the Fever. You'll keep the peaking magic and raging hormones. The fun part."

I gave her a pleading look.

"It will mean my death if anyone found out," she said in a hissed whisper.

I felt a sharp twinge in my heart. Nerissa was my friend. I didn't want her to die.

"Does the potion leave any traces?" I whispered to her.

"By the time it's discovered that your Fever cycle was unsuccessful, there will be no trace of the potion left in your body. But if anyone tests you in the next few days…" She looked ill.

"I swear I won't tell anyone, and I won't give them any reason to suspect me. But if you still don't want to do it, I understand. It is dangerous."

Nerissa met my eyes for a few long moments. "Screw it." She pulled a bowl off one of her shelves and began mixing things into it. "You saved my ass more times than I can count." She poured the potion into a cup and handed me the steaming concoction. "I have to warn you, Leda, this won't taste very good. In fact, it's supposed to taste like old socks."

I plugged my nose, trying to block out the stench rising up from the cup. "It certainly smells like old socks."

"Medicine rarely tastes good. Its palatability is not a top priority."

"Well, if I made medicine, taste would be *my* top priority. I'd create a collection of sensational delights. Strawberry cheesecake. Banana split. Blueberry muffin. That's medicine people would gladly take."

She chuckled.

"Mint chocolate chip. Mint chocolate chip," I repeated to myself over and over again, trying to summon the memory of that particular taste. Then I chugged down the terrible potion, hoping it wouldn't come back up again.

"All good?" Nerissa asked.

I responded with a thumbs up—and a grimace. "Thanks, Nerissa." I frowned at the empty cup that had contained the foul potion. "I think."

"In your place, I'd do the same thing," she said solemnly.

My phone buzzed in my pocket. I pulled it out and read the screen. I froze.

"What is it?" Nerissa asked me.

"Monsters are gathering on the Black Plains outside the wall, close to Purgatory." I looked up from my screen, meeting her eyes. "Beasts wearing control collars."

"Like the ones in New York?"

"Except there are a hell of a lot more of them this time."

"How many more?"

"Thousands," I said darkly.

Light flashed, and an explosion boomed outside, shaking the ground. My phone buzzed again.

I read the text—and immediately drew my sword.

"What happened?" Nerissa asked.

"The Magitech barrier is down. The monsters are swarming into Purgatory."

CHAPTER 29

CUTTING TIES

*N*ero and I ran through the dark streets of Purgatory, rushing toward the wall to intercept the invading monsters. With the Magitech barrier down, the wall was no stronger than the bricks that formed it. And bricks were no match for the monsters of the Black Plains. They'd already made a hole in the stone wall, and an unceasing river of beasts was streaming through it. The fallen barrier also meant no magical protection from the air. Winged monsters were circling over Purgatory like vultures over a rotting carcass.

There weren't yet many Legion soldiers here in Purgatory—certainly not enough to protect the town from the monsters streaming through the opening in the wall, or from the avian beasts' aerial bombardment. So I'd called for every paranormal soldier stationed here to help us protect the town. I didn't even have to call for my family; as soon as trouble broke out, they went out to meet it.

Hollering in terror, the townspeople fled from the monsters. The monsters took chase. Paws and hooves pounded the roads. Savage snarls sent the people into a state of complete, unbridled panic.

"Gin is working on getting the Magitech barrier back up," I told Nero, watching as my sister made a run for the power building.

Tessa and Damiel were keeping close by her side. Tessa's presence didn't surprise me. She and Gin had always been close, but ever since we'd escaped the demon Sonja, the two of them had been completely inseparable. They went absolutely everywhere together.

But I did wonder why Damiel had chosen to serve as Gin's bodyguard rather than jump at the stream of monsters gushing through the hole in the wall. Then again, Damiel was a thinker as much as he was a fighter. He probably realized that Gin getting the Magitech barrier back up was our best shot at saving the town. There were too many monsters for us to defeat by sheer brute force alone. We needed the power of the wall, the Magitech spell on it, to kill the flood of beasts...

I watched the flow of monsters for a moment. They definitely weren't coming in wildly or at random. Their movements were controlled and calculated.

Sure enough, each and every one of them wore a shining control collar, lit up with magic. I knew those collars well. I'd seen them on the necks of the beasts in the dark New York alley—and in broken pieces on the ground at the monster owners' villas. I'd seen Arina reassemble one from little more than shattered debris.

The control collars. Except now there weren't only just two or even two dozen of them; there were thousands of them, directing the monsters' every move.

"Controlled by those collars, the beasts are completely focused on their targets," Nero said. "We can't distract them, easily trick them into traps, or ignite their emotions. A rational mind is behind this, which is a far more formidable foe than savage, mindless beasts running purely on instinct."

Nearby, Nyx and Ronan stood back-to-back, fighting off a flock of giant green birds. They slashed and sliced with their swords as they unleashed barrage after barrage of spells. They worked as one being, one body. Every movement was perfectly synchronized, perfectly balanced with each other.

Past them, Ronan's two godly soldiers battled a pack of winged tigers. From their excited expressions, they considered facing monster armies much more fun than babysitting the Angel of Chaos. They didn't even seem to mind that they were severely outnumbered.

As Nero and I moved to help them, the Magitech barrier sizzled to life on the stone wall that separated Purgatory from the Black Plains. The monsters flying overhead dropped dead to the ground. Magic zapped the life out of any monsters within a few feet of the wall. The spell didn't reach the beasts who'd already made it deeper into the town, however. The battle was far from over.

"Gin did it," I told Nero, my nose tingling with the stench of burnt monsters. "Now it's up to us to clear away the strays."

There was a loud pop. There went the Magitech generator again. The golden barrier sizzled out.

"That didn't last long," I sighed.

Monsters streamed into the town once more.

A big blue giant pounded his fists against the wall like it was a punching bag. Splintered shards shot in every direction as the beast chiseled away at the stones.

Another giant, this one red and orange, hurled rocks

and other heavy objects at the wall. Without the magic barrier to protect it, it wasn't faring well. Monsters burst through the growing holes.

I lit up my sword with fire, cutting through the beasts, even as I tried to gain control over their minds. The control collars were making that task near impossible. At this point, I didn't even care if I triggered the collars' self-destruct mechanisms; it was preferable to the beasts destroying the town. I wasn't making any headway with overpowering the collars' influence, though. There were just too many monsters.

The battle was burning hotter with every passing moment. Alec stood beside Calli, his face lit up. The two of them seemed to be competing to see who could shoot down the most monsters.

Nerissa and Lucy were fighting out here on the battlefield—or on the rooftop, to be precise. The cauldron they had between them bubbled over, spilling out a waterfall onto the beasts on the street below. Lucy tossed exploding sleeping powders. Nerissa shot sticky goo out of a cannon at winged monsters, gluing their wings to their bodies.

Harker was there too, fighting with us. So were Drake and Ivy, Basanti and Soren. Even my cat Angel was helping out. The fierce, clever little warrior was currently helping Ivy tackle a hairy trio of wolf-sized spiders.

We had an army of elite fighters, of angels and gods. But would it be enough? There were just so many monsters, and every second the Magitech barrier remained down, the monstrous force grew larger.

The gold barrier slid over the wall, but it sizzled out before it made it even halfway. Despite Gin's best efforts, she couldn't seem to keep the magic barrier up.

"The Guardians are targeting the Magitech generators," Nero said.

"But why now?" I wondered. "Why are they attacking us after so many millennia of doing nothing? And why attack the Earth rather than another of the gods' worlds?"

"I don't know." Nero swung his sword, killing a monster that had jumped at me. "But let's live long enough to find out."

"Agreed."

The Guardians thought they could come here—to my world, my territory, my town—and destroy everything. They thought they could kill everyone under my protection. Oh, no. No way. I was not letting that happen on my watch.

The Fever surged in me, powering my magic, boosting it. My angel instincts were burning hot. I had to protect what was mine from the invading forces who would destroy it. They were trying to take this town from me. I would not stand for it.

I reached for the monsters' willpower, cutting the collars' ties, stealing control away from the force that bound the beasts. I felt them suspended inside my head, held there by my siren's song. All of them. All the monsters in town.

I hadn't thought it possible, but it was. Not only had I finally truly tapped into my angel magic, I could feel a different kind of magic deep inside of me, a well of potential waiting to be unleashed. I'd only just dipped my toe in that power, and look what I'd done. I'd seized control over all the monsters, control collars be damned.

I quickly sent the beasts rushing back onto the Black Plains as fast as they could move, far away from the town. Before…

The monsters suddenly all exploded. Apparently, my control hadn't been absolute. The collars self-destruct mechanism had kicked in. But at least the beasts had blown up outside of town, not in it.

As the Magitech barrier flared to life, Ivy walked up beside me. Her gaze panned over the town, over the dead monsters strewn across the ground. Her eyes settled on the wall, once again glowing and humming with magic.

"I can't believe it," she said. "We won."

"Of course we won." I grinned at her. "I am here."

Ivy snorted. "I hope your arrogance wears off with the Fever."

Harker joined us. "Leda is an angel now. I think the arrogance is a permanent accessory."

"Good." Nero's eyes slid over me. "I like it."

"Because it's a quality becoming of an angel?" I tried to keep a straight face.

"Very."

His hand stroked my cheek, tracing over my neck, down my ribcage, and dipping over my hip.

"We're going to get into trouble," I whispered.

"Yes," he said against my lips. "Very big trouble."

The ground shook so violently that for a moment I thought the giants had returned. But there were no giants in sight, and it wasn't just the ground that was shaking; the sky was booming too. Deep, incomprehensible shouts echoed off the storm clouds. It sounded like someone was hollering up there in the stratosphere.

I took a big step away from Nero. "Ok, Nyx. I get it. I'm moving away from him now."

"It's not Nyx," Nero told me.

"Then who?"

I didn't see anyone in the clouds. Granted, gods had

their fair share of tricks. I wouldn't be surprised if making themselves invisible were one of them. As far as I knew, only gods and Nyx could do that cool, freakish voice-projecting trick. Unless…

"I really hope a demon doesn't pop up in town," I sighed.

That would just be the exploding cherry on this catastrophe cake.

"Demons can't come to Earth," Nero reminded me. "Long ago, the gods wove a spell around this world that keeps them out."

The gods had also woven spells to keep the monsters on the wild side of the wall, but as we'd just seen, spells could fail. Who was it hollering out of the sky? A god? A demon? A Guardian?

I shook my head. It couldn't be a Guardian. Somehow, it didn't seem like their style.

There was a blinding flash of magic, then the goddess Meda appeared on top of the tallest building in town: the new Legion of Angels office building.

The Goddess of Witchcraft and Technology was dressed in a suit of red armor. It seemed to be made of dragon scales. And over her armor, the goddess wore a silver-white cloak that flapped and snapped fiercely in the wind. She held a majestic gigantic shield in one hand, a large glowing spear in the other.

Meda opened her mouth, and the echoing, frightening words of an all-powerful god thundered against my eardrums. "People of Earth, you have failed the gods." Her dark hair whipped in the wind, sparkling like lightning. "You speak of fealty and faith, all the while conspiring with demons and traitors, plotting treason. Our judgment is final and our punishment swift. Prepare to die."

CHAPTER 30

WEB OF MAGIC

I looked up at Meda, standing high above us all, proclaiming our imminent doom. "It looks like we celebrated too soon."

Nero's eyes hardened; his jaw clenched.

"Why have the gods turned against us?" I asked.

Ronan set down on the ground in front of us. "We haven't."

Nyx landed beside him. Their wings—hers white dusted with gold, his sparkling like diamonds—stretched out wide, then folded neatly against their backs.

"If the gods haven't turned against us, then what the hell is Meda up to?" I demanded.

"It would seem that Meda's connection to the Guardians runs deeper than just using their Life potion."

"But why? Why would she ally with them?"

"Why does any god ally with anyone else? To unite against a common enemy," said Nyx.

"The other gods? She is turning against the other gods to ally with the Guardians?" I shook my head. "It doesn't make sense."

"No, it does not," Nyx agreed. "None of this makes any sense. And yet here Meda is, trying to purge the Earth."

I frowned. "To pave the way for her Guardian allies."

"Or for herself," Ronan said.

"If Meda wants to rule the Earth, killing everyone on it isn't the best strategy," I replied. "What does she want with a dead world with no people on it?"

"Leda has a point," Nyx told Ronan. "The Earth's power, the reason the gods fight over it, is for its people."

I hadn't known that. I'd thought the Earth was just another battleground to the gods, just another world. Then again, there was only one Legion of Angels, and it was on Earth. The gods must really want this world if they'd created an army to protect it.

"Explain," I said.

Nyx exchanged loaded looks with Ronan, then she turned her eyes on me. "The Earth is a special place. For centuries, supernatural refugees from other worlds have fled here. People with magic have always been drawn here. Telepaths hid here from the gods and demons who tried to enslave them. Phoenixes and djinn like your sisters hid here as well. And they're not alone. Many others have come here over the ages."

"But why? What is special about the Earth?" I asked.

"I don't know," said Nyx. "The gods and demons eventually traced the fleeing supernaturals to this place. The deities followed them here, and here they clashed. That conflict tore the Earth apart. The monsters that the gods and demons had maintained perfect control over for so long began acting oddly. Some went rogue. Light bred with dark, and both gods and demons lost control over the monsters."

"We think something about this place sparked the strange behavior in the beasts," Ronan said. "And that same 'something' was what attracted so many supernatural refugees here from so many worlds. There is something special about the Earth. We just cannot pinpoint what it—"

Magic burst out from Meda like a spider web, cutting through Ronan's words. Tentacles of twinkling white magic slammed against the wall around Purgatory. The gold Magitech barrier stuttered.

Gin, Tessa, and Damiel ran up to us.

"It's going to go down," Gin said, her voice shaking. "Meda's magic is overloading the barrier."

"She's not just overloading this barrier," Nyx said. "She's overloading every barrier on every wilderness wall on Earth." She showed us her phone screen, which was littered with alerts from Legion offices all over the world.

"How is this possible?" I gasped.

"Meda used the Purgatory wall to inject her spell into the entire Magitech network." Gin read some information from the tablet in her hands. "The whole thing is going down, and not just the walls keeping out the monsters. All Magitech power everywhere." She chewed nervously on her lower lip. "I don't even know how she did it."

"Meda designed the Earth's Magitech network," said Ronan. "She would know better than anyone how to take it down."

My body twitched with the urge to do something. "We have to stop her."

Damiel glanced up at the web spiraling out from Meda. "That web isn't just destroying the Magitech network; her spell is like a shield. It's sucking up all the

magic from the world's Magitech generators and channeling it into a ward to keep us out. There is so much
power surging in there, it will instantly kill anyone it
touches."

Which meant that at the rate the web was expanding,
we'd all be dead in minutes. The town wasn't that big.

Damiel scrutinized Meda's magic field, his eyes narrowing. "It will absorb any unfriendly spells as well."

"What about weapons?" Calli asked as she, Harker, and
Alec joined us.

"It will also disintegrate bullets and other weapons,"
said Damiel.

"That might be true of mundane weapons, but what
about immortal weapons?" I asked.

Nero shook his head. "It's too dangerous, Leda."

He knew me well. He knew I was thinking of using the
weapons of heaven and hell to go after Meda.

"The armor has protected me from unfriendly magic
before."

"But not like this. Not the power of all the world's
Magitech generators, funneled by a goddess."

"I don't see that we have any choice, Nero."

He caught my hand. "Don't go."

"I am the only one who can go, the only one who can
wield the weapons of heaven and hell," I reminded him.

"The Pilgrim Valiant wore the armor. It protected
him."

"It protected him a bit, but it did not work as
completely as it would on me."

Stubbornness was etched into his face. "That's a chance
I'm willing to take."

He wanted to take the weapons of heaven and hell

from me and go after Meda himself. I could see it in his eyes.

"But I'm not willing to take that risk. Nero, I'm going. The weapons of heaven and hell are meant to be part of me, to work with my magic. The armor and shield protect me better than anyone. The sword and gun can only deal killing blows if I wield them."

And chances were we'd have to kill a goddess if we were going to survive this.

"She's right," Ronan told Nero. "The weapons of heaven and hell were made for someone with her kind of magic, someone with a perfect balance of dark and light. Like the original Immortals."

"I have Immortal blood," he declared.

Shock flashed in Ronan's eyes. And he wasn't the only one. Damiel looked pretty taken aback by the statement as well.

"You and Mother have Immortal blood as well," Nero told his father. "It appears the Guardians had something to do with you two coming together. And with my being born."

Damiel's eyes drifted upward in thought, as though he were mentally rewinding his entire life, trying to figure out how and when the Guardians had interfered with it.

"So that's why the Legion considered your father dark," Harker said. "At least darker than expected of an angel. And why you battle that same darkness in yourself."

"You might have Immortal blood, but it's buried under all the Nectar, beneath all the Legion's leveling up. You can't use more than a fraction of it," I said to Nero. "But I can use it all, light and dark, the whole spectrum. It has to be me who wields the artifacts and goes after Meda."

"She's right," said Ronan. "Only Leda can truly tap

into the power within the weapons of heaven and hell. And only with that power can we hope to stop Meda's spell."

The weapons of heaven and hell suddenly materialized in Ronan's hands. He must have summoned them here from my room. I wondered if that was how he and Nyx had stolen them from Nero. But Ronan wasn't stealing them this time. The god held them out to me, offering them freely. I moved toward him, but Nero stepped between us.

"I won't lose you," Nero said, his face pained, his voice dry as gravel.

"You won't have to." Smiling, I took his hands and gave them a squeeze. "I'll be fine." I pointed at the spreading web of magic. "Meda's spell is growing. I have to get to her before it destroys this town and the whole world beyond."

Nero set his hands on my cheeks. "Swear it. Swear you will come back to me."

"I swear it." I flashed him a smirk. "And you know how stubborn I am."

He captured my lips with a slow, searing kiss. Beneath my skin's surface, my blood rushed like a burning river, supercharging my veins with a jolt of magic. A shudder rippled down my spine.

Then he pulled away, and it was a good thing he did. The rational part of my brain had lost its way.

"I'm going to hold you to that promise, Pandora," he whispered, his breath melting against my lips.

"I'll make it." My voice shook, more from lust than fear. "It's the only way to avoid the ten thousand pushups you'd assign me as punishment if I fail."

"Only ten thousand?" He looked offended. "You know very well that I'd never let you off that easy."

"Twenty thousand then," I said, grinning. "But they

won't be necessary. I'm going to knock the evil right out of Meda."

I put on the armor. I holstered the gun, then I took up the shield with my left hand and the sword with my right. My wings unfolded from my back—dark, deep black on top, a gradual gradient to bright white at the tips. Right now, they were mirroring the unity of light and dark magic inside of me, bolstered by the weapons of heaven and hell.

I launched high into the air and flew at the web of magic. A sparkling tentacle snapped at me. When it hit my armor, it hissed like a piece of burning-hot metal plunging into a pool of cool water. The impact sent me wobbling off balance, but I managed to stay in the air. The armor's magic had protected me from Meda's spell. I only wished I'd figured out the art of flight a little better. Going in a straight line would have been a lot faster than zigzagging toward the goddess.

With each bolt of magic swinging at me, however, I was getting better. I was flying straighter, dodging better, and most of all, I was getting pretty damn good at putting up my shield fast enough to counter the web's lightning whips. I guessed when it was a matter of life or death— when the fate of the Earth lay in the balance—that was a pretty effective way to learn fast.

Having navigated through the twisting, winding web, I landed on the rooftop in front of Meda. I didn't botch my landing this time. I set down in a low attack crouch, my wings extended wide, my weapons at the ready.

"Pandora." Meda's red lips spread wide. "The Angel of Chaos." Her halo sizzled like a pan of hot oil.

"That's me."

A hissing, magic tendril zapped out from her. I put up my shield, deflecting her attack.

"What do you think you're doing here?" she demanded.

"You come to my world to kill every living being, and you ask what *I* am doing here? What the hell are *you* doing here?"

Meda didn't dignify my question with a response—at least not a verbal one. Her response was decidedly less civil. She sent another magic bolt at me. I deflected that one too. When I deflected her next bolt as well, she rushed me, her spear swinging high. She moved so fast that I barely got my sword up in time. Our weapons clashed, a geyser of sparks showering us.

Damn it. Meda was holding an immortal weapon too. It wasn't an immortal weapon like the ones I was wielding, ones that could only be wielded by someone with light and dark magic. Hers was of the more common kind, the kind any deity could use.

Under normal circumstances, my four immortal artifacts would clearly trump her one, but this was not a normal situation. Meda was feeding off the Earth's entire Magitech grid. It was providing her with a hell of a power boost.

Even as we fought, Meda's web continued to expand. Soon it would consume the town, killing everyone in it. From there, it would move on to the rest of the world. I had to stop this. I had to stop Meda.

I scored a hit, breaking off the clasp that held Meda's cloak. The web, bursting with wind and lightning, sucked away the silver-white sheet of silk. With the cloak gone, Meda's neck was left exposed but not bare. A collar pulsed on her neck.

"A control collar." I looked at her, my eyes wide. "None

of this is your doing. You're being controlled." My voice scraped against my throat. "Just like the beasts."

Meda hadn't turned against the gods. The Guardians had enslaved her mind. And if the Guardians' collars could control a god, they could control anyone.

CHAPTER 31

CHILDREN OF THE IMMORTAL

"*R*elease Meda's mind immediately," I said to Meda, knowing it would reach the Guardians pulling her strings.

"All in good time," she laughed, her voice hard and horrible. "After the Goddess of Witchcraft has fulfilled her purpose."

"What is…" I stopped, the Guardians' grand plan finally coming into focus. "The collars have never been about controlling the monsters. That was just the test run. This is about people—or gods, to be exact. You used Meda's research experiments on beasts and the archangel Osiris Wardbreaker to adapt your magic formula. Then you added that potion to the control collar you bought from House Leviathan." I stared through Meda's eyes to the Guardians beyond. "Your plan is to use the collars to control the gods and demons." I chewed on the thought, trying to work out why the Guardians wanted to do that. "You're using Meda to wreak devastation on the Earth because…" Why? "Because you want to turn the people against the gods, so you can weaken them. The people's faith boosts the gods' power."

"But no longer," Meda sneered. "The gods and demons, the favored children of the Immortals, the worthy descendants, will finally serve us."

Favored children of the Immortals? Worthy descendants? What did she mean by that?

"The gods and demons will serve us," she prattled on, her voice lifted, victorious. "They will serve us just as we were forced to serve the Immortals for millennia. For far too long, those chosen ones, the Immortals' beloved prized warriors, were set above us. But no longer. We're turning the tables."

There seemed to be a long and jaded history between the Guardians and the Immortals, gods, and demons. Arina had told me that the Guardians' betrayal of the Immortals had led to their downfall, but I didn't know anything more than that. The gods and demons must have risen to fill the power vacuum, and as 'children' of the Immortals, they'd fought over the worlds like normal children fought over toys. Somewhere in all that, the Guardians seemed to have been left on the sidelines—and they'd been plotting their revenge ever since.

"You would kill everyone in this world just to 'turn the tables'?" I demanded.

"A select few will be saved."

I assumed she meant people like Nero and Damiel, those with Immortal blood. Somehow, they were part of the Guardians' plan of ascension. I just couldn't figure out how they fit in.

"What do you want with people of Immortal blood?" I asked.

A crooked smile twisted her lips. "You can't expect me to hand you all the answers, can you?"

Yeah, that would have been too easy. And as I'd learned early on, living as a child on the streets of Purgatory, life was very rarely easy. Or fair.

"And am I to be among the saved?"

Meda's smile grew wider—and even more crooked. "What do you think?"

I already knew the answer. I just had to keep her talking as I tried to figure out a way to stop her from killing nearly every person on Earth.

I had no doubt that I would be among the casualties. The Guardians would never allow the Angel of Chaos, the unwanted aberration in their plans, to survive. In fact, maybe they were invoking the apocalypse, wiping out nearly everyone on Earth, just to get rid of me. I wouldn't have been surprised. Sure, I'd like to think no one was *that* evil, but I wasn't betting on it.

How could I stop Meda's spell? There was no guarantee that knocking her unconscious would end it. And if I knocked her out, she might explode. The beasts' collars had a self-destruct program built in; I bet Meda's collar had the same feature. Killing her wouldn't necessarily stop the spell either. Not to mention that killing a goddess would weaken the gods' position, which would also play right into the Guardians' hands. They wanted to weaken the gods so they could rise to power.

Plus, if I killed a god, the gods would certainly kill me. They wouldn't care that I'd done it to try to save the Earth. The gods saw themselves as above entire worlds; they believed their lives were worth more than all the people on a planet, all put together. Killing Meda to save the Earth— if killing her even saved the Earth—was a surefire way to earn my own death sentence, no matter how much the gods wanted to hold on to the Earth and its people.

And if I died, the Guardians won. They wanted to be rid of this uncontrolled, wild variable. Me. Had they set up this whole battle to manipulate me into killing Meda?

Meda swung her magic-charged spear at me. I rolled out of the way, still trying to decide what to do. The Guardians wanted to be rid of me because they couldn't control me; they couldn't predict me either. They feared me and what I could do. If the Guardians were right about me —if I really represented a big potential monkey wrench in their plans—that meant I could find a way to save Meda, the Earth, and myself.

Meda swung her spear again, and this time I was too slow. The magic-tipped head snapped off a piece of my armor. The silver metal clunked to the ground. Meda's magic, bolstered by the Magitech of Earth's monster barriers, was too powerful, even for my set of immortal artifacts.

Come on, Leda, I told myself as the goddess took another swing at me. *You can win this. You can find your way out of this conundrum. It's nothing more than dirty fighting on a cosmic scale.*

Meda snapped off another piece of my armor. And another. My armor was scattered across the rooftop. If I could only get to all the pieces, I could fasten them back on again. I snorted. Yeah, *only*. Meda was attacking like a windmill, over and over again, never stopping. I barely had time to defend myself against her strikes, let alone go collect my fallen armor.

Meda's weapon slammed down so hard that she knocked the shield out of my hand. It dropped over the edge of the building. The impact also caused her to lose her hold on her spear, but she hardly seemed to notice. She switched to bombarding me with psychic and elemental spells. Her true weapon was not the immoral artifact, but the web of magic swirling around her, feeding off all the world's Magitech generators.

A sparkling silver tentacle snapped out from that web and slammed into me. Without my armor to protect me, my body took the full force of the attack. It shot me backward. I hit the ground with so much force that I slid clear across the rooftop. My fingers clawed and scratched, reaching for something to catch myself on. They gripped onto a pipe just in time. Another moment and I'd have tumbled over the edge and been fried on a net of sizzling magic.

I swung my legs over my head and landed back on the rooftop. The world was spinning too. I reached out to touch my head. My fingers came back covered in blood. Meda's spell had hit me hard.

I had to get to her. I had to kill her, even if that meant my death. It was all I could think of to do. I just had to hope that her spell would die with her. That killing her would save the Earth.

I moved toward her, struggling to walk in a straight line. Meda's spells shot at me. I hopped aside, dodging them.

They were coming at me so fast.

I couldn't dodge them all.

I fell, my head spinning with pain, my mind swimming with half-baked plans. How could I stop Meda?

A crazy idea popped into my head. I wasn't sure it would even work, but if it were to have any chance of success, I had to get to my feet again. I had to get to Meda.

I tried to push off my hands, but my arms collapsed under my own weight. My face hit hard stone.

A hand gripped my arm, pulling me to my feet. How had anyone managed to get through the web of magic to make it up here? I turned around to face my ally.

It wasn't Nero or anyone else from the Legion. It wasn't Ronan or his soldiers either.

It was Cadence Lightbringer, Nero's mother. And she was wearing my armor.

"What are you doing here?" I asked in surprise.

"Helping you." She lifted up a shield to block a ribbon of fire magic that Meda had shot at us.

Wait, that was my shield. Cadence was wielding two artifacts from the weapons of heaven and hell. And she was tapping into their magic every bit as much as I could.

"But *how* are you here?" I asked.

"It's a long story. After we're done here, I'd be happy to share it."

"All right," I said, then stared across the rooftop at Meda.

"From the calculating gleam in your eyes, you have a plan," said Cadence, her golden hair rippling in the wind.

"I do," I confirmed. "But it's insane. And I'm not even sure it will work."

"I'd say that in this situation, we don't have much of a choice." Her eyes panned across the expanding web of magic. "What do you need me to do?"

I glanced at my armor and shield, sitting nicely on her body. "You wield them well."

"I am a dual angel—light and dark—now," she reminded me.

Which meant she could access the full spectrum of magic, light to dark. She'd realized the potential of her

Immortal blood—with the Guardians' help. But why did the Guardians want her to gain more magic, especially now that she was using that magic against them?

"You distract Meda," I said, handing her my sword. I wouldn't need it to carry out my plan. "So I can get close to her."

Nodding, Cadence rushed toward Meda. She didn't even ask me what I was going to do. It was just as well. She'd probably have thought I'd lost my mind.

"Is this how you repay us, Cadence Lightbringer, for all that we've done for you?" the Guardians spoke through Meda. "We saved you from the shackles of gods and demons. We freed you from their games. We made you powerful, and now you betray us."

Ah, so this wasn't part of the Guardians' plan. They hadn't anticipated that Cadence would come to my rescue. There it was again, that unpredictable element: me. Whenever I was involved, even the best-laid plans seemed to crumble to pieces.

"You betrayed me before I'd ever met you," Cadence said to the Guardians. "It was not freedom you offered, but instead shackles. You used me, just as you are using Meda."

Meda had recovered her spear. She brought it up to meet Cadence's sword. Magic exploded between them, shaking the building. Meda had more power, but Cadence was faster. She moved like a lightning storm.

I kept to the edge of the rooftop, circling around behind Meda as Cadence drew her attention. She was keeping Meda busy, at least for now.

I snuck up behind Meda. I was only a few steps away from her when the web of magic overpowered Cadence, dropping her to the ground. Meda spun around and unloaded a fresh barrage of spells on me. She was so close that I didn't have time to evade. Her magic hit me hard, jolting me like a shock of lightning.

Grinding my teeth, I stayed on my feet and made my way toward her, one agonizing step at a time.

"You really are so stupid and stubborn," she cackled. "Like a street dog."

"I am so tired of being talked down to because I'm different," I ground out, pressing forward.

I shot my magic at her. A tornado of swirling dark and light threads slammed into her. She doubled over and stumbled back, recovering her balance.

But I was faster this time.

"I am no street dog. I am Pandora, the Angel of Chaos," I declared, grabbing the goddess.

My hands closed around her collar. The glowing metal burned my hands, but I didn't let go. I gripped it harder. Meda bucked, trying to throw me off of her. As I held on, I concentrated my siren's magic on breaking the collar's control over her mind.

I felt it—that sharp pop the second I stole control over her mind from the collar's spell. The collar froze for a moment as its programming tried to access the self-destruct spell. It was building up.

I prepared to unlatch the collar.

I couldn't toss it away. Arina had told me the power of the self-destruct spell was proportional to the power of the being it had fettered. The monsters weren't all that power-ful, but Meda was a goddess. Even if I tossed the collar as far away as I possibly could, it wouldn't be far enough. The explosion would still destroy the whole town. The shock wave might even reach as far as New York City.

Since I couldn't simply toss the collar away, I had to overpower it with my siren magic. Arina had also said that if I could overpower a collar completely and all at once, I could knock out the self-destruct mechanism too. I hadn't been able to do that when it was on Meda. It was time for a different approach. A direct approach—one the Guardians would not expect, and hadn't accounted for.

I unlatched the collar from Meda's neck and closed it around my own. That put me into direct contact with the spell that powered the collar. Unfortunately, it also presented me, front and center, as its next target.

The compulsion spell crashed against me like a stormy ocean wave. I fought back, countering its magic with my own. It tried to enslave my will; and I tried to put it under my power. Around and around our magic went like two great tigers circling each other in a battle for supremacy.

My head hurt. *Everything* hurt. The world hadn't stopped spinning since Meda had knocked me down. And my battle of wills with the Guardians' spell had sent everything whirling out of control.

I felt a hand on my back. I glanced behind me. It was Nero. He froze when he saw Cadence. Beside him, Damiel was gaping at her like he couldn't believe his eyes.

Nero set his hands on my shoulders, his eyes honing in on the collar around my neck. "Leda, what have you done?"

Meda was waving her hands around, quickly reeling in the sparkling web, pushing the magic back into the Magitech network. She was back to normal. The world-killing web had dissipated.

"We did it," I told Nero, smiling. "Purgatory is safe. The Earth is safe. We've won. And you're all going to be all right."

The iron fist of the collar's magic locked around my mind, dropping me to my knees.

CHAPTER 32

GUARDIANS OF MAGIC

"*L*eda broke the spell over Meda," Cadence told everyone as they closed in around me. "To stop the collar from self-destructing and taking all of us with it, she put the collar around her own neck."

"Giving it a new target," Nero said.

"Yes. And now the collar is trying to take over her mind."

"It appears to be winning." Ronan's face suddenly came into sharp focus in front of my eyes. "And if it succeeds, we'll have a very big problem. Leda's magic is even more dangerous than Meda's."

"She'll beat the collar," said Nyx.

Ronan frowned. "I hope you're right."

"I'm not waiting to find out." Nero waved his hand. "Tessa, get over here."

When had Tessa gotten here? And how much time had passed since I'd put on the collar? Everything was bleeding together. I was so dizzy, and my head hurt. It hurt so much.

Voices echoed in my head. So many voices. They

promised they could take away my pain, but they were all liars. They were just part of the spell the collar was weaving around me. It wanted me to give in.

"The moment I get the collar off of Leda, open a portal and send the collar through it before it explodes," Nero told Tessa.

"I haven't completely mastered my magic." My sister's voice trembled. "I can't guarantee that I can create a portal to another world right when you need it." She swallowed hard. "Or at all."

"You can because you have to," Nero said. "Or Leda will die."

Tessa nodded, her fists clenching with determination. "Leda saved me from hell. I will save her."

"Stop." Damiel's voice cut through their plans. "We can't send the collar to another world. The power of its self-destruct spell is proportional to the magical capacity of its last prisoner."

"This is Leda we're talking about," Nero growled. "I won't allow the collar to take her mind."

"Yes, this is Leda," Damiel replied calmly. "And we both know how powerful she is. With both her light and dark magic to power the self-destruct spell, the explosion would be catastrophic. You would be sentencing another world to destruction."

"I refuse to let her die," Nero said, his voice almost savage with desperation.

"And she won't," Cadence said to him. "She is fighting the collar."

"That's the problem. If she wins, the collar explodes, killing her and everyone else. And if the collar wins, it takes control over her and forces her to kill everyone anyway."

"I don't think so," said Cadence. "She is the Angel of Chaos. There's another way."

"Like what?"

"I don't know, but Leda did. She knew what she was doing when she grabbed that collar."

Well, at the time, I'd *thought* I'd known what I was doing. I was starting to question that conviction now. I hadn't anticipated the collar would put up such a fight, or that it would hurt so damn much. The Fever wasn't exactly doing wonders for my self-control right now. I was holding on to it by the tips of my fingernails and ends of my teeth.

"She's losing it," Damiel said, drawing his sword.

What he hoped to do with it was anyone's guess. If he killed me, the collar exploded. He knew that, but I supposed having a weapon in his hand made him feel better. It made him feel like he was in control.

"She'll make it." A potion vial appeared in Cadence's hand. "But she could use a helping hand, Nero."

"How can I help her?"

"You and Leda are connected by magic," she said. "You've marked each other. I can sense it. You need to use that connection you share to offer her your strength."

Nero looked at the potion inside the vial, the sparkling silver liquid moving as though it were alive. "That's Life potion."

"That's right," she said. "It will activate the other side of your magic, the side that has remained dormant your whole life. Your dark magic."

"You know about our Immortal blood," Nero said.

"Yes, and this is the key to unlocking it." She set the vial of Life in his hand.

Not hesitating for a moment, Nero uncapped it and drank the potion down in one go.

I blinked. I didn't know how much time had passed. All I knew was everything had gone blurry. I couldn't hear anyone anymore. The only voices left were the ones in my head, the voices of the collar as it worked its magic on me…no, wait. There was something else, not a voice but a presence.

Nero. He was lending me his strength. He was helping me fight the collar's spell. His magic popped with power, a firestorm and a blizzard both at once. The Life potion had worked. It had ignited his dark magic, blending it with the light. And the end result was beautiful. His magic burned through my veins, hot and cold, gentle and explosive.

Thank you, I told him, hoping he could hear me.

With Nero to strengthen me, I pushed back against the collar's spell.

The voices grew louder. More voices joined in. The collar was fighting back.

My mind followed the connecting strand between the collar on my neck and the Sanctuary. I felt like I was there on the Guardians' world, inside an unfamiliar room. It was hot. And the voices were louder here.

That was when I realized they weren't voices at all. They were machines.

Racks and racks filled with humming computers surrounded me, their lights flickering rapidly. The machines were powering the collar around my neck. Collectively, they were fighting me.

The lights raced faster. The machines stared at me like they were alive.

The humming had grown louder. The fans spun faster. The machines' mocking rumble was deafening. The noise crashed against me, trying to crush my freewill.

I buried my fear beneath my resolve to silence the

machines once and for all, to never again allow the Guardians to use them to enslave anyone's mind.

There was a sizzle. One machine exploded.

A pop. A computer melted.

A click. Another machine blew up.

Sparks flew. Parts snapped. One by one, the Guardians' machines were destroyed—until there wasn't a single one left. But I didn't stop there. As my connection to the Guardians' machine room died, I sent a final jolt of magic across the spell that linked my collar to it. The burning, melting machines burst into flames. The last thing I saw before my mind whipped back to Earth was the roof of the building crashing down.

The collar's clasp clicked open, and the metal ring dropped to the ground. I looked down upon the now-inert metal piece, smiling. I'd beaten it. I looked at Nero. *We* had beaten it. And with the Guardians' machines destroyed, it would be a very long time before they could try that trick again—if they could *ever* try it again.

"You know, you really should listen to your mother." I smirked at him. "My plans always work." I took a step forward, stumbling.

Nero was right there, catching me before I fell. "Your plans are always dangerous."

I looked into his eyes. "I swore that I'd come back to you, and I did."

"Technically, I had to come to you," he pointed out.

"Don't be such a know-it-all, General."

"Even if I know everything?"

I laughed. "You are insufferable."

"And you are reckless," he countered. His thumb massaged deep circles into my palm. "Will you still marry me?"

"Of course I will, you crazy angel." I reached up and touched my hand to his cheek. "There's never been anyone else but you."

His hands closed around my waist. "Good." His mouth swooped down on mine, and he drew me into a deep kiss that made my knees buckle.

But we weren't alone. The loud chorus of clearing throats reminded me of that. As Nero drew back, I threw a sheepish glance at our audience.

"Behave yourself, Pandora," Nyx chided me. "I'd hate to have to arrest you after you saved the world."

"Come on. Surely, I'm allowed to kiss Nero by now." I pointed at the pink and blue splashes lighting up the horizon. "Look, it's already morning. A new day is here." I winked at Nero. "Our wedding day."

"Don't count your wedding bells before they ring, Pandora." Nyx's voice cracked like a whip. "You're not married yet. And formalities must be observed."

"Of course they must," I said with a heavy sigh that rattled my chest.

"Cadence, is that really you?" Damiel reached his hand toward his wife.

She touched her palm to his. "Of course it's me." Her blonde brows peaked. "Don't you know your own wife?"

"My memory's a bit fuzzy. I need to reacquaint myself with your qualities." His eyes slid over her body.

Cadence folded her arms over her chest and shot him a sassy smirk. "I'm sure you do."

He reclaimed her hand, kissing the top. "Will you be my date at our son's wedding?" His voice was formal and polished, like he was proposing marriage, not a dinner date.

"That depends," Cadence said.

Damiel's brows lifted. "On what?"

"On whether or not you can keep your hands to yourself, Damiel."

He folded his hands together. "I will be a perfect gentleman."

"Will you?" Her smile faded. "How disappointing. After two hundred years apart, I was hoping for a warmer welcome."

Magic flashed in Damiel's eyes. "That can be arranged."

There were sparks flying between him and Cadence. Literally. It was a full-on fireworks show.

"Sooo," Harker said to me, looking away from Cadence and Damiel. "How did you beat the collar anyway?"

"Through sheer force of will—and a little help from Nero." I winked at my husband-to-be. "But only just a little."

"Admit it," Nero said, his voice like a slip of dark silk. "It feels good to shed your modesty."

I bit my lip. "I'm not done shedding my modesty yet, honey."

His hand traced my sleeve. "I cannot wait to witness more…shedding."

"Nor can I." Then I glanced at Harker. "In the end, the collar failed because it didn't know how to deal with my balanced chaos magic."

"Chaos magic," Harker repeated. "Truly a contradiction to stump even the most brilliant scientist."

I brushed off my hands on my pants in an exaggerated display of accomplishment. "Then my work here is done."

Harker laughed. "But willpower alone wasn't enough, was it? There was a trick to it."

"Tricks? Why, I would never stoop so low."

"You toss water bottles in sword fights," Harker reminded me. "And you get your opponents twisted up in ropes during training."

I shrugged. "I do what works."

"And what worked here?" Nyx asked. "Every other time you wrestled control over a mind from the collar, the collar exploded."

"This time, the collar was fighting me for control over my *own* mind, not another's mind." My gaze flickered to Nero. "And this time I had some help," I added, more solemnly this time. It was all in good fun to tease Nero with my angelic ego, but the truth was that he had helped me a lot. "Together we fried that collar's magic, through and through."

Gin plucked the collar from the ground and looked it over. "She's right. Everything is fried. It's no longer functional at all."

"The Guardians can't handle anything outside their way of thinking, anything outside of the box." I pointed my thumbs at myself. "Like me. And that's why they want me dead."

Damiel laughed.

Nero scowled at him. "This is hardly funny."

"The joke is on the Guardians," replied Damiel. "What made her a target is also what saved her life."

Meda strode up to me, looking very regal, once again draped in her long cloak. "Leda Pandora, it appears I owe you a debt." She said it like the words hurt.

I gave my hand a dismissive wave. "Don't mention it."

"I know," she hissed, her voice low. "I know who you are. *What* you are. You're the child born from Faris and Grace. That's the only way you could possibly have had enough magic to do this." She pointed at the broken collar.

"I felt your light and dark magic at work in my mind, unraveling the spell's control over me."

Then she vanished in a puff of purple smoke, but the bitter taste of her damning accusation still lingered in the air.

"Well, Meda sure knows how to leave a girl hanging," I said quietly. "At this point, I'm not sure if she's going to throw me a party for saving her life, or light my funeral pyre in punishment for what I am."

"I have to go," Ronan said to Nyx, then he vanished too.

"Gods," I sighed. "They do love making an entrance. And an exit."

"Ronan will speak in your favor," Nyx said.

Well, I guess that answered the whole will-Meda-expose-me-to-the-other-gods question.

No, I wasn't going to think about that now. The cat was out of the bag, and there was no putting it back in again. From my personal experiences with a feisty feline, I knew that was impossible.

"How did you get back to Earth?" I asked Cadence. "I thought the Guardians still had you under observation."

"They do, but I've been doing some observing of my own on them. And after I heard what they were planning to do with Meda and the collar, I had to come here to help you."

"But why now? Why not leave earlier?"

"I knew from the start that the Guardians were up to something, but I kept those thoughts buried deep inside my mind."

A smart move. The Guardians had many telepaths under their 'care'.

"I had to learn what they were planning," said

Cadence. "And now, finally, after all these years, I know. Quietly, secretly from the shadows, they have been pitting gods against demons for millennia, ever since they betrayed and destroyed the Immortals."

"Do you know what the Guardians did to the Immortals?" I asked.

"Yes, I do. They killed them and trapped their souls away inside immortal artifacts."

My mouth fell open. "All of them?"

"Yes. The Immortal magic smith Sunfire designed the process of creating immortal artifacts. The Immortals used it to capture the souls of their own who died in battle or otherwise; they wanted their magic to continue to serve after death. The Guardians forced Sunfire to use his magic against his own kind. Against the other Immortals.

"Then, with the Immortals out of the way, the Guardians moved on to the next stage of their plan. They pitted the gods against the demons, keeping them busily locked up in this immortal war, as the Guardians manipulated events to further their agenda."

"But why?" I asked her. "What do they want?"

"Magic," Cadence said. "The Guardians want magic. They have no magic of their own. In fact, they aren't simply devoid of magic; they nullify it completely. And for that reason, they cannot even gain magic from Nectar, Venom, or anything else. If they drink a potion, their bodies instantly break down the magic inside of it; if they try to use a magical artifact, they nullify the magic inside that artifact forever. You see, that's why the Immortals made them the guardians of magic, the keepers of their potions and objects of power. With no possibility to gain magic, the Guardians would not be tempted to steal the potions or artifacts for themselves. They were supposed to be the perfect magic keepers."

"Until they got resentful," I said.

"Yes, the Guardians got resentful, and then they got even. And now they are trying to get what has been denied them since the beginning: magic. That's what all of this is about. Meda's monster experiments. Creating people with more concentrated Immortal blood. Their manipulations even led to the birth of Earth's first demigod." Cadence dipped her chin to Nyx. "And the creation of the Legion of Angels."

"An army of people who'd once had no magic but grew to be more powerful than any other supernatural on Earth. The Guardians think they can use the Legion to gain magic themselves," I realized.

"The Legion and everything else they've sunk their teeth into over the past few millennia," said Cadence. "They manipulated the demons into stealing angels, into turning their magic and making them dark angels. Because of the Guardians, the demons' Dark Force came to be. And I'm sure there's a lot more they manipulated in their long quest to gain magic."

Fear tightened my throat. Dread dropped like a stone in my stomach. I couldn't help but marvel at how much the Guardians had accomplished without any magic—and shudder at the thought of all they would be able to do if they finally gained it.

"We will stop them," Nero said.

"Yes, we will. Together." I took his hand. "Your new magic will come in handy."

"Haven't I always been handy, Pandora?"

I giggled at his innuendo. "There's one thing I don't understand, though, Cadence. How is it the Life potion worked on Nero immediately? I thought it took the Guardians centuries to balance your magic with Life potion."

"The Guardians exaggerated the process."

I looked at her in confusion.

But Nero wasn't confused. "The Guardians need an excuse to keep people cooped up in their Sanctuary for many years. So they can condition them. Brainwash them."

"Yes," said Cadence. "In truth, the Life potion has a powerful balancing agent, one designed by the Immortals. The effect is instantaneous on people with enough Immortal blood. It balances light and dark magic. For others, the process takes a bit longer, but it's a matter of months, not centuries."

The Guardians really loved their mind games. Honestly, I much preferred the direct, honest fight.

"There's more," Cadence told us. "The Guardians have plans for the telepaths they have 'rescued'. Including your brother, Leda."

"What are they going to do to them?"

"I don't know. I didn't hear any details. I only know that the telepaths are critical to the next step in the Guardians' plan."

"Can you help me free Zane and the other telepaths?"

"The Guardians have locked me out of their Sanctuary. I can feel it. The way there is now closed to me. But I promise you that we will find a way in. We will save your brother and the other telepaths."

My gaze panned across Nero, then Cadence and Damiel, Nyx, and finally Harker. They were my new family. I looked at Gin, Tessa, and Calli—my old family.

"Together," I declared. "We're going to save Zane and the other telepaths together."

I'd started this journey alone. I hadn't even told Calli what I was doing when I ran off to join the Legion of Angels, not until it was too late. I'd thought I had to travel this perilous road alone, but I'd been wrong. And now here I was, nearly two years later: an angel but far from alone. I was surrounded by friends and family, and I was stronger because of it. We would save Zane and the other telepaths. And we'd do it together, united by friendship and love.

CHAPTER 33

UNITY

I stood in front of the mirror, watching as my sisters Tessa, Gin, and Bella put the final touches on my wedding wardrobe. The ceremony would begin in a matter of minutes.

"The dress truly is stunning," I commented.

"Yes, it is, isn't it?" Tessa replied, triumphant. "Mind you, it wasn't easy creating something that both satisfied the Legion's regulations *and* had all the flair of the Angel of Chaos's unique personality. The Legion excels in regulating all the fun out of everything. The fabric of an angel's wedding dress must be white."

Tessa indicated the icy white color of the fabric, but the dress wasn't white at all. It was completely covered in gems that sparkled, the tiny precious stones changing color depending on how the light hit them. Right now, the dressed was predominantly blue and purple.

The chameleon dress was an ode to my hair and wings. They changed color too.

Bella squinted at me. "People are going to have to wear sunglasses when they look at you."

"Precisely," Gin said.

She and Tessa exchanged crisp, satisfied nods.

"I love it," I told them.

"Of course you do," Tessa cooed. "Your sisters have excellent taste."

I laughed.

"The Legion regulations don't stop with the dress's fabric color," Gin said. "They also define that the neckline must not dip below the collarbone."

She indicated the thick strap of beaded fabric over my collarbone. Below it, there was a decided absence of fabric. A deep v plunged between my breasts, which were covered in fabric shaped to resemble mermaid shells—and covered in gemstones. A diamond-shaped cut in the dress over my waist exposed my bellybutton. This dress was certainly not what the author of the Legion's wedding regulations had envisioned.

"The hemline of the dress must touch the floor and have a train in back," Tessa said.

The dress's long skirt hugged my hips in a mermaid cut, and there was indeed a train in back. Naturally, the dress's train was also covered in gems. A slit cut into each side of the skirt allowed my legs to move freely, enough to kick my leg straight up to my head if the need arose. Not that I had any intention of showing the wedding guests what was up my skirt.

In tune to my thoughts, Nero leaned in to whisper into my ear, "Especially since you aren't wearing any underwear."

I glanced over at him, meeting his smoldering eyes. Oh, he liked that I wasn't wearing any underwear. He liked it a lot.

"I thought it best to remove the temptation of

throwing them at you. It's unquestionably against the Legion's wedding regulations." I slid my hand over the hard leather hugging his chest.

"Unquestionably." He caught my hand, bringing it to his lips to kiss it softly. "But if your goal was to remove temptation, I'm afraid you have produced quite the opposite effect." His other hand rolled over my hip and slid across the slit in the dress, teasing the bare skin of my leg under the skirt.

Harker entered the room and declared, "It's time to begin."

Nero dropped his hand from my leg, but his eyes remained locked with mine, undressing, seducing, unraveling me in a way that rivaled his touch.

"How long does this ceremony last?" I asked Nero, impatience flaring in me.

It was Harker, however, who answered. "Just a few minutes."

"But then there's the party afterwards," Tessa added quickly. "I've scheduled so much fun."

"Why does this 'fun' sound like an assignment?" I asked Nero with a sigh.

"We can skip it," he promised me.

"Oh, no," Tessa said, completely horrified. "No, you don't. You aren't skipping a single second of the party. Not after all the work I put into it."

"We really must take our seats now," Harker said.

Tessa handed me my flower bouquet. "The Legion stipulates golden roses for an angel wedding."

I looked down at the bouquet. The roses were indeed golden, but rainbow glitter sparkled on the soft petals. That was yet another touch of individuality, another way

Tessa had gotten around the rules while still following them.

"Thank you." Smiling, I squeezed her hands. "For making this more than just any Legion wedding."

"Damiel helped," she admitted. "A little. He knows the regulations and laws backward and forward—and how to circumvent them without sinning."

I looked at Nero, laughing. "So that's where you learned it."

"He never allowed *me* to get away with circumventing anything."

I laughed again.

Tessa and Gin headed out the door. Harker went next. He extended his arm to Bella. She glanced at me, at him, then cautiously took his arm. They followed behind Tessa and Gin. Nero and I were finally and truly alone.

"I have something for you, Leda." He took a present box from a side table and handed it to me. "My final engagement gift to you. We were so busy yesterday that I didn't have a chance to give it to you."

Busy saving the world. Again. That was the story of our lives. I wondered if that would ever change, if we'd ever truly be at peace.

I opened the box and pulled out a black tank top. The words 'Angel of Chaos' were written in sparkly text across the front. There were other tops in the box too. One read 'Kick Ass Angel' and the other 'Pandora's Box', a tribute to my family's bounty hunting business.

"I love my gift," I said, throwing my arms around Nero to draw him into a hug. "You were right."

"Yes." His tone was easy, arrogant—and irresistibly sexy.

A flush warmed my cheeks. "In fact, I love it so much,

I think I'll wear it the next time we meet an angel." I buried my lust beneath an impressive smirk. "Or a god."

Beyond the door, an orchestra began playing. I stole a peek into the ballroom. What I saw there startled me.

"There are cameras. The wedding is being broadcast to the other Legion offices, just like my introduction ceremony."

"Actually, it's not just being broadcast to every Legion office, but to the whole world, to every city and town on Earth."

I grimaced. "You're the groom. I thought it was your job to make me feel better."

"No, it's my job to not bullshit you." He folded his arms around me and kissed the top of my head. "And I never will."

I chuckled. "Save your vows for the altar." I stole another peek into the ballroom. "There sure are a lot of cameras. How many do they really need to film a wedding?"

He shrugged. "A lot. Tessa wanted to make it look cinematic."

"Then you'd best put on a show for them all," I teased, nudging him toward the door.

Nero winked at me, then he threw open the double doors and marched into the ballroom. As he strode down the red-carpeted aisle, magic flashed, and his wings unfolded from his back, extending big and formidable behind him. Gold sparks sizzled on the black, blue, and green feathers, lighting him up like he was encased in a field of lightning. His wedding suit was a black leather uniform, as he always wore—with the added embellishment of a gold headband shaped like a pair of wings, folding forward to embrace his face.

Dramatic, angelic music—the swells of strings and wind instruments over deep, echoing percussion beats—accompanied his procession down the aisle. Oohs and aahs rose from the chairs, our audience's reaction to Nero's dominating halo of power. Even the floral arrangements seemed to weep in his presence.

The moment he stepped onto the raised stage, the music changed to something decidedly more melodic. Harps, soft but strong, sang a beautiful tune. That was my cue. I adjusted my tiara and stepped into the ballroom.

My cat Angel trotted up to me, and together we proceeded down the aisle. Flower petals and butterflies fluttered in the air. The frisky little kitten pounced at them as we made our way toward the stage.

The aisle seemed to go on forever, and everyone was staring at me. I heard a few wowed comments about my dress. My sisters had really outdone themselves today.

As I followed the red carpet, I saw more examples of my sisters' love for me. Glitter sparkled from all the golden roses in all the floral arrangements. It made me smile.

Not that I was having any trouble smiling, not with Nero waiting there at the end of the aisle. A force was pulling me toward him. I had to fight the urge to break into a run, to get to him as fast as I could possibly go.

Finally, I reached the end. Beyond Nero, the First Angel Nyx and Noble, the head Pilgrim of Purgatory, waited on the stage.

I took Nero's hand, the warmth of his skin melting into mine. Here we were, side-by-side, hand-in-hand, about to be married. When I'd set off on the train to New York, the plan to save my brother fresh in my mind, I hadn't predicted this. I'd never thought that my joining the

Legion would lead me here, standing at the altar, about to be married to an archangel.

"Citizens of Earth, honored soldiers from the Legion of Angel, welcome," the Pilgrim began his speech.

As the head Pilgrim of Purgatory, he represented the Faith, the voice of the gods—just as Nyx represented the Legion of Angels, the hand of the gods. Both the Pilgrims and the Legion were supposed to give a speech at an angel's wedding.

"Many of you know that Leda Pandora, the Angel of Purgatory, grew up in this humble town at the edge of the Frontier," the Pilgrim continued. "She was once a human like all of you. Before she had magic. Before she was chosen by the gods." He paused for dramatic effect. "But by the virtue of her pure, unwavering faith, she became something more. At the Legion, her faith propelled her quickly up the ranks. She became an angel, achieving the highest order a human can aspire to become."

That was a pretty generous stretch of the truth. Yes, I'd spent much of my childhood in Purgatory. And yes, I was now an angel. But my faith was neither pure nor unwavering. In fact, back when I'd lived in Purgatory, I'd teased the Pilgrims when they cornered me on the streets to sell me the gods' holy message. I supposed the real truth didn't fit Noble's agenda nearly as well as his embellishment did.

"Today she is wed to Nero Windstriker, archangel, son of the angels Cadence Lightbringer and Damiel Dragonsire," said the Pilgrim, his voice ringing with conviction. "Born from angels, forged in holy deeds, General Windstriker—"

A flash of magic cut through the Pilgrim's words. I blinked back the bright spots dancing in front of my eyes. When my vision settled, I saw that Zarion, God of Faith, now stood on the stage. What was he doing here? Wasn't he still in the middle of his one-month sentence of training under Faris?

Surprised whispers rustled across our audience. Noble looked pretty damn shocked himself to see Zarion.

"Honored Pilgrim, step aside," Zarion said, his voice booming with the power of the gods. "I will take over from here."

Noble bowed deeply to the god, then left the stage.

My grip on Nero's hand tightened. Whatever this was, it couldn't be good.

"Leda Pandora." Zarion's steely eyes flickered to me, before his gaze fell upon the guests. "This angel is a shining example of how a human can aspire to be something greater: a champion of the gods' will."

That was all he said, but the message was powerful. The gods were endorsing me. They were naming me their champion. That just didn't make sense. They considered me a nuisance at best; or, at worst, a precursor to all-out anarchy.

Before Nyx could give her speech, there was a second flash of magic, and Faris appeared on the stage beside her.

"Leda Pandora isn't just the champion of the gods' will," Faris said. "Our newest angel is the champion of the people." His gaze panned to me, then he addressed the cameras. "And we know she will inspire them."

The gods now sat front and center in the audience. Ronan, Valora, Meda, Maya, and Aleris had joined Faris and Zarion.

"You all know Leda Pandora," said Faris. Why was he speaking for the Legion instead of Ronan? "She has saved the Earth countless times. Her rise from humble human to holy angel will inspire you to join the Legion of Angels.

Her selfless dedication will inspire you to persevere and level up your magic. And her compassion will inspire you to fight for this world. And for the gods."

So the gods were making me the poster child of the Legion. They expected me to inspire the masses to join their army and fight for them.

"For she truly is the Angel of the People."

Yay, another title.

"Her image will be everywhere—on banners and billboards, on buildings and trains."

Oh, great. Just what I did *not* want. My image everywhere, the center of the gods' latest advertising campaign.

"Not as the Angel of Chaos, but as the Angel of Hope."

And there was another title. No matter that I already had so many. I supposed titles were like shoes; you never could have enough of them.

"A symbol of harmony and perseverance. Of ascension. An example that lights the way for all hopeful humans to follow."

"The archangel Nero Windstriker shall have an important role in this bright future as well," Zarion said. "He is the only offspring ever born from two angels, the epitome of holiness on Earth."

"Heaven and Earth are united now in Leda Pandora and Nero Windstriker," Faris said, picking up where Zarion had left off. Though the two brothers rarely got along, right now their words were in perfect harmony. "You have the gods' blessing."

The gods are all present, sitting in the audience, putting on a united front, I said silently to Nero. *Have they resolved their differences already? Or are they just that good at putting on a show?*

The gods do excel at putting on a show, Nero replied.

We pressed our hands and foreheads together to declare our vows for all to hear: to serve the gods and their will, to grow the Legion and make it stronger.

They are putting on a united front because everyone is watching, Nero told me. *After Meda's outburst, they cannot afford to do anything else. They need to show the Earth—all their worlds really—that they are united and strong, that they aren't splintering from the inside.*

That made sense. The gods drew some of their power from people's faith. That usually meant solemn prayer, but it was also expressed in acts performed in the gods' honor: courage in battles fought for the gods. And weddings like this one.

That's what the gods are all doing here, I told Nero. *They're drinking in the magic of people's faith, of this ceremony. It's a vessel of great power—all the people of Earth praying at once right now, boosting the gods' magic. Hijacking my wedding was a very smart move on their part.*

Faith, Leda. That's why the gods made you a symbol for humanity. A human angel is relatable. It's a powerful image, one that will encourage people to join the Legion, of course. But it also has another purpose. The gods needed a symbol to renew the people's faith, and that symbol is you.

What about Meda? Do you think she's told them what she knows? I asked.

I do not know.

As we spoke privately, publicly we declared our vows, pledging ourselves to each other, to the Legion, to the gods. A twinge of guilt hit me when I spoke the pledge of procreation; I'd already broken that vow by taking Nerissa's potion. I'd have felt guiltier, however, about bringing a child into this shattered world, at least as it was now. My first duty was to that child, our future daughter from

Nero's dream. We first had to create a world safe for her before bringing her into it.

Nero's hand squeezed mine, bringing me out of my mind. *I am going to kiss you now, Leda.*

I beamed at him. *Then do it. What, are you waiting for permission?*

You should know by now. His eyes ensnared mine. *An angel never asks for permission.*

Or forgiveness?

Of course not. That would be an admission that we'd erred.

One of his hands closed around my waist. The other curled around the back of my neck. He dipped me back slowly, as his mouth came down on mine. His kiss was not gentle or teasing; it was full-throttle. There, in front of the Legion of Angels, the gods, and the whole world, he gave me a deep, devouring kiss that made my head swim and my body buzz.

He kissed me like I was the only woman in the world —and yet there were millions of people watching us. Heat flashed through my body in raging, roaring cascades, a feverish explosion of raw lust and a rebellious desire to hightail out of here and skip the rest of the party.

I grabbed Nero's jacket, pulling him against me. Chuckles echoed from the audience, then hands pulled me and Nero apart, dragging us to opposite sides of the ballroom. Party music displaced the dignified orchestral tune.

Tessa was right beside me. She was one of the hands that had pulled me away from Nero. The others belonged to Calli, Bella, Gin, Ivy and Nerissa. Even Basanti and Leila were here.

Across the room, Nero was surrounded by Harker and a whole lot of other guys.

A new song pumped over the speaker system, and the crowd cheered.

"And now?" I asked.

"And now you go to your honeymoon suite," Leila told me.

Her smile looked genuine, but I remained suspicious. It sounded too good to be true.

"This is a trick."

"No, it's not," Tessa laughed. "But you should have seen the look on your face earlier when I spoke of hours of planned activities."

I planted my hands on my hips and scowled at her. "That wasn't nice."

"Don't frown, or your wedding pictures will be crap." Her eyes twinkling with delight, Tessa pulled out a chair. "But before we send you off to the honeymoon suite, there's just one short order of business."

"Oh?" I asked, my suspicion reignited.

She pointed at the chair. "Sit."

I sat. "And now?"

"Now Nero is going to throw your garter belt to all the single ladies."

"I thought that the groom was supposed to throw the garter belt to the guys."

"You're Pandora, the Angel of Chaos," Tessa said. "It's time to turn these traditions upside down."

A chorus of catcalls broke through the music's heavy beat. Nero was striding toward me, his walk smooth, his face determined—like the ground he was going to conquer and claim lay right before him. He knelt to the floor in front of me. His hands slid under my skirt.

Thankfully, the cameras were gone. The party wasn't being broadcast across the world. The only people watching us were those right here in this room. Another round of catcalls trilled from our live audience. I noted that the gods were gone. They'd just popped in and out again, twice as fast.

Nero's hands slid slowly up my leg. I tensed.

"Don't fidget, Pandora," he chided me, his lips twisting with satisfaction.

"Easy for you to say," I hissed.

He chuckled. Then, fire in his eyes, his fingers closed around the flower band fastened around my thigh by a single frail ribbon. He began to untie it—very, very slowly. As the ribbon released, the tip of his fingers brushed between my legs, a kiss of fire against my naked lips. I bit back a moan. Through it all, his eyes never left mine. Scorching and seductive, they never stopped drilling into me.

Then, just as slowly as his hand had slipped up my leg, it slid back down and emerged from my skirt. He rose to his feet and lifted my garter garland of flowers victoriously over his head.

Nero tossed it at the women. Tessa dove and Gin jumped, but they both missed. The rest of the crowd ran frantically in every direction.

"Amusing, isn't it?"

I glanced back and found Damiel.

"A Legion of highly-trained soldiers, reduced to this." His eyes tracked two women colliding.

I rose from my chair. "There's no way that tiny piece of fabric can possibly stay up in the air for that long," I said, pointing at the garter belt that still hovered somewhere close to the ceiling.

"Why not?" Damiel looked positively amused.

"It defies the laws of gravity."

"So do angels." He winked at me.

The garter belt had dipped lower now, which only made the women more frantic. Bella calmly reached out and caught it out of the air. Her action must have been pure instinct because she was now staring down at the lacy piece in surprise. Everyone cheered. Grinning, Tessa and Gin patted her on the back.

"Now the bouquet!" Tessa waved at me. "Throw it to the guys!"

I rose from the chair. "Don't you want to participate?" I asked Damiel when he didn't join the other male soldiers.

"I already have everything I need." His tone was serious, not joking, this time.

I watched him walk off toward Cadence. The guys were yelling at me to hurry up, so I tossed my bouquet at them —well, at Harker actually. When he caught it, I winked at him. Then Tessa and Gin swooped in to drag him and Bella together for a dance.

I felt the pull of Nero's magic. He was close. When I turned around, he was right in front of me, extending his hand out to me. I took it, then we spread our wings and flew up through the open skylight in the ceiling.

We rose higher and higher over Purgatory. I didn't know where we were going, but Nero seemed to. He led me to the highest balcony of a tall, white-and-gold building across town. I followed him inside, my wings fading away as I walked.

We passed from room to room. They seemed unending. I looked around at the house—no, *castle*. It was more extravagant than mine. A former district lord's home, it had clearly very recently undergone cosmetic surgery. The paintings on the ceilings featured angels and gods. The floors featured black marble and the walls white marble.

Accents of color punctuated the black-and-white palette. Cherrywood furniture, warm and rich. Crimson silk curtains. Gold and green tapestries.

"Why are we here?" I asked Nero.

"You have a suite in the Legion of Angels building. And I have a house in this town."

"This is all yours?"

"Yes. All mine and everything in it." His eyes pulsed with dark intentions; his voice was a dangerous caress.

I flashed a smile at him. "This house might be yours, but this is *my* territory. And, therefore, it and everything in it is mine as well."

"Good."

I stared at him. He watched me. Neither of us spoke.

We crashed together in an explosion of passion. His hands tugged the wedding dress off my body. I yanked at the bindings of his armor. Silk and leather hit the floor.

Both of us now completely naked, he grabbed my hips and lifted me up. My back bumped the cold marble wall, as cold as his body was hot. His skin burned against mine. Fire and ice collided.

His mouth lowered to my neck, and he inhaled slowly, deeply. "You smell like chocolate and cherry blossoms, with a hint of vanilla."

Nero smelled like angel and sex. Delicious and masculine, his hot, spicy scent flooded my nose and seared my senses. His fangs teased my throat, tracing my throbbing, pulsing vein. Blood blossomed beneath my skin. He paused to exhale. My body jerked as his breath melted against my skin.

His mouth lifted from my neck, and he looked up at me. "Do you know how much I love you?" His hand stroked my cheek.

"Yes." My heart thumped. It seemed to expand to fill my whole chest. I could feel his love inside of me, burning hot, flooding my mind and body. "Can you feel my love for you?" I asked him.

Nero kissed my fingers. "Yes." He set my hand over his forehead. "Here." He moved my hand to his chest, right over his heart. "And here."

I plunged my hand lower. "And here?" My brows arched, my mouth twisted.

He surged forward. He moved so fast that the next time I knew it, my back was flat on the mattress of the enormous bed. Nero knelt over me, big and unbreakable.

"You're mine, Leda." A savage, deeply possessive smile stretched his lips. His hands clamped down on my wrists, pinning me to the bed.

"I think my Fever has gone to your head." I struggled against his hold.

He gripped so tight that it hurt—in the very best way. "Yes." Slowly, he lowered onto me, his muscles tensing.

I gasped as the hard wall of his chest kissed the peaks of my breasts. He was so close now; I was drowning in his scent. His mouth closed over the thumping vein in my neck, teasing it between his teeth as his hands plunged lower. He traced my inner thigh, parting my legs. An ache throbbed inside of me, empty and hollow—coupled with a deep, intense longing for him to fill that emptiness.

Pain and pleasure shot through my body as he penetrated me in two places at once: his fangs pierced me; he thrust fully inside of me in one hard, forceful stroke.

My whole body pulsed with the heavy beat of my speeding heart. A river of fire flashed through my body. Savage longing consumed me from the inside out, leaving me gasping for breath.

ANGEL'S FLIGHT

He began to move inside of me, each thrust measured.

A slow, steady pressure was building up in me. My body shook with desperate anticipation. Forget slow and steady. I wanted fast and hard. I wanted Nero with an intensity that crossed the line into sheer madness. Gripping him tightly, I ground myself against him. My fangs sank into his neck.

A low, feral groan broke his lips. He gripped me harder, his thrusts growing rougher, deeper.

I drank from him, drawing his blood into me, claiming his body as he claimed mine. The taste of him surprised me, almost as much as it excited my hunger. He didn't just taste amazing; he tasted…no, there were no words to describe the incredible, unbelievably divine flavor of his blood. It eclipsed anything on Earth, anything in heaven or hell either. It was so complex, so complete. So sweet. The taste of him shot a sudden, merciless wave of desperate longing through me.

We moved together—fast and hard, relentless and insatiable. Every taste, every stroke, every jolt of our colliding bodies, was an explosion of magic and pleasure. I could feel myself inside of him, making him mine. Just as I could feel him inside of me, making me his.

"Leda," he growled.

"Nero." A shock wave rippled through my body.

"I love you." His whole body shuddered, his eyes rolling back, his face twisting in rapture.

"I love you too."

The pressure inside of me burst like a flash of lightning. Ecstasy spilled over me, wave after wave, again and again, each one building from the last. Dizzy, feverish, I thrashed beneath him. My body was convulsing. My mind was long gone. But through it all, I felt his mind inside of mine, his blood inside my veins, his body inside of me—sharing every moment together.

When the waves finally subsided, Nero lowered to the bed. He folded his arms around me, embracing me from behind. His hand crested my hip and trickled slowly, seductively, up my ribcage.

I chuckled. "General Windstriker, I don't believe your intentions are entirely honorable."

"No," he agreed. "They most certainly are not."

His fingers pinched my hard nipple, shooting a fresh surge of unchecked lust through me.

"So," I gasped, drawing in a sharp breath that seared my lungs. "You're not satiated?" I threw a coy wink over my shoulder at him.

"When it comes to you, Leda, I can never get enough."

His mouth came down hard on mine, and we gave ourselves up completely to the feverish magic pulsing through us, bonding us together.

CHAPTER 34

DADDY DEAREST

J glanced at the clock on the nightstand. The date printed on the display was quite a shock.

"It's been five days," I told Nero groggily. "Do you think we should get out of bed?" I nestled my head against his chest.

"No." He folded his arms around me, holding me to him. "The moment we get out of bed, something truly terrible will happen."

"Like yet another maniac will try to destroy the world?"

"Exactly." He kissed my forehead softly. "And we're currently on vacation from world-saving duty."

"You're right. Let's stay in bed. I'm not sure I could get up if I tried."

"Wear you out, did I, Pandora?" he said with a self-satisfied chuckle.

"No," I lied.

I couldn't very well admit that five days and nights of passionate sex had done me in. I was an angel. I had an image to maintain.

"I'm not worn out." I grinned at him. "I'm satisfied: body, magic, and soul."

"How romantic," said a dry, sardonic voice.

I twitched at the nearness of that voice—and the person it belonged to. Faris.

"Do you mind?" I snapped at him, pulling the blanket up to cover up all of me and Nero. "You can't just barge in here, unannounced and unwanted."

Faris folded his arms over his chest. "I grew impatient of waiting."

"You should work on that," I replied with a smile. "I hear patience is an immortal virtue."

"Don't be sassy with me." Faris leveled a hard, commanding stare on me. "I allowed you to have many days alone with your new husband." He said it like he was being enormously generous. "You've had your fun, and now you will listen to me. The fate of the known universe hangs in the balance."

I glanced at Nero. "The fate of the universe is always in the balance. We keep saving it, and it never does anything for us."

Nero snorted softly.

"Take this seriously," Faris chided us. "I will be in the lounge downstairs. I will not tolerate being kept waiting for long."

He disappeared. A normal person would have walked over to the bedroom door, opened it, and taken the stairs down, but doors and stairs were apparently beneath the God of Heaven's Army. Just like manners were.

"I really hate it when they just pop up like that uninvited," I told Nero as we rose from the bed.

"Perhaps it's time you turned the tables on the gods."

He collected the pieces of his leather armor and began putting them on.

I wished I'd had some armor of my own to put on before we went down to face Faris, but I'd come here in a wedding dress.

"Turn the tables?" I asked. "You mean drop in on them?"

He nodded. "Given your origin, the ability must lie somewhere within you."

"I'd love to see the looks on the gods' faces when I popped up in the middle of the council meeting chamber." Giddy with glee, I tapped my fingers together like a maniacal cartoon villain. "I'd most likely need Nectar and Venom to unbury that power, but maybe you can already teleport, now that Cadence gave you the Life potion to activate the magic in your Immortal blood. Hey, we could do it together."

He arched his brows at me.

"Not do *that*, you dirty-minded angel," I chuckled. "We could pop in on the gods. You know, for fun."

"For fun." Nero didn't sound convinced.

"Yeah, fun. Spreading chaos is fun." I picked up my wedding dress, but there was nothing on the floor beneath it. "Hey, you don't recall what happened to my underwear, do you?"

"I recall you weren't wearing any." His eyes captured mine. "Distinctly."

I almost got lost in the silver and gold swirls of magic gleaming in his eyes. But duty called, and his name was Faris.

"What do you think Faris wants?" I asked Nero.

"Nothing good." Nero tossed me a pair of tight shorts and a tank top. "Here."

I slipped them on, then glanced at myself in the mirror. "Angel of Chaos." I grinned when I read the glittery text on the tank top. "How did my fabulous new shirts make it here?"

Nero snapped his fingers. "Magic."

I laughed. "I love my shirts so much that I want to spread the love. I'm thinking of getting you one. Or maybe a pair of shorts with 'General Hard Ass' printed on the back."

"Funny."

"I think so."

"Too funny," he added. "I'm sure there's a Legion regulation against angels having a sense of humor."

"Actually, I'd be surprised if there is only one regulation against angels having a sense of humor." I swayed my hips for his benefit. "Say, you know what would be *really* funny? I should totally get Faris a t-shirt that reads 'Daddy Dearest'."

"I doubt he'd be amused by the gesture. He doesn't share your appreciation of irony."

"You're probably right." I turned in a tight circle in front of the mirror, looking at myself from all angles. "Is it obvious that I'm not wearing a bra?"

His eyes dipped unapologetically to my chest. "Yes." His gaze panned lower. "As is the fact that you're not wearing any underwear."

I shrugged. "I've survived worse."

Nero took my hand, and we left the bedroom and descended the stairs to the level below. Baskets of fruit, muffins, and other tasty treats waited for us on the dining table—and Faris waited for us in front of a glass wall with a view onto Purgatory.

I chose the more enticing encounter and went to the

breakfast table. Nero made the same choice. It hurt to walk. I limped a little. Coincidentally, Nero seemed to be suffering from the same ailment.

"You haven't been training enough," I teased him.

His eyes twinkled at me. "Neither have you." He pulled out his phone and hastily typed away on it. "To remedy this problem, I've ordered your team to set up an obstacle course beyond the wall."

"You can't be serious," I said.

Proving how very serious he was, he showed me the impossible obstacle course he'd brought up on his phone screen.

"You are serious," I sighed.

"About training. Always."

I took a blueberry muffin for comfort. "I was planning on just taking it easy today."

"Which is why I started out with the easiest course I've designed."

"How many courses are there?" I asked, fearing the answer.

"There are over two hundred distinct variations."

I sighed. That served me right for teasing Nero about training. Training for Nero was a serious affair.

Faris watched us in calculating silence.

"What?" I asked him.

"All this banter isn't particularly efficient. It's so off target."

"So was officiating our wedding." I smirked at him. "Did the prospect of your daughter's wedding make you feel unusually sentimental, Faris?"

"Hardly," he said coolly. "Your wedding served a very important purpose."

"An opportunity to eat lots of cake?"

"No."

"No? Are you sure? Because there was an awful lot of cake. And a lot of people eating cake. That served a very important purpose: once and for all proving to the gods that you can indeed have your cake and eat it too."

Faris's mouth tightened into a hard line. "It's puzzling that you haven't gotten lost in your own meandering tangents yet."

"What do you want, Faris? Or did you just come for the muffins?" I grabbed a second muffin, this one chocolate with chocolate chips.

"No, I am not here to eat muffins." He turned up his nose at my muffin. "I am here to outline your duties."

"Well, you already covered my duties pretty thoroughly on my wedding night. I'm to be the face of the Legion, the symbol that encourages Earth's citizens to join up, so we can clear the plains of monsters, bring harmony to the world, and all that jazz."

"There is more."

"Oh?" I sat down at the breakfast table. I didn't like the sound of this 'more'. I was definitely going to need another muffin—no, make that *several* muffins.

"You are obviously wondering why it was I who spoke for the gods at the ceremony."

"You mean, besides your burning need to say a few words at your daughter's wedding?"

He gave me a flat look. I smiled back.

"Ronan wanted to speak for the Legion in his role as Lord of the Legion. Just as Zarion spoke for the Pilgrims in his capacity as God of Faith," Faris said. "But the council has decided that we need to take a more active role in the affairs of Earth."

Alarm bells were going off in my head. Nothing good

ever came of the gods taking an active role in the affairs of Earth.

"We decided to have the council speak, not just the Lord of the Legion, to show that all the gods were united."

"And mitigate the damage done by Meda's very public damnation of the Earth and all its inhabitants," I said.

"Unfortunately, that will take time. But we are confident that you can do it."

"I?" I gasped. "*I* am supposed to fix your mess?"

"It is the Guardians' mess."

"Right, and you didn't contribute to it at all." I rolled my eyes.

"The Guardians set themselves on this path long ago, Leda. What you discovered about their crimes is shocking. We'd always known that the Guardians had betrayed the Immortals, but we didn't know how they'd done it. We had no idea that they'd killed them all and channeled all their magic into immortal artifacts."

"How did you find out about that anyway?"

"Meda told us. She told us a lot of things." He gave me a pointed look.

I slouched in my seat. "The gods know about me. They know what I am."

"Yes," Faris confirmed, his face impassive. "They know."

"What are they going to do?" I hardly dared to ask.

"There was a debate."

My hands were sticky and sweaty. "They want to kill me."

"There were calls for your immediate execution."

Of course there were. A god-demon hybrid didn't fit into the gods' vision of how the universe should be.

"But Meda spoke in your favor," Faris told me. "As did Ronan."

"And you?"

"Your death would hinder our efforts, especially now that the Guardians have shown their cards. You possess unusual skills: the ability to access light and dark magic, the power to control monsters. The other gods recognize the essential role you will play in the days to come."

"So they're not going to kill me?"

"No," said Faris. "The Guardians have been plotting their ascension for millennia, and we had no idea. My colleagues on the council have come to recognize the necessity of your continued survival. Your chaos is the best weapon against the Guardians' perfectly-laid plans."

"So I'm the monkey wrench you're throwing at the Guardians' machinations?"

"You have an important role to play, Leda." He looked at Nero. "You both do, archangel of Immortal blood."

So the gods knew about Nero's origin as well.

"Wait a moment here." My forehead furrowed with suspicion. "Just a few weeks ago, you tried to sell me on the story that Nero is the enemy, that he was using me, that he was engaged in some underhanded scheme. You manipulated me. You tried to put a wedge between me and Nero, in the hopes that I'd then lean on you for support. And now you've proclaimed him a champion of the gods."

"I was misinformed."

I laughed. "You're actually admitting that you were wrong?"

"Not wrong. Misinformed." His marble facade did not crack. "I knew that Nero Windstriker had taken an interest in you from the moment you joined the Legion. The only logical conclusion was that he knew of your origin and wanted to use you."

"That wasn't the only logical conclusion, and if you weren't so jaded, you'd have realized that. Nero had a dream about me before we met, of me and him, together as angels. *That* is why he took an interest in me."

"No, I did not predict an angel's humanity," Faris said, his words dripping with disapproval. "The Legion's training regimen was supposed to wash the humanity out of its soldiers by the time they became angels. Ronan has been far too lax, far too easy on the Legion's soldiers. He is too attached to humans and his Legion soldiers. But Ronan is not solely at fault. As head of the council, Valora should have managed him better."

"Which is why the gods replaced her," Nero said.

Gold sparked in Faris's bright blue eyes, a hint of emotion peeking through his mask. "Indeed so."

"Replaced her?" I asked. In gods' speak, that meant kill. "But Valora was at the wedding. She's not dead."

"She is still the Goddess of Shifters. She is just no longer the Queen Goddess. The council judged her unfit to lead us, so she was replaced."

"By whom?"

"By Faris," Nero told me.

I looked at Faris. A hard, victorious smile was etched into his face, like a sculptor had chiseled it from a block of stone. It was the smile of someone confident in his own supremacy.

"You?" I blinked. "The other gods made *you* King of the Gods?"

"We now face a crisis far worse than our war with the demons. The Guardians have been plotting our demise for millennia. Even without magic, they destroyed the Immortals. They are the greatest threat we have ever faced. The other gods recognized that I, the God of Heaven's Army, am the one best suited to lead them now in this time of war."

I shook my head. "I can't believe this."

"Believe it. I am king, and you two are crucial to my plan."

That was what I was worried about.

"We might already be too late," I said. "All your planning could be for nothing."

"Explain." Faris's voice rang with the note of command.

"Someone wanted me and Nero to meet," I told him. "Someone sent him those dreams of me. I can't imagine it was the Guardians. They want to keep me and Nero apart. After all, I am the wild variable that's messing up all their equations. It wouldn't do to mix that chaos with their plans for Nero and the Immortals' other descendants, whatever those plans might be. But someone else did send Nero those dreams. There's another player at work here."

"Someone with powerful telepathic magic," Faris said, his voice…bored?

"You know who this other player is," I realized. "You know who sent Nero the dreams of me."

"I am reasonably certain, given the available facts."

"Just as you were reasonably certain a few weeks ago that Nero was manipulating me?"

Faris brushed off my quip. "Recently, my telepaths have had visions to back up my theory."

Faris's chorus of telepaths was the reason he always knew more about what was going on than anyone. It was probably a contributing factor as to why the other gods had put him in charge as well. The Guardians had a chorus of telepaths too. Knowledge truly was power.

"So who is it?" I asked Faris. "Who sent Nero dreams of me?"

"We both know they weren't merely dreams, Leda," he said, smooth as silk. "They were visions of the future. A future with you, Nero, and your *angelic* daughter."

Shit. Shit. Shit. I hadn't told anyone about our daughter's presence in Nero's dream, but somehow Faris knew. That must be the vision his telepaths had seen. They'd seen the same thing Nero had, and now Faris knew it too. He recognized what our daughter meant, what she represented.

Somehow, Faris would find a way to use my child who did not yet exist, a child with the power of gods and demons and Immortals. That would be his perfect, ultimate weapon. I was just a temporary stand-in until he could replace me with my daughter.

I'd felt divided about my decision to take Nerissa's contraceptive potion. But now, knowing what Faris would do to my child, that he'd steal her from me to make her his weapon, I was no longer conflicted. I knew that I'd made the right choice. I had to protect her, even if she didn't exist yet.

"Who sent this dream to General Windstriker, you ask?" Faris wore the confident, unfading face of a king. "My Orchestra has not seen this, but when magic fails, you need only apply logic to the problem. It takes a powerful telepath to catch a fleeting fragment of the future, to make it solid and concrete, real and true, and then pass on that vision to someone else in the form of a dream."

"The dream could be a fake, a forgery," I pointed out.

"No, only a true vision of the future has the potency to

provoke such a deep, emotional response in a trained angel like Nero Windstriker. Only a real vision could ring so true, could take such a powerful hold over him that he'd set aside his other duties to train you. Only a real vision could compel him to want to know you before he even saw you, could press him to figure out why you were in his dreams and how you were his future."

"That was almost poetic," I said. "If I didn't know better, Faris, I'd say you were having a fatherly moment."

"But you do know better."

"Yes, I do. So, tell us, who is this powerful telepath?"

"Gods and demons did not always possess the power of telepathy. Do you know how we acquired it?"

"You bred it into your magic by mating with powerful telepaths."

"Native telepaths are one of the many branches of supernaturals descended from Immortals. They are not natural, direct descendants like you." He glanced at Nero. "But rather bloodlines created by the Immortals in their many experiments on the nature of magic."

"What kinds of experiments?" I asked.

"The Immortals were experimenting on isolating specific magical abilities from the rest. The ghosts—or telepaths—came into existence as a result of one of those experiments. Shortly before our war with the demons began, the ghosts went into hiding."

"You hunted them down so you could breed with them?" I demanded, my voice shaking.

The whole idea of hunting down these poor telepaths to breed their powers into the gods' magic made me sick.

"Finding telepaths was easy. Finding a pure, undiluted telepath proved nearly impossible," Faris said, unmoved by my anger. "But eventually the gods managed. Unfortunately, so did the demons."

"You're saying a god or a demon sent me those images of Leda?" Nero asked him.

"Despite our best efforts to gain the power of telepathy, it is not as strong in us as our other magic abilities," Faris admitted, looking annoyed. Hunting down people to breed them hadn't bothered him, but this failure to fully acquire their magic clearly did. "Furthermore, future-gazing is a difficult art that requires much magic and training to perfect. Most deities do not possess enough telepathic magic to capture and redirect future visions. In fact, of all the gods and demons alive today, there is only one who wields that power."

"Who?" I asked.

"Grace."

My mother. Demon of the Faith and Queen of Dark Vampires.

"Grace channels the future-gazing ability through prayer and meditation," said Faris. "She uses her followers' faith to boost her telepathic powers."

I frowned at him. "You knew that she had this ability when you used her to create me."

Faris laughed. "Grace allowed herself to be 'used'. You can bet she has her own plans for you, Leda. She was undoubtedly furthering that agenda when she sent Nero dreams about you. She brought you together, and you can be sure her motivation wasn't motherly compassion. Grace isn't looking out for your best interests."

"Neither are you," I told him.

There wasn't a shred of regret on Faris's face.

"So what is Grace plotting?" I asked him.

"Ask her yourself when you see her."

"I wasn't planning on paying her a visit."

"Your plans have changed," Faris told me. "The gods have decided to broker an alliance with the demons, at least until the Guardians are dealt with. And you, Leda, child of god and demon blood, are our emissary to hell. You'll leave at once."

AUTHOR'S NOTE

If you want to be notified when I have a new release, head on over to my website to sign up for my mailing list at http://www.ellasummers.com/newsletter. Your e-mail address will never be shared, and you can unsubscribe at any time.

If you enjoyed *Fairy's Touch*, I'd really appreciate if you could spread the word. One of the best ways of doing that is by leaving a review wherever you purchased this book. Thank you for your invaluable support!

The ninth book in the *Legion of Angels* series will be coming soon.

ABOUT THE AUTHOR

Ella Summers has been writing stories for as long as she could read; she's been coming up with tall tales even longer than that. One of her early year masterpieces was a story about a pigtailed princess and her dragon sidekick. Nowadays, she still writes fantasy. She likes books with lots of action, adventure, and romance. When she is not busy writing or spending time with her two young children, she makes the world safe by fighting robots.

Ella is the *USA Today, Wall Street Journal,* and International Bestselling Author of the paranormal and fantasy series *Legion of Angels, Immortal Legacy, Dragon Born,* and *Sorcery & Science.*

www.ellasummers.com